TRANSCENDER:

First-Timer

Transcender Trilogy Book 1

Vicky Savage

Copyright © 2011 by Vicky Savage

This book is a work of fiction. Names, characters, places, and incidents are either products of the author's imagination or used fictitiously. Any resemblance to actual events, locales, or persons, living, dead, or undead, is purely coincidental. All rights reserved. No part of this publication can be reproduced or transmitted in any form or by any means, electronic or mechanical, without permission in writing from the author or publisher.

ISBN-10: 0-9859019-0-X
ISBN-13: 978-0-9859019-0-5

In loving memory of Tug and Jo Savage.

Dying is a wild night and a new road.

~ Emily Dickenson

ONE

Headquarters of the Inter-Universal Guidance Agency (IUGA):

Senior Guidance Agent Constantine Albrecht Ralston was *pissed*—not in the British sense of 'totally wasted,' but in the American sense of 'mad as hell.' He'd never even spoken the word before, but he believed it described his mood precisely this morning as he stood in the office of IUGA's new director, Braxton Zarbain.

"Agent Ralston, thank you for coming so promptly," Director Zarbain said, motioning him to take a seat in front of the director's chrome and glass desk. The desktop bore a single item—a crystal plaque with the motto: *Destiny is Our Duty.*

"I apologize for this unexpected disruption of your field work." Zarbain said, plucking an imagined bit of lint from his sleeve. "I am aware you are fostering a high-value subject, and that one of his crucial events occurs tonight, but we have received information that requires your efforts be redirected immediately."

Ralston opened his mouth to protest, but the director held up a hand. "A Transcender will arrive in your sector today, the appearance of whom will have a direct impact upon your subject's crucial event and threaten to unravel all the important work you have accomplished to date. I was certain you would wish to be the agent in charge of containing the damage."

"But this is outrageous," Ralston spluttered. "A Transcender interfering with a crucial event? I am not aware of a Transcender applying to my sector."

"As you know, they are not *technically* required to apply. It is more of a courtesy. Regardless, I am speaking of a first-timer. A young woman—a child really—seventeen years of age. She does not even know what is about to happen to her. She is coming from Earth 7Y12. Resides in the state of Connecticut, I believe. It is critical for you to initiate contact with her, monitor her every move, and return her home at the first possible opportunity. All of this must occur without her discovering she is a Transcender."

Ralston removed his glasses and massaged the bridge of his nose, his anger now overshadowed by a sense of duty. "Yes sir, I see. An American teenager. She'll be disoriented and frightened. But why is she not to know that she's a Transcender?"

"Outside of the obvious undesirability of allowing the Transcenders to add to their ranks, a more important consideration exists. She has a prior connection with your primary subject and she must not become aware that there is a choice about her leaving."

Agent Ralston narrowed his eyes. "By a prior connection, you mean …"

"There is a pre-existing Perpetual Contract between the two. Nevertheless, eternal love cannot and shall not be permitted to interfere with the galactic order. Destiny must prevail."

"But sir, don't we have an absolute obligation to honor such a contract? In all my years at the agency I've never heard of a Perpetual Contract being ignored."

Director Zarbain waved this off. "The parties could not possibly have foreseen the present situation. The legal department assures me that under such circumstances, we are free to disregard it."

Ralston replaced his glasses, frowning internally. *This does not comport with my understanding of the law at all, and I see another, larger problem as well.*

To the director he said, "Sir, if I may, how am I to transport this child home without informing her that she's a Transcender and allowing her to use her gift?"

"That is indeed the tricky part. It has been done in the past with accidental shifters who were not Transcenders. You needn't worry about it, though. I will have a team of agents working around the clock to engineer her expeditious return. While she is in your sector, however, you will be solely responsible for her every move—within the guidelines of our charter, of course."

"Yes, sir, that goes without saying," Ralston replied, although he suspected the entire operation drew perilously close to the outer limits of IUGA's authority. Despite these misgivings, he added, "You can count on me, sir. I will handle it."

"Excellent. A copy of the file is waiting for you in research. I knew I could depend on you, Ralston." Zarbain rose from his chair.

Agent Ralston shook his outstretched hand and turned for the door.

"Oh, by the way, there is one additional complication of which you should be aware," the director said, smoothing his silver hair with a manicured hand. "The mirror for this Transcender, her twin in your sector, is the Crown Princess Jaden Beckett of Domerica."

Ralston flinched. *Good God, he waited until now to tell me this?* "Princess Jaden? The one who is slated to pass on tonight?"

"The very same. Makes for an interesting assignment, don't you agree?"

TWO

It's prom night, but I'm not going. Not because I didn't get asked, but because tomorrow I'm moving across town—to the wrong side of the tracks. New home, new school, new life. So while my best friend, Olivia Wallace, is preparing to lose her virginity (for the second time), I'm stuck here packing up the kitchen. It sucks. In fact, if zombies really existed they'd make excellent movers because when it comes to packing up boxes, the fewer living brain cells you have the better. I've been at it for hours, and I can actually feel the gray matter shriveling up inside my head.

I reach for my phone. No messages. Everyone's out partying except me.

I dial 4-1-1.

"How can I help you?" the information lady asks.

"Hi. I was just wondering. Who do I talk to about exchanging my life for a new one? See, there's been this huge mistake. I did *not* order the giant super-deluxe shit sandwich."

She kind of snorts. "Girl, would I be working this crap job on a Saturday night if I knew the answer to that one?"

Good point. She clicks off.

I pitch the phone on the counter and open another drawer. Dish cloths, dish towels. I toss them in a box. Six packages of white paper doilies. I wish someone would explain the purpose of paper doilies to me. I consider calling information again ... nah, two prank calls in one night is a little much even for me.

"Hey, who're you talking to?" My brother Drew shambles into the kitchen in his rented tuxedo looking ready to break someone's heart.

"Just my travel agent."

"Yeah? Where you going?"

"I'm thinking anywhere but here would be good." I stuff the doilies into the garbage can and open the next drawer.

Drew laughs. "What's with the attitude? Not looking forward to adventures in condo living?"

"Oh, it's not that. I can't wait to figure out how to cram all my stuff into that cute jail-cell-sized room. The new school's got me worried, though. I don't have the handgun skills or the requisite number of tats to get into any of the honors clubs."

He cups a hand under my chin looking at me seriously. For a second I think he's got something on his mind. But one side of his mouth quirks up and he says, "Just crank up the eyeliner and get some black lipstick. I'm sure the Emos will think you have enough street cred. You got that vacant look they all aspire to."

I slap his hand away and he heads for the back door.

"Whoa, dude," I say. "Where do you think you're going? You're not getting out of here without a couple of pics of you in that monkey suit." I grab my camera from the table and pop off the lens cap.

"No can do. Don't have time." He looks at his watch and grimaces. "I told Sherry I'd pick her up fifteen minutes ago."

"So she's already pissed, what's a few more minutes?" I put one hand on my hip, cock an eyebrow, and give him a glare that plainly says 'no' is not an option.

He slumps his shoulders. "Okay, just make it quick. Where do you want me?"

"Stand by the staircase. It's the only box-free spot in the house."

We step into the hall and he leans casually against the banister, arms folded across his chest. I check him out in the viewfinder. "God, what happened to your hair? Did you comb it or something?"

"No!" He straightens up looking pained and ruffles his fingers through his tawny curls. "Does it look like I combed it?"

"Just kidding. You look good."

He beams and resumes his pose. I snap a few shots.

Drew's my big brother by virtue of his being thirteen months older than me. Really, he's about an inch shorter than my five feet ten inches, but he thinks he's a rock star so everyone else does too.

"Dad still on duty at the hospital?" he asks.

"Yeah, double shift in the ER."

"They still shorthanded on nurses?"

"So he says."

But Drew and I both know the alleged nurse shortage is only an excuse for avoiding this house and us, or anything that reminds him of Mom. After she died, Dad just kind of checked out. It's like he crawled inside his own head and can't find the exit. She's been gone about twelve months now, and he's still MIA.

"You know I hate leaving you here all by yourself to finish up the packing," Drew says. "But someone has to represent the badass Becketts at this little soiree, and it might as well be the pretty one, right?"

"Yeah, too bad *you're* showing up instead." I pop the lens cap back on my Canon, and Drew makes for the door. "Have fun and try not to embarrass yourself," I call after him. "Remember, disco is dead."

He waves—or flips me off—I can't tell which.

I trudge back to the kitchen. Pots and pans are next. Whoopee. I'm thinking maybe I should've gone to the prom after all.

I had a date with the charming and ever-so-hot Jason Fallon. But I found out last week that Liv was going to make a huge deal out of it being my last hurrah at Madison High, and I have a definite aversion to epic farewell scenes. So I cancelled on Jason and told Liv I had to stay home and get ready for the move. I plan to ease out of here in my own way. Like smoke from a candle, *poof*, I'm gone.

The house seems unnaturally quiet tonight, or maybe I'm just feeling alone. I search through the clutter on the kitchen counter for my iPod. It's not there. I spot a box with my name on it. Maybe it got packed in there. I rip off the tape and pry open the top, but it's just my old yearbooks and Tae Kwon Do trophies from the den. I make a mental note to look for my iPod later and get back to my packing. I hum a little Arcade Fire, but my voice sounds tinny and makes the place seem even lonelier.

Thunder rolls in the distance, rattling the kitchen windowpane. Storm's coming in. I open the door to the back porch. The air has a metallic tang to it, and dark clouds mushroom across the sky, blotting out the moon and stars. I make sure all the boxes and things we stacked out here for the movers are well under the roof. Looks like it might be a soaker.

I wind my way through a maze of crates, bicycles, and garden tools to a wicker patio chair by the porch railing, and I curl up on the cushion to watch a little Mother Nature in action. I'm awed by the super mega-watt power of a dozen dazzling lightning bolts as they blaze across the sky, eerily illuminating the manicured neighborhood lawns and trees.

I was afraid of thunderstorms when I was a kid, and Mom used to comfort me by saying it was only "heaven's fireworks." She was amazing like that, always seeing the positive side of things. I haven't let myself think about Mom a lot over the past year. Sure, random thoughts of her float through my head a hundred times a day. But I usually just push them out, forcing myself to think of something else.

Tonight though, with the rain falling softly on the new spring grass, I let her settle gently on my mind—her warm smile, the bright green eyes I was lucky to inherit from her, her amber and spice scent. I close my eyes, conjuring up the feelings of comfort and security I used to have whenever she held me in her arms.

As I sit lost in my memories, the storm grows steadily faster and fiercer. Rain sheets across the back lawn in gust-driven torrents, pulling my thoughts away from Mom. I know I should go inside and finish packing, but the porch is still mostly dry so I linger on, mesmerized by the powerful downpour.

Without warning, an immense shaft of lightning stabs the earth uncomfortably near the house. The intense flash of light blinds me momentarily, and the sonic boom of thunder makes me jump. When I recover my vision, the churning cloud bank in front of me looks exactly like a bunch of guys on horseback, kicking up dust as they speed toward my house.

I rub my eyes to shake off the strange optical illusion, but a second burst of lightning gouges the air, this one brighter and louder than the first. My hands fly to my ears, and in the stark light I see them again, more clearly now. Horsemen!

I spring from the chair. My head's telling me it's not real—just a trick of the storm, like a mirage. But another lightning bolt rips the sky, and there they are again, in IMAX 3-D, bearing down on my back porch at breakneck speed. Real or not, all my instincts scream at me to get the hell out of here. Now!

There's no time to find a path to the door. They're closing in too fast. I can hear their shouts above the storm.

"There she is!" "Take her alive." "Don't let her jump!"

My nearest escape route is over the porch railing into the remains of Mom's rosebushes. It's a three- or four-foot drop into thorns and mud, but it's my only shot at getting out of here before being trampled by dozens of thundering hooves. My heart tries to kick its way out of my chest as I scramble like mad for the rail and dive to the other side.

THREE

I'm floating a few inches above my body. It feels bad, but in a good way. I know I'm not supposed to be outside my body, but I'm so light and carefree. Muffled voices hum in the background. The words are unclear, the tones low and serious. Something's wrong. I don't remember what, but my attempt to compose my thoughts pulls me back down to earth. *Zip!* I'm back in my body and, oh man, I ache all over.

I try to move. I try to speak. I hear a low moan. Did it come from me or someone else? The background voices change abruptly, becoming more urgent. Someone sits down beside me and places an icy cold object on my forehead. It stings like hell. I move my head to make it go away.

A soothing voice says, "Be at peace. Rest assured you are safe."

My brain commands my eyes to open, but they don't obey. It's maddening. I want desperately to see what's going on. I concentrate very hard, and with enormous effort I open my left eyelid a slit. That's when I see the angel.

He's the most radiantly beautiful being I've ever laid eyes on. A golden glow emanates from the light coppery skin of his muscular arms and smooth face. His eyes are summer-sky blue and his hair shiny and black as a crow's feather. I stare at him brazenly, enthralled by the movement of his full lips.

He's speaking, I realize belatedly. The angel is speaking to me.

"Are you well, Princess?" he says.

"Uh, that depends … am I dead?"

The angel throws back his silky hair and laughs a thrilling, throaty laugh. "No, thank the spirits, you are not dead. You gave us quite a scare though when you launched yourself from the cliff. You could have been killed."

His long fingers lift a stray lock of hair from my face and tuck it behind my ear. "Whether bravery or idiocy I do not know, but I hope you will not attempt such a thing again."

The background voices burble with soft laughter.

What is this guy talking about? I know I didn't jump off a cliff, but something sounds familiar. A wisp of memory struggles to break the surface of my mind. I close my eyes and try to coax it to the top, but I lose the thread. Something touches my forehead again, accompanied by another cold stab of pain. My eyes fly open and I see the beautiful man dabbing at my forehead with a strange kind of instrument.

"Dude! That hurts!" I push his hand away. He smiles with that hauntingly perfect mouth and my heart contracts inside my chest.

"Ah, I see you are going to be difficult," he says. "I regret your pain, but you must hold still. I wish only to staunch the wound on your forehead, Princess. There will be dire consequences if I do not return you in perfect condition."

Princess? "Who are you?" I ask.

"Ryder James Blackthorn, at your service, Your Highness." He bows his head.

"Are you making fun of me?"

His head flies up. "Of course not. I am concerned for your well being."

"Why? What am I doing here?"

"You are here because I have need of you until your mother can be persuaded to, uh… accede to certain reasonable requests."

"My mother?" Okay, I must be dreaming or hallucinating. I close my eyes and try to think. I have a dim recollection of a storm, but then … nothing. My mind's a spilled jigsaw puzzle.

The cold stinging is back on my forehead. "Stop that!" I shove him away again.

"This is necessary to prevent infection, Princess. If you allow me to tend to your injury, all will go smoothly. If you do not, I shall be forced to restrain your hands, and I do not wish to do that."

"What's that thing you're putting on my head?"

"A healing wand. See?" He shows me a small slender metal rod with a rounded tip that glows white light.

"It hurts only for a moment, and it will close your wound, *if* you will be still," he says.

I've never seen an object like the wand before, but it looks relatively harmless and he seems to want to help me, so I let him touch it to my forehead again. It burns intensely for about ten seconds—icy and hot at the same time. Then the pain fades to a cool, dull throb. Not so bad, really. I relax a little.

"Better?" The corners of his mouth turn up, and a fraction of my fuzzy brain is pleased that I made him smile. I open my mouth to ask how I got a gash on my forehead, but my weary eyelids droop involuntarily and I nod off.

When I come to again, Blackthorn is still sitting at my side watching me intently. I peer over his shoulder into the dimly lit room, but I can't make out anything. The air smells weird in here, though, like wet dirt and old gym socks.

"Where am I and how did I get here?" I ask.

"That is not important at the moment. What is important is that you are safe, Princess. No harm will come to you regardless of the outcome of our negotiations with your mother. I give you my oath on that."

His words are obviously meant to reassure, but they send a shiver of fear through me. This guy may be breathtaking, but he's either a nut job or he's got the wrong girl. Either way, I think I'm in trouble.

"Do you even know who I am?" I ask. "My mother's dead. She died last year in a car wreck."

He considers this. "I do not know what you mean by *car wreck*, but I know who you are. We were introduced years ago at a Coalition Meeting at Warrington Palace. You may not remember me, but I have not forgotten you, Princess, and I happen to know your mother is very much alive."

Huh? "You need to get a clue Blackthorn, or whatever your name is. The only palace I've ever been to is the Ice Palace in Hartford to see *Disney on Ice*. I was five. I doubt you were there. And quit calling me Princess!"

"Do you prefer Your Highness?"

I scowl at him. "Worse!"

"What then? Jaden?"

He knows my name?

"Victoria?"

And my middle name? He has my complete attention now.

"Surely you do not wish to be called Hanover," he says lightly. "Lady Beckett, perhaps?"

I'm still a little bleary, but he definitely said my name—my *full* name—Jaden Victoria Hanover Beckett. Nobody knows my full name. Not even Liv. God, it's too embarrassingly pretentious to ever tell anyone. I try to sit up, but the room starts to spin, so I ease back down.

"How do you know my name?" I ask.

"It is a wonderful name. It suits you." He brushes his fingertips along the cut on my forehead, and I feel a slight crackle of electricity.

"I told you. We have met, and by now Queen Eleanor will surely be anxious regarding your whereabouts. Since your wound is looking much better, I must make certain my messenger is on his way. Please excuse me." He stands and I'm able to see him completely for the first time.

Whoa! The guy's huge. He's at least six foot five. His size makes it hard to guess his age. Twenty, twenty-one, maybe.

He snags a piece of black leather garb from the floor, puts it on over his head, and buckles himself in. It looks like the body armor my cousin wears for downhill mountain biking. An enormous sword is strapped to one of his hips, and a wicked long knife is sheathed on the other. He looks Terminator-dangerous, except for that amazing face. A flicker of hot fear slices through me. This guy's no angel—a fallen angel maybe, or maybe something more sinister.

"Can I trust you to mind yourself and not try to escape?" he asks.

I nod meekly, and he turns to go. A brown and white bird feather on a beaded cord dangles from the back of his hair. It doesn't fit with the rest of his outfit, but hell his whole look is straight out of *Lord of the Rings*, so I guess anything goes.

"Wait!" I call after him. "Does my dad know where I am?" He must be insane with worry by now, coming home from his shift at the hospital and finding me gone.

"Your father?" Blackthorn seems taken aback by the question. "It was my desire to avoid involving your father in this business, since he has always been a friend to the Unicoi. But you are right ... uh, what am I to call you?" He raises a questioning eyebrow.

"Jaden," I say.

"You are right, Jaden. He is certain to be drawn into this one way or another. Once we are securely outside of Domerica, I shall send word to the Enclave that you are safe and will remain unharmed. It would be callous of me to cause him unnecessary concern."

He bows slightly and strides away on his mile-long legs, stopping for a moment to speak with a group of really big guys standing near a fire. No, not a fire—more like a pile of glowing rocks. *Glowing Rocks?*

I don't understand why everything is so freakin' confusing. My head throbs like a churning caldron of kimchi, and my eyes are collecting data that my brain can't process. Who is this mind-bogglingly gorgeous madman? He seems kind of nice, but he's holding me prisoner for some reason. He's speaking English—kind of formal English—but I can't make any sense of it. All I know is that I need to get home before Dad and Drew get too worried.

I close my eyes, trying to think. Mom always used to say that the best way to approach any problem is to use logic. Okay, the logical approach is for me to take stock of my surroundings. Maybe something will look familiar or give me a clue about what has happened to me.

I'm lying on top of soft blankets spread out on a stone bench that seems like it was carved out of a stone wall. Slowly and carefully, I slide my legs off the side of the bed and sit up. I rest my head in my hands until I have my equilibrium. Through blurry eyes I examine the room—if you can call it a room. It looks more like a cavern, with rough stone walls and a dirt floor.

My bed is in a cool, dark alcove separated a few feet from the rest of the cave. On one side of the room is a makeshift table—just a board, really, propped up on some stones with papers and scrolls scattered across the top. In the center of the room is the fire pit with the weird rocks that give off a soft yellow glow. Several large men dressed in leather armor with big swords similar to Blackthorn's are clustered around that area, talking and laughing.

Logical conclusion: I'm being held captive by a bunch of giant-sized psychos who like to dress up in creepy outfits, tell jokes around a fake campfire, and hang out in caverns. Great!

My eyes find the cave entrance where a tall, willowy girl, about my age, stands gazing out into the rain. Her sable hair is pulled back in one long braid, with a beaded band around her forehead. She's wearing the same leather armor as the guys, only in a lighter russet shade. A small sword hangs at her side.

Logical conclusion: escape isn't going to be easy, but this woman is the most vulnerable target in the group—and she controls the door.

I sweep my eyes around the rest of the room, taking in more details. I'm shocked when I happen to glance down at my legs and notice for the first time that I'm also wearing unusual clothing. My pants are a buttery leather, streaked with dirt and split at one knee. My top, which is also caked with dirt, is made of a soft white fabric with a lace-up front. The problem is I don't remember changing out of the jeans and hoodie I had on last night.

Up until now I've managed to keep my panic in check. But nausea swells in my stomach, and I think I'm going to be sick. Did these people change my clothes while I was passed out? Or worse, have I lost a chunk of time, a block of memory that would make all the pieces fall into place?

"Where are my clothes?" I say out loud.

The girl turns and glowers at me, folding her arms over her chest. She has Blackthorn's golden skin and high cheekbones, but her eyes are a deeper, stormier blue. She's over-the-top fabulous-looking, and it crosses my mind that maybe I'm being punk'd on TV and these people are a bunch of actors.

"Do you have a complaint?" She asks, marching to my bedside.

"Where are my clothes?" I say, a little intimidated.

"Those *are* your clothes."

"This isn't what I was wearing last night."

"Those are the garments we found you in. They became soiled and torn when you hurled yourself from the cliff."

"But they're not mine!" I insist.

"Their ownership is of no concern to me, and I will not be drawn into a discussion regarding your wardrobe. This is not Warrington

Palace, and I am not your servant. You shall remain in that clothing until you are safely stowed away inside of Unicoi. Whining will change nothing." She turns and stalks away muttering "pampered little princess," under her breath.

I want to scream at her to stop calling me Princess, but I get the feeling it's not in my best interests to anger this Amazon just yet. I need to stay chill if I'm going to find a way out of this live-action spin-off of *Dungeons and Dragons.*

These lunatics have obviously kidnapped me under some crazy-assed notion that my mom's still alive and they have something to gain by holding me. Maybe this whole thing has something to do with one of the cases mom presided over as a judge. It's possible one of her rulings angered these people. But what do they want? Revenge? Ransom? My heart sinks at the thought. God knows Dad could never scrape up enough money for that. And why are they dressed so strangely? Are they part of some cult?

I have a zillion questions, but no answers. Logic is getting me nowhere fast. What I need is a plan of action. My best chance is to stay alert and wait until a path becomes clear. Maybe I can steal a cell phone or a weapon, or slip away while everyone is sleeping, or eating, or doing something else. Maybe they'll let me go when they find out my mom really is dead. Maybe my dad and the police will be able to find me. Someone has to be searching for me by now. Although I don't even know how long I've been gone.

All this stressing is making me tired, and I bury my face in my hands again. I thought my life reeked to high heaven before—this is a whole new level of putridity.

If I ever get out of here, I'm going to appreciate what I have—cramped condo, ghetto school, whatever. Be it ever so humble ... and all that.

"Princess," a soft male voice says.

I've had just about enough of the 'Princess' thing, and I'm about to snap off the head of the unsuspecting speaker, when I glance up to see a slight, middle-aged man with wire-rimmed glasses holding out a cup for me.

"Tea?" he asks.

I hesitate before accepting it. "Thanks," I say.

He smiles kindly. His looks are markedly different from the rest of the group. Besides being normal-sized, he wears no armor or weapon. Instead he has on a tan shirt, the same shade as his sandy-colored hair, a taupe vest, camel pants, and brown boots—he's a study in earth tones. Only his pale blue eyes lend a hint of color to his appearance.

The tea smells okay, so I take a sip. It's delicious. The sweet, warm liquid soothes my churning insides and makes me feel slightly better.

After I've drained my cup, the man asks, "More?"

"No, thank you," I say, feeling a little like I've taken candy from a stranger.

"I'm Ralston," he says with a slight British accent. He makes a little bow and reaches for my cup. As he takes it, he slips a small, folded piece of paper into my palm. I look at it curiously, and he briefly touches his index finger to his lips, with an infinitesimal shake of his head. Okay, I get it—keep my mouth shut.

When he leaves, I lie down on the bench with my back to the room so no one can see what I'm doing. I unfold the paper, and in the dark I can barely make out the message: *I will help you escape when the time is right. Be patient. Do not do anything foolish.*

A tiny flame of hope ignites inside me.

"Jaden, are you awake?" Blackthorn has returned.

I crumple the tiny piece of paper, discreetly pushing it into a dark corner of the bench. I roll onto my back and meet Blackthorn's bottomless blue eyes.

"Yes?" I say.

"Are you feeling better?" He sits down next to me again.

"Yes."

"The rain will cease in ten minutes. Then we must be on our way."

"On our way?" Panic flares in my gut again. I'm pretty sure my chances of escaping or being rescued are much better if we stay in one spot. Plus, the prospect of getting into a car with these yahoos and moving to another mysterious location makes me a little crazy.

I glance at the opening of the cave. It is dark outside and still raining heavily. "I don't know," I say. "It looks pretty socked-in to me. I think we should stay put for now. That rain's not stopping anytime soon."

"Yes it will. It's nearing five o'clock," Blackthorn says.

"So?"

"So, the rain in Domerica always ceases at five." His dark eyebrows knit together. "Are you certain you are well?"

"No! No I'm not! I don't understand any of this. I want to go home." My voice echoes shrilly in the cave. "Please don't do this. Please let me go."

A flicker of emotion darts through his eyes. Concern? Guilt maybe? I don't know. But he sets his jaw and turns away from me without response.

"It is time to move," he tells his men.

FOUR

I sit on the edge of my bench-bed while my captors break down the camp. They pack their stuff, including the glowing rocks, into leather saddlebags. Blackthorn assigns the cranky Amazon to babysit me while this decamping is going on. She stands with her back to me, impatiently shifting from foot to foot.

I may not know much about my present situation—where I am or why I'm here. I do know one thing, though: *I'm not going anywhere with these guys!* I'll find a way out of here somehow.

Amazon girl doesn't realize it, but she makes an easy target with her back exposed like that. I know I can take her down with a few simple Tae Kwon Do moves. She's taller than I am, but her height is no match for my black belt. My problem's going to be making it to the door. The big burly guys will be all over me in a red hot minute, unless I can figure a way to bob and weave my way around them— under the table, over the rock pit to the door. I'm pretty fast, and the element of surprise will be on my side.

I begin to plot a strategy. Most of the big boys are clustered to the left near the rock pit, so I'll stay to the right. I scan the room for something to use as a weapon. Before I come up with anything, though, the man with the wire-rimmed glasses steps directly into my line of sight. His eyes laser into mine, and he gives a nearly imperceptible shake of his head, like he knows exactly what I'm thinking. It creeps me out, yet it's enough to make me abandon my half-formed plan. He's definitely a strange bird, but he may just be my ticket out of here.

The rain stops at exactly five o'clock, as promised, and the men begin carrying out the bags.

"Get up," Amazon girl orders. I stand, and she shoves me roughly toward the opening of the cave. "Move quickly. Do not attempt to escape."

When we reach the threshold, I freeze. For the first time I can see outside the cave, and I'm totally freaked. It's daylight, but there's no visible sun in the sky. In fact there is no sky at all—just a swirling, shimmering, silvery mass high above my head.

The lushness of the land is astonishing. Steep hills tangled with vegetation slope gracefully into a wide valley splashed with colorful wildflowers. Blossoming trees line a dirt lane adjacent to a rushing creek that churns up foam across slick black and gray stones. Everything is lit from within by a supernatural silvery light. I'm rooted to the ground, dazed and disbelieving. My original thought that I'd died and gone to heaven is momentarily revived until Amazon girl shoves me again, hard.

"Keep walking." she barks.

"Get the hell away from me!" I bat her arm down.

She reaches for her sword, but Blackthorn catches her hand before she can unsheathe it.

"Catherine! Don't be reckless. Go find your horse." She jerks away from his grasp and tramps off.

Horse? Oh crap! Ahead I see the others sitting astride horses waiting for us. I turn to Blackthorn. "You're kidding right? You guys kidnapped me on horseback?" Then something pings in the back of my mind. *The riders in the storm*! A shard of memory slides into place.

Blackthorn takes my elbow and guides me to a terrifyingly enormous gray stallion. The horse stomps and snorts impatiently, but calms immediately at Blackthorn's touch. I've never been so close to an animal this huge. Someone the size of Blackthorn probably needs a monster charger like this one, but it scares the hell out of me.

"Mount up," he says.

"Huh?"

"As you have lost your mount, you will ride with me."

"I'm not getting on that thing."

"Yes, you are." His voice leaves no room for argument.

"Fine! But how am I supposed to do that? Do you have a ladder?"

He raises his eyes heavenward for a moment. Then he grabs me around my waist, swings my legs up, and unceremoniously shoves my butt into the saddle. He climbs up behind me, taking the horse's reins in his right hand.

"We have a long journey ahead of us, which will pass more agreeably for you if you cooperate," he says, urging the horse forward onto the dirt road. The others fall into step behind.

"Where are you taking me?" I ask.

"I've arranged comfortable quarters for you in Unicoi."

"Where's Unicoi? Are we still in Connecticut?"

He sighs. "I fear the blow to your head has left you a bit muddled, Princess ... er, Jaden. I am sorry for that. I am certain you will recover yourself soon enough."

I sure as hell hope he's right because at the moment it's like I've fallen down the rabbit-hole, and I'm wondering how in the world I'll ever get out again.

We ride along in silence for a time, and the steady cadence of the horse's gait calms my jangled nerves a bit. I goggle at the spectacular scenery, searching for clues to my whereabouts. The air is warm and sweet with spring perfume. Flowers in carnival colors blanket the hillsides. Fallen saffron-colored petals from hundreds of blossoming trees carpet the path before us. It reminds me a little of the road to Oz.

After several miles, though, the lavish green hills and blooming valleys give way to a thick, piney forest and rockier terrain. The rushing creek narrows into a small brook that trundles crookedly alongside the roadway.

My mind gradually accepts that this is not the Connecticut countryside. Nothing is familiar to me. The land is primitive and unspoiled—not a building, paved street, or telephone pole in sight. They must have taken me to another state or country while I was out cold. Could be another planet, for all I know.

Cranky Catherine pulls her animal alongside ours, and though her horse is smaller than the gray monstrosity Blackthorn calls Tenasi, it falls easily into step with us. "There is so much waste here," she says, gazing at the countryside. "This land should be farmed or settled or put to good purpose. Instead it lies fallow and useless, all for the selfish pleasure of the queen." She shoots me a ferocious sneer and I recoil.

"That's enough Catherine," Blackthorn says. "Jaden is to be treated with the respect she is due. I'll not have you taunting her. We will soon have our audience with the queen."

Catherine huffs off on her pony and rejoins the others.

Soon the path becomes steep and gouged with ruts. Our horse stumbles slightly. Blackthorn wraps his free arm tightly around my waist to secure me in place. This simple gesture has a profoundly unsettling effect on me. I'm intimidated by the man—his arm is powerful, hard with muscle, and I'm his unwilling prisoner. But his body is warm next to mine and his scent surrounds me—a pleasant mixture of soap, leather, and sweat. His protective embrace feels strangely comforting and oddly intimate under the circumstances. It occurs to me that if he wasn't in the process of kidnapping me, I'd feel a strong attraction for this man. It troubles me to realize maybe I'm drawn to him anyway.

Oh God, I hope I'm not developing some "Stockholm

Syndrome" crush. I don't need that kind of weirdness on top of everything else.

The road evens out again and Blackthorn loosens his hold, but still keeps his arm around my waist. I wonder what will happen when he finally figures out my mom really is dead. Will he take his anger out on me? Will he abandon me in some dank isolated cave? The thought makes me shiver.

"Are you cold?" he asks.

I suck in a shaky breath. "No, I'm scared. I don't know what you plan to do with me, and I want to go home."

"It is not my preference to place you in the midst of all this. Perhaps this is not the best manner in which to resolve my issues with your mother, but we have exhausted all diplomatic avenues and precious little time remains." He pauses and adds more gently, "You have nothing to fear from me. I truly regret you are injured and frightened."

Something in his voice convinces me he's being straight. I shift in the saddle so I can see his face. "Please take me home."

He refuses to look at me. "All in good time," he whispers, urging the horse forward.

As night falls, the road grows narrower, and with no moon or stars shining above us, it soon becomes difficult to see. Blackthorn commands the party to stop. The men climb from their horses and unpack small lanterns from the saddle bags. The lanterns shine with a yellowish light similar to the glowing rocks from the cave. They hook the lanterns to the front of their horses' harnesses like single headlights and we set off again—Blackthorn and I in the lead, the others in single file behind us. The night is still and silent except for the gentle clop of our horses' hooves.

After a mile or so Blackthorn pulls up on Tenasi's reins and holds up a hand, bringing the others to halt. He listens for a moment and climbs down from the horse.

"Stay where you are," he says to me, unhooking the lantern. He disappears up the trail.

After about ten minutes he returns, silently signaling his men to join him on the ground. They form a huddle.

I don't know what in the hell is going on here, but no one is paying any attention to me, so I consider my chances of escape. There's no way I can ride off on this horse by myself, but if I can slip off his back without killing myself, I may be able to sneak away in the darkness. I glance over my shoulder, but that Ralston guy is staring straight at me, so I decide to stay put ... for now.

I strain to hear what Blackthorn is saying. "A group of a dozen or so patrols has stopped to rest ahead," he tells his men quietly. "I see no way to avoid them. We will have to render them ineffective. Catherine, you remain with Jaden. The rest of you, come with me."

Catherine clutches Blackthorn's arm. "I will not stay behind with her. I am part of this mission. I came for the sake of my country. Tell Ralston to remain with her. I do not understand why you allowed him to come along anyway. He is a teacher not a warrior, and he's not even Unicoi."

"Must you always be so obstinate?" Blackthorn says.

"Only when combat is involved." She grins.

"Very well." He turns to find Ralston. "Will you please remain with the Princess, Professor? We shall return soon."

The warriors quietly thread their way into the trees, and Ralston silently motions for me to climb down from the horse. I fall on my butt clambering off the overgrown beast, and Ralston frowns at all the noise I'm making.

"Shhh," he says, pulling the saddle bags from the back of his horse and slinging them across his shoulders. He takes my arm and leads me off the trail a few yards to the edge of a large meadow.

"Once the fighting has begun, run straight for that herd of animals on the other side of this field," he whispers, pointing across the clearing. I can barely see the outline of the herd.

"The animals and the darkness will provide cover for us. I know of a cave in that rocky hill just behind the herd. We will be safe there until I can transport you home."

"Okay. But what is Blackthorn doing? Are they just going to kill all those men?"

"Of course not. They're not savages. They're going to disarm them and take their horses so they can't follow. The whole thing will take a matter of minutes. The Unicoi warriors are larger and considerably better skilled than the Royal Guard, so we must hurry."

"But—"

"Shhh." He shakes his head. "Wait for my signal."

I don't know this guy from Adam, but I'm guessing I'll have an easier time escaping from him than from the others, so I decide to go along with his plan. I mean, how dangerous can a guy be who brews his own chamomile tea?

A blood-curdling battle whoop cuts through the night from the direction of Blackthorn and his men. I nearly leap out of my skin. Sounds of clanging metal and ferocious shouts ring out into the night. Ralston nudges me with his shoulder. "Now!" he says.

I run. Instinctively I run away from the sounds of the violence. I run faster than I've ever run before. Sharp rocks bite into the thin soles of the odd boots I'm wearing, bruising my feet. My heart pounds wildly, and my lungs scream for air.

When we finally reach the outside edge of the herd, we're assaulted by a sickeningly sweet, fetid stench so strong it almost knocks me to the ground. Ralston takes my wrist and pulls me behind one of the animals.

"Put your sleeve over your nose, and breathe through your mouth," he says, demonstrating with his sleeve.

"What's that smell?" I cough, trying not to gag, as we snake our way through the grazing animals.

"It's the fargen."

"The what?"

"These beasts. They're fargen."

For the first time I focus on the odd animals we're hiding among. They look like a cross between wooly mammoths and Texas Longhorns—enormous and ugly. Their coats are matted dreadlocks, so long that they brush the ground. Cruel-looking, curved horns perch on either side of their fat heads. They stink something fierce! Like a porta-potty stuffed with rotting garbage and rolled in cow manure. I pull down the bottom of my sleeve, clamping it over my nose to filter the stench.

"Careful where you step." Ralston points to a massive pile of dung. "It's slippery."

We make our way quickly to the back of the herd while the peculiar animals graze serenely, oblivious to our presence. Once we reach the rocky prominence, Ralston says, "The cave is about halfway up. Follow me."

He begins to scale the steep hillside, holding onto bushes and finding footholds in the rocks.

"I can't do this," I say.

"Yes you can. It's easier than it looks. Come on."

I grab a sturdy looking bush and hoist myself up. It *isn't* easier than it looks. In fact, I expect to fall to my death at any minute. I lose my foothold several times, cut my palm on a sharp stone, and rip a couple of nice new holes in my flimsy leather pants. Finally, I make it to the ledge where Ralston crouches, waiting for me.

"I can't go any farther," I wheeze, completely gassed.

"It's all right. We're here.

FIVE

Ralston quickly locates the opening of the cave, even though it's entirely obscured by a thick growth of bushes. He rearranges the foliage after helping me inside. The cave is inky-black and smells like Drew's running shoes on a Friday afternoon. I stay perfectly still, disoriented in the darkness. Ralston fumbles with the saddlebags and pulls out one of the glowing rocks.

"You have to be careful how you handle these," he says, deftly removing the leather wrapping. "They can burn you if you touch the middle part barehanded."

The rock gives off some illumination, and I can see that this cave is similar to the one we've just come from. A few stone benches are carved out of the walls. A rock pit sits in the middle of the floor. Everything is grimy and covered with about six inches of crud.

"What is this place?" I ask.

"It was once a hunting camp, but no one has been here for years. These lands belong to the Crown now."

"The Crown? What do you mean? Where are we?"

"Jaden, I'm certain you have many questions. I'll answer them as best I can, but let's set up our camp first. We're going to be here all night."

"All night!"

"Yes, unless you want to meet up with Blackthorn and his men again. They will be scouring the hills for you by now. Once it begins to get light, they'll be forced to flee to Wall's Edge or risk being captured." Squatting in front of the pit where he placed the glowing rock, he pulls his saddlebags close to him, rummaging through the contents.

"Do you have a cell phone in there? We can call my dad. He'll send help."

He shakes his head. "Sadly, no. But it would be of no use here anyway."

"No bars, huh?" I scan the area looking for a spot to sit that isn't covered with layers of muck. My head is pounding again, and I realize I haven't eaten since—well since I don't remember when.

"I'll make tea, while you roll out the bedrolls," he says, handing me two foam-like cylinders. He fills the teapot from his canteen, carefully balancing the pot on the flat center of the glowing rock.

"Now let's see what we have to eat," he says, dipping back into the bag. "I have some bread, cheese, and a few pommeras. That should get us through until morning."

"Why are you helping me?" I ask, laying out the bedrolls on two stone benches. Each roll has a foam pad and a light blanket.

"Ah, now that is the quintessential question, my dear. Within it is the key to this entire dilemma. Sit down, and I'll tell you over tea."

"I'm not in a tea party mood," I say. "I'm scared, I'm tired, and I want to go home."

"Yes, I know. But I'm afraid we're stuck here for awhile, so we should make ourselves comfortable." He takes his sweet time steeping the tea and decanting it ceremoniously into our cups. I stifle the urge to scream at him to haul ass.

We sit next to each other on the dirty ground. He clinks his tin cup with mine. "To new adventures," he says with a smile.

I sip at my tea, while Ralston sets out napkins. He divides the bread, cheese, and the weird things called pommeras between us. I pick up a pommera. It looks a little like an apple but feels more like a peach. The skin is a light pink, but when Ralston cuts one in half, the inside is blood- red. I cautiously take a small bite. It is unquestionably the most delicious thing I've ever tasted. I quickly devour it, seeds and all.

"Now, where shall we begin," he says while I eat. "Ah, yes, you would like to know why I'm helping you. The simple answer is that I am a Senior Guidance Agent with the Inter-Universal Guidance Agency, or IUGA for short. As such, my assignments take me wherever the greatest need exists, to ensure the orderly unfolding of events in my designated sector. At the moment, that is right here. I've been assigned to assist in returning you home as quickly as possible."

"What?" Pommera juice trickles down my chin and I swipe it with my hand. "You're like in law enforcement or something?"

"In a manner of speaking, yes. Actually, I'm more of an *order* enforcement agent."

"I don't get it. I've never heard of IUGA."

"No, you wouldn't have. It's not an earth-established agency. You see Jaden, you're not at home any longer. You've been … well, *shifted* to another realm, so to speak. Actually, you have been diverted to a different world."

I squint at him. "Okay. Is this still part of your little role-playing game where you and a bunch of your really big, scary friends get together on your horses and try to capture the princess? Because I still don't understand."

"It's not a game, Jaden. I know it seems a bit surreal, but that is exactly what has happened to you. You are no longer on earth … well, earth as you know it, anyway. You are in what we call an alternate world."

I put down the remnants of my second pommera and fold my arms across my chest. "Exactly how stupid do you think I am?

Kidnapping's a serious crime—you know that, don't you? I'm not a willing participant in your little entertainment, so you and your deranged friends better get me home right now or you'll spend the rest of your pathetic lives in prison."

"All right, all right." He raises his hands to calm me. "Humor me for a moment, please. Let us use logic. Like your mother used to say, 'the best approach to any problem is the logical approach'."

That weirds me out. How does he know about that?

"More tea?" he asks.

"No!"

"All right, think back for a minute. What do you last remember before you hit your head?"

I mull it over a moment. "I remember a big storm, thunder, lightning, you know. I was on my back porch watching it all. Then I jumped off the rail."

"Why did you jump?"

I scrunch up my forehead straining to remember. It hurts my cut, so I stop. "I thought I saw some guys on horses. They were barreling straight for the house. That must have been you and your buddies. Right?"

"Didn't that seem a bit odd to you? Horsemen in your backyard in a storm?"

"Uh, *yeah*. In the middle of Madison, Connecticut, that would be a little out of the ordinary. Why do you think I jumped?"

I go over the scene again in my head. "You know, it didn't seem real, though. It almost looked like a 3-D movie. But I got really scared, because it felt like they were looking for *me*."

"Well, they were—and they weren't. They weren't looking for Jade Beckett of Madison, Connecticut. They were looking for Princess Jaden Victoria Hanover Beckett, heir to the throne of Domerica."

"What are you talking about? What's Domerica?" I say, irritated with this whole screwy conversation.

"You're in Domerica now, Jade. We don't know exactly how it occurred. It likely had something to do with the intense electrical storm, but you were shifted from your life in Connecticut to another existence in Domerica."

"Huh? You're saying I'm not *me* now. I'm somebody else? Like I'm really going to believe that. How does someone get 'shifted' to another existence?" I don't know what the point of this bogus scam is, but this guy must think I'm pretty gullible.

He looks at me over the top of his glasses. "Nothing like this has ever happened to you before, has it?"

"Seriously, dude?"

"I didn't think so. Well, I assume you've heard of a time-warp? This is more like a person- and place-warp, similar to a worm-hole or a parallel universe. Can you understand that?"

"Understand what? The load of crap you're trying to feed me?" Now I'm pissed. I jump to my feet, adrenaline pumping wildly through my veins. Its fight or flight time.

"Okay, buddy, who the hell are you? What are you trying to do to me? Is this some kind of sicko mind-game you're playing?" I silently thank my mom for forcing me to go to Tae Kwon Do all those years. I know I can deck this wiry little freak and get the hell out of here. There has to be a sane person somewhere nearby who can help me.

"Please sit down, Jaden," he says calmly. "Think about it. Somewhere in the deepest part of you, you *know* what I'm saying is true. Your mind may not be willing to accept it, but you know this is not the same earth on which you grew up. You can't even see the sky or the sun. Look at yourself, you have on different clothing." He gestures to my peculiar outfit. "Your hair is significantly longer than it was."

My hair, which I normally wear loose, is tied back and woven into a thick braid. I reach around to grab it, and I'm shocked to find that it hangs below my waist. I pull the braid around to examine it. It's the same gold-brown hair I've always had, split-ends and all, only it's grown about two feet.

Ralston says, "People are riding horses for transportation, Jade. Have you seen a car or an airplane since you've been here? Have you ever heard of a fargen, or a pommera, or a healing wand?"

I sit down hard on the dirt floor, sending up a cloud of dust. My mind zooms in a million different directions. It's true that a lot of the things I've seen since I woke up don't make any sense to me. My brain has taken it all in, but hasn't figured out how to process it. I just thought my faculties were addled from the fall, but that doesn't explain this mysterious skyless land or the differences in my appearance. His words bring all the curious things I've witnessed into focus, causing my pulse to quicken and my breath to come in short spurts.

"Okay, okay. Help me out here," I say. "The logical explanation for all this bizarre stuff is that I'm hallucinating, or dreaming, or drugged. The logical explanation is *not* parallel universe. Parallel universe is not the logical explanation for *anything*. That's insane!"

"It is perfectly understandable that you should feel that way," he says soothingly. "In general, people on your earth do not accept the reality of other universes. They are the stuff of science fiction and fantasy, but rest assured they do exist. Whether or not you believe me now does not matter. You will soon know beyond a doubt that what I am saying is true."

"This can't be happening," I say, covering my face with my hands. How did I get stuck in this god-forsaken cave with a certifiable lunatic?

"I know it is hard to believe, but I can guarantee that you are safe here. This shift is only temporary. We will get you home within a short period of time, and meanwhile, I'll be here to help you through it all."

"You're going to take me home?" I ask quietly.

"I promise you, as soon as it is safe to do so, we will return you home."

He gets up and pours more tea for me. I take some sips, and my breathing slows a little.

Can it possibly be true? Could something so bizarre really happen to me? I think I'm pretty open-minded about most things. I like the idea of reincarnation, and I'm pretty sure earthlings can't be the only life forms in the universe considering the billions of other planets out there. But a parallel world? It's too far-fetched. I don't buy it. And, if it is true, why me? Why is this shitstorm happening to me? Out of all the billions of people in the world? I can't be that unlucky.

"Jade," Ralston says after a moment. "You'll be pleased to know there is a bit of good news in all this."

I don't reply. I stare at my teacup trying to figure out what I did to deserve this kind of rotten karma.

"Your mother is alive in this world."

My head snaps up. "My mother? My mother is here? She's alive?" That rockets me out of my little pity party.

I nail him with my eyes. "If you're lying to me, I swear I'll ..."

"I'm not lying, my dear. I would not be so cruel. Remember Blackthorn said she was alive."

"When can I see her? Can we go now?" I spring to my feet.

He shakes his head. "It's not safe yet. Morning will be here soon enough and besides, we have a few things to discuss first."

"Like what?" But before he can answer, another question occurs to me. "Wait a minute, is this my *same* mother?"

"Yes and no. She is basically the same person you've always known. But Jade, she really *is* a queen—the Queen of Domerica. She is running a decent-sized country in a world that is far different from the one you know. She may have certain traits you are not accustomed to. She may appear more formal, more devoted to duty than before. But she loves you and is terribly worried about you right now."

"Is my dad here, and Drew?" I sit back down on the cave floor.

"Yes they are both here. Your father doesn't live at the palace with the rest of you, though. He has his own pursuits, still within the healthcare field. He is a physician and lives in a community within Domerica, but independent from it."

"Are my parents divorced?"

"No. They've parted ways. They remain on good terms, though. He sees you and Drew frequently.

"In this world, your brother is known as Prince Andrew William Hanover Beckett. Domerica is a matriarchal society, Jade. That means that even though Drew is the eldest, you are the heir to the throne."

"Me? So, that's why everyone was calling me Princess?" It scares me to realize I'm beginning to buy into this alternate universe story. I remind myself to be on my guard, but certain things are starting to make a little more sense. Maybe I just want to believe I'll see my mom again. But maybe, just maybe, it's true.

"So, what happened to the real princess? The Jaden that was here before I got shifted?"

Ralston takes off his glasses and massages the bridge of his nose. "She is your *mirror* in this world—your twin here. In all honesty, she was supposed to have died as a result of the fall from the cliff. That did not occur because you shifted into her body."

"Whoa, shut the front door! She was supposed to have *died* from the fall, but she didn't? Now I'm here in *her* body and going on with her life? That's just creepy!" I examine my hands. They look just like my hands, except the nails are beautifully manicured, and I'm wearing an unfamiliar carved gold ring on my right hand.

"One might consider it—"

34

"Wait a minute, wait a minute! What is happening with my life back in Connecticut? Does my family think *I'm* dead? Did I just disappear? Is my dad okay?"

"Jaden, calm down. I will answer all your questions. One at a time, please."

"You're telling me to be calm when my whole world has turned into a bad *X-Files* episode. I want answers!" I ball my hand into a fist and smack it on the ground for emphasis. It hurts like hell.

"Ow!" I shriek.

"Keep your voice down. They will be searching for us," he says. "In answer to your questions, without getting into all the technicalities, I can tell you that when you return—and I promise you will return—it will be within a few minutes of the time you departed. Your life will continue on just as it would have had you never been shifted to this world. No one will have an opportunity to miss you or think you're dead. We can manage that part at least."

He drags his hand over his wispy hair. "I can't say exactly when you will be able to return. We're working on that. These things can be tricky."

"How tricky?"

"Very. Many factors must favorably coincide for such a precisely timed return."

"What's that supposed to mean?"

"Let me try to explain, as best I can. I warn you, though, I will *not* be able to do a thorough job tonight. You will still have lots of questions. I can give you the basics, and we can fill in the details later."

"The basics would be good."

He sits cross-legged, facing me. "All right, try for a moment to imagine your life as a computer model. At the instant you were born, billions of paths for your life became possible, based upon trillions of different variables, including all the choices you might make during a lifetime." He leans forward earnestly, brow knitting together. "An illustration you are familiar with might help. Have you ever watched the news when a hurricane is approaching the United States?"

I nod.

"Excellent. You've seen what they call the 'spaghetti models' that the meteorologists use with all the different colored lines extending out from the storm?"

"Yeah."

"Those lines represent the computerized prediction of the myriad possible paths the hurricane *might* take, based on many meteorological variables. But sometimes, something happens that the meteorologists don't anticipate, and the hurricane veers off on a path completely different from any of those predicted by the computers. Are you with me so far?"

"I don't know. I think so. Please get to the point!"

"Take that spaghetti model and layer it on top of the spaghetti models for each of the innumerable universes in existence—that is the number of potential paths your life might take."

"Hang on a sec; you're saying there are zillions of other universes out there?"

"Trust me on this, Jaden, there are." He stares at me with steely conviction.

"Now this is the important part: *You,* the spark that is uniquely you—call it the soul or whatever you like—can be on only one of those paths at a time. So even though all the possibilities exist in their entirety, just like in the spaghetti model, the hurricane can follow only one path at a time. Just as you can follow only one path at a time. Except you jumped paths in midstream, so to speak."

I stare at him for a minute, processing this explanation. "Okay, so you're telling me I got shifted from the path I was on in Connecticut to this path in Domerica, or wherever the heck I am, because of something like a computer glitch?"

"Yes. Well, that's a very good analogy."

It sounds complicated. "So how do I get home?"

He shrugs. "As I've said, we are working on that. Many factors must coalesce at the exact moment in order for your homecoming to be timely and successful. I don't know how long it will take—maybe a week, maybe a month, or maybe more. But you will get home. No one who has shifted has ever failed to get back. It's vital to galactic order that you return home."

This information makes me dizzy. "I'm not sure I understand all this stuff about possible lifetimes and other universes and spaghetti models."

"That's all right. Those details are unimportant right now. What is important for you to understand is that your presence here has already altered the course of this universe to an extent. We must minimize the effects of this cosmic accident by ensuring that things proceed in an orderly fashion while you are present in this world, and by returning you swiftly and safely to your own world so the course of *that* universe remains intact. That is my job."

"Yeah? Just how do you plan to do that? We don't have to stay in this cave the whole time, do we?"

He chuckles. "No, my dear. In fact, you have quite a comfortable home here in Domerica. It's called Warrington Palace. But I need to educate you on a few things first. You will be required to play the role of Princess Jaden until this situation is resolved. So, you will have to learn certain things about this world and your specific situation before we return to the palace."

"No way! You're going to try to pass me off as a princess? Good luck with that." I laugh nervously, but I'm feeling queasy.

"What if they find out I'm an imposter? What will they do to me? I'm sure the penalties for impersonating a princess are pretty steep."

"That's not going to happen. You are in Princess Jaden's body.

You know all the players—well, your family members, at least. At most, they will think you have been traumatized by your ordeal. We can finesse the rest." He lifts my half-empty teacup and hands it to me. "Here, drink some more tea. You'll feel better."

I do as I'm told and, remarkably, I do feel better, more calm and confident. I'm beginning to believe everything will be okay, especially if I get to see my mom again. In fact, come to think of it, I'm feeling a little *too* good under the circumstances.

"Hey, is this tea drugged?"

Ralston drops his eyes. "It contains a mild mood elevator."

"What!" I fling the cup at the opposite wall. It clatters and bounces against the stone. "That's just great! "You're supposed to be my what? My sponsor, my guardian, my protector? And you drug me without my knowledge? Why should I trust you at all?"

"You're right, Jade. I'm sorry. It's just that most people would be in utter shock if this happened to them. I wasn't sure how badly you'd react. I thought it would make things easier for you, but I shouldn't have done it without telling you. Truly I meant no harm." His whole body sags, like the stuffing's been ripped out of him. "Please forgive me."

I glare at him, considering my options. Let's face it—I don't have a lot of other options. I blow out a long breath. "Okay. Just don't lie to me again," I say sternly.

"I won't. I swear it." He straightens up.

"Let's get on with it, then. Make me a princess."

SIX

*R*alston rubs his hands together eagerly. "First, I shall tell you about this world in which you currently find yourself. It's quite extraordinary! We have time only to touch on the essentials; the particulars can be filled in later."

"Fine. Just go slow," I say.

"The year is the same as in your world, and technically you are on the planet known as *earth*, but this earth is vastly different from the one you are used to."

"Different, how?"

"An astronomical event, commonly known as the Great Disaster, took place more than three hundred years ago. It wiped out the majority of this earth's population and drastically altered its atmosphere, making it hostile to all but the hardiest forms of life. Consequently, most of this earth's population now lives inside domes."

"Domes? You mean like geodesic domes?"

"No, I mean like enormous domes with their own ecosystems, capable of housing entire countries."

I gape at him. "You mean we're in a dome?"

"Yes, we are. *Domerica* to be exact, one of the three existing dome nations. It is roughly the size of your state of Massachusetts and is located at the foot of the Appalachian Mountains. Domerica houses most of the surviving North American population—approximately five million people. *Cupola de Vita* stands where Peru once existed and domiciles the South American survivors. On the European continent is *Dome Noir*, located roughly where Paris, France, used to be."

My eyebrows shoot up. "That's it? Only three?"

He nods.

"What happened to Africa? Asia? Australia?"

"They, and Antarctica, were mostly wiped out. The land that didn't fall away into the oceans was destroyed by thermal heat, tidal waves, dust clouds, fire storms or noxious gases. You name it. Every possible catastrophe occurred."

"That really sucks! What caused all that to happen?"

"Back in 1758, a small celestial body, known on your planet as Halley's Comet, was supposed to pass so close to the earth it could be seen with the naked eye. Instead of making its peaceful journey 50 million kilometers outside the earth's atmosphere, it collided with another asteroid, which altered its trajectory and caused it to slam into the Pacific Ocean."

"A comet hit the ocean? But that would wipe out the entire earth. I mean, that's what all the disaster movies want you to believe."

"Most of the comet burned up before it ever reached earth, but what was left was enough to destroy eighty percent of the earth's surface and permanently rip a hole in its atmosphere, making the rest of the planet uninhabitable."

It takes me a few minutes to wrap my mind around that. It's straight out of a fantasy novel—global destruction, scorched earth. Knowing that it really happened is seriously disturbing.

Ralston sits quietly sipping his tea and watching me.

TRANSCENDER: *First-Timer*

When I find my voice again, I ask, "How did *anyone* survive? These domes couldn't have been around in the 1700s. I mean they have their own ecosystems, so they must be climate controlled, right? That's pretty sophisticated technology."

He half-smiles. "Actually, IUGA interceded."

"Agents? Like you?"

"Yes. You see, the asteroid that collided with Halley's Comet was a cosmic accident, a fluke, something which was not foreseen. It threatened the entire galactic order and put the destiny of this universe in jeopardy. So, when the Agency became aware of the rogue asteroid, it felt compelled to step in quickly in an attempt to minimize the inevitable catastrophic consequences.

Erecting the domes and stocking them with all the essentials to begin a new society was the easy part. Convincing the people they needed to take shelter in the domes was something all together different."

"So how did you manage that?"

"Not very well at first. We tried telling them the truth—that a cataclysmic event was about to occur which would annihilate the world's population. That was a mistake. We convinced some people, others believed we were instruments of the devil—witches or heretics—trying to capture their bodies or souls for evil purposes. A public outcry went up for the arrest and imprisonment of all IUGA agents. It was a chaotic time."

"What happened?"

"Actually it was rumor and superstition, with a bit of religion thrown in, that saved much of the population. To this day, we don't know how the rumor originated, but the story began to circulate in South America that the *end of days* as foretold by the Bible was coming, and we agents were actually angels of mercy, emissaries of God so to speak, sent to save the chosen ones. Some even likened the domes to Noah's Ark." He laughs, shaking his head.

"Soon people were flocking to the Dome in Peru faster than we could accommodate them. The word quickly spread, and the domes began to fill up. I have to admit, when we saw how well the story resonated with the people, we did nothing to quell the rumor or convince the populous otherwise. Grateful for our good fortune, we heartily welcomed all those who wished to be saved and did our best to appear angelic."

"That's wild!" I shake my head in wonder.

"Yes. It was a little frenzied. When the comet actually hit, the survivors were at once horrified and relieved. Equal amounts of grieving and rejoicing ensued in the domes. A new church was formed shortly thereafter—the Church of the Chosen, or the COC. Its doctrines are based on the myth that the people in the domes were hand-picked to survive because they were somehow more worthy." He chuckles. "It is the largest religious denomination in the world today. Membership in the church is mandatory in Domerica."

"People in Domerica are *required* to attend the COC?"

"Yes, they are," Ralston replies.

"And my mother is okay with this?"

"She's the one who made it mandatory."

I have to chew on that for a minute. It doesn't sound like Mom. The whole idea of freedom of religion was a big deal to her.

This is all so enormous and so implausible, and all at once, I'm very fatigued. I have no idea what time it is or how long Ralston and I have been talking. More than anything at this moment I just want to close my eyes and go to sleep right here on the grimy floor of the cave.

"Ralston, are we almost finished? I'm beat, and I'm not sure how much more information my head can hold tonight."

"I know, old girl," he says. "You've had a pretty eventful day. We've only a few more things to go over. I need to fill you in on what to expect at the palace, so you won't be completely overwhelmed. Why don't you get up and move your legs a little. I'll make some more tea—without any additives, this time."

I stand up and shake out my legs, then I do a few jumping jacks to get my circulation going. It occurs to me that although I've spent several hours on a horse, I don't feel saddle sore at all.

"Hey Ralston, the princess must ride horses all the time, huh?" I say.

"Actually she's an accomplished horsewoman. Why do you ask?"

"I can tell her saddle muscles are in shape." I pat my thigh. "Where's her horse?"

"I'm afraid he didn't survive the fall," Ralston says. "A beautiful animal ... such a shame."

"They went over the cliff together?"

He nods.

"Oh man, that's depressing! And by the way, when it comes to horses, I don't know the first thing. That beast I was on today was as close as I've ever been to one."

"That's all right. I can teach you enough to get you through. Toning the muscles is fifty percent of the battle, so you are already half-way there."

I'm not sure I believe him, but I'm too tired to argue. Instead, I wander around the cave wondering how far it extends into the hill. I peer into a long, dark hallway.

"ARGGHHH!" I let out a loud shriek.

Ralston drops the teapot with a clunk and a splash. "What is it? What's wrong?" He's at my side instantly. I'm impressed the old guy can move so fast.

"I saw something. Some eyes back there."

Ralston squints into the darkness. "It's just a Hillcat, Jade. They're harmless. They live in the caves. Probably looking for a morsel of our dinner."

He retrieves his fallen teapot and checks to see how much water is left. "By the way, may I remind you that we are being pursued by your kidnappers. Please keep your blood-curdling screams to a minimum."

"Yeah, sorry about that." I break off a piece of cheese from the remains of my meal and go back to hunt for the Hillcat. "Here kitty, kitty," I call softly. I crouch near the spot where I saw the eyes. The cat doesn't reappear.

"Tea's ready," Ralston says. I leave the cheese and rejoin him at the rock pit. "The cat's probably long gone by now. Many of these caves are interconnected."

I pick up my tea, and we settle ourselves on the ground again.

"We have only a half-cup each," Ralston says. "We must conserve the remainder of our water for morning. I'm not certain how long it will take us to find a search party or one of your mother's patrols."

He regards me thoughtfully. "How are you holding up?"

"Oh just great, for someone who's been dropped into the middle of a bizarre sci-fi nightmare."

He offers an indulgent smile. "Jaden, my best advice for you is to look at this as a grand adventure—one that few humans ever get to experience."

I respond with an exaggerated eye roll.

"It's not that bad, really. You're a princess here. Something most girls can only dream of."

"Yeah, that's another thing. Why am I a princess? Why of all people is my mom the queen?"

"Surely you are familiar with your mother's lineage? Your ancestors were British, as were mine. But yours were part of the House of Hanover—the British royal family. When the disaster occurred, your five-times great grandfather, Lord Malcolm, happened to be the highest ranking member of the royal family present in the British Colonies. At the time, he was Governor of New York. Consequently, he was the natural choice to become the first King of Domerica.

"Unfortunately, he died two years later, and his eldest child, Prince Richard, became king. I'm afraid it was something of a calamity. Richard was a notorious alcoholic and gambler. He nearly brought the newly formed country to its knees, before finally drinking himself to death a few years after his coronation. His mother Lady Amelia and sister, Princess Mary—later Queen Mary—were the only reasons the country did not fall into chaos. So, rather than ousting the House of Hanover altogether, it was decreed that thenceforth only female heirs of the queen could succeed to the throne of Domerica."

"Are you serious? I always thought my mom was exaggerating with all that stuff about Queen Victoria. So the Revolutionary War never happened? This country's still a monarchy?"

"Actually, no wars have occurred since the time of the disaster, but I'm afraid you will find this world quite backward compared with your own. The disaster caused quite a set-back for the advancement of enlightened forms of government, as well as for industry and technology. Many of the greatest inventors, scientists, and statesmen of your time were never born in this world, their ancestors having been wiped out."

"You mean no Alexander Graham Bell, Albert Einstein, or Steve Jobs?"

"That's right. Even though Henry Ford was born and lived his entire life in Domerica, combustible engines, and all other machinery or industry that pollutes the air, are strictly prohibited within the domes. Any type of flame or fire is banned completely in Domerica. The risks are too great. A large fire could potentially destroy all life in the dome."

"For real? So it's kind of like living in the dark ages?"

"It's not quite as bad as that. In fact, the inhabitants of this earth have a few things that have not yet been developed on your earth."

"Like what?"

"The domes are quite complex technologically, requiring a significant power source to keep them operating optimally. Each dome is equipped with a completely self-regenerating, perpetual power source called an *Xtron* energy cell. It works on a concept called x-fusion. Nothing even approaching this type of natural, self-perpetrating power has yet been developed on your earth. It has many uses here. Although I suspect you may be more impressed by the lack of uses developed to date." He shrugs. "More's the pity."

"Ralston, how am I going to keep all this stuff straight? What if my mom sees right through me or thinks I have permanent brain damage or something?"

"Not to worry, we'll have time to review everything later. In fact that's enough Domerican history for tonight." He gets up and begins to clear away our tea things. "I should tell you a few things about Princess Jaden, though. Enough for you to finesse it through the next few days until we have a better idea when you will be going home."

"Is she anything like me?" I ask. "Or is she some prissy, stuck-up diva who says things like 'let them eat cake'?" I sit on top of my bedroll and pull off my decimated boots.

"Fortunately she looks and sounds just like you." He chuckles at his own joke. "But, of course Princess Jaden has been groomed from an early age to inherit the throne. She is gracious and articulate; fluent in both French and Spanish; an excellent swordswoman. She can outride anyone in Domerica, man or woman. Social causes are high on her agenda, making her truly beloved by the people of Domerica."

"And I'm supposed to be her? You're kidding, right?" My stomach suddenly hits the spin cycle.

"No, Jaden, I am quite serious. I know you can do it." His eyes tell me I have no choice.

"Well, that's just insane! I suck at Spanish, I don't know any

French, I've never held a sword in my life and I've already shared my vast knowledge of horses with you."

"That's another thing we need to work on," he says shaking a finger at me, "your language."

"What do you mean?" I don't remember cursing in front of him.

"You must try not to use American slang while you are here. First of all, princesses do not employ the word 'suck' as a descriptive term. Secondly, wellborn young people say mother and father, not mom and dad. And please use the word man or gentleman where appropriate, not dude or guy. If you make an effort to stick to proper English, you'll be fine."

"Okay! I never asked to be a princess, you know."

"I know, Jaden, but even the word 'okay' is out. It has no meaning here. In fact, I'm not sure where it originated on your earth. Just say 'all right' instead."

"All right!" I say. "What about everything else?"

"Well, I plan to ask your mother to let me stay on in some capacity at the palace. I have every reason to believe she will grant my request. We can work on some elementary French. I can give you riding lessons without her knowledge." He scratches his head thoughtfully. "We won't worry about the swordsmanship. As regards your royal demeanor, the best advice I can give you is to stand up straight and pretend you are an actress playing the part of a princess."

"Oh man, I don't think I can pull this off," I say, holding my stomach.

"You'll be fine, Jade. Nobody will be the wiser. If you get into trouble, I shall be right beside you."

"I hope you know what you're doing," I say, although I'm pretty sure he doesn't have a clue.

"I do. Just get some sleep. We can talk more in the morning."

I climb into my bedroll and pull the thin blanket up to my chin.

Ralston putters quietly, repacking his saddlebags.

I close my eyes and my head swims, like I've spent the whole day on a rollercoaster ride. Gradually my tensed-up muscles begin to relax, and my stomach settles a bit. No sense trying to compose my thoughts tonight, though. Tomorrow promises to be another mind-blowing day.

SEVEN

*T*he good news is I slept like a rock. The bad news is I slept *on* a rock—a rock bench. In the morning, my whole body throbs like a toothache, and my mouth tastes like I've been sucking on fargen fur. I need two Tylenol and some Listerine badly. But, oh yeah, I'm stuck in some backwoods dome-world where pain reliever and mouthwash don't exist.

Ralston glances at me as I stretch to work the kinks out of my neck. "Your accommodations will be much more agreeable tonight, Jaden." He's already packed up his bed roll and is fussing with the teapot.

"Do they actually have real beds in this god-forsaken place?" I ask.

"I think you'll find Warrington Palace much to your liking."

He nods toward the foot of my bed. "I believe you've made a friend."

A pile of dirty straw lies at the end of my bed. On closer scrutiny, I realize it's an animal. "The Hillcat?" I ask softly.

He nods.

"Hey buddy." The cat turns her head toward me and twitches her bushy tail. Traces of old scars mar her otherwise noble face. She has a proud nose, piercing amber eyes, and she's about double the size of a normal house cat. "Aren't you a pretty girl," I say, reaching out to pet her. She darts out of my reach and back into the dark recesses of the cave.

"They're not used to people, but she was apparently grateful for your cheese," Ralston says, checking his pocket watch. "We have time for a quick cup of tea. Then we'd better get going. Your mother will have patrols spread over these hills by now. The sooner we flag one down, the sooner you will get to see her."

My mother! I'd almost forgotten. My mood brightens immediately, and my stomach quivers with anticipation. I'm going to see my mother! It's a miracle. Being kidnapped was worth it, being "glitched" into some creepy, post-Apocalyptic dome-world was worth it, for a chance to be with Mother again.

"I'm not thirsty," I say rolling up my bedroll. "Let's go."

Ralston smiles, quickly repacking his teapot. "Whatever you say, Your Highness." He exaggerates a bow in my direction, and hitches his saddlebags over his shoulder.

The day is bright, but the sky is empty of sun or clouds. A giant silvery mass glimmers high above our heads. Ralston explains that a protective layer of gases is maintained between the two layers of impenetrable clear material forming the dome. According to him, the silver gases let in enough sunlight for the plants to perform their food and oxygen-making functions, but not enough to burn the skin or damage the eyes.

Ralston scans the adjacent hills and the valley below before we begin our descent from the cave.

"You don't think Blackthorn and his men are still looking for us, do you?" I ask.

"No, it's too dangerous with everyone in the country searching for you ... and them. They'll be racing toward Wall's Edge by now to a secret underground tunnel. That is how we got into the dome yesterday. That is how they will get home."

"Who are those guys anyway? Why were they trying to kidnap

me?"

"That was young Chief Blackthorn, the son of the Chief of Unicoi. The woman was his sister Catherine. The others were Unicoi warriors."

"What's Unicoi?"

"Ah well, that's an interesting story, most of which can wait until later. All you need to know for now is that when the Great Disaster occurred and the domes were put in place, a few pockets of survivors completely escaped our notice for a number of years. The Unicoi lived on the edge of the Appalachian mountain range in what would be the state of Tennessee back in your world. They weren't supposed to have made it at all. But due to certain serendipitous factors, such as the prevailing winds and the protection of the mountains, a rather large group actually survived.

"The population was made up mostly of Cherokee Indians, along with a collection of Spanish, British, and Irish settlers. They moved into a series of caves near Domerica where they devised ways to filter most of the impurities from the air through the use of animal skins and fabrics. It was tough going those first few years. There was an underground source of fresh water, though, and eventually they learned to raise their own crops and livestock inside the caves."

Traveling down the rocky hill is much easier than climbing up and, by a stroke of good luck, the fargen have moved off to graze in another area of the meadow.

"Ralston, what are those fargen things exactly? I mean, do people eat them?" I ask.

"Some people do, but the meat is tough and gamey tasting. They're raised for their wool. One fargen produces as much wool as thirteen sheep, yet eats only as much as three or four. They look large, but they're mostly hair. Fargen wool is the major source of fabric for clothing, bedding, rugs, and just about everything else in Domerica. That top you are wearing is made of fargen wool."

I check out my soiled, torn, formerly white sweater. It's very soft and must've been nice at one time. Hard to believe the sumptuous fabric came from those smelly beasts.

"The main road is about a mile that way." Ralston points ahead. "If we travel in that direction, we're sure to be discovered in no time."

Walking along the dusty trail Ralston chatters away, filling me in on more details about how the domes operate. "It's quite ingenious really; everything is climate controlled. The temperature is always a perfect seventy-two degrees. It rains on Monday, Wednesday, and Friday from three o'clock until five in the afternoon, leaving the weekends completely storm-free. The air is recycled through ionized filters every twenty-four hours to ensure it is properly oxygenated and entirely devoid of pollutants."

"That's awesome. Do IUGA Agents take care of all of that?"

He stops and looks at me. "Remember, Jaden, don't say 'awesome,' that's uniquely American and appallingly overused. Say 'my but that's remarkable,' or something similar."

I roll my eyes, and we continue on.

"The answer to your question is 'no.' Domerica has a Dome Operations Center and crews of dome maintenance workers who handle the day-to-day operations. IUGA hasn't been directly involved in the affairs of the Domes since the Great Disaster."

I tilt my head and give him a look. "Oh, so you just operate behind the scenes now?"

He cuts his eyes toward me. "Let us say that we maintain a presence here to ensure continuing order. Our charter does not allow for direct interference with events on this planet." He shrugs. "That provision was added after the Great Disaster. Some felt we should not have erected the domes in the first place."

"They think you should have just let everyone die?"

"Yes, well, even cosmic accidents can be looked upon as a type of destiny. Reasonable men hold differing opinions on that point."

TRANSCENDER: *First-Timer*

We reach the main road in about twenty minutes, but see no patrols. Ralston suggests we continue walking in the direction of the palace, rather than waiting for someone to find us. We stroll along the dusty road, and I pepper him with more questions.

"You never told me why Blackthorn was trying to kidnap me," I say.

"Ah, now that is an unfortunate story. The population of Unicoi is slowly and inescapably being poisoned. Its citizens are falling ill and dying at an alarming rate."

"Poisoned! How?"

"By long-term exposure to the radiation and gas emitted from naturally occurring Uranium. Uranium, once contained deep in the mountain, has been exposed by all the excavation for underground building. The spread of the poison cannot be contained. They have no choice, but to leave their cities or die."

"They're all going to die? Why haven't they just cleared out of there?"

"The only way they can survive is to become a part of Domerica or some other dome, or to have a dome of their own. Your mother and the other dome rulers have refused to allow the Unicoi to relocate into the existing domes."

"But, that's insane! Why would they refuse? I don't believe my mom would do that."

"It is a bit complicated, Jade. The queen is genuinely concerned about allowing the Unicoi population into Domerica for several reasons. The major one being that she believes, as many others do, that the disease killing the Unicoi is communicable. No one in this world really understands the nature of chronic radiation poisoning. It has never been studied because it was never an issue before. In her mind, she would be placing her own people at risk."

"There's got to be someone who understands it and can explain it to her," I say.

"Yes, well, perhaps that will occur in time, but many political and practical considerations must also be dealt with when relocating an entire country. How will the population be fed and housed? Will they submit to Domerican rule or demand a chief of their own? Will they join the Church of the Chosen? Thorny issues, all. It's a daunting proposition and one which your mother has been unwilling to address to date."

"And they kidnapped me to force her to do something?"

"Yes. It was a foolish plan, but Ryder Blackthorn is young and fervent in his desire to save his people," he says. "Ryder's mother died last year due to Uranium exposure, and his father has contracted lung cancer from breathing the gas. Chief Blackthorn has become physically debilitated, although his mind is still sharp. Young Blackthorn has taken on a great deal of the responsibility for running the country. A huge burden for a twenty-year-old."

He pauses and looks over at me. "He is a very good man, Jade. Please don't judge him too harshly based upon his treatment of you."

"Oh, you mean don't be angry with him just because he tried to abduct me and almost got me killed?"

"He was attempting to save hundreds of thousands of lives."

"Well, I don't hate him or anything," I admit. "Actually, he was kind of nice. I sort of liked him."

"I'm not surprised. He's quite an appealing individual, isn't he?"

"Umm," I mumble, remembering the shared horseback ride. "Hey, Ralston?"

"Yes."

"What were *you* doing with those guys?"

"I was young Chief Blackthorn's teacher and trusted friend for the past two years. He knows nothing about the IUGA or my being a Guidance Agent, but I rarely left his side. I suspect he may be a bit put out with me just now."

TRANSCENDER: *First-Timer*

"So if you're a Guidance Agent, and you go where you're most needed, why were you with him?"

He looks at the swirling mass above our heads for a moment. "Because Ryder Blackthorn is the key to the survival of this planet— or at least he was before this little snafu."

"You mean the survival of Unicoi?"

"No. I mean this version of earth. I mentioned that there has been no war on this planet since the time of the disaster, but war will come eventually. Blackthorn is the only one who can prevent total annihilation of the domes."

I stare at him for a beat. "Holy crap Ralston, don't you think you ought to be back there with him instead of with me? I mean ... geez ... the whole damn planet?"

"I think I can keep an eye on you both for a while."

We walk along not speaking while I consider all this. Then something else strikes me.

"Ralston, how come the Blackthorns have such light skin and blue eyes if they're descended from the Cherokee?"

"Well, for one thing, their mother was mostly Irish. For another, no copper-skinned Cherokee exist anymore. After three hundred years of living underground, the population of Unicoi is generally fair skinned."

"How come they're all so ... well, gorgeous?"

He laughs. "Not *all* Unicoi are as handsome as the Blackthorns. No sunlight for three centuries helps. I suppose you noticed their flawless skin. Also, a kind of natural selection took place in the beginning, when the living was very rough. Only the strongest men and the most beautiful women survived and had offspring. I suppose you could say they come from a good gene pool."

We follow the road a few more miles, when we finally spot a group of riders coming our way. "Excellent. This looks like a royal patrol," Ralston says, grinning and waving to the men.

One rider breaks away, making a beeline straight for us. Frightened, I turn to run in the opposite direction, but Ralston catches my arm. "It's all right, it's Prince Andrew."

Andrew? Drew? "Drew!" I yelp, sprinting toward him.

He jumps from his horse in mid-stride and catches me up in his arms. "Oh, Jade, we were so worried." He hugs me fiercely, then holds me at arm's length to look at me. A flicker of fear licks my insides, and I pray he can't see I'm an impostor, but his eyes hold only concern.

"We found your horse. We weren't sure if you were alive or dead," he says.

"I'm fine, Drew. Really."

"What did they do to you, Sister?"

Nothing, I just fell," I say, gingerly touching my forehead. I'm so happy to see his sweet face. His untidy curls are a bit longer than normal, and he's dressed all weird, in a white poet's shirt, leather vest, dark pants, and riding boots—but it's still Drew.

"Truly? You're all right?"

I nod.

He grins, taking my chin in his hands and examining my gash more closely. "I thought perhaps they tried to rearrange your face for you. I could have told them it was no use."

Yup. Same old Drew! I knock his hand away.

"And, who's this?" he asks, stepping back to look at Ralston.

"This is Ralston. He helped me escape."

"Professor Constantine Albrecht Ralston, at your service, Prince Andrew," he says bowing. That's the first time I've heard his full name. No wonder he likes to be called Ralston.

Drew eyes him suspiciously. "You don't look Unicoi. Who are you?"

"I am a scholar, a student of the world," he says. "I lived in both Dome Noir and Cupola de Vita before taking a position as teacher and trainer to young Chief Blackthorn in Unicoi."

"You're Blackthorn's teacher! Why, pray tell, did you help my sister?"

"While I respect young Blackthorn, I do not condone kidnapping," Ralston says. "I felt it my duty to ensure that Princess Jaden was returned safely to her family."

"And, how can I be certain you're not a spy?"

"Oh, Drew, please," I say. "The man just rescued me. He hid me in a cave all night and brought me safely to you. You should be thanking him. We're tired and hungry and I want to see Mom ... er, Mother. Let's go home."

Drew's posture relaxes. "Of course you are right." He holds his hand out to Ralston. "Thank you Professor Ralston for saving my sister and delivering her safely to us. You have the gratitude of all of Domerica. You shall be handsomely rewarded."

Drew signals two of the patrols. They climb from their horses and offer the reins to Ralston and me.

"Uh, Drew, can I ride with you? I'm beat," I say.

His brow creases for a half-second. "Of course. You *must* be tired if you're willing to ride with me on Glacier."

He climbs on his pure white horse, which thankfully is regular-sized, and holds his arm out for me. I take it and clumsily clamber up into the saddle behind him. I can hardly believe I'm on my way to see my new home and the mother I thought I'd lost forever.

EIGHT

Drew sends a man ahead to tell Mother I've been found safe. He tells me she's been "wretched with worry" since Blackthorn's messenger arrived with the news of my kidnapping. Drew's speech is a lot different here, but I'm grateful for his familiar company and relieved that, as usual, he's a one-man gab-fest.

He keeps up an animated, mostly one-sided conversation about the frantic dome-wide efforts to locate me, the fantastic rumors flying around about my fate, and the poorly-timed arrival of the Ambassador from Cupola de Vita at the palace. I'm glad I don't have to talk much because I'm so tired I'm afraid I might screw up and say something I shouldn't.

When Warrington Palace finally comes into view, I nearly gasp out loud. Gleaming, white and enormous, it's set like a pearl in the ravishing countryside. It looks like a fairy-tale castle straight out of the Brothers Grimm—with square towers, rounded turrets, and those saw-tooth looking things running the length of the roof. Ivy crawls along the walls, and dozens of mullioned windows sparkle silver in the soft dome-light. I can hardly believe this luminous citadel is going to be my temporary home.

We ride along the front promenade toward the massive palace entrance. Drew stops our horse near a rail post with a water trough underneath—the place where people park their horses, obviously. He dismounts and helps me off Glacier's back.

The gigantic palace doors burst open, and Mother sweeps out onto the portico. Oh God, it's her. It's really her! My heart soars. So many times I've thought if only I could see her one more time, if only I could say all those things I never said, if only I had one more chance .... It takes me a second to collect myself. But I suck in my breath and fly up the stairs straight into her arms. We hug each other tightly, both weeping for joy.

"Jaden, darling," Mother sobs. "I was worried sick. Thank God you are alive. They didn't harm you, did they?" She pushes a lock of hair off my forehead, tenderly touching my wound.

"No, Mother, I'm fine." I smile through my tears. "The cut is from a fall. It's nothing. I'm just so happy to see you."

"And I you, child." She dabs at her face with a lace handkerchief. She is more beautiful than in my memories, even with red, swollen eyes. Her gown is dark blue silk, and her hair flows long and loose down her back. Quite a change from the business suit and short bob she always wore back home.

"Come inside, dear. You must be tired and hungry." She leads me into the palace. "Oh God, Jaden, I believed I'd lost you. I did not think I could bear it."

The interior of the castle is even more striking than the outside. Prisms of light dazzle from crystal chandelier, to gilt-framed mirror, to marble floor, and back again. Thick tapestries cover towering stone walls. Massive wooden chests bearing huge vases of fresh spring flowers, line the hallway. Interesting objets d'art are tucked into every corner, crying out to be appreciated but it's all going to have to wait, because right now I only have eyes for my mother.

We enter a large room with floor to ceiling windows overlooking an inviting courtyard. Chairs and sofas are arranged in clusters around the room. Mom settles next to me on a green satin-covered loveseat facing one of the windows. Her arms encircle me again, and I rest my head on her shoulder, drinking in her wonderful amber-spice scent. I cry like a three-year-old reunited with its mother after going missing in a department store. I'm a complete puddle of ooze, but I don't care. I have my mom back!

A dozen or so people hover unobtrusively in the background while this little scene plays out. I assume they're servants—a fact which is confirmed when Mother subtly lifts her hand, and a uniformed butler comes scurrying forward.

"Samuel, please bring us some tea and have cook prepare a small breakfast for Princess Jaden."

Samuel, a buttoned-up man with a pathetic comb-over and fluttery hands, bows obsequiously. "Yes, ma'am, and may I say how happy we are to have Princess Jaden back with us. Blessed be the Chosen."

He doesn't make eye contact with either me or Mother. She smiles vaguely in his direction. "Thank you, Samuel. Yes, we are overjoyed that our Jaden has returned safely."

She holds me close again, rocking back and forth, not saying a word. After a few minutes, she puts a finger under my chin, raising my face to hers. "Jaden, when you feel ready, I hope you will be able to tell me what happened."

It's so nice just to sit here with my head on her shoulder. I don't really want to rehash all the bizarre events of the last two days, but I suppose I need to come up with a story about what happened to me. Explaining my capture is going to be a little delicate since I can't very well tell her I was sitting on my porch in Connecticut when a bunch of armed horsemen snatched me.

Based on things Blackthorn told me, I'm able to give her a sketchy account of my leaping from the cliff and waking up in the cave.

I act as though the bump on my head made the sequence of events a little hazy, which it did. She doesn't question me too closely. I tell her about Ralston and our escape, and I pretty much go over everything else that happened right up to the point of meeting Drew and the patrol on the main road. Of course, I leave out the part about Ralston being an IUGA Agent and me not being *exactly* the same daughter who went missing yesterday.

"Did Blackthorn or any of his men harm you or treat you harshly in any way?" she asks, her eyes probing mine.

"No, Mother, he was a little scary, but he was a gentleman with me."

"They didn't bind your hands or blindfold you? Or make you do anything, well … repugnant?"

"No, Mother. Other than being held against my will, I wasn't mistreated."

My breakfast arrives, interrupting our conversation. Samuel pours tea and offers to be of further assistance. Mother waves him away.

I'm famished. I lift the silver dome covering my plate, hoping there won't be any unrecognizable food. It turns out to be good old scrambled eggs and biscuits. I dive into my meal while Mother talks.

"Darling, we were so fearful for your safety. I want to assure you that this heinous deed will not go unpunished. Young Blackthorn and all of Unicoi will pay dearly for this."

I look up from my feeding frenzy and gulp down a mouthful of eggs. "What do you mean?"

"I mean, we know where their secret tunnels are. I have men stationed there now. He and his gang of criminals will be apprehended before they can escape to Unicoi." She pats my arm. "If he thinks he can trespass on my land and kidnap a Princess of Domerica with impunity, he has rather an unpleasant surprise waiting for him." Her smile is almost sinister. This is a side of her I've never seen. Whatever she has in mind for Blackthorn, it isn't good.

"Mother, I wish we could just forget about it. Everything's fine now. He made a stupid mistake. He was just trying to get help for his people. I'm sure he won't try it again."

"You can count on it, Daughter. That, I promise you." She pats my arm again, sending chills down my spine.

"Now what about this Ralston character?" she asks. "Do you

think he's a spy?"

"No!" I say a little too quickly. "He's really a gentle, kind, scholarly type of person, Mother. He's not even from Unicoi." I choose my next words carefully. "It is my strong desire that he be treated as a hero, not a villain, Mother. Please."

She raises her eyebrows. "If you wish it, it shall be so." She signals Samuel. "Bring in Professor Ralston, please."

Ralston is escorted into the room, and he bows deeply to Mother.

"Professor Ralston, I understand I owe you a large debt of gratitude for rescuing my daughter," Mother says. "I would like to reward you. You may take your recompense in gold if you like. Or, if you wish to make your home here in Domerica, we will furnish you with a small farm and sufficient working capital."

"Thank you, Your Highness. You are most generous and kind. But, if you please, ma'am, I humbly request that I be given a post here at Warrington Palace. You see, I'm no farmer. I am an academic and a world traveler. I have been fortunate enough to have held posts at both Chateau de Ciel Bleu in Dome Noir and Castillo de Angeles in Cupola de Vita. Most recently I was employed at Sequoyah Hall in Unicoi."

"My children have already had an excellent education. What else do you have to offer?" she snips.

"Mother," I interrupt. "Ralston knows so much about our neighboring domes and their governments and cultures. In my brief discussions with him, I can tell he would have a lot to teach me."

She looks at me oddly. I swallow hard, hoping I haven't said anything wrong. Her eyes return to Ralston.

"If you please, Your Highness," he says. "I am certain both King Philippe and King Rafael will recommend me to you. I am also well acquainted with your cousin, Lady Lorelei Bartlett. I am confident that she will vouch for my character and credentials as well."

This piques Mother's interest. "Oh? How do you know Lady

Lorelei?"

"I had the privilege of being her professor when she studied abroad in Dome Noir. She was one of my brightest pupils. We've kept in touch these many years. I've dined with her and Lord Bartlett on a number of occasions."

Mother gazes at Ralston, speaking slowly, as though composing her thoughts. "I suppose your travels and your knowledge of other governments would round out Princess Jaden's education nicely. Andrew could also benefit, I have no doubt. Lord knows even *I* could do with some greater insights into our neighbors to the South and East." She seems to be warming to the idea of having a distinguished professor in residence at the palace.

"Yes. You may start immediately," she says. "Samuel will arrange rooms for you on the children's floor. You will find a laboratory, a classroom, and a modest library on that floor. I have quite a nice selection of literature, poetry, and biography in my office which you are welcome to borrow also. Let Samuel know if you require any additional books or equipment."

"Thank you, ma'am," Ralston says. He bows again and turns to leave.

"And Ralston, please join us at our state dinner tonight," Mother adds. "We are honoring our esteemed guest, Ambassador Garcia of Cupola de Vita."

He nods. "As you wish ma'am." Samuel leads him from the room.

"Thank you, Mother," I say relieved.

"He seems harmless," she sniffs. "Did you get enough to eat, dear?"

"Yes."

"Good, now we must get on with our day as much preparation remains to be done. You look a fright, Jade. It will take Sylvia all day just to get the mats out of your hair."

I frown. "But Mother, I was hoping we could spend some more time together."

"Oh, I know Jaden, I was too." She takes both my hands in hers. "But all of this could not have come at a worse time. What with Ambassador Garcia visiting, and King Rafael still in a snit with me about our new trade agreement with Dome Noir, I have some work to do with the ambassador—you know, smooth over hard feelings. We lost all of last night. After we heard of your abduction, the whole palace was in chaos."

I heave a sigh and form my mouth into the best pout I can muster.

"Please darling, don't be cross with me. I know you've been through a nightmare, but we'll have plenty of time together once the ambassador leaves. Why don't you go upstairs to bathe and rest for a while? I'll send Sylvia up later with your dress." She kisses me on the forehead and rises from the sofa. "Oh, and Jaden, the Skorplings have been very upset over your disappearance. You know how they get. They kept half the household up all night long with their carryings on. I'll have Drew bring them to your room for a few minutes before you rest, so you may calm and reassure them."

My mind freezes. Who the heck are the Skorplings? "Uh, sure, that'd be great," I say.

"Samuel!" Mother calls as she strides briskly from the room.

NINE

*M*y head is reeling from meeting my mother the queen. It isn't quite the homecoming I had envisioned. She isn't exactly what I was expecting, but she's beautiful and commanding and impressive and I'm over the moon to see her again. I'm a little crushed that she didn't want to spend more time comforting me after my ordeal, but I get it—being queen is a lot of work. I stand to leave and stop dead in my tracks. I realize, to my horror, I don't have the slightest idea where I'm going.

The look on my face must give away my confusion, because a pretty girl in a maid's uniform hurries to me. "May I get you something, Princess?"

"Uh, no. I think I would like to go to my room now."

"Yes, ma'am." She curtseys, and turns to leave.

Ma'am? Is she talking to me? I guess it's some royal term of address.

"Uh, would you mind helping me to my room?" I say. "I'm feeling a little faint."

"Oh, yes, ma'am." She takes my arm and leads me from the room. The other servants gawk and whisper behind us. My paranoia tells me they know I'm not the real princess. My common sense tells me they just love to gossip.

The princess' room is in the east wing of the family quarters, second floor, seventh door to the right. I know because I counted the doors on our way. A trick I learned when I was a freshman at Madison High, so I wouldn't embarrass myself by walking into the wrong classroom.

When the maid opens the double doors, I nearly swoon. I don't know what I was expecting, but this room is beyond my wildest dreams. Bright and enormous, it has everything a princess could want, including a sitting area, kitchenette and fireplace. I'm thinking that cheering and jumping up and down on the Wyoming-size bed, would not be in keeping with my princess persona, so I try to stay cool. Instead I walk over to the French doors, which open onto a large balcony and take in the spectacular view of the countryside.

"It's a beautiful day," I say. But then I realize that every day's probably perfect inside the dome.

The pretty maid smiles. "I am happy you are home safely, ma'am." She walks to the fireplace, flipping a switch to activate the fire, which is actually a pile of crystalline logs. They sparkle with gold and red light, simulating a real fire and lending a warm glow to the room.

"Would you like me to draw your bath before I go?" she asks.

"Yes, that would be nice, uh ..."

"Maria. I know you don't remember me, but I've helped you before when Sylvia was not available."

"Of course, I remember you Maria. I'm just not myself today. Bump on the head, you know." I touch the cut on my forehead.

Maria walks to the bathroom as I tag along behind. I nearly weep for joy when I see there's indoor plumbing. The cream-colored marble floors and counters softly reflect the light from the glittering chandeliers. The bathtub looks large enough for a small pool party, and baskets stuffed with fluffy white towels sit at either end. Oh man, I could really get used to this.

Maria turns on the water faucet and sprinkles some divine

smelling bath salts into the tub, while I sit at the dressing table attempting to free the rest of my hair from its badly mangled braid. Most of my thick mane has already escaped on its own, but the matted remainder isn't coming undone easily and I'm not used to dealing with hair down to my butt.

"Let me help you with that," Maria says. She snips the band at the bottom of my braid with a delicate pair of silver scissors, and begins to gently and expertly unplait my hair. When she's finished she takes a golden hairbrush from the drawer to work on the snarls. In a short time my Rapunzel-like tresses are smooth and tangle free, although still smelly, filthy, dirty.

"Your bath is ready," she says, turning off the water. "Shall I help you undress?"

"Uh, no, thank you. I'll do that myself." I'm not sure how pampered Princess Jaden really is, but I'm going to handle the dressing and undressing part on my own.

Maria disappears abruptly. I hope I haven't hurt her feelings. I strip off my grimy clothes, and toss them on the floor. I'm dipping a toe into the steaming water when she reappears holding a soft ivory colored robe.

"Here is your robe, Princess. I hope your bath is enjoyable." She smiles sweetly completely unfazed by my nakedness.

My whole body blushes. "Thank you, Maria, for everything." She smiles, curtseys, and closes the door softly behind her.

The bath is glorious. Soaking in the warm, aromatic water makes me realize just how exhausted I really am. I finish bathing and wrap myself in the luxurious robe. After searching without luck through all the drawers in the bathroom for a hair dryer, I decide to check the closet. My weary eyes are completely unprepared for the magnificent spectacle that assaults them when I open the closet doors. It looks like a mini-Bergdorf's in there, packed with glorious outfits and accessories. Hundreds of pairs of shoes, dozens of dresses, scads of scarves, tops, pants, and every color of fargen wool sweater imaginable to man, neatly stacked, folded and hung in a floor-to-ceiling fashionista's dream.

I'm not able to handle the sensory overload just now, so I quickly back out of the closet, close the double doors, and promise myself to spend hours in there tomorrow exploring all the lovely things temporarily at my disposal.

I towel dry my miles of hair and pull down the coverlet on the princess' gargantuan bed. The sheets are cool and silky, the pillow a velvety cradle for my weary head, but a knock at my door disturbs me before my eyes have a chance to close.

"Who is it?" I call.

"Jade, open up. I've brought Fred and Ethel." It's Drew.

I don't feel like company at the moment. And who might Fred and Ethel be?

"Just a second, I'm coming." I drag my protesting body out of bed, cinching up my robe. As I open the door, a gray furry object hurtles through the air, hitting me in the chest and knocking me flat on my back. My arms fly protectively to my face, and the little fur ball jumps up and down on top of me.

"Jay! Jay!" it cries in a little Munchkin-like voice. "Jay home."

Drew comes over and scoops up the beast. "Fred, get off of her; she can't breathe."

I sit up gasping for air, gaping at Drew, who's holding two small gray creatures that look like a cross between a monkey and a Koala bear. The one that attacked me is wearing a miniature gold, satin coat.

"Sorry Jade," Drew says. "Fred really missed you."

It dawns on me that these must be the Skorplings Mother mentioned. The smaller of the two holds out her arms to me. "Jay," she says in a tiny musical voice. She's wearing a doll-sized pink dress, and I swear she is smiling at me. I take her from Drew. She puts her little arms around my neck, nestling her furry head beneath my chin. I instantly fall in love.

"Ethel love Jay," she coos. "Jay pretty."

"Ethel's pretty, too," I say, stroking her fur. "I like your dress."

She shocks me by kissing my cheek. What kind of startling creatures are these? I hold out my other arm for Fred. He comes more quietly this time. "Jay home," he squeaks, toying with a strand of my hair.

Ethel also seizes a handful of my hair. "Ooooh, wet." She holds it up to her nose. "Smell good."

"Thank you Ethel. I hear you two were naughty last night."

"They were vile," Drew says with a groan. "They wouldn't shut up all night. Cook threatened to make Skorpling stew for lunch today."

Fred shakes his head. "No, no Jay, Fred good." Ethel is too occupied with my hair to worry about Drew's slander.

"You look tired, Jade. You should try to nap a little before the big gala tonight." Drew reaches for Fred. "God knows you can use the beauty sleep."

"Thanks a lot." I swat his arm. "And thanks for bringing Fred and Ethel to me." I kiss Ethel's furry head and hand her over to Drew. I scratch Fred's ear.

"Bye Fred, bye Ethel," I say. "You two be good. I'll see you later."

"Bye Jay," they say in unison.

"I am glad you're home, Sister, if only to calm these rascals down," Drew says, bouncing them in his arms.

"It's nice to be home," I say. *And what a nice home indeed!*

TEN

I don't know how long I've been asleep—hours maybe—when a loud rap at the door startles me awake. Before I can respond, the door flies open and in marches a gaggle of pretty, colorfully dressed teenage girls, led by a severe looking older woman outfitted in black who is carefully balancing what appears to be a green ball gown in her arms. It takes me a few seconds to remember where I am.

"What? Who?" is all I manage to get out.

The woman in black, who could pass for twin sisters with the Wicked Witch of the West, lays the gown on the foot of my bed. "Princess, ze queen wishes for you to get dressed now," she says with a French accent. "We 'ave a lot of work to do. You must not lie abed all day. Come, come."

Grasping my hand in her bony claw, she pulls me to my feet, appraising me critically from head to foot. A sour look organizes itself on her clay-like face. She makes a clucking noise with her tongue and shakes her head. "Oh mon Dieu, what are we to do with you?" She lifts a strand of my hair. "No, no, no, zeez will never do. Celeste, go and get ze wigs, we will 'ave to use a wig tonight."

"A wig?" I ask.

Ignoring my question, she barks, "What is zeez?" She uses her thumb to push hard against the newly healing scar on my forehead.

"Ow! That hurts!" I yelp.

TRANSCENDER: *First-Timer*

"We will 'ave to use ze thick makeup," she says. "Rose, go. Get ze makeup tray." Another girl scurries from the room. "I think we shall dress you before we do ze wig and ze makeup." She reaches for the belt of my robe.

"Whoa, lady," I say, yanking my belt out of her hand. "What do you think you're doing? I'm naked under here."

"We must get you dressed. I 'ave seen you naked 'undreds of times!"

"Well not today! Get out of here!"

"What?" Her entire body forms a questions mark.

"Get out of here. All of you. Now!" The girls scatter immediately, but Witchy Woman's eyes bore into mine. I suspect she's casting a silent curse. After a moment she turns, gathers her skirts, and moves slowly out the door, which I slam and lock behind her.

"Arrgh! I can get myself dressed," I mutter.

Everything is laid out on the bed. I mean how hard can it be? The underwear is easy to figure out, even though it isn't what I'm used to. There's a very French looking, lacey push-up bra and a microscopic pair of panties. The princess is obviously more daring in the undie department than I am, but *when in Rome,* right? I put them on and examine the other items.

The long silky white thing looks like a slip, so I figure it must go on next. I pull it on over my head. No problem there. The dress is another matter, though. The fabric is exquisite. I rub it between my fingers. Some kind of silk, I think. The color is the exact shade of my eyes, but it's iridescent and takes on a slight golden hue when the light hits it just right. The design is classic—square neck, square back, long sleeves, flowing skirt, and about five thousand tiny pearl buttons. The trouble is I can't figure out if the buttons are supposed to go in the front or the back. There's no tag to help me. The dress is obviously custom made. I'll just have to try it on both ways.

I begin to undo the endless trail of buttons when someone else knocks at my door. Crap! "What is it?" I shout.

The door knob rattles. "Jaden, it's Mother. May I come in?"

I dash to the door and fumble with the lock. When I manage to get it open, I nearly fall over in awe. My mother is dressed for dinner in a very low-cut, red velvet gown. Her hair, styled on top of her head, is held in place by a magnificent jeweled crown. She's heavily made up, but on her it looks killer.

"Wow, Mother you look outstanding," I say.

"Thank you dear." She touches my cheek softly. "Now, what is the trouble? Sylvia says you banished her and my ladies from your room."

"She was so rude, Mother. I don't like her. She manhandled me worse than the kidnappers did."

"Jaden, I know that Sylvia can be rather coarse sometimes, but you need help getting dressed, and I need to be downstairs greeting our guests. Please let me send her back to you."

"No!"

I know I'm acting like a child. I also know I'll never get that dress on by myself, but there's no way I'm letting that old cow back into my room. "What about that Maria girl? Is she around?" I ask.

"Maria Alvarez?"

"Yes, I like her. Would you see if she'll help me?"

"Of course, dear. I'll send her right up." She glides to the door. "Jaden, please don't keep our guests waiting. Dinner is promptly at eight." She tilts her head to the side, smiling at me. "I'm glad you're home, darling," she says and floats out of my room. I've never before fully appreciated what a great beauty my mother is. She's absolutely stunning!

Maria arrives within a few minutes, carrying what looks like a make-up case. She suggests I wear my hair up like my mother's, but with a small pearl tiara to match the buttons on my dress. Although

I'm not a big up-do person, I like the effect when she's finished.

"May I do your make-up now?"

"I don't really like make-up," I tell her. "Maybe just a little concealer to hide the cut on my forehead."

She studies my face for a few seconds. "I have been learning all about make-up, and I think tonight you may wish to wear a little more. You have wonderful skin and eyes. I will only make them a bit more dramatic. Will you trust me?"

Judging from my mother's appearance, make-up is part of the royal get-up for this event, so I reluctantly agree. "All right. Just don't give me raccoon eyes or anything." Maria looks confused. "Never mind," I say. "Just use a light hand."

She quickly gets to work, refusing to allow me to look in the mirror until I'm completely dressed. I don't get really nervous until she brushes a little golden glitter under my brows and across my cheekbones.

When she's satisfied with my make-up, Maria helps me into the dress. It turns out the buttons are supposed to be in the back. Go figure. She holds my shoes for me, and I slip my feet into them. Then she takes my hand, guiding me to the full-length mirror. I've never worn a long gown, since I missed the prom, and it feels weird walking with so much material flowing around my legs.

"Close your eyes." She positions me in front of the mirror. "Now open them."

When I do, I let out a startled "Oh!" The person staring back from the mirror looks nothing like me. She looks sophisticated and regal. She looks like a princess. I smile involuntarily, feeling like a little girl playing dress-up. I hold out the sides of my skirt, turning from side to side. The fabric glistens in the light.

"Ah, lovely," Maria says.

"Thank you so much. I love it—even the glitter. You did a great job." I hug her.

"You'd better go, it's almost eight o'clock. The queen will be looking for you."

"Wish me luck!" I call heading out the door.

ELEVEN

*M*y insides squirm like a bucket of eels as I traipse down the hallway to the stairs, careful not to trip over my dress. Even though I now look the part of a princess, I have serious doubts about whether I can carry off this act in a room full of strangers—most of whom I'm supposed to know.

Thankfully, Ralston's waiting for me at the top of the stairs. "You look quite beautiful, Jade," he says, offering me his arm. "Just follow my lead tonight. You'll do fine. I'll step in if I sense that you require some assistance."

"Thanks Ralston," I mutter. My mouth's gone dry.

"Hold your chin up," he whispers, as we near the entrance to the grand hall. "Remember, act like a princess."

I straighten my posture, and do my best Marie Antoinette imitation. As we enter, every head in the great dining hall turns our way. By now the entire country has heard about my abduction and rescue, but I'm not prepared for the roar of applause that greets us. My cheeks burn bright crimson, but I keep a smile on my face and hope I look more gracious than terrified. We move slowly up the red-carpeted aisle toward the queen's table. Everyone along the way bows or curtseys to me. I follow Ralston's lead, nodding occasionally to the adoring assemblage.

About halfway through the crowd, a guy steps out onto the carpet and bows deeply in front of me. His unexpected appearance rattles me, but when he raises his head, I recognize him.

"Jason!" I say. I can't believe it's my almost date to the prom.

"Yes." he takes my hand and kisses it softly. "Forgive me Princess. I wish only to tell you how happy we are that you have returned safely to us."

It's wonderful to find a familiar face. "Thanks, Jason. It's good to see you."

He bows to Ralston. "Thank you sir, for bringing our Princess Jaden home unharmed."

"It was my privilege, Sir Jason," Ralston says with a nod. He gently nudges me forward along the carpet.

"Jason Fallon's a 'Sir'?" I whisper under my breath.

"Yes," he says quietly. "For future reference, he's quite smitten with Princess Jaden."

I'm psyched to hear that, but I hope it won't present a problem. I'm counting on things going smoothly with no complications until I get shifted back to my real home. A love interest is the last thing I need.

When we reach my mother, she stands and kisses me on both cheeks. She shakes Ralston's hand. The guest of honor is standing beside her, and Mother formally introduces us to Ambassador Diego Reynaldo Garcia of Cupola de Vita.

The ambassador is a balding middle-aged man with a dark mustache and a prominent paunch. His appearance is completely unremarkable except for his peculiar outfit, which resembles white pajamas with a red sash. A brown woolen serape is draped across his shoulders, and a thin golden sword hangs at his side. He reminds me of an overweight Jedi warrior.

Ralston greets the ambassador in Spanish. Apparently they've met before. Ambassador Garcia seems genuinely pleased to see Ralston. I hope that isn't lost on my mother.

TRANSCENDER: *First-Timer*

Ralston and I are seated to Mother's right, the Ambassador and Drew to her left. Various other dignitaries of one kind or another fill out the rest of the queen's table.

Shortly after we take our places, the feast begins with a great flourish of music and activity. Exactly on cue, uniformed waiters march into the dining hall bearing tray after tray of meats, vegetables, and other accompaniments. I recognize pheasant, venison, beef, and chicken, as well as the normal fruits and vegetables one might see at a spring banquet, along with some not so normal looking items that I decide to steer clear of.

Other delicacies soon follow—caviar, quail eggs and some odd looking dishes I don't recognize. Baskets of bread and pastries arrive, and with an additional splash of fanfare, the desserts appear, looking more like art than food. The most spectacular creation is an enormous cake sculpted in the shape of Warrington Palace, complete with turrets and climbing ivy. I've never seen so much food in my life. Heavenly aromas fill the hall, and I realize I'm starving.

An orchestra plays tedious elevator music throughout our meal, but the food is delicious and I stuff myself. I even try something called Baked Weigel, that looks a little like fried puke, but tastes okay—kind of smoky and earthy. By the dessert course, my stomach is aching, and I'm worried that I might pop all the tiny pearl buttons on my fitted gown.

Ralston leans in to tell me to expect some interesting entertainment after the final course. He's heard that Ambassador Garcia brought a traveling menagerie of exotic animals with him from Cupola de Vita. After meeting the Skorplings, I'm looking forward to seeing that.

I push my plate away and sip slowly from my water goblet, taking a moment to admire the grand hall. The room is enormous with towering white columns, ornate moldings, and gold patterned wall paper—exactly what I'd expect a grand hall to look like. Judging from the smiling faces and audible good cheer, the finely-dressed guests are enjoying the evening's festivities immensely.

I'm grateful to have Ralston by my side. His presence helps keep my creeping paranoia in check. No one has acted the least bit suspicious of me, and I believe the evening has gone pretty well so far. I'm beginning to believe we might just pull off this whole charade, when the doors at the opposite end of the hall fly open, and a group of armed soldiers bursts into the room.

The music immediately ceases, and the crowd falls silent. I'm convinced they've come for me, the princess-pretender, but Ralston smiles reassuringly.

"It's all right," he mouths.

The soldiers clatter up the red carpet toward our table. When they're about five yards away, they come to a halt. The soldier in the lead steps forward and bows to my mother. He's large and attractive, in a kick-ass kind of way, with a shaved head and a giant ruby stud in his left ear. He has a tough-guy arrogance about him.

Mother rises from her chair, concern lining her face. "General LeGare, what is it?" she asks.

"Your Highness, I apologize for interrupting your elegant dinner, but I thought you would wish to know right away—we have captured three of the criminals who abducted Princess Jaden." He motions to three men in shackles being held by the guards. "Some of the others had already escaped. We have their leader, though. We have young Chief Blackthorn!"

He half-turns signaling to his men. Two soldiers step forward with a shackled Blackthorn propped up between them. They drag him to face my mother, and roughly force him onto his knees. I gasp involuntarily. Ralston places a warning hand on my arm.

Blackthorn's armor is gone, his white tunic torn and caked with blood. A gash disfigures the biceps of his right arm, and dried blood covers his forearm. His head is bowed, his face hidden behind the dark curtain of his hair.

Mother's expression hardens. "Good work, General LeGare. Thank you for bringing the prisoners to me immediately. I have always believed in swift justice."

She nods to LeGare, then focuses her attention on Blackthorn. "Young Chief Blackthorn, I am very disappointed to see you here. What have you to say for yourself?"

He does not reply, but keeps his head bowed. LeGare rams the hilt of his sword into the wound on Blackthorn's arm, causing it to gush fresh blood. Blackthorn grunts in pain.

"Answer the queen!" LeGare says.

Blackthorn springs to his feet, swinging his shackled wrists upward, catching LeGare under the chin. The blow sends the general sprawling into the crowd. Three guards immediately subdue Blackthorn, forcing him to his knees again. LeGare regains his balance and charges toward Blackthorn, a murderous expression distorting his face.

"Enough!" Mother cries. "General LeGare, I will not have brawling in the middle of my feast."

LeGare regains control of himself, taking his place next to Blackthorn, his fists tightly clenched at his sides. "I apologize, Your Highness," he says.

"Young Blackthorn, you are not doing yourself any favors by attacking my general." Mother says. "You stand accused of grievous crimes against Domerica. You are charged with abducting Princess Jaden, holding her against her will, and causing her bodily harm. These are offenses of a most serious nature. I am offering you the opportunity to speak before I pass sentence upon you."

Blackthorn raises his head, a defiant expression on his handsome face. "Your Highness, I have nothing to say in defense of my actions, other than that they were committed not to inflict harm, but only to persuade you to speak with my father in an effort to save the Unicoi from certain death."

"Nonsense! Does your father know what you have been up to in Domerica?"

"No. My father knows nothing of my actions, nor would he condone them if he did. I beg you not to hold my transgressions against him or Unicoi. They are mine alone."

"Ha! A Chief should be able to control his own son, else how can he command a whole nation?"

"He is ill, ma'am," Blackthorn says quietly.

"I regret that he is ill. He is a decent man. *You* on the other hand are a disgrace to your family and your country. You entered into Domerica illegally and cruelly abducted my daughter, Princess Jaden. These are momentous crimes for which you could be summarily hanged."

Her words cause a ripple of commotion in the crowd. Ralston tightens his grip on my arm. Mother holds up her hand for silence.

"But I am known to be a merciful sovereign. Since my daughter was not seriously harmed, and out of respect for your father, I shall not hang you. I believe, however, that reeducation would be in order." This evokes still more murmurings from the crowd.

She pulls herself up to her full height, glaring at Blackthorn. "Accordingly, I sentence you, Ryder Blackthorn, to be taken at first light to the prison at Wall's Edge for reeducation, after which you shall be returned to your father. Your comrades shall also be reeducated. They, however, shall remain our prisoners at Wall's Edge, in servitude to the crown for the remainder of their lives."

A wild chorus of whoops and applause erupts from the crowd. Cries of "Blessed be the Chosen" ring throughout the hall. Mother receives this adulation with a regal smile. LeGare signals the guards and they pull Blackthorn to his feet.

"Your Highness," Blackthorn's voice is forceful and carries above the din. The crowd falls silent again. "With all due respect, ma'am, my men and I would prefer the hangman's noose to your reeducation program."

"Well now, that is the drawback to electing the path of the criminal, young Blackthorn," Mother says. "*You* do not get to choose. Remove them!" The soldiers drag Blackthorn and his men from the great hall. The mind-numbing music instantly resumes.

Okay, I don't really know what just happened, but I know it's got to be bad. I'm pretty sure reeducation doesn't have anything to do with going back to school. But what does it mean? I stare bewildered at Ralston, who looks pale and shaken.

"What's reeducation?" I whisper.

He shakes his head. "We can't talk here."

I'm not about to take 'no' for an answer, but unfortunately, Ambassador Garcia chooses that exact moment to ask me to dance. I can't come up with an excuse, so I take the Ambassador's outstretched hand, and the crowd parts, making a path for us to the dance floor. I only hope it's a short song.

I'm an okay dancer. My mother taught me the basic ballroom dance steps when I was in middle school, and I can hold my own with just about any partner. On the other hand, I'm flunking out of Spanish II this year, so I hope the Ambassador doesn't try to converse with me in anything other than my native tongue.

"You are very light on your feet, Your Highness," the Ambassador says in perfect English.

"Thank you." I manufacture a smile I don't feel. I need to talk to Ralston.

"When do you turn eighteen, my dear?" the Ambassador asks.

The question seems odd, but maybe it's his version of small talk.

"In August."

He nods. "You still have some time, then. Are you ready to announce?"

"Announce what?" I ask, afraid I've missed a vital piece of the conversation.

"Your selection."

I wrinkle my brow in confusion.

"Of a husband, a consort. That is still the law in Domerica, is it not?"

I gulp loudly, not knowing the answer to that. "Uh, yes, but why rush these things?"

"I was wondering whether you have met Don Francisco Ferrera del Rio Martinez?"

"I, uh … don't believe so."

"He would make a very good match for you. He is handsome and rich. He comes from an ancient Peruvian royal blood line. You should ask the queen to invite him to the palace for a visit before you make up your mind."

"Yes, I will. Gracias, Ambassador."

"Ah, *me olvidé de que usted habla español con fluidez,*" he says with a smile.

Uh-oh. I have no idea what he just said, so instead of responding, I begin to cough loudly. We pause our dancing. I cough some more.

"Are you all right, Princess?" He pats my back lightly. The dancers nearest us stop to stare.

"Uh, yes," I croak. "I have something in my throat. Will you help me to the table?"

He takes my elbow, guiding me back to my seat, while I continue my bogus coughing fit. The Ambassador looks completely flustered. He helps me into my chair and hands me my water goblet. Both Mother and Drew come over to check on me.

"Are you all right, dear?" Mother asks, taking my hand.

"Yes, I'm fine now. Just something in my throat. Thank you for helping me, Ambassador Garcia." He bows and retreats to his seat.

"Always have to be the center of attention, don't you?" Drew says with a smirk. "Getting kidnapped wasn't enough?"

I scowl at him.

"Andrew, be kind," Mother says. "She has been through a lot these past two days." Drew doesn't reply, but winks at me and walks away.

"Mother, I am a little tired. Is it all right if Ralston escorts me to my room?" I say.

"But darling, you'll miss all the entertainment."

"I know, and I'm sorry. I just need some rest." I try to look pitiful.

"Of course, darling," she helps me to my feet. "I hope you sleep well, knowing that the monster who kidnapped you has been captured. He will receive his just punishment."

"Yes, Mother, thank you."

She pauses for a moment. "Darling, you are rather pale. Do you need a doctor? Would you like me to accompany you?"

"No, no, Mother. I'll be fine." She kisses my forehead and turns me over to Ralston, who leads me back down the red carpet and out of the dining hall.

TWELVE

*R*alston and I walk in tension-filled silence until we reach my room. Once inside I turn on him. "Okay Rals, spill it! What does reeducation mean? Why would Blackthorn prefer to be hanged?"

"May we sit for a moment?" Ralston clutches the back of an armchair near the fireplace.

"Yeah, sure. But please tell me, fast."

He sits on the edge of the chair cushion, placing his hands on his knees. His features are strained. "Reeducation is a euphemism for a nasty bit of brain alteration. It's practiced only in Domerica. The locals call it a 'mind wipe,' which is an apt description."

"Mind wipe?"

"Yes. When it works properly, which is not very often, it essentially wipes out the entirety of a person's memory. The victim is still able to function on a rudimentary level—breathe, eat, speak and such. But everything else is gone. The person's identity, history, ability to recognize friends and family. All gone. Wiped out. What's worse is the person becomes incapable of forming new memories, so he is not able to regain an identity. Each day he must begin anew with a blank slate, so to speak."

"Are you kidding me? That is *seriously* screwed-up!"

"More than you know, Jade. Most victims do not live much

longer than a year or two after the surgery. They either die of some complication from the surgery or they take their own lives."

"But how does it work exactly? How do they do it?"

"You don't really want the details. It involves inserting ionic rods into a certain part of the brain and *zzzzzt!*" He makes a zapping sound.

"No way! How did it come to be used as a punishment?"

"Oh, a bright young general in your mother's guard—you remember Charles LeGare—heard of a strange medical case where the doctors were trying to cure a man of epilepsy, but erased his memory instead. LeGare had the brilliant idea that the procedure could be perfected for use on prisoners. It makes them so much more docile while they are performing hard labor on the royal farms at Wall's Edge."

"And my mother's okay with this?"

"I'm afraid so. In fact, Queen Eleanor is the one who coined the term 'reeducation'."

"But, this can't happen!" I say. "I mean you're the Guidance Agent. Isn't Blackthorn supposed to save the world or something? You should have stayed with him instead of coming with me."

"Unfortunately, everything went a little haywire after you shifted, Jade. None of this was meant to occur. Blackthorn should have escaped with the others. But the whole path shifted when you did. Now everything is in jeopardy."

"Because of me?" My head reels making the room spin. I stagger unsteadily to the bathroom and heave the contents of my stomach into the sparkling porcelain toilet bowl. Sitting on the floor in my lovely ball gown, I yank the tiara out of my hair and fling it against the wall. Dozens of tiny pearls break away, ponging across the marble floor.

Tears stream down my face, washing away all the golden glitter. Ralston kneels beside me, and I throw my arms around his neck, weeping huge blubbery tears into his crisp white shirt. "I just want to go home," I wail.

"I know child. Soon."

I cry on his shoulder for a minute, but I understand it won't do any good for me to fall apart. That doesn't solve anything. I know because I watched my dad do it, and it didn't bring mom back. This is all happening because of me. I have to figure out a way to make it right.

"I won't let this happen," I say, drying my eyes with my fingers. Ralston helps me up off the floor. "I can't let them do that horrible thing to Blackthorn and those men. I've got to go to my mother to plead for mercy for them."

He scratches his chin thoughtfully. "Yes, that might work. But, I'm afraid all it would accomplish is getting them hanged or sentenced to hard labor at Wall's Edge for life. Queen Eleanor would never just set them free."

"In that case, we'll just have to get them out of here somehow," I say.

"Yes, we will—and I think I may have a plan," he says. "Only, I need to take care of this alone, old girl. We can't risk your being involved. If something else goes wrong—"

"No, Ralston!" I cut him off. "Don't even try to talk me out of this. I'm going with you. I'm responsible for this. I need to fix it."

"It's not your responsibility, Jade. What happened is no fault of yours. But, if we are caught, I'm afraid I can't predict what your mother will do. It might be rather unpleasant."

"Then we won't get caught. Now what's the plan?"

THIRTEEN

Ralston studies me a moment, like he's considering whether it's worth an argument. I give him a steely stare. At last, he gives in.

"This particular castle, Warrington Palace, is old and has a number of interesting features, many of which are unknown to the current inhabitants."

"Like what? Like a secret passage or something?"

He nods. "I know of one such passageway that leads to the prison under the palace. We'll have to get into your mother's office, though. That's where the entrance is."

"Don't tell me—the door's disguised as a bookcase."

He smiles sheepishly.

"No. Really?"

"I have some arrangements to make," he says. "Your job is to get the key to your mother's office."

"But, how do I do that?"

"You already have it somewhere. Since you are the heir to the throne, you possess keys to all the important rooms and government facilities. Have you seen anything like a ring of keys in your room?" I shake my head.

"They may be in a safe, or locked in a drawer, or someplace similar to that. Search the room, see what you can find, and I'll return at midnight. Dress in something dark and easy to move in. We may have to hide or make a quick getaway."

Ralston slips out of my room, and I begin my search for the key. I check the closet first, since that is the most logical place for a safe. I look behind racks of fabulous dresses, through shelves of folded sweaters and drawers of socks and frilly underwear. I examine row upon row of shoes and boots. It's hard not to get distracted in here, but I manage to look over, under, and behind everything. I find no safe hidden anywhere.

Next, I check the princess' desk. The main drawer is locked. I rattle it, but it doesn't budge. I run my finger across the brass keyhole in front. It's an odd cylindrical shape. It would take a special key to open it—something round or ring shaped. I wrack my brain trying to remember if I've seen anything like that among the princess' things. I poke around the stuff on the top of her desk, and my eye is drawn to the carved ring on my own hand. Could it be? It's worth a try.

I twist the gold ring off my finger and slide it into the key slot. It fits perfectly. I turn it to the right, and half-way through the turn, the lock releases with a click. Yes! Two books, a stack of papers, and a couple of weird-looking writing instruments take up most of the drawer, but unfortunately no keys. I'm about to move on to the dressing table when someone knocks at my door.

Irritated by the interruption, I open the door a crack and peer out. It's Maria.

"Hey Maria, what's up?"

She curtseys shyly, "I'm sorry to disturb you Princess, but I heard you left the feast early. I thought you might like some assistance getting undressed." She eyes my smeared make-up and wild hair.

My first impulse is to send her away, but I realize I'll never be able to get out of the dress-of-a-zillion-buttons by myself. Plus, she may know where the keys are. "Sure, thanks. Come on in."

She helps me out of the gown and into my robe. I sit on the bench at my dressing table, while she pulls the rest of the hair pins out of my destroyed up-do. She gently runs the brush through the length of my hair, over and over. Oh man, it feels so good ... I have to remind myself not to get too used to this lifestyle.

"Would you like me to get your nightgown for you?" she asks, after she has tamed my hair into a single braid.

"Uh, no," I say, remembering my assignment. "Maria, you haven't seen my keys anywhere, have you? I think I misplaced them."

"They're not in your jewelry safe?" She glances at a large ornate chest perched on top of my dressing table.

Of course, the jewelry chest! I casually walk over to the safe and tug at the small knobs on the front panels like I know what I'm doing. The doors don't budge. I fiddle with the latches for a moment, but no matter how I try I can't get the thing to open.

"Did you forget the combination?" she asks.

I had overlooked the five small, numbered dials on the front of the chest. "Uh, yeah, I'm pretty bad with numbers. Do you know it?"

She shakes her head. "No. Sylvia is the only person who knows the combination. She would never tell me."

Oh, great! The one person in the palace I've already alienated is the only person who knows the combination. "I'm not very good at remembering numbers either," she says, "so I write them down and keep them in a safe place for when I need a reminder."

"Yeah, that would be the smart thing to do," I say. "Well, don't worry about it. I'm sure I'll figure it out. Thanks for everything, Maria."

"Goodnight, Princess." She curtseys again and leaves. But, she's given me an idea. After closing the door behind her, I go back to the princess' desk to examine her books and papers more closely. Two small, leather-bound volumes are tucked inside the main drawer. The first book is an appointment calendar—nothing too interesting, just a daily log filled with events and meetings. The Princess is a busy girl.

The second book looks more promising. It has reminders of important dates like family birthdays, christenings, and the like. I flip through the pages, noticing that the other Jade has recorded things like names of the royal families of Dome Noir and Cupola de Vita. This book will definitely come in handy. There's also a listing of the names of the ruling family of Unicoi: Chief Seneca Blackthorn; his wife, Caitlin Ryder Blackthorn (deceased); their children, young Chief Ryder James Blackthorn and Catherine Fitzpatrick Blackthorn. She drew a tiny star next to Ryder's name. I'm curious as to what it means.

In another section is a record of every horse she's ever owned, the date she got the horse, it's coloring and specific markings, as well as certain special characteristics like "fond of pommeras" or "likes to be rubbed behind the ears."

Leafing through the rest of the book, I find things like pressed flowers and line drawings of formal gowns. One page has a detailed map showing the location of the "Sacred Caverns." Maybe a tourist spot. This is all interesting but useless information. I'm about to give up when, on the second to the last page, I find an inventory of the contents of the princess's jewelry chest, and BINGO! It's here. The five-number combination I've been looking for: 5-7-9-5-5.

I hurry to the sturdy chest and spin the dials to the designated numbers. Voila! The doors open out, revealing a collection of glittering, gleaming objects of desire—necklaces, earrings, rings, bangles. But no keys. A number of small drawers line each side panel, and I search through each one. It requires a huge effort on my part not to get sidetracked by all the alluring adornments inside. I'm a little giddy with the knowledge that these tantalizing treasures temporarily belong to me.

Tucked inside a black velvet pouch, I find a large golden key with a pentagram shaped head. It's unlikely this is a key to a door, so I put it back and continue my search. Another velvet pouch in the same compartment contains a silver oval-shaped ring holding six different keys. I set it to the side while I finish my search. I find no other keys, so I'm pretty sure one of the keys on the silver ring is the one I need.

TRANSCENDER: *First-Timer*

Pleased with myself, I carefully put everything back into the jewelry chest and lock it securely.

The next order of business is to choose an appropriate outfit for breaking someone out of prison. Ralston said to wear something dark, but the princess' closet, as plentiful as it is, doesn't have a lot of basic black. I settle on a black, long-sleeved sweater, a pair of black leather riding pants, and some black boots. I hurriedly dress, and then check myself out in the mirror—a little Goth for my taste, but it will definitely fit the bill. We *are* going down to the dungeon, after all.

When I'm finished, the desk clock says it's after midnight. I shove the key ring into my pocket and pace the floor waiting for Ralston.

A sharp tap at my door makes me jump. I tiptoe to the door. "Who is it?" I ask quietly.

"It's me, let me in," Ralston whispers.

Once inside, he asks, "Did you find the keys?" I smile and jingle the key ring in front of him. "Good work."

"Now what's the plan?" I ask.

He explains that a small prison lies beneath the palace, although prisoners are rarely kept there. Blackthorn and his men are the only prisoners there now.

"Two guards are on duty, but they are not much of a concern," Ralston says. They are part of the palace guard, not LeGare's men. They play cards half the night and sleep the other half. I don't believe they'll be much of a problem, even should we cross paths with them."

"So what do we do with Blackthorn and his guys after we get them out?"

"I've already taken care of that. I have a friend in town who will ensure their safe passage. They should be back in Unicoi by morning."

Ralston has a leather pouch slung across his shoulder, and he's brought a metal box with him.

"What's with the bag and the box?" I ask.

"Just a few things we'll need." He reaches into the pouch, pulling out a black knit cap. "Here, put this on, we don't want anyone recognizing you." I wind my braid around my head and pull the cap securely over the top.

"You'd make a decent cat burglar," he says, eyeing my outfit.

"I'll keep that in mind for after graduation. Can I help carry something?" I reach for the metal box, but I can barely lift it. It must weigh fifty pounds. "What's in that thing?"

"You'll see." He picks up the box, and checks the hallway to make sure the coast is clear. We make our way swiftly and silently to the stairs. The darkened third floor hallway, where Mother's office is located, is deserted. We creep along the corridor until we reach her door. A slit of light shines from beneath it. Ralston presses his ear against the wood and motions me to the other end of the hallway. We duck into a small alcove.

"She's with someone," he whispers. "We'll have to wait."

FOURTEEN

My heart drums so loudly in my ears, I think it might wake half the palace. It's only a minute or two until the door opens, but it feels like an eternity. Mother steps out into the hall followed by LeGare. They pause, silhouetted in the doorway. "Goodnight, Charles." She smiles, extending her hand.

He leans in and kisses her lightly on the cheek. "Goodnight, Ellie."

The whole scene is a little too cozy, and it makes me feel weird. LeGare walks quickly to the stairs and disappears. Mother locks the door, and leaves also.

We wait in our hiding place for about ten seconds before sneaking back to the door. Hands trembling, I slide one of the keys into the lock. Thankfully, it opens on the first try. Mother has left the lamp on, and Ralston is able to quickly find the bookcase we need. He runs his hand down the back and does something that makes the edge of the bookcase pop away from of the wall a crack. He wedges his fingers into the gap, and swings it open like a door. I follow him inside.

It is pitch black on the other side, except for the slice of light coming from the office. Ralston takes a penlight from his bag and examines the wall to his right. He clicks a tiny lever on the wall, and the bookcase silently closes behind us. We're standing on the small landing of a narrow, curving, stone stairway. I cautiously follow

Ralston as he descends in the darkness, the penlight our only illumination as we go. It feels like we've gone fifty feet straight down by the time the staircase dead-ends into a small rectangular landing. We're surrounded by gray stone walls with no doors or openings of any kind. It's unpleasantly tight and claustrophobic in here and I hope Ralston knows what he's doing.

He hands the penlight to me and shows me where to shine it. He takes a small folding knife from his pocket, opens the blade, and inserts it into the mortar to the left of one of the smooth stones. I hear a click. He removes the knife, puts a finger to his lips, and slowly pushes on the wall, which turns out to be a concealed doorway.

The door opens out into a short, dimly lit hallway. The walls here are also smooth, gray stone. The floor is hard concrete, and it feels about ten degrees cooler down here than in the rest of the palace. To our right is the arched opening of a tunnel. The air is damp and musty, and I hear water lightly lapping inside the tunnel. I figure it must be an underground stream or aquifer, maybe the palace water supply.

I follow Ralston as he moves to the left. We inch our way slowly along the wall to another, larger hallway. He cautiously peers around the corner, drawing back abruptly. "Guard!" he whispers. My eyes widen and he adds, "Going the other way."

We hug the mildewed wall for a minute or two; then Ralston steals another look around the corner. He waves me forward. In this hallway, the stone walls are interrupted every few feet by a barred cell door. We slink past a cell where Blackthorn's men are lying asleep on bare cots. Neither of them stirs. In the next cell, Blackthorn sits on a similar cot, his head down, his hands and ankles shackled.

I examine the cell door for a lock, but don't see one. "How do we get in?" I whisper.

Ralston sets down the metal case and opens it. He withdraws a high powered magnet like ones I've seen in science class. "Magnetic locks," he says softly. He passes the magnet down the side of the door, and the lock releases with a loud clack. Blackthorn's head snaps up and he eyes us warily. When he recognizes Ralston, he springs to his feet.

"Traitor!" he cries.

"Calm down, Ryder, I'm no traitor." Ralston says.

"I trusted you, I thought you were my friend. You betrayed me!"

Fearing a loud, angry tirade, I kick the side of Blackthorn's boot to get his attention. "Shhh. Pipe down," I hiss. "We're trying to get you out of here." He wheels around on me in anger, but his expression turns immediately to one of amazement.

"Princess Jaden?" he says.

I pull off my cap and my braid tumbles out. "Yes, it's me. We're trying to *help* you. So shut up and sit down."

He looks to Ralston who nods in agreement. He turns back to me. "Why would you help *me*?"

"Because Ralston convinced me you're worth it. Don't make me change my mind." He obediently sits on the cot.

"I told her you were a good man who made a stupid mistake," Ralston says, opening his bag and laying out our tools. "I believe there is still hope for you Ryder, but you're going to have to resist being so reckless, for your own sake as well as that of Unicoi."

We quickly get to work on Blackthorn's shackles. Ralston shows me how to use an ionic torch he brought with him to cut through the metal cuffs on Blackthorn's wrists and ankles. Ralston uses a crudely fashioned pair of pliers to pry the metal apart once the torch has cut through.

I feel Blackthorn's gaze on me as we work. I glance up at him, but his eyes are difficult to read in the dim light—curious maybe, • grateful certainly, and something else I can't quite make out. His left eye is swollen, his face is marred with fresh cuts and bruises. LeGare obviously exacted his revenge after being humiliated in the grand hall.

Once he is free from the manacles, Blackthorn stands, rubbing his wrists. "My men?" he whispers.

"They're next door," Ralston says. "How is your arm? Are you injured anywhere else?" I'm glad to see that Blackthorn's arm has been cleaned and bandaged.

"I'm fine. Let's go."

We move on to the next cell, and Ralston uses his magnet to trip the lock. It takes only a few minutes for us to free the astonished men from their bindings. The five of us steal silently back to the small hallway where Ralston and I first emerged. We bypass the concealed doorway and head to the tunnel entrance. The tunnel houses a wide canal with concrete walls on either side. A narrow ledge extends down its length.

Ralston points to a small boat moored about thirty feet down the canal. "Take that boat downstream to the mouth of the river," he says to Blackthorn. "Pull it out of the water, and hide it in the trees on the left bank. You'll be met by a woman who will bring your horses. Her name is Lorelei. She will find you."

Blackthorn nods. Ralston puts a hand on his shoulder. "Ryder, it is important that you do *exactly* as she tells you. She knows how to get you safely back to your home. She is your only chance. Do you understand?"

"I do, and thank you for what you have done, Ralston. I value your advice. For what it's worth, you were right all along. It was an ill-advised plan. I am sorry."

"We learn the most from our mistakes, young friend. You must work to find a more constructive solution to Unicoi's problems. I'm confident that you will. Now go before the guards discover you are missing."

Blackthorn and his men make their way carefully along the concrete ledge toward the boat. About midway there, Blackthorn stops to say something to his men, then he turns around and comes back to where Ralston and I stand. He positions himself directly in front of me and, astonishingly, he falls to his knees.

"No. What are you doing? Get up," I say stupidly.

He gazes up at me, blue eyes glittering fiercely. "Princess Jaden, you have put me to shame. I abducted you and treated you in the poorest manner possible. Yet you have shown me nothing but compassion and mercy. I humbly apologize for all my offenses. I beg your forgiveness. You have risked much for me, and I am forever in your debt. I pledge to you that from this day forward, I shall act only to serve and protect you."

He bows his head, and I instinctively reach out to touch his lovely ebony hair. "I forgive you." I whisper. "Just return safely to your people, they need you."

He catches my hand and presses his lips fervently into my palm. The kiss sends a jolt of electricity coursing through my arm. I gasp, and the look in his eyes tells me that he felt it too.

He gets back to his feet. "Until we meet again, Princess Jaden," he says, and strides into the tunnel.

I don't understand the sense of loss that pulls at me as he leaves. I know he must go quickly, but I want him to stay. I want to call after him to come back. I want to touch his injured face and tell him I'm sorry for what they did to him. I want him to know how much I admire him for what he is trying to do. I stare into the tunnel, a mass of confusing emotions tearing at my heart, as the small boat disappears into the darkness.

Maybe if we had met at some other time, in some other place, we would have meant something to each other. Even though I'll never see him again, I know I'll never forget him.

FIFTEEN

*R*alston tugs at my sleeve. "We must go, Jade."

I follow him to the hidden doorway. We retrace our steps up the staircase and back into Mother's office. Everything is just as we left it.

Ralston closes the bookcase, and I head for the door. He grabs my arm, pulling me back. "Someone's coming," he whispers, shoving his bag and the lead case behind a chair. In one smooth motion, he pulls a small book from the shelf and tosses it to me. I catch it just as the door opens.

My startled mother stares first at me, then at Ralston. "What are you doing here, Jaden?"

"Oh, I ... well, we ..." I stammer.

"Good evening, Your Highness," Ralston says. "Princess Jaden was having difficulty sleeping after the excitement of the past few days. She asked if I could recommend a good book to soothe the mind and help sleep come more quickly. I suggested some poetry might do the trick. She recalled the rather nice collection in your office, so in light of your kind invitation earlier, we've come to borrow a book."

"What have you there?" She gestures to the book in my hand. I give it to her.

She examines the cover. "Ah, William Blake, a nice choice." She hands it back to me, appraising my odd outfit. "You must be feeling better if you're up and dressed, dear. I hope you weren't planning to take a midnight ride. You know it isn't safe, especially in light of what has happened recently."

"No, Mother, I just couldn't sleep."

"Ralston, I hope you will keep an eye on her for me," she says. "My daughter tends to act impulsively when she gets an idea in her head."

"Yes ma'am, I shall."

"Very well. I had forgotten some papers I must read before morning." She picks up a file from the top of her desk. "I trust you two will lock up when you have finished here?"

"Yes, Mother."

"Goodnight then. Sleep well, my dear. Goodnight, Professor." She closes the door behind her.

My knees are quaking, and I hold onto the back of the desk chair for support. "Oh man, that was close! She nearly caught us. Nice save on your part, Rals. Thanks."

He chuckles, retrieving his bag and the lead box. "Take a deep breath, and let's make our retreat before we have any further surprises."

We reach my room without running into any other castle inhabitants, but I'm still wired from the night's activities, and I have a few things on my mind. "Ralston, can we talk for a minute?"

"Of course." He stows his gear inside my door, and we settle into the armchairs facing the faux fireplace. The glass logs twinkle a cheery red and gold.

"How long have my parents been separated?" I ask.

He leans his elbows on the arms of the chair, steepling his fingers beneath his chin. "Over ten years, I believe."

"What split them up?"

"Oh, the usual reasons. They did not see eye to eye on a number of things. Reeducation was one of the issues. You see Jade, your father believes that it is inhumane, while your mother believes it is preferable to the old physical punishments such as hanging, flogging, maiming, and some of the unspeakable tortures used in the past. I suppose it is a matter upon which reasonable people may hold differing opinions."

"Is my dad happy? I mean being separated from my mom?"

"Yes he is. He misses you and Andrew, of course, but he has established The Enclave, a little walled city near Wall's Edge. Your father's city is quite insulated from the rest of Domerica. It is a progressive community of scholars, inventors, artists, and other free thinkers."

"I'd like to see it ... and I'd like to see my dad *soon.*"

He smiles. "I think we can arrange that. It would be most educational for you. Your father has successfully re-socialized many victims who have been surgically reeducated, and he has welcomed exiles from other domes as well. It's really a remarkable little society."

"Ralston, is my mother in love with LeGare?" I blurt out. "Is she going to end up with *him?*"

He clears his throat. "Now *that* is one of those questions I cannot answer, my dear. It is a private matter. You will have to take that up with her." He rises to leave.

I stand also, but I'm not ready to let him go yet. "You know I can't ask her. Why won't you answer me?"

"Princess," he tilts his head, looking at me over the top of his glasses, "love is a very complex, very personal thing. We cannot always choose with whom we fall in love."

"That's a bunch of bull!"

"And that is language unbefitting a princess."

"Whatever." I throw up my hands, slumping back into my chair. "Okay, fine. But one last thing—now that he's free, will Blackthorn succeed? I mean, will he save the planet?"

"That is what I am trying to ensure. At this point, I really cannot say. Goodnight, Jaden. Pleasant dreams." He grabs his stuff and walks out my door. Technically, I think he's supposed to be dismissed or something, but I guess I'm not in a position to make a big deal of it.

I undress and slide between my acres of sheets, my mind reeling once again from the events of the day. My heart is lighter now that Blackthorn is on his way home. I wonder what will happen when Mother finds out he's gone. What if she discovers I had a hand in his escape? I feel uncomfortably like I don't really know my Domerican mother. She is capable of things, both great and terrible, that I never dreamed of. She's a queen, but is she a fair and just ruler? I want to believe she is, but how can she think reeducation is okay? Maybe that's LeGare's influence on her. I'm too fatigued to reason it out now, so I push it out of my head, allowing my exhausted mind to wander aimlessly.

Eventually it winds its way back to the mysteriously alluring, dangerously impulsive Ryder Blackthorn. I press my palm to my cheek as if to transfer his kiss. Thoughts of him warm me, but I know it's best to erase him from my heart and mind altogether—he's double off-limits. He belongs to this world, not mine. By morning he'll be the most wanted man in Domerica. But, oh, that glorious face, and what a fierce heart he must own. I wonder what it would feel like to be held by him, to be kissed …

I need a distraction—some way to stop thinking about him. I wish I could listen to my iPod or watch *Conan* or go online. Instead I pick up the slim volume of Blake's poetry lying on my bed. The cover is smooth, supple leather; its red color darkened over the years by the touch of many hands. I run my fingers across its patina and absently open the book to a random page, to a poem entitled "Love's Secret."

Never seek to tell thy love, Love that never told can be;
For the gentle wind doth move; Silently, invisibly.

I hope that is how Ryder Blackthorn is making his way home tonight. Silently, invisibly ... like the gentle wind.

SIXTEEN

*D*espite my gloriously plush bed, I toss and turn all night. I wake up feeling frazzled and anxious, even as the dawn of the new Domerican day frosts my whole room with a silver glow.

The escape of Blackthorn and his men is not "officially" discovered until early morning. LeGare and his soldiers arrive to take them to the stockade at Wall's Edge and find them gone. The two guards left in charge of the prison have also vanished, leading to speculation that either they assisted in the escape and fled to Unicoi with the fugitives, or they were killed or taken hostage by Blackthorn and his men. No one guesses the truth, which, according to Ralston, is that they high-tailed it out of there, fearing the queen's wrath if they reported the escape during their watch.

Queen Eleanor is in a royal rage. The majority of her ire is directed toward LeGare. Couldn't happen to a nicer guy, in my opinion. An official edict is issued declaring the young Chief Blackthorn and his two accomplices enemies of Domerica. A huge reward is offered for information leading to the capture of the fugitives. The entire palace is placed on high alert. Several regiments of the Royal Guard are dispatched to search for the criminals, although everyone pretty much knows that at this point a search is futile.

I'm eager to spend as much time as possible with Mother, but Ralston says it's best to give her some space for a day or two until the general palace uproar dies down. I suspect he's happy for the chance to get in a little intensive royal training before I spend too much one-on-one time with the queen.

Our classroom on the third floor is arranged so we can sit in comfortable chairs and have tea while Ralston gives me my lessons. We quickly fall into an easy daily routine, beginning each morning with an update on the IUGA's progress toward getting me home—which is usually a big zero. After that, while I'm supposedly learning the finer points of dome governance, Ralston conducts a kind of Princess Boot Camp. He fills me in on the rules of royal etiquette and the essentials of life at the palace. Afterward, he drills me with questions to see what I've learned.

In the afternoons, we go for nature walks, and he points out any unusual trees or plants I should be familiar with. Sometimes Fred and Ethel join us. They've quickly become my best buddies. Fred is a total cut-up, frequently needing to be scolded for his pranks. Ethel is sweet as honey. She has me wrapped around her furry little finger. Not a day goes by that I don't wish I could take them back to Connecticut with me.

Afternoons are also for working on my riding skills. To my complete surprise, I find I have a knack with horses. Ralston has selected a gentle bay mare named Roxanne for me, and we take small excursions around the palace each day. We can't go into town, though, because Mother has forbidden me to leave the grounds until she's certain Blackthorn is no longer on Domerican soil.

Evenings are my favorite times of all. That's when I get to be with Mother. We usually have dinner together—Mother, Drew, and me. Other people join us from time to time. We even have to put up with General LeGare occasionally, but the mood is always light, and Mother seems more relaxed than she is during the busy daylight hours.

Tonight Mother has invited Ralston to join us for dinner. She is scheduled to leave for a Coalition meeting in Dome Noir in a few days, so she wants to pick Ralston's brain about the other domes.

Ralston already explained the *Coalition of Dome Nations* to me. It's an alliance to facilitate cooperation among the domes and help to maintain world peace. "Similar to your United Nations," he says.

Mother asks Ralston all sorts of questions about what he observed while working in the other domes with the other royal families. He answers her thoughtfully, and she seems impressed with his knowledge and his insights. I'm happy that she respects Ralston enough to value his opinion.

After dessert and coffee are served, Mother says, "By the way, Professor Ralston, your friend, Lady Lorelei, has designed some unique gifts for the royal family of Dome Noir. One of my staff will pick them up tomorrow. You should really see them before I depart."

"I would be happy to pick them up for you, Your Highness," Ralston tells her. "An excursion into town would be an enjoyable diversion. I need to replenish some of my supplies and, of course, I would be pleased for an opportunity to see Lady Lorelei again."

"I couldn't impose upon you to do that," Mother says, "and I do not wish to interrupt Jaden's lessons. She so enjoys your daily sessions." She smiles fondly at me.

"Perhaps Princess Jaden would like to accompany me." He cuts his eyes toward me. "She hasn't been outside the palace grounds for days."

Mother frowns.

"Oh please, Mother," I beg. "I haven't been to the village … in ages."

After a moment her features ease. "I suppose it would do you good to get away from the palace for a while. You may go along, on the condition that you have an armed escort." I open my mouth to protest, but she holds up her hand. "Don't even think of arguing, Jaden. That is my decision."

~ ~ ~ ~

I'm thrilled to have a chance to see the village, even if we have to drag four armed guards along with us. Ralston and I ride in a horse-drawn carriage, so I don't have to worry about staying on top of my horse. Over the past few days, I'd gotten more relaxed about my own situation and less obsessive about asking Ralston when I can go home, so I'm freer to enjoy the sheer amazement of being in an alternate universe.

We pass some farms along the way. Most have industrial looking barracks-like buildings on the property instead of houses, and scads of workers dressed in white overalls toil away in the fields. Ralston says Domerica grows ninety percent of its own food. Few products are imported from the other domes since transporting them is so expensive.

"What are those buildings?" I ask.

"They are dormitories, to house the workers. As you already know, young adults are required to formally declare a marriage partner by age eighteen. Young men and women who fail to marry by age twenty are given a choice to work on a communal farm, such as the ones you see here, or in government offices in town. Based upon their choice, they are assigned to a post."

"Is it some kind of punishment or something?"

"I don't believe your mother would consider it as such. Every person is provided with a job and a place to live among people of a similar situation. They are comfortably taken care of for the remainder of their lives, as long as they perform their duties satisfactorily. They work alongside people of their own age, and retire with their cohort when the time comes."

"People are okay with this? They don't mind the government forcing them to marry by a certain age, work at a certain job, and live in a certain place?"

"It's been that way almost from the beginning, Jade. Every Domerican grows up knowing what their choices are and accepting that."

"But these people, the single ones, are they ever allowed to marry and have children?"

Ralston focuses on the road as he answers. "That gets a bit

complicated. On rare occasion a couple is allowed to marry late, if they apply for and receive special dispensation from the queen. They must show a compelling reason for the late marriage—perhaps one party was lost at sea for years or something similar. *Love* is not considered a compelling reason."

"That's harsh," I say.

"As for children, these late-marrying couples may adopt up to two children, but they cannot have children of their own. All single workers are surgically sterilized before they are assigned to a post."

"What?" I cry. "They're forced into sterilization? That really blows!"

"Jade, settle down; the guards will hear you," Ralston says quietly. "It's a choice they make, and it's not such a bad life, really. No poverty or overcrowding exists in Domerica as in the other domes. There is also very little crime because, as you have witnessed, justice is swift and harsh."

"Why do you try to make it all sound so rosy? It's totally oppressive. Why haven't the people revolted?"

"They don't have any weapons, for one thing. It is illegal to possess arms. Guns are strictly prohibited. Possession of one is grounds for immediate imprisonment. Only the royal family and members of the Royal Guard are allowed to own swords. For another thing, life is better here than anywhere else on this earth. Your mother makes certain the people are constantly reminded of that."

"I can't believe my mother would support that kind of government interference with people's lives. When she was a judge, she was a maniac about protecting individual constitutional rights. I don't get it."

"It's quite consistent, really. Remember, Queen Eleanor inherited this system when she ascended to the throne. She is enforcing the Constitution of Domerica, just as your Connecticut mother ardently supported the Constitution of the United States. It is the constitutions that are different, not your mother. Don't be too quick to judge, Jade. You really know very little of life on this planet."

I guess what he says makes sense, but some of the Domerican policies offend my most basic sense of morality and justice. And I still haven't come to terms with Mother's refusal to lift a finger to help the Unicoi.

As we approach the village, my attention is diverted back to the unique scenery. Most of the buildings in town are plain, multi-storied structures that appear to house a lot of people. They look sturdy, but lack any trace of art or style. Other structures, though, are grand, fashioned out of marble, stone, and metal, with elaborate and interesting architectural features. Ralston points out that these more elegant structures are government buildings and places of worship for the COC.

The main street of Warrington Village is lined with a variety of quaint, small shops. A wooden sidewalk stretches along both sides of the street. At intervals along the way, rails and troughs mark the designated areas for parking horses and carriages. Ralston pulls into one of these, and the guards dismount and tie up their horses. Ralston suggests that two of them wait with the wagon and horses. The other two clatter along behind us down the wooden sidewalk on the way to Bartlett's Silversmiths Shop.

Our presence raises quite a commotion in the village. As news of our arrival spreads, people stream out of the shops and restaurants to greet us. The crowd applauds and people call my name. Every few feet someone bows or curtseys, saying how great it is that I'm home and safe. Others assure me that Blackthorn will be found and brought to justice; still others throw flowers or small lace handkerchiefs to me.

A kind of hot-looking guy boldly steps forward from the crowd. He has the most startling pale green eyes I've ever seen. Something about his clothing is different also. I don't have time to figure it out, though, because he gets a little too close and my guards quickly step in to steer him away, but not before he smoothly slips a small piece of paper into my hand.

He melts seamlessly back into the crowd, and I stuff the paper into my pocket as Ralston and I continue to plow our way through the throng of well-wishers. The outpouring of affection is touching and seems genuine. The townspeople obviously like Princess Jaden very much, and I can't help but beam at the adoring faces.

Our love fest is soon broken up, however, by the appearance of a group of Royal Guards escorting three prisoners in shackles and leg irons. The villagers part to make way for them. The prisoners' faces are forbidding and weather-worn. They wear strange tan outfits resembling hazmat suits, helmets swinging loosely at their sides.

"Who are those people?" I ask Ralston.

"Outlanders. One usually does not see them this far inside the dome. They wear those suits to protect themselves outside. They must have been apprehended committing a crime."

"They don't live in the dome?"

"No. One or two small settlements of Outlanders exist near here. They are usually individuals running from the law, or free spirits who do not care for being restricted by dome walls or rules. Their dwellings protect them from the elements and are equipped with filtered air, but they must wear those suits when they venture outside."

The whole spectacle has a chilling effect on the crowd, and I'm relieved when we finally reach our destination. The guards station themselves by the door to the silversmith's shop, while Ralston and I step inside.

Bartlett's is impressive even by modern standards. Lighted glass cases form a square in the middle of the store, displaying sparkling pieces of silver jewelry. The walls are lined with shelves showcasing larger gleaming treasures like platters, bowls, and jeweled swords.

A uniformed security guard greets us inside the door. He bows and says, "Your Highness, please come with me." He leads us to a private chamber in the back of the store, and asks us to be seated in some red velvet chairs arranged in front of a polished wooden table.

"Lady Bartlett will be with you shortly." He bows again before leaving us alone.

"I saw that young man pass a note to you," Ralston says. "What does it say?"

I take the paper from my pocket and read it to him. *"Jaden — It is urgent that we speak about your current predicament and your astonishing gift. I can't get near you at the palace, but I will find you. —Asher."* The muscles in Ralston's jaw tighten as I read.

"What's wrong?" I ask. "You don't think he's dangerous, do you?"

"Probably not. We cannot take the chance, though. If you see him again, steer clear of him and call for help immediately."

"Okay, but what do you think it means?" I ask.

Before Ralston can answer, however, a radiant young woman glides into the room. We both rise to greet her. Technically, I'm supposed to remain seated, but she looks so regal I can't help it. The lady warmly embraces Ralston. After a small curtsey she embraces me also.

"You look well, cousin. It is so nice to see you again." Her voice is like tinkling crystal.

So this is Ralston's former student and friend Lorelei—the one who helped Ryder and his men return to Unicoi. Ralston told me she's an enlightened thinker who strongly opposes reeducation. She's also a great supporter of the Unicoi cause, which is why she readily agreed to help Ryder and his warriors escape.

A curtain of wavy yellow hair falls across her slender shoulders, softly framing her elegant features. Elaborate jewelry of polished silver twines like delicate vines around her pale neck and right wrist. It's impossible to guess her age. She looks quite young, but she carries herself with the sophistication of a much older woman.

"It has been too long since we have seen each other," she says to me. "You are a grown woman now. I am overjoyed to hear that

Professor Ralston has agreed to tutor you for a time." She smiles, placing a small hand on Ralston's arm. "He is a very wise mentor. You must listen carefully to his advice."

"I'll try," I mutter, feeling clumsy and dumb just being in her presence.

"Please sit down." She gestures to the chairs and we all take seats. "I trust you are feeling better after your ordeal," she says to me. "I'm certain it could not have been pleasant for you."

"I'm fine, thank you."

"Is your family well? I haven't seen your father or Prince Andrew for quite some time."

"Drew is the same," I tell her. "I hope to see Father soon myself."

"Excellent. Please give him my best."

I nod.

"May I offer you some tea or other refreshment?"

I glance at Ralston. He's waiting for me to answer. "Uh, no, thank you," I say.

"Very well, shall we get down to business? I have the pieces Queen Eleanor commissioned. I think you will be very pleased with them." She tugs on a tasseled cord hanging from the ceiling. Seconds later three men enter the room carrying carved wooden boxes. They place the boxes on the table in front of us. On a signal from Lady Lorelei, they simultaneously lift the lids, revealing three jewel-encrusted silver chalices.

"The chalices bear the names and birthdates of each of King Philippe's three sons," she says, pointing to an inscription on the base of the first chalice, *"Gilbert Auguste, Ne 25 Mai, MCMLXXV*. He is the crown prince, first born, and heir to the throne. These are for his brothers Jean Louis and Damien René."

"They're beautiful," I say, gawking at the gleaming pieces. "I'm sure Mother will love them."

"May I?" Ralston asks, reaching for the first chalice.

"Of course. Please have a closer look."

Ralston removes the chalice from its satin lined box. He examines it closely, holding it up to the light, revolving it in his hands. "Exquisite. I believe I recognize your hand in some of the more elaborate workmanship, Lorelei." She smiles modestly.

"Queen Eleanor will surely be delighted. If you will have them wrapped we will take them with us," he says.

"Certainly." She nods to her men. They remove the boxes from the table and disappear through the door.

Lady Lorelei settles back in her chair. "I have something for you," she says to me.

"For me?" I look at Ralston, confused. He shrugs.

She pulls a dark blue velvet pouch from a drawer in the table and hands it to me. "It is from our raven-haired friend. He was wearing it the night we assisted him. He asked me to give it to you as a token of his gratitude."

My heartbeat quickens. Blackthorn has left something for me? Inside the pouch is a long, elaborately woven silver chain with an intricately carved wolf-head pendant.

"He gave you this? For me?" I ask.

"Yes. He said it had a special significance for him. He wanted you to have it. Shall I put it on for you?" She comes around the table, and I place it in her hand.

"The workmanship is exceptional," she says. "It must be very old. The chain and pendant are undoubtedly Cherokee. I polished it for you, and repaired the clasp. I think it must have been through a lot!" Her laughter is light and melodic.

She slips the necklace over my head, centering the delicate wolf-head on my tunic. "Charming," she says smiling.

"I ... I don't know what to say. Thank you. Are you sure this is for me?"

"Of course, Princess. It was a most compassionate and courageous thing you did for our young friend."

My cheeks flush red. Mostly because I don't feel courageous at all. I feel like the scared, homesick kid I really am.

SEVENTEEN

*R*alston says I have *Dome Fever*—not unusual for someone not accustomed to being so confined. I've been in Domerica for over two weeks now. I still get daily updates on IUGA's efforts to coordinate my return home, but it's always a different version of "we're working on it." I admit I've been moping around since Mother and Drew left for Dome Noir three days ago.

The Coalition meeting is supposed to last for several days, and I'm annoyed that I couldn't tag along and check out Dome Noir myself. I've heard it's a lot different from Domerica—kind of dark and edgy. It's called Dome Noir because the gases in the dome shell are darker silver, nearly black. Ralston says the queen and the crown princess are never allowed to travel together outside the country. So I'm stuck here on my own.

As a remedy for my malaise, Ralston has planned a little picnic for us to a nearby lake for art lessons. I swear to him that I don't have an artistic bone in my body, but he insists that a princess should know how to paint and he describes the lake as a "painter's paradise." He sends me to my room to change while he arranges for a picnic basket and art supplies to be loaded into an open-air carriage. The picnic part sounds fun at least.

I throw open the doors to the princess' well-stocked closet to choose an outfit (one of my favorite daily activities). I'm tired of wearing riding clothes every day, so I decide that a dress would be the perfect choice for a picnic. The princess has so many cool dresses it's

TRANSCENDER: *First-Timer*

hard to settle on one. I finally pick out a sweet, spring green, sleeveless number that just brushes the tops of my knees. The style is simple, but the silk is gorgeous. I wear my hair loose with a woven headband of pink and green ribbons.

When Ralston comes to fetch me, his eyes grow wide. "You can't go out like that, Jade," he says.

"Why not?"

"Because that's an under dress—like a slip. Haven't you noticed that ladies do not wear sleeveless or short dresses during the day? It is considered immodest."

I frown. I guess I hadn't noticed, but now that I think about it, I haven't really seen any mini-dresses in the palace.

"Well hell, a little help would be nice," I say. "How am I supposed to know what passes for appropriate fashion in this backward little snow globe?"

He steps past me into my room. "Let's have a look in your closet, shall we? And watch your language, Princess."

Ralston examines the contents of my closet. "I think you understand the pants. Tops should have sleeves and should not show your midriff." He picks up a camisole. "Though women may wear this as a top in Connecticut, this is *not* a top in Domerica, it is underwear."

I nod. "Got it."

"These are your day dresses, he says, waving his arm at one rack. Notice they are ankle length or longer, with some sort of sleeve. They normally have buttons or ties, lace or cuffs, or some kind of trim, and possibly a pattern in the fabric." He points out several examples. "As you know, an evening event is the exception. Then you may throw out all the rules. Elegance is the only imperative, and you've done well with that, so far."

I smile at the compliment.

He pulls out a dusky pink, U-neck dress made of lightweight fargen wool and embroidered with small flowers. "This would be an appropriate dress for our excursion today." It's ankle length with long, belled sleeves. Kind of retro 70s, vintage hippie, but I like it.

"Underneath, you should wear a swimsuit. The lake will be perfect for swimming this afternoon. You might enjoy a dip." He opens several drawers in the lingerie chest. "Ah, here we are." He pulls out what looks like a white workout tank top and a pair of matching stretchy shorts. "This is a swimsuit," he declares.

I squint at the suit, and then at him. "Are you sure? That doesn't look like a swimsuit to me. It looks more like a yoga outfit or something."

"Trust me Jade, this is considered risqué in Domerica. Just wear it. No one is going to see you anyway. I'll wait for you in the carriage. And don't take all day, we're losing the light."

"Yeah, yeah, yeah. I'll be right there."

When I reach the carriage, I find Ralston waiting for me—alone. Somehow he managed to convince our guards that we don't need an escort today. He sent them into town on an errand. I'm sure they'll be spitting mad when they get back to the palace and find us gone, but it's liberating to be rid of our constant, noisy companions.

~ ~ ~ ~

Ralston didn't exaggerate about the lake, it's idyllic. Wildflowers are strewn across the broad meadow leading down to the silvery-blue water. A small waterfall is visible on the far side of the lake, where fifty-foot spruces form a border along the bank. We set up our outdoor classroom beneath a welcoming, ancient oak.

Ralston props a fresh canvas on the easel, and begins my lesson with a flourish. He deftly demonstrates various methods for making globs of oil paint look like flowers and trees. I'm fascinated by his movements as the canvas comes to life with each brush stroke. He does a good job of making it look easy.

Then it's my turn. I select a brush and attempt to imitate

Ralston's flamboyant strokes. The result is beyond dismal. My painting looks like someone sneezed tossed salad all over the canvas. Ralston patiently makes suggestions for ways in which I might improve my technique, but after a whole slew of failed attempts, and several spoiled canvases, even he is forced to admit defeat. He mercifully suggests we break for lunch.

We spread a blanket under the tree and open the basket to see what goodies Cook has prepared for us. I'm happy to find baked chicken instead of Weigel or some other local delicacy. Crusty rolls, sharp cheddar cheese, and juicy pommeras round out the menu. Two jars of sweet peach juice are included for drinks, and two thick wedges of blueberry pie for dessert.

"Ralston, how did Mother and Drew travel to Dome Noir if the atmosphere outside is deadly?" I ask, enjoying the delicious and slightly messy cuisine.

"They wear protective clothing when they're exposed to the open air, but for the most part they stay inside enclosed vehicles. Motorized conveyances take them to the harbor, and high-speed hydrofoils transport them across the ocean. The hydrofoils are quite amazing. They travel at speeds similar to that of a jet plane."

"We have some high-speed ferries like that back in Connecticut," I say. "What's this Coalition meeting all about anyway?"

A look of unease flashes across his face. "I do not know, my dear. It could be anything really, especially now that this world has veered from its predicted course. I am certain we shall find out upon your mother's return."

He gathers up the remains of our lunch. "Now, are you ready to get back to our lessons? Your first foray into oils was rather disheartening, I must say. Perhaps watercolors are a better medium for you."

"No more painting, pleeeease." I beg.

He shoots me an exasperated look.

"Ralston, teach me to sword fight."

"What? No! It's too dangerous."

"But I'm supposed to be a sword-meister, right? So I at least need to learn the basics. What if I'm ever called upon to use my skills? I'll be exposed as a fake…if not maimed or killed."

"I seriously doubt that you'll be challenged to a sword fight in Domerica, Jaden. Not to mention that you are normally surrounded by a number of armed guards even if you were."

"Come on Rals. It'll be fun. We don't even have to use real swords. Just show me the down and dirty."

He tries to purse his mouth, but the corners turn up into an almost-smile, and I know I've won. "All right," he says. "You finish cleaning up lunch, while I find something we can use for swords."

He stalks into the trees and is back a few minutes later with some sturdy branches he has stripped and cut to roughly the size of a sword. "These are lighter than real swords. But, they'll do for practice." He tosses one to me. We stand facing each other under the tree.

"Your footwork is as important as your swordplay," he says. "We'll start with that first. You seem light on your feet, so just watch and follow."

What Ralston lacks as an art teacher, he makes up for as a fencing instructor. He's graceful and athletic, and surprisingly strong for his size.

I'm not too bad with my stance and footwork. My Tae Kwon Do experience helps me with balance and speed. When it comes to my grip, though, Ralston says I'm a hopeless case. No matter how many times he demonstrates the proper grip, I can't get the hang of it. After a while he just shrugs and says maybe I've invented my own style.

It doesn't take long for me to become completely absorbed in the lesson. I love the new challenge, physically and mentally. After two hours of intensive swordplay, I'm totally whipped and soaked in sweat. My arms and shoulders ache.

TRANSCENDER: First-Timer

"I need to rest," I say, plopping on the grass.

"Too much for you? Taking on the old Swordmaster?" Ralston's still fired-up from the sparring and kind of full of himself.

I have to smile. "Yeah, Rals, you kicked my butt!"

"Why don't you take a swim, while I pack up the art supplies? You've done remarkably well for a novice—much better than your abysmal showing as an artist."

"Hey, you got to play to your strengths, right?" I laugh. "A swim sounds great, but I'll help you pack up first."

"No. You go on. There's not much to do here, and I'm not even winded," he boasts, folding up the easel.

I drag my tired bones to the edge of the lake. The sparkling water looks cool and inviting. I peel off my dress, hang it on a tree branch, and dive in. It's heaven.

I swim out to the little waterfall. The chilly curtain of water cascades across my head and shoulders, refreshing my aching muscles. Hoisting myself up on a rock beside the falls, I let the dome-filtered sunlight warm my skin. I wonder what Mom and Drew are doing right now in that mysterious place called Dome Noir. I hope they'll be home soon. Maybe if I practice enough, I can challenge Drew to a sword fight. I'd love to see his face if I beat him.

I close my eyes and my thoughts drift idly to the place where they hang out a lot these days—to that incredible face, jet black hair and sexy smile. I flex the fingers of my right hand recalling the electrical charge when Blackthorn's lips met my skin. A flicker of bittersweet pain passes through my heart again, remembering his face as he left that night.

I dive back into the water to clear my head. I swim underneath the falls and discover a small, protected alcove carved out of the rock on the other side. It shelters a tranquil little pool with a sandy bottom. Silver-green light filters through the veil of water, dancing and sparkling across the pool. The sounds of the cascading falls are peaceful and soothing, and I wonder how many people know of this tiny hidden haven.

As I explore the little grotto further, I realize that if I position myself to one side of the waterfall, I can see the entire lake without being seen myself. I scan the shoreline looking for Ralston and our picnic tree. When my eyes find him, I'm startled to see that he's talking to someone. It looks like ... but, no, it can't be. Ryder Blackthorn!

My heart skips a couple of beats and a wave of hot emotion surges through me. What is he doing here? I'm ecstatic and frightened at the same time. He shouldn't be here! He's a wanted outlaw with a hefty bounty on his head. How can he be so reckless? I dive under the falls, quickly swimming for shore.

EIGHTEEN

I see Ralston hand Blackthorn some towels, which he carries down to the water's edge. By the time I reach him, I'm hopping mad and sopping wet.

"What in the hell are you doing here, Blackthorn? Didn't we just move heaven and earth to help you escape Domerica? Why don't you just ride straight over to the palace and turn yourself in?"

He half-smiles, "Nice to see you too, Princess."

"Oh really? Are you completely out of your mind or do you just have a death wish?"

"I need to speak with you." He hands me a towel.

"So you just trot on over here to see me despite the fact that there's a huge reward on your head, the Royal Patrols have been doubled, and everybody and his brother are looking for you!"

He steps closer to me, so I have to look up at him. His expression is amused and his manner relaxed. "Please calm yourself, Princess. Put on some clothes, then we shall speak."

I look down at myself and realize that the oversized Domerican swimsuit I'm wearing, while modest by anyone's standards when dry, is something else altogether when wet. The dripping fabric clings to every embarrassing curve of my body—like I just entered a wet T-shirt contest. A small "Oh" escapes my lips and my face burns scarlet. I quickly wrap the towel around myself.

"I need a few minutes to wash up," he says, pulling off his armor. "It's been a long ride."

Hurrying to the tree where I left my dress, I dry off and quickly put it back on. I run my fingers through my wet hair pulling futilely at the mass of tangles. I soon give up, however, and twist the whole snarled mess into a knot at the base of my neck.

I peer around the tree. Blackthorn is kneeling at the lake's edge. He has stripped off his tunic and is splashing water on his face and shoulders. With each movement, his smooth skin ripples across the muscles of his back. When he's finished washing, he rakes his hands through his hair, picks up his things, and turns toward me.

My heart nearly catapults out of my throat. God he's gorgeous! More striking even than my overactive imagination had remembered. Water beads down the skin of his bare chest and arms. My eyes follow the trail of droplets as they travel down his ripped abdomen to the top of his riding pants. My knees turn to spaghetti.

A pink scar from the injury to his arm is visible, and I notice a few other long-healed disfigurements along his torso, but they only make his body more interesting. His face is almost completely healed now, with only faint traces of bruising. He smiles and strides to my tree. I have to remind myself to breathe.

"Are you ready to be civil now?" he asks.

I nod.

"Will you walk with me while we talk?"

I lower my eyes, "I think you'd better put some clothes on too, Chief Blackthorn. If you want my full attention, that is."

He raises an eyebrow, laughing his wonderful laugh. "Princess, the way you speak! I've never met anyone quite like you. You are very direct." He slips his shirt on over his head.

"I guess I am." I laugh too. "Is that a bad thing?"

"No, not bad. It just throws me off balance sometimes." He leaves his armor and his sword near the carriage. We tell Ralston we're going for a walk. Always the mother hen, he warns us to be back before dark, and cautions us to keep an eye out for patrols.

Blackthorn and I walk along a footpath that follows the perimeter of the lake. He seems reluctant to speak, so I ask him a question to get the ball rolling.

"Did you have any problems getting back to Unicoi after you left the palace?"

"No. No problems on our journey. Ralston's friend Lorelei attended to everything. She brought our horses, as well as food and fresh clothing. Her people had a secure tunnel which we used to get out of Domerica. She took a great risk in helping us."

He stops for a moment and gazes across the lake at the small, rocky waterfall shimmering in the afternoon light. "It's so beautiful here. I do love this land. The silver light illuminates everything from within." He turns to me. "Even you are glowing."

My face warms at his comment because I know that if I'm glowing, it has more to do with his sudden appearance than any effect of the lighting.

"It is uniquely impressive," I agree, realizing it must be very different for him living inside a mountain. "Do you have any natural light in Unicoi?"

"None at all. But the lighting technicians have become very good at recreating a feeling of daylight inside. The technology improves every year." He turns back to the path, and we continue our walk. "In any event, I owe you, Ralston, and Lady Lorelei a great debt of gratitude for rescuing me from my own stupidity. My father was not quite so understanding when I reached home."

"Yeah, parents can be that way. What did he do?"

"The details aren't important. It is enough to say that I have never felt so ashamed or humbled in all my life. He is enormously disappointed in me, and justifiably so. I know he still loves me no matter how asinine I have acted, but I must walk a long road to make things right again." A flicker of pain passes across his face, quickly replaced by a sad smile.

"Your eye is healing nicely." I say, reaching up and touching my fingertip to the small scar on his cheek. He flinches slightly.

"Oh, I'm sorry. Does it hurt?"

"No." He runs his own fingertips along the small cut. "It's just that when you touch me, I feel a ... jolt."

"Oh that." I look down at my feet, suddenly shy.

"Do you feel it too?"

"I do," I admit quietly. We walk in silence again, my hand unconsciously fingering the woven silver chain at my neck.

"I'm glad you are wearing the necklace I left for you," he says

"Yes, thank you. It's lovely. You know you didn't have to do that."

He stops and his eyes find mine. "I want you to have it. It has very special meaning for me. It is good to know that it is with you now, Princess."

"I thought you weren't going to call me Princess anymore."

"I beg your pardon, lady." He bows formally. "And I would appreciate it if you would not call me Chief. I'm not really a chief yet. People use it to acknowledge my assumed future status."

"But you will be chief one day, right?"

He grins. "Unless your mother succeeds in having me hanged or reeducated."

"So, is being chief just like being king?"

"No. It's not like a king. In Unicoi, the chief has certain powers, but a council elected by the people makes most of the laws and policies. The chief steps in if they cannot agree."

"Oh, kind of like a democracy?'

He arches an eyebrow. "Has Ralston been teaching you government?"

"Not today!" I tell him about the art lessons, but skip the part about fencing. "So, if not *Chief*, what do people call you?" I ask.

"My friends call me Ryder and my enemies—well they have many names for me, none of which shall be repeated here. I would be honored if you would call me Ryder."

"Done. Now that we have that out of the way, why are you here, Ryder?"

"Let's walk," he says, and we continue down the path. "I have been to see your father."

"My father?" I say, surprised.

"Yes, I needed to apologize to him for my treatment of you. I have known him since I was a boy. He has always dealt fairly with my father and my people. I owed him better."

"That must have been an interesting conversation. What did he say?"

"He said he was troubled by my actions, but understood my motivations. I asked his permission to come to you, to speak with you about something."

"Oh yeah? About what?"

He's silent for a time, collecting his thoughts. When he finally speaks his voice is strained. "I have come to ask something of you, something I have no right to ask."

"What is it?" My brain starts shuffling the possibilities.

"I would like you to visit my country. To meet the Unicoi people, and my father, and to see first-hand why I am dedicated to saving our people."

That's not what I expected. "But why? Why me? What good will it do?"

"Jaden I don't know you well, or at all really. I know of your reputation for helping others, and I sense something in you—an openness, a kindness—that leads me to hope you will not let a whole nation of innocent people die if you can do something about it."

I stop in the middle of the path. "But what can *I* possibly do? I don't have any power over these things."

"Come, sit for a minute." He leads me to a crude wooden bench at the edge of the path. We sit facing each other, our knees nearly touching. It's awkward for me to be this close to him. I have a physical reaction to this guy that I can't control. My pulse races and my temperature shoots up a few degrees. It's uncomfortable, like some kind of itch I can't quite scratch. I try to listen to what he's saying but it's hard to focus on his words.

"You can come to Unicoi and draw your own conclusions," he says. "Should you decide to help us, you can speak to the queen. She will listen to you. Unicoi has much to offer your country. We've tried to tell your mother about our progressive agricultural methods and our advances in medicine and technology, but she does not believe us. She refuses to come and see for herself."

"She's just afraid that the disease spreading through Unicoi is contagious," I tell him. "She's worried about protecting her own people."

"That is what she says publicly, but I believe her real motivations may be something altogether different."

"What do you mean?"

"I believe she fears our culture will infect her people. She does not approve of our views on government and religion."

"Don't the Unicoi belong to the Church of the Chosen?"

"The Unicoi believe in many paths to God. A variety of faiths are practiced in Unicoi. Mainly the ones practiced by our ancestors before the Great Disaster. The COC teaches that those who fled to the domes are the 'chosen ones.' Some argue that excludes the Unicoi and others living outside the domes."

This is news to me.

"What the queen fails to recognize is that we would be powerful allies for Domerica. We could coexist peacefully, while sharing our many great advances with the Domerican people." Conviction burns in his eyes as he speaks.

"Ryder, honestly, I've already tried to talk to my mother about this. She's still a little prickly about you trying to kidnap me. She won't even discuss it with me."

"I understand. But consider that it might make a difference if you have been to Unicoi, met with the people, and witnessed the technological advances, as well as the realities of the disease. You could explain it to her from first-hand observation."

He leans in toward me, and I have to swallow my heart. It's thrilling to hear him speak with such passion, but his sensuous mouth makes me think of things … well, completely unrelated to the subject matter, so I stare at my hands as he continues.

"You can persuade her. I know you can."

I glance at him briefly, lowering my eyes again. "Listen Ryder, your plan will never work. The chance that my mother will allow me to visit Unicoi is less than zero, and I'd never be able to sneak out of the country without her consent. You don't understand—I'm guarded 24/7. Ralston and I were able to slip away today, but that's not likely to happen again."

"I have thought about that," he says, "and I think I have a solution. You can arrange a visit to your father at the Enclave. Wall's Edge is at the dome's western-most border. Unicoi is only three hours from there through the tunnels. We have many tunnels still undiscovered by your mother's soldiers. I will meet you at the

Enclave and escort you to Unicoi myself. You can spend a day, maybe two, and I will deliver you safely back to your father."

I look up in surprise. "You spoke with my father about *this* and he agreed?"

"He gave me permission to ask you. He said it is entirely your decision. He trusts your judgment completely." Ryder lifts my hand. The buzz of electrical current flows through my arm. I suck in a breath and turn away from him again.

"Please look at me," he says. I do. Big mistake. His eyes are so crystal blue that I want to dive inside them and lose myself in him.

"Won't you at least consider it?"

"Do you even know how stunning you are?" I blurt out.

His face falls, and he drops my hand. "Are you mocking me?" he says, an edge of irritation in his voice.

"No! No, I'm sorry. That was totally inappropriate." I stand, throwing my hands into the air. "Arrgh! It's just that you've got me so confused. I don't want to lie to my mother. It's important to me not to hurt her. Besides, I'm not sure that going to Unicoi is the *right* thing to do anyway."

According to Ralston, my accidental presence in this world has already thrown the whole future of the planet into question. Who knows what my going to Unicoi might do?

"The way the queen chooses to deal with Unicoi is her call, not mine," I say. "I shouldn't be interfering at all. It's really none of my concern."

He responds quietly, "People are suffering and dying. How can that *not* be your concern? My people believe that all of creation is connected—the pain of one is the pain of all; the honor of one is the honor of all. Whatever we do affects everything in the universe."

"See what I mean?" I stretch my arms out wide. "See what you do? This is the whole problem! I'm trying to be practical and you go all Yoda on me. You sit there looking the way you look—how am I supposed to refuse you?"

He stands to face me. "I respect that you do not wish to deceive your mother. That is what makes it so difficult to ask it of you. But I want to make things right ... with you, with my father, and with my people. I am convinced that if you see with your own eyes what I am fighting for, you will understand what I was attempting to accomplish by holding you against your will. If my father sees that you have forgiven me, that you trust me enough to make this enormous concession, perhaps he will not look at me with such hurt in his eyes."

I shake my head. "Look, Ryder, I want to help you. I really do. But I'm not convinced it'll work."

"Perhaps it will not, but won't you try? At the very least, I am certain that I can convince *you* that the Unicoi deserve life as much as any other humans do. One day you will be Queen of Domerica. If any of us are left at that time, I know you will help us." He smiles sadly. "Will you at least sleep on it and give me your answer tomorrow? I'm staying in the village tonight. I will meet you here again tomorrow, if you are able to come. If not, send Ralston with your answer."

My heart leaps at the prospect of seeing him again tomorrow, but hanging around Domerica doesn't sound like a good idea for Blackthorn. "Whoa, Ryder, are you sure it's safe for you to stay in the village? I mean, it's well known that you're wanted by the Crown, and you don't exactly blend in with the rest of the villagers."

"True, but Lady Lorelei has agreed to put me up. I will be safe with her."

"Lorelei? You're staying with Lady Lorelei?" Beautiful Lorelei? My stomach clenches at the thought of him spending the night with her.

"Yes. She's your cousin isn't she?"

"*Distant* cousin. We're not close."

"It sounds as though you do not care for her."

"Of course I do. It's just that she's so … well, she's just so … *pretty.*"

He laughs, and I feel a little stupid.

"I hardly think that's grounds for disliking someone. If it were, you wouldn't have a single friend."

"Ha, ha. I'm serious, Blackthorn. Just be careful, wherever you stay, because I don't want to have to come to your rescue again."

"Very well, my lady," he says, bowing, "I shall endeavor to stay out of harm's way for your sake."

"And I will endeavor to meet you in person tomorrow to give you my answer. Just don't be upset with me if I decide I can't go to Unicoi."

"I could not be upset with you—not after everything you have already risked for me."

We walk along the path without speaking for a time, but I know I need to clear the air about something.

"Hey Ryder."

"Yes?"

"You know back there … what I said about you being so gorgeous and all, well I didn't mean to insult you, especially when you were spilling your guts to me."

He stops and looks at me, his expression indecipherable. I'm pretty sure I'm about to seriously embarrass myself again, but I plow ahead anyway.

"It's just that meeting you was so … unexpected. You kidnapped me, but I couldn't hate you for it. After Ralston and I helped you escape, I was sure I'd never see you again. Even so, I've spent an incredible amount of time over the past two weeks wondering what it would be like to kiss you."

Lowering his eyes he says, "Jaden, I must tell you something."

Uh-oh. That doesn't sound like good news. I hold up my hands. "No. No, Ryder, you really don't have to explain anything to me. I mean I realize you might have a girlfriend, or you may not find me in the least bit attractive, so it's all right. Really. You don't have to say anything." God, what an idiot I am! I can't stop blithering on.

He touches a finger to my lips. "Shhh," he says softly. "This is something that concerns you."

"Me?"

"Yes. I told you we have met before. I know you do not remember, but I will never forget. It was the first time I ever saw green eyes."

"What? Really?"

"Yes. You must know that no one in Unicoi possesses green eyes?"

"No green eyes? How can that be?"

"Well, I'm certain a few original settlers must have had green eyes, but over time they have ceased to exist in our society. Whether it is the lack of natural light, or simple genetics, I do not know."

"That's crazy. I've never heard of that before. So, how did we meet?"

He puts his hand on my elbow, steering me off the path into a small clearing. A large dried-out tree stump sits at the center. He gestures for me to have a seat, and he leans against a tree opposite me, arms folded across his chest.

"I remember our introduction clearly," he says. "It was during a Coalition meeting at Warrington Palace. That was back when my father was still invited to Coalition meetings. I was fifteen. You were twelve."

I narrow my eyes at him. "Are you making this up?"

"I swear I am not." He raises his right hand. "Stories had circulated throughout the tribe that you and your mother possessed green eyes. I always believed it to be a myth—an exotic fairytale. We met in a reception line in the grand hall. You smiled at me and said, 'I am very happy to know you, young Chief Blackthorn.' I was so awed, I could not even reply. You must have thought me deaf and dumb."

"And you must have thought I was some kind of freak!"

"Not so. I believed you were quite possibly the most beautiful creature on earth, with your lovely smile, your golden hair, and your impossible emerald-colored eyes. In fact I was certain you were some sort of enchantress," he says smiling, "because I could never get you out of my mind."

His eyes lock onto mine and his expression turns serious. "So you see, I have spent an incredible amount of time over the past five years wondering what it would be like to kiss you."

Our eyes hold for a heartbeat, then we're in each other's arms. Weeks and months and years of longing collide in that moment. Well, okay, so technically it's not me he's been longing for all those years— but close enough.

His arms pull me in tightly. I melt into him as if it is where I belong, where I've always belonged. My body trembles and I surrender all my senses to everything that is Blackthorn—his taste, his smell, his touch, his warm mouth on mine, giving and demanding at once. The hot, sweet sensations of hunger and thirst are fulfilled, then renewed with each movement of his mouth. His body presses against mine, and I respond in kind. Nothing in my life has ever felt so miraculously right and I'm certain nothing else ever will.

After much too short a time, he tears his lips away. I whimper in protest, but he takes my face in his hands and gazes at me with such tenderness, I'm sure my heart will break.

"Ah, Jade," he whispers hoarsely, "I have dreamed of this." He gently kisses each of my eyelids, then each ear and each cheekbone— whispering my name softly between each kiss … Jade … Jade …

Jade. I cling to him, helplessly lost in a rapture I've never known. I believe I could die right here, right now, and be perfectly happy.

When his lips reach my throat I moan involuntarily. Abruptly he straightens up, sweeps me into his arms, and carries me determinedly back toward the path.

"Wait, where are you taking me?"

"Back to Ralston," he says, his breath ragged. "I believe that you are in need of a chaperone."

"Whoa. Whoa, wait a minute. Stop!" He stops.

"Put me down!" He obeys, refusing to meet my eyes.

"Ryder, look at me." When he does, his face holds something unreadable. Shame? Regret?

"Oh God! You don't regret kissing me, do you?"

"No. I regret that I almost could not *stop* kissing you," he says angrily. "I seem always to behave poorly in your presence."

I cover my face with my hands, tears of relief spilling down my cheeks. "Please don't apologize for that. Don't spoil one of the most amazing moments of my life."

"Was it really?" he asks.

"Yes."

"For me also." He takes me in his arms again, gently this time. He presses his cheek to the top of my head. "Thank you," he whispers.

After a few moments, his breathing returns to normal, and my tears are mostly dry. I pull away from him slightly. "See," I sniff, "no chaperone required. We're both responsible people. Right?"

"We both undoubtedly have our share of responsibilities," he says. "You're not angry then?"

"Hardly. I thought I'd died and gone to heaven. You really should behave badly more often."

He grins, shaking his head. "It seems I can't help myself when I'm near you. It must be something about you."

"Ha! I bring out the worst in you, then?"

"Or the best. I'm not sure." He laughs.

I take his hand and we head back to the carriage.

It's weird; I feel a connection with him and not just because of the kiss. I've heard of something called *cell memory*, and I wonder if the princess's body remembers Ryder from their childhood meeting—she did draw a little star by his name. Maybe she felt something too.

Ralston has everything packed and is waiting for us upon our return. It doesn't escape his notice that Ryder and I are holding hands, but he doesn't comment.

"I look forward to our next meeting," Ryder says. "I must speak with Professor Ralston for a few minutes. Please excuse me."

He releases my hand, which I take as my cue to go pick some wildflowers or something. I assume he's going to fill Ralston in on his plan to have me visit Unicoi and our agreement to meet here tomorrow for my answer. I can guess what Ralston's reaction is going to be. I only hope he doesn't lock me in my room for the rest of my stay in Domerica.

When I hear Ryder whistle for his horse, I rejoin the two men. The atmosphere is cordial enough, so Ralston didn't blow a gasket when Ryder explained his plan. The men say their goodbyes, shaking hands.

"I shall meet you here tomorrow, Jaden," Ryder says bowing politely. He hops onto the back of his horse.

"Tomorrow, then," I say.

And he is gone. And the empty feelings of loss that enveloped me last time he left me are back, only stronger this time. I hug myself against the ache.

NINETEEN

*T*he ride home is bumpy and dusty. No rain in Domerica on Thursdays. I'm still flying high on Ryder's kiss, content in my own thoughts. It was an unexpected thrill to see him again. And the kiss, well ... I shiver all over just to think of it. He's so brave, so kind, so irresistibly sexy, and he likes me! Well maybe not *me* exactly, but he definitely likes Princess Jaden. A lot. I touch the silver necklace, remembering to tuck it inside my dress. I always wear it hidden at the palace. I don't want any questions about where it came from.

Despite my warm feelings for Ryder, I'm uncomfortable every time I think about his invitation to visit Unicoi. I want to help him and the Unicoi people, and I want to spend as much time with him as possible, but I'm pretty sure Ralston's going to say it's too dangerous, that interfering in the affairs of this world can only lead to disaster. I don't even want to think about Mother's reaction if she ever finds out. I'll be the star pupil in her reeducation program. My stomach gets twisted, and my temples throb just thinking about it. How can my life be so hopelessly messy and so spectacularly wonderful all at the same time?

Ralston seems to be nursing a mood of his own. He hasn't said a word for the entire ride home, clucking to the horses occasionally or humming to himself. As we near the turn-off to the palace drive, I can't stand it any longer.

"So, what do you think of Ryder Blackthorn's idea about me visiting Unicoi?" I ask.

"What I think about it is not really pertinent, Jade. What *you* think about it is what matters," he says, keeping his eyes on the road.

Hmm. That wasn't quite what I expected to hear.

"I'm just so torn about the whole thing," I say. "I'd like to help the Unicoi if there's anything I can do in the short time I have here, but so many things can go wrong with the plan. Plus, my mother will probably kill me if she ever finds out. Even on the outside chance I can pull it off and actually visit Unicoi, there's no guarantee it'll make a difference anyway. Mother isn't willing to listen to me at all where Unicoi is concerned."

Ralston clucks softly to the horses, continuing to stare ahead. "Uh huh," is his only response.

"Hey, I'm looking for some help here," I say. "Aren't you supposed to advise me and guide me? Don't you have an opinion on this? Or are you even listening to me? I'm trying to figure out what to do. I don't want to disappoint Ryder. I don't want to disappoint my mother either, and the whole thing could just blow up in my face."

He stares straight ahead and remains infuriatingly silent.

"I want you to tell me what to do, damn it!"

He pulls the horses to a stop and faces me. "Jade," he says in a voice a patient mother uses with a petulant child. "I know you are frustrated with having been plucked from your quiet life and transported into a tense situation not of your own making, but is it really necessary for you to brow-beat me when you already know what you are going to do?"

"What? I ..." My mouth moves, but no words come out. I start to tell him he's nuts—I have no idea what I'm going to do but, oddly, the noise in my head just stops, and I know he's right. There's only one thing I can do. I have to go to Unicoi.

"So you're not going to try and stop me?" I ask. "You're not going to tell me this isn't my world and this is not my affair so I should just butt out?"

"Would it make you feel better if I tried to stop you?"

"No."

"Would it change your mind?"

"Not a chance."

"Well then ..."

"But you wish I'd make a different decision?"

"That would be like wishing fire didn't burn one's fingers, Jade. You are uniquely *you.*" He smiles kindly. "You must do what you feel is right, and I must not interfere with your free will while you are here."

I slump back in my seat. "I'm sorry to be so cranky, Rals. I guess I'm just a little scared."

"That's healthy." He snaps the horses' reins to get us rolling again. "It could be an interesting trip. Of course I'm going with you," he adds. "You might as well see a little more of this world, as long as you are here. Think of it as part of the adventure."

"Yeah, some adventure." I lean back against the seat, clasping my hands over my roiling stomach.

"Have you considered that a personal element may be involved in young Blackthorn's invitation to you?" Ralston asks, avoiding my eyes again.

"What do you mean?"

"I mean, he seems rather taken with you."

"Yeah, I like him too," I admit. "I wish I didn't, but he's just so freakin' likable."

"He is that," Ralston says mildly. "Just be careful, my dear."

I get it. This is his way of giving me a gentle warning, but I don't want to talk about it right now. Mainly because I don't need him to tell me what I already know—that falling for Ryder is not a smart thing to do. That depressing fact hangs heavy in the dusty air between us.

Our four guards are totally ticked at us by the time we reach the palace. No one has known our whereabouts for several hours, and they've been preparing to send out a dome-wide alert for us.

Ralston smoothes everything over, though. He tells them I changed my mind after they left, insisting we go out to the lake to paint wildflowers. Rather than have me pout all afternoon—you know how girls can be—he gave in to my wishes ... yada, yada, yada. By the time Ralston finishes with his story, the soldiers are apologizing to him for being so needlessly worried. As a little *just-between-us-boys* gesture, Ralston actually shows them some of my artwork, which causes a few exaggerated grimaces and some barely concealed laughter. I'm sure I'll be the butt of a few jokes around the Royal Guard mess hall this evening, but it was worth it to see Ryder again.

I eat a light supper in my room, preferring to be alone with my thoughts. I'm not avoiding Ralston exactly, but after such an awesome day, I don't feel like getting into a big discussion about the dead-end street in front of me if I get involved with Ryder. I haven't quite turned that corner yet, and I don't need Ralston flashing any big stop signs at me. I'm not sure I'm even capable of steering clear of Blackthorn at his point. I just hope I'm strong enough to make the right decision and live with it.

Maria appears at my door, while the maids are clearing away the remains of my meal. "May I help you with your hair tonight, Princess?"

"I was going to just forget about it, but, yeah, come on in," I say.

Maria massages my scalp with creamy shampoo smelling of rosemary and basil. She applies a lightly perfumed tonic from Copula de Vita and combs it through to the ends, saying it will work wonders on my wild mane. The whole process is divine and relaxing.

"How did your hair get so matted?" She asks, expertly working the comb through the snarls and knots.

"I went swimming in the lake, and … oh, speaking of which …" I hop out of my chair and unroll my wet swimsuit from its towel, "do I have anything decent to swim in other than these?" I hold up the damp garments.

She giggles. "You swam in your underwear?"

"Um … apparently," I say, silently cursing Ralston for his faulty fashion advice.

"Your bathing clothes are right here. Did you forget?" She goes to a drawer in one of the chests.

"Well, yes. You know me—can't remember a thing."

"I think Sylvia used to lay out everything for you. That is why you are a little confused." She pulls out several one-piece suits. They are still modest and old fashioned looking, but at least they are made out of thicker, stretchy fabric like a normal swimsuit.

"Yeah, I'm sure you're right. She hates me now, doesn't she? Sylvia, I mean."

"She doesn't hate you, but I think that maybe she used to keep an eye on you for your mother. Now that she cannot do that, she doesn't have as much access to the queen anymore. She is not as admired by the others as before, if you know what I mean."

"Yeah, I think I know what you mean—she was spying on me. That figures." I thank my lucky stars that I dumped Sylvia my first day in the palace.

"I like the blue one." She holds up a suit for me to see. "It is a good color for you, and the square neckline is very flattering."

It's pretty, although it looks like something my grandma would wear. "Leave it out for me, would you please? I'm going to the lake again tomorrow." My heart does a little flip-flop when I think about seeing Ryder once more.

Maria finishes with my hair and bids me goodnight. I climb into my princess bed, my body dog-tired, my mind swirling with questions. What will Unicoi be like? What is my father like in this world? What will my mother do when she finds out about my secret trip? Will Ryder kiss me again tomorrow? What are Ryder and Lorelei doing right now? What are Ryder and I doing?

Round and round in circles, so much to think about, so much to look forward to. I'm completely caught up in all the drama and intrigue of my new life. Then it hits me all at once—I haven't thought about home all day.

The realization shakes me up. I kick off my covers and sit up in my bed. I don't want to admit it, not even a little bit, but I'd be crushed if I had to go home right now. I want to see Unicoi. I want to see my dad and his little community. I haven't spent nearly enough time with my mother. But most of all, I want to see Ryder Blackthorn again ... badly.

TWENTY

I look a little wrecked because I hardly slept all night. I dress in a cheery spring frock with my pretty blue swimsuit underneath. My hair still looks fresh and smells great thanks to Maria's special treatment. But I can't eat a bite of breakfast because millions of baby butterflies are flitting around in my stomach, tapping out Ryder's name with each tiny wing-stroke.

I arrive in the palace courtyard to find Ralston waiting for me in a carriage, packed and ready to roll. He's already gotten rid of the guards. The man's a genius!

"It's a beautiful morning, Jade! A wonderful day for a picnic," he says. "Climb on board."

"You're pretty chipper this morning. Why the sudden good mood?" I ask.

He snaps the reins and the carriage clatters down the palace road. "You'll be happy to hear that we've made some real progress on your case. Things are coming together nicely and we should have a time-frame for getting you home soon."

"What do you mean? Like I'll be leaving in a few days?"

"I'm afraid we're not *that* good. It will still be a little while, two to three weeks, maybe. Not months, as I had originally feared."

My feelings are jumbled up at this news. Thoughts of going home

TRANSCENDER: *First-Timer*

make me glad and sad at the same time. A few more weeks, maybe less … not much time.

When we reach the lake, Ryder is nowhere in sight. Ralston unhitches the horses and lets them wander down to the water's edge where they can nibble on the sweet grasses. I spread our picnic quilt under the shade of the old oak tree and sit down to wait for Ryder.

An uncomfortable hour passes without him making an appearance, and I'm getting worried that something terrible has happened. He's just too reckless sometimes. He has no business being within a hundred miles of Domerica or me anyway. I curse myself for agreeing to meet him again. It was stupid, stupid, stupid! I should have sent him straight home.

Ralston spends the time placidly fishing and attempting to reassure me that Ryder can take care of himself. "Jade, quit fretting. Go for a swim or take a walk. We can eat lunch now if you like. Are you hungry?"

"No! I want to wait for Ryder."

I'm on the verge of hitching up the carriage to go and look for him myself, when he finally rides into view. I'm so relieved to see him, I forget to be angry.

He jumps off his horse grinning. "Sorry to be tardy, Jade. I ran into one of your mother's patrols. I was forced to double back and find another route—several miles out of the way."

"We were worried about you," Ralston says, cutting his eyes toward me to let Ryder know that I was the one worried about him.

"I am sorry to have worried you. I'm fine. No one saw me."

Ryder looks different today. Very different. Instead of his usual black leather riding clothes or his body armor, he has on a billowy white shirt with a high collar and brown wool pants with black riding boots. His hair is pulled back in a ponytail tied with a leather thong. He looks darkly dashing in a weird pirate sort of way.

"Is this an attempt at a disguise?" I ask him. "Because if it is, I don't think it will work. You're still a foot taller than most Domericans, and nobody else on earth has hair quite like yours."

He laughs. "No. Lorelei thought my riding clothes needed cleaning and mending. Jacob lent these to me. He is nearly as tall as I am but, you know, slimmer. The trousers are a bit tight." He turns around displaying his amazing backside for me. Oh, yeah, delightfully tight.

So Lorelei is cleaning and mending his clothes? That means he has to go back to her place tonight. I don't like that idea at all ... for more than one reason.

"You're staying in the village again?" I say.

"No. I must return to Unicoi tonight. Jacob will meet me on the road leading out of town this afternoon with my clothes."

"Who is Jacob?" I ask.

"Lorelei's husband, Lord Bartlett. I thought you knew him."

Oops! "Oh him ... Well, I told you we aren't close."

"Yes, well," Ralston interrupts, "since young Blackthorn has arrived safe and sound, may we have lunch? I am famished, and we need to be on the road home before the rains begin."

"Let's eat," I say, turning to follow Ralston to the carriage. Ryder catches hold of my hand.

"I am sorry, Jade. I'm not a very patient person. Will you have mercy on me and inform me of your decision before lunch?"

I get the part about not being patient. "Yes. I will go to Unicoi," I say.

"Wonderful!" He rewards me with a brilliant smile.

"I'm not sure when I'll be able to get away, though. I have to wait until my mother gets back from Dome Noir. I'll also need to make arrangements with my father."

"I understand. We shall accommodate whatever arrangements you must make. He lifts my hand, placing the back of it against his warm cheek. "Thank you," he whispers.

I'm not sure if he's thanking me or the spirit gods.

Ralston spreads out our portable feast on the blanket. Cook has outdone herself with pheasant, roasted vegetables, baked breads, and fresh pommera pie. Our lunch conversation is light and happy. Ryder and Ralston have an easy rapport. They banter back and forth on many subjects. Ryder doesn't hide his enthusiasm for my upcoming visit. He's anxious for me to meet his father who he speaks of with a kind of reverence.

"I fear I'll never be capable of completely filling his shoes." Ryder says. "He is wise and unfailingly just. Some of my recent actions have caused him concern over the fate of our people after he is gone. If I could undo anything I've ever done, I would take back what I did to you Jade. It was dishonorable and stupid."

"Hey," I say trying to lift his mood, "look at it this way, if you hadn't abducted me, we wouldn't be here right now, and I wouldn't be going to Unicoi. Maybe something good has come of it."

"You're much too easy on me. I'm not sure I deserve it."

"Your father has been chief for forty years," Ralston says. "It takes time to learn how to be a wise leader."

Ryder half-smiles. "You should know from being my teacher, I can be rather thick-headed at times. I hope forty years will be long enough for me." I'm glad to hear the lightness back in his voice. He stands and holds out a hand for me. "Shall we go for a walk?"

"Absolutely!" I say, taking his hand.

"Ralston? Join us?" Ryder asks.

"No, no. You two go ahead. I think a little nap would be just the thing right now." He leans back against the trunk of the old oak and closes his eyes.

Ryder and I take the same lake path we strolled along the day before, but in the opposite direction. Everything glows silver and gold in the afternoon light. I can't decide if it's the illusion created by the dome, or my own bright spirits that make the scenery so intensely vivid.

Ryder stops to admire the lake. "It looks brilliant this afternoon."

"I was thinking the same thing."

He cocks his head to the side. "Would you like to take a swim? Jacob was kind enough to furnish me with a bathing suit."

I have a fleeting suspicion that he may be hoping I'm wearing that underwear swimsuit again. "I'd love to."

I sit on a boulder to take off my shoes. I pull my dress off over my head revealing my demure, blue swimsuit.

"Very nice," Ryder says, taking off his boots and stepping out of his trousers. Underneath his pants he is wearing a pair of black swimming shorts made from the same fabric as my suit.

I dip my toe into the lake to test the water. The temperature is perfect—probably controlled by the dome maintenance workers.

Ryder unbuttons his shirt. "May I?" he asks before removing it. "It seems to have unnerved you a little yesterday."

I kick water at him, soaking the front of his shirt. "Well, it's wet now anyway, so why even bother?"

He's momentarily stunned by the spray of water, but throws off his shirt and starts after me.

"Race to the waterfall," I call, diving into the lake. I figure I can beat him. He's stronger and longer, but I'm lighter and a decent swimmer. Plus I gave myself a generous head start.

I win by a nose.

"You cheat!" he says, out of breath.

TRANSCENDER: *First-Timer*

"I like to win!"

He dunks my head underwater, and I swim beneath the waterfall to the small, hidden alcove I discovered the day before.

"Jade? Jade where are you?" he calls after a moment.

I don't answer. The water in the small pool is shallow enough for me to balance on the bottom with my head above water. He dives underwater. A few seconds later, his head pops up next to mine.

"You found me!" I say.

"Of course. I shall always find you, no matter where you are hiding." He kisses me playfully.

"Oh really?"

"Really."

"How would you find me?"

"You draw me to you like a magnet. I feel your pull even when I'm back in Unicoi and you are here."

In the weak light that filters through the curtain of the waterfall I can see by his face that he is serious. "When did you discover this?" I ask.

"I don't know." He smoothes back his wet hair, which has fallen loose. "On that first day, I believe."

"Oh, you mean when you kidna—"

He puts his hand to my mouth to quiet me.

"Yes, when I ruthlessly abducted you. I knew I had seriously miscalculated the moment I saw you go over the cliff. I was panicked … then relieved that you weren't badly hurt. I wanted to take you straight home to your mother right then, but I couldn't force myself to let you go. I convinced myself you would understand everything once we reached Unicoi, and you wouldn't hate me.

"When Ralston helped you get away, I was furious at first, but I quickly realized that it was for the best. I trusted he would return you safely home."

"Why didn't this magnetic thing work when Ralston and I were hiding out?" I ask, skeptical, but intrigued.

He shrugs. "It did. We easily tracked you across the field to the hills where the herd of fargen grazed. Unicoi are talented trackers even in the dark. Dozens of caves exist in those hills. I knew exactly in which one you were hiding, but I sent Catherine and most of the men back to Unicoi, saying I was certain we would never find you.

"My two most trusted friends, Alexander and Makoda, stayed with me. I told them I knew where you were, but planned to let Ralston escort you home. I'm certain they thought I was mad, especially after all the trouble we went through to capture you. But, they did not question me."

He pulls me over to a rock ledge at the back of the alcove and lifts me up. We sit side by side, our legs dangling in the water.

"We waited until morning," he continues. "When we saw you and Ralston emerge from the hillside, we followed until Prince Andrew found you. Then we made for Wall's Edge. By that time, your mother's soldiers had discovered our escape tunnel. They ambushed us inside the entrance."

I look at him curiously. "You let me go?"

He nods.

"And you waited until my brother found me?"

"Yes."

"But you could have been executed, or *worse!*"

"I know and I was miserable afterward. I made a terrible mess of the entire situation. I had failed Makoda and Alexander and shamed my family, on top of causing injury to you. But when you helped me escape from the palace, I knew ..." He trails off.

"Knew what?"

He laughs nervously. "I don't know what I knew. Perhaps that it had all been for a reason. That something exists between us … a bond." He slides off the ledge into the water and looks up at me. "Am I mad or do you feel it too?"

I hesitate. I don't know if I'm ready to be quite as honest with my feelings. It's a little scary. But what do I gain by lying? I don't really have time to play hard-to-get.

"I feel it," I admit. "But, I don't think it affects me in the same way as you. Besides that electricity thing when we touch, I feel it mostly when we part."

He's not laughing yet, so I go on. "When you leave me … it hurts. It's like a piece of me—of my heart—is being torn away. God, that sounds so stupid!"

He pulls me into the water and wraps his arms around my waist. "No, it doesn't. It's good to know I'm not a complete fool. I am sorry for causing you pain, though."

"It's not that bad," I say. "So, this magnet thing—do you think it works anywhere?"

"Probably. It's quite strong."

"Over space and time?" I ask.

"I believe so."

"What if I were to just suddenly disappear one day, without a trace? Do you think you could find me then?"

He looks at me oddly and pulls me closer to him. I clasp my arms around his neck, buoyed by the water. "Of course," he whispers, nuzzling my ear. "That would not stop me. I'd find you no matter what."

My arms and legs twine around him, and he holds me in our own private alcove. His mouth covers mine—warm, sweet, and moist. Heat and electricity course through my body. He kisses me deeply, hungrily. I hold on tightly, melding into him, like he's part of me now, sharing everything vital inside me. Blood blazes in my veins. I'm certain if I open my eyes steam will be rising from the water surrounding us.

His lips break away from mine and we face each other silently, reading each other's eyes, feeling each other's thoughts, glimpsing each other's souls. This is all happening so fast. I hardly know him, yet it seems I've known him forever.

He carries me toward the backside of the waterfall and with one swift motion positions us both directly under the cascading falls. The cold shock of water on my head startles me.

"Why did you do that?" I choke.

"I needed to cool off," he says, laughing. "Can you even imagine how desirable you are to me?"

"Uh, yeah. I was on the other side of that kiss. Is this you behaving badly again?"

"Rather trying not to," he says. "Come on."

We swim to the large flat rock next to the waterfall, then hoist ourselves up. The rock feels warm and inviting. We lay on our backs, gazing at the swirling silver ceiling above. I roll onto my side and prop myself up so I can see him.

"What is it?" he asks.

"I want to know more about you," I say.

He tilts his head to the side. "What do you wish to know?"

"Well, I guess I already know some things from what you've shared with me and what Ralston has told me, so tell me something I don't know. Tell me three things about yourself that would shock me."

"Oh, you want shocking things, like I was raised by wolves?"

"Yeah, like that. Were you?"

TRANSCENDER: *First-Timer*

"I'm sorry to disappoint, but no. My upbringing was strictly human." He looks pensive for a moment. "Hmm, shocking things .… All right, number one: I love to dance."

"That's not shocking," I say. "But it is kind of hard to believe." I can't picture this giant warrior dancing.

"It's absolutely true. I do not know whether it is my Cherokee or my Irish heritage, since both cultures include much ritualistic dancing. War dances are my specialty, but I can hold my own in a ballroom also."

"All right, I believe you. That's great. I like to dance too."

"I hope we have the opportunity to dance together one day," he says.

I like the visual that conjures up. "All right, what's number two?"

He grins. "It is embarrassing…but I get choked-up at weddings, baby christenings, any solemn occasion."

"Really? Like you cry or something?"

"Fortunately, I have learned to control it fairly well, but last month when my friend Alexander got married, I had to leave the ceremony to avoid making a scene."

"Why? I like a man who can show his feelings."

"I doubt it would favorably impress the Unicoi people to see their future chief bawling like a baby."

"Good point. I guess you have to worry about 'appearances' all the time, huh?"

"As do you," he reminds me.

"Yes, well, so you like to dance and you're a cream puff when it comes to weddings, what's number three?"

"You're enjoying this aren't you? Learning all my darkest secrets?"

151

"I'd hardly classify those things as 'dark.' Although, I suspect there may be another side to you, judging from the way we met. But, I'll get those secrets out of you later."

"Well, number three," he says, stretching languorously, "is that I can fall asleep anywhere. Allow me to demonstrate." He closes his eyes and feigns sleep.

"You're just trying to avoid answering me."

His eyes remain closed, a slight smile playing at his lips.

"All right, I'll let you off this time," I say. "But you still owe me one."

I get no reply from his reclining form, so I steal the opportunity to stare shamelessly at his seriously impressive body. He's beautifully put together—long limbs, muscled but lithe, broad well-defined chest, muscular abdomen, firm, flat belly. Simply put, he's splendid. The Cherokee prince, not yet quite grown into himself.

I watch the rhythmic rise and fall of his chest. His blue-black hair fans out like a sunburst beneath his head. His face is peaceful and perfect in sleep, and my heart swells with the sheer joy of just being near him. There is so much more to him, and I want to learn it all.

At that moment I'm struck by a stunning realization—I'm happy! Truly happy, for the first time in more than a year. I'd almost forgotten what it feels like, and I welcome it back into my life like an old friend.

I lay back on the rock, allowing the good feelings to wash over me, cleansing me of the pent up sadness and fear I've carried around for so long. I refuse to let thoughts about the future intrude on this moment. A sweet serenity descends slowly upon me making my limbs feel heavy and my mind go pleasantly fuzzy. And, for a moment I sleep, a blissful sleep beside Ryder Blackthorn, my new crush.

TWENTY-ONE

I'm not sure how long I've slept, when I'm roused by Ralston's voice carrying loudly across the water. He's talking to someone. I raise my head to get a better look, and a wave of icy panic passes through me. Ralston is speaking with two soldiers.

They're standing with their backs to the lake, so I figure they haven't seen Ryder and me yet. I touch his shoulder. "Ryder! Soldiers!" I hiss in his ear.

In a split second, he rolls onto his stomach, silently slipping into the water. The alcove behind the waterfall will hide him well. I also slide into the water and make my way for the shore as soundlessly as possible. I pray the soldiers won't spot me before I reach our clothes.

I locate the spot where we entered the water. I hide Ryder's clothing under some bushes, and pull my dress on over my wet swimsuit. Walking quickly toward the soldiers, I wring the water from my hair and straighten my dress. I steel my nerves and try to calm my trembling hands.

When they see me, the two men bow. "Your Highness," they say in unison.

"Princess, this is Captain Hill and Sergeant Scott of the Queen's Royal Guard," Ralston says. I recognize the mustached Captain Hill. One of LeGare's men.

I nod to them. "What is it? What's the matter?" I say.

Captain Hill speaks, "Nothing's the matter, ma'am. Although I must say, I am greatly distressed to see you here without your guard. There will be some serious reprimands when we return to the palace. I will personally see to it that more reliable men are assigned to your protection."

"Please Captain, that isn't necessary. It was on my personal insistence that the guards didn't accompany us. I needed a little … alone time." I smile. "I do not want the men punished for allowing me my privacy."

"As you wish, ma'am," Captain Hill says, lips pinched tightly below his black mustache.

"What brings you here, Captain?" I ask.

"A significant increase in the number of highwaymen and livestock thieves has been reported in this part of the realm. We've added patrols to all the major roads. We're also warning the residents of this district to limit their nighttime travels, and to be extra vigilant in guarding their livestock. We think the Unicoi are growing bolder in their incursions into Domerica."

"Unicoi? What makes you think it's the Unicoi?" I ask.

"Just a hunch," he glances knowingly at the sergeant. "In light of the recent kidnapping of Your Highness, it is evident they are becoming more desperate."

"I wouldn't assume too much, Captain," I say tartly. "Very well, continue with your mission."

The captain and sergeant exchange looks again. Captain Hill gives a little cough. "Yes, uh, we didn't expect to find you here, Princess Jaden, but since we have, we will remain with you and Professor Ralston to ensure your safety."

"Thank you, Captain. There's no need for that. We were just about to pack up and return to the palace anyway," I say.

"In that case, we will accompany you back to Warrington, ma'am," Captain Hill says.

"It's only three miles, Captain. Ralston and I are perfectly capable of making it safely on our own."

The corners of Captain Hill's greasy black mustache rise in a fake smile. "Princess, I'm certain the queen would be most disturbed if she learned we had left you alone in this dangerous area. You do not even possess weapons."

"Ah, but we do," Ralston says, fishing two swords from the back of the carriage. He hands one to me and straps the other around his hips.

I buckle the sword over my damp dress. It feels heavy and awkward.

"Well, there you have it Captain," I say, straightening the sword on my hips. "We are set and ready for battle. That will be all."

"But Princess—"

"Surely you don't question my ability to defend myself," I say, raising my eyebrows.

"Of course not, but—"

"Fine. You're dismissed." I use a tone of voice I've heard my mother use with tiresome subordinates.

Captain Hill winces as though I struck him. "Yes, ma'am." He bows to me and glowers at Ralston, his face growing red as pommera juice. "You'd better make certain she arrives safely at the palace," he says to Ralston, "or you'll have me *and* the queen to answer to."

Ralston bobs his head in reply. The two soldiers climb on their horses and gallop away.

The second they are out of sight, my knees give out and I crumple onto the blanket. To my surprise, Ralston falls on the blanket too—writhing in a fit of laughter.

"What's so funny?" I ask irritably, waiting for my heart rate to slow.

"You're dismissed"? he chortles. "That was priceless, Jade. How did you come up with that? I thought the Captain was going to burst a blood vessel."

I laugh too. "Oh, I've heard Mother use it a few times. It works every time. But, you were the brilliant one, Rals. Where did these swords come from?"

"I thought we might get in some practice this afternoon, so I threw them in, just in case. Where is our young friend?" he asks, scanning the lake.

"Behind the waterfall. He probably saw the whole thing. I'd better get his clothes out of the bushes."

By the time I retrieve Ryder's clothes, I can see his dark figure swimming across the lake. I wait for him on the shore.

"That was close," he says shaking the water from his hair. "How did you get rid of them so quickly?"

"They weren't looking for you, thank God." I hand him his things. "They're out here warning the residents about a rash of highway robberies and livestock thefts. They were going to stay to make sure I get home safely, but we talked them out of that."

"Did the sword have anything to do with that?" he asks, eyeing my new accessory.

"I didn't threaten them, if that's what you mean. They just needed to be convinced we can take care of ourselves."

"I take it you're pretty good with a blade?" he says, slipping into his shirt.

"My reputation is far greater than my skills."

"Nevertheless, I think you should wear it when you're not at the palace, especially if highwaymen are about. You never know … someone may try to kidnap you."

I smirk at him. Funny guy.

He finishes dressing, and we walk back to the carriage where Ralston is packing away the remnants of our picnic.

"They headed due south," Ralston says. "I believe they intend to stop in on the surrounding lake residents. Keep your eyes open, my boy. They say extra patrols have been assigned to all major roads."

"I shall return the way I came," Ryder says. "It will take longer, but it is more isolated."

"Ryder, please be safe," I plead, still shaken by the close call.

He lifts my hand. "I promise I will, if you will promise me the same."

"I promise."

He pushes the wet hair off my face, and smiles down at me. "Jade, you've made me very happy today. All of Unicoi will rejoice at word of your upcoming visit. Send a message to Lorelei when you know your travel plans. I will meet you on the road and escort you to the Enclave. We shall travel together to Unicoi."

"No! Ryder, don't come back. It's not safe," I say.

"That is why I shall escort you." He whistles for his horse. "I am in your debt once again," he says to Ralston and me. "You have saved my neck for a second time." He takes my hand, pressing his lips into my palm. "Until we meet again …"

He climbs on Tenasi's back, and rides away with a small wave—taking that part of me that always goes with him, leaving the emptiness behind.

~ ~ ~ ~

The ride home is uneventful. We don't run into any highway men or fargen thieves. But we're late leaving the lake, so at three o'clock on the dot the afternoon rain begins to fall. The carriage is uncovered, but Ralston pulls a rain poncho from the back and hands it to me.

"Better put this on," he says.

"You're not wearing one?"

"No, I don't mind the rain. I find it rather refreshing." He reaches for his hat. "It does fog up my glasses, though."

We ride along in silence, raindrops plopping gently on our heads. After a while I say, "Hey Ralston, can I ask you a question?"

"You can ask." His stock reply meaning *I may not answer.*

"You said Princess Jaden was supposed to have died from that fall?'

"Yes."

"Well, what was going to happen after that, before everything went off track?"

"The scenario, if you had not arrived on the scene, would have unfolded like this: Queen Eleanor would have discovered Ryder's involvement in the princess' death and would have declared war on Unicoi, believing that Domerica would easily crush its much smaller neighbor. She would be wrong." He glances at me meaningfully.

"You mean Unicoi would have won? But how could they?"

"The Unicoi have been unfettered by treaties not to develop weapons or wage war, which the Domes entered into hundreds of years ago. Consequently they have developed advanced weaponry. They also have a sizeable army of highly skilled warriors. Domerica has only the Queen's Royal Guard consisting of a few thousand trained soldiers and a volunteer militia of farmers and townspeople. Also, the Unicoi are experts with explosives, which were perfected early on for underground expansion."

"So how would they have won? Would they have blown up the dome?"

"Heavens no! I said they were skilled warriors, not idiots, Jade. You watch too much American TV. The declaration of war would have reached Unicoi, and triggered a secret attack by the Unicoi army through the series of tunnels that pass beneath Domerica. The war would have been short-lived and relatively bloodless. Warrington Palace would have been captured almost immediately and, with the Royal Guard out of commission, the militia would simply have given up. A few local skirmishes would have ensued, but nothing big. The Unicoi population would have relocated, lock, stock, and barrel to Domerica."

"What would've happened to my mother?"

"The royal family would have been spared. Queen Eleanor and Prince Andrew would have been exiled to the Enclave, on your father's word that no talk of sedition or of retaking the throne would be tolerated. They would have lived out their lives in relative peace."

"And what about Ryder and Chief Blackthorn?

"Chief Blackthorn would have died shortly after the war. Ryder would have become chief. The Unicoi parliamentary form of government would have been put into place in Domerica, and the country would have been renamed the United Federation of Unicoi.

"Over the years Ryder would have led the combined country through some difficult times and, as I alluded to before, he would have eventually been responsible for saving the planet from needless destruction. End of story."

"Wow!" I say, thinking through what he told me.

The horses and wagon squish along the muddy road, and the quickening rain trickles down the front of my poncho, soaking the bottom of my dress and my shoes. Ralston's hat soon becomes soggy, the brim drooping over his forehead.

The sixty-four million dollar question still looms in the air above my head, begging to be asked. I'm not sure I have the courage to hear the answer, but I swallow hard and turn to Ralston. "So, what's going to happen now?" I ask. "Now that I showed up and threw everything off course?"

"Nobody knows for certain, Jade." His glasses are all fogged up, so I can't see his eyes, but his voice is somber. "We can run some models, make some educated guesses. At this point, nobody knows.

Once you're back home, things will be easier to predict."

"Is there something special I should be doing in the meantime?" I ask.

He grins at me, rain dripping from the tip of his nose. "Just continue being yourself, old girl."

I smile back. "I think I can handle that."

TWENTY-TWO

It's a typical morning, Ralston and I spend the early hours working on my studies. I don't see the point since I'm going home soon, but he takes great delight in lecturing on the differences in the governmental structures of the three dome nations. Bor-ing. Especially because the two other domes are stuck in backward monarchies similar to Domerica's.

My mind wanders back to the lake, to Ryder, and stolen kisses. My hand idly touches the small bump in the fabric of my tunic beneath which lies the delicate wolf-head pendant. I wonder if Ryder can sense me thinking of him. The feel of him is with me all the time now, like a promise waiting just out of reach. I count every heartbeat until I'm with him again.

Finally responding to my obvious lack of interest, Ralston calls off the lesson and suggests we sneak away for some fencing practice. We stride across the courtyard, swords strapped to our sides.

"I have a little surprise for you," he says.

"What kind of surprise?"

"I've found a spot on the palace grounds where we can train without worrying about being discovered."

I follow Ralston to an old barn used for storing hay and old saddlery. Not much of a chance anyone will interrupt us while we spar here. A large area of clear floor space in the center of the barn serves as our training area, offering plenty of room for pursuit and retreat.

We take our positions on the floor. "All right," Ralston says. "What are we always focused on?"

"Tempo, measure, and footwork," I say.

"Very good! Let's begin."

We spend an exhilarating two hours thrusting, parrying, and perfecting my form. I've been working on my technique, which is improving daily, but I suspect that I'd still be bested by my eight year old cousin, Max—an expert with a light saber.

"It just takes time and practice," Ralston says, handing the water canteen to me. "You may want to check into some lessons when you get back to Madison, if you are really interested."

The mention of home is bittersweet. I miss my dad and all the old familiar places and faces that used to bring me comfort. But my new life in Domerica is so novel and exciting. I feel to be an important part of an unfolding drama. For the first time ever, I believe I can make a difference in the world. It's a potent sensation, and I worry about how I'm going to readjust to my old, mundane existence back in Connecticut.

I sit on a bale of hay, wiping the sweat from my brow. "Can we talk for a minute, Rals?" I ask.

"What's on your mind today, old girl?" He props his foot up on the side of the bale.

"It's just that yesterday when I was with Ryder he said something to me, and I wondered if it means anything."

"What did he say?"

"He said there's this sort of connection between us, that he feels drawn toward me like a magnet's pull. The pull is so strong he's able to find me no matter where I am. Why is that, Rals? What's that all about?"

An odd expression flits across his face, but he resumes his previous light air. "Well, you are two very attractive young people. I suppose it's only normal that you would feel drawn toward each other."

I scowl. "Oh please, Ralston! I'm not talking about a couple of kids with raging hormones here, and you know it. I feel a connection too, and it's not *normal*. Give me a straight answer."

"Forgive me Jade, I'm sorry. I didn't mean to be flippant." His tone is gentle, and I detect a trace of pity in his eyes. "All I can say is that the two of you were never supposed to have met in this life."

"That's not an answer! Anyway Ryder says we already met when we were kids."

"That is true, and it was significant, but that was not *you*, Jade. That was Princess Jaden. Their paths were not meant to have crossed as adults. *You* were never supposed to have met Ryder Blackthorn."

"What in the hell does that mean? I did meet him and now there's this *thing* between us. I want to know if it means something … something about why I'm here, what I'm supposed to be doing here. I mean, am I here for a reason?"

"Hold on Jade, just stop right there!" he says harshly. "Don't even start down that road. I told you why you are here—it is a mistake! There is nothing you are supposed to be doing here. You aren't even supposed to be here! The whole damned system has been bollixed-up because you *are* here!"

I feel like I've been punched in the gut. I stare at him, my mouth hanging open. Anger and hurt ripping my insides.

He exhales a long breath and sits down beside me on the bale of hay. "Forgive me child, I didn't mean to be cruel. Of course, none of this is your fault. I miscalculated. I never should have allowed you to assist in Ryder's escape from Warrington."

I blink back the tears pressing behind my eyes. "I don't get it. Why?"

"Because it emboldened him to come to you at the lake. I didn't think he'd risk it."

"Geez, Ralston, the guy kidnapped me. You can't get much bolder than that. Besides, you couldn't have stopped me from helping him. It was my fault he was there in the first place. I had to do it for *me*."

He studies my face a moment. "Sometimes you are wise beyond your years, my dear. Life has a way of taking its own course, doesn't it? I shouldn't have to be reminded of that."

I have a strong sense he's holding something back. "Ralston, what *aren't* you telling me?"

"All I can say for certain, Jade, is that you are going home soon. That should make you very happy. Cherish the moments you have left with your mother. Your time with her is short."

"How short?"

"Two weeks, perhaps three at the outside."

"Will I still have time to visit my father?" I ask in alarm. There are so many things I want to do before I go.

"Yes."

"And spend more time with my mother?"

"Yes."

"And go to Unicoi?"

"And travel to Unicoi, if that is still your wish," he says.

"Are you saying I should cancel my trip?"

"I'm not saying anything. That has to be your decision. You must divide your remaining time as you see fit."

I stand and face him. "Quit handling me, damn it Ralston! Just tell me the right thing to do."

"Jade," he says with infuriating calm. "There *is* no right or wrong here. It has to do with the choices we make. It must be your decision. That's how it works."

"You know you're not much help for someone whose whole purpose here is to guide me. Are you sure you read the whole IUGA handbook, because I think you skipped the chapter on giving advice and counsel."

"It's still *your* life, my dear, no matter where you are living it. I can do my utmost to keep you safe. I can gently nudge you back onto the proper path if you are straying far afield, but I cannot make the hard choices for you."

"Yeah? Well thanks for nothing!" I snatch my sword from the floor and storm out of the barn.

By the time I reach my room, I've cooled off enough to feel a little guilty for biting Ralston's head off. I toss my sword in the corner and flop face down on my bed, smearing sweat and grime all over the satiny white coverlet. Who cares? A fresh one will replace it in the morning anyway.

Ralston's right, of course. I have no future here. I belong in another world. I'm not doing Ryder any favors by letting this— whatever it is—blossom between us. He has enough on his plate without getting involved with someone who's about to disappear from his life forever. It won't be easy keeping things impersonal between us, especially since we've already gone a bit beyond personal, and I'm not totally sure I can make the trip to Unicoi without finding myself in serious lip-lock with him again, but I have to try. I need to find some courage of my own … somewhere.

I wash up and change into clean clothes before I realize I'm starving. I need to order up some food, but I have one stop to make first.

The door to Ralston's room is slightly ajar. I knock softly and stick my head inside. He's in an easy chair near the fake fireplace, engrossed in an ancient looking book.

"Hey," I say, and he looks up.

"Jade, come in." He stays seated, smiling at me. As a matter of royal etiquette he's supposed to rise when I enter the room, but he doesn't strictly observe the technicalities when no one else is around.

"How about some lunch?" I ask.

"Thank you for the invitation, but I've just eaten." He nods at a tray with the remnants of some sort of meat pie in a dish.

"Okay. Well," I suck in a deep breath. "I'm here to say I'm sorry, Rals. I was such a ... well, you know. I'm sorry I was so rude to you, and I know you're right. There's no future for me in Domerica or with ..." I stare at the floor for a moment. "Ryder Blackthorn." It hurts to say it out loud.

"Sit down, my dear," he says and I take the chair across from him.

"Thank you for your apology. It is I who should be apologizing. I know this entire situation is stressful for you. But take heart, you will be home soon."

"That's great," I say with more enthusiasm than I feel. "Ralston, about Unicoi ... I think I still need to make the trip, because I committed to go, and because I'd like to try and help those people."

He closes his book and his eyes find mine. "That's honorable, Jade. I respect your decision. I will do all I can to ensure that things go smoothly for your trip."

"Thanks."

"Would you like to take a little ride after lunch?" he asks.

"That would be nice."

"Shall we venture into town, or would something else interest you today?"

"Actually, I do have something in mind. On our trips to town I noticed a sign that said 'Princess Jaden Home' with an arrow pointing down a road to the east. I was wondering," I say a little sheepishly, "if I have a home of my own, you know, other than Warrington Palace?"

He gazes at me a moment like he's formulating a reply. "The answer to your question is yes. You do have a home of your own. It is called Meadowood, and it is very charming. But the sign you saw was not for Meadowood. It refers to a children's home that was founded by Princess Jaden."

"Oh, you mean like an orphanage?"

"Well, yes, some orphans are in residence there." He lifts his glasses and pinches the bridge of his nose. "But the majority of the home's occupants are 'redundant' children."

"What does that mean?"

"It means children who are born illegally. By law in Domerica, married couples may have only two children. If a child is born to a family that already has two children, the child is considered redundant and is placed in such a home."

I gape at him. "Are you serious?"

"I would not joke about such a thing."

"Did my mother make that law too?"

"No. It has been in place for more than one hundred years."

That makes me a little sick inside. "Ralston, I can't get used to this ... this dystopian-like society. I'm sorry, but my own mother seems so heartless sometimes."

"Try to understand Jade, the law was instituted when a sudden population explosion caused a serious food shortage in Domerica. Fearing a future famine and severe overcrowding, Queen Caroline, the ruler at that time, put the law into place. It has stayed on the books. The children in these homes are treated very well. They are educated, clothed, and have all their needs provided for. Candidly, the law has served its purpose in Domerica. No food shortages or threats of overpopulation have occurred since that time."

"But these kids are taken away from their parents! They're not allowed to be with their families. That's inhuman. How can you defend such a ridiculous law?"

"I am not defending it. I am simply saying that a reasonable person could view it as protecting the wellbeing of the realm. I believe your mother views it that way."

"Oh, so you're defending her! Are you sure she deserves it? Some of the things she does are totally ruthless."

"She's a good person, Jade, I assure you. I hate to sound like a broken record, but spending a few weeks in Domerica does not make you an expert on its people or what it takes to govern this land. Please do not judge her too unkindly."

I'm silent for a few seconds, confused, as usual. "Right and wrong seem a little less black and white here than they did back in the good old USA," I tell him.

"Nothing is ever really black or white, Jade. It's all a matter of degrees."

"If you say so." I rest my head in my hands. "I don't think I'm up for a ride, after all."

"Why don't you eat and rest up for a bit, old girl. I think you may change your mind. I believe a ride in the fresh air would be just the thing to lift your spirits, and Roxanne hasn't had a good exercise all week." He leans over to pat my hand. "In any event, it's better than sitting around here stewing about things."

"Okay," I say dully. "I'll meet you at the stables in half an hour."

"Better make it an hour. I'm still recuperating from our little sparring session this morning. I'm afraid I'm not as young as I used to be."

"Yeah, neither am I." I sigh, feeling terribly old myself.

TWENTY-THREE

*O*ur afternoon ride is refreshing and rejuvenating. We solemnly swear to stay within the palace lands, so we don't have to drag our guards along. The blossoming beauty of the countryside always takes my breath away. I understand my mother wanting to preserve this lovely way of life, but is the cost worth it? I'm still not sure.

I'm in a much better mood as we make our way back to the palace. We ride placidly along until the courtyard comes into view and we catch sight of dozens of soldiers milling around the grounds—some on horseback carrying large banners, others clumped in small groups talking or playing dice.

"What's going on?" I ask Ralston.

"It appears your mother is home, and she has brought some visitors with her. Those standards are from Dome Noir," Ralston says, nodding to several large black and gold banners flying from long poles held by the liveried soldiers.

"Mother's home!" I yelp. "That's fantastic."

"I'll put Roxanne away for you if you want to go straight inside."

"Thanks Rals." I bound from Roxanne's back, hurrying across the courtyard to the palace steps. I feel the eyes of the soldiers following me as I run, probably thinking my behavior unbecoming of a princess. But, I don't care. I want my mother.

I take the steps two at a time, and Samuel opens the huge doors before I even reach them. "Where's the queen?" I ask.

"In her office ma'am," he says, bowing.

I dash to the third floor and throw open her door without knocking, startling my mother and the group of people gathered around her desk.

"Jaden." She rises to hug me. "It's good to see you, darling."

I scan the collection of people in her office: LeGare, Cook, the head of housekeeping, the gamekeeper, and two others I don't recognize.

"Mother, I'm sorry I interrupted. Is everything all right?"

"Yes dear ... well no, actually. I sent a messenger from Dome Noir two days ago to inform the palace I would be arriving home today with a visiting dignitary. Unfortunately the messenger never reached the palace. I am disappointed to find that Warrington is completely unprepared for our arrival and, of course, I am concerned for the welfare of my messenger."

"I'm so sorry Mother."

"Yes, it is rather troubling. But, in any event, I am pleased to tell you that we have Prince Damien of Dome Noir with us for the week." I remember his name from the silver chalices at Bartlett's— King Philippe's youngest son.

"You haven't seen him since you were children. He plans to stay, sample our hunting, and spend some time renewing his acquaintance with you." She puts her arm around my shoulder and steers me to the door.

"You must make yourself presentable now, dear. We have a private audience with the prince in two hours, before the dinner guests begin to arrive. Oh, I do hope we can gather a respectable turn-out for this important occasion on such short notice," she says. "LeGare, are you certain you sent your fastest riders?"

"Yes, ma'am. And a number of nobles are already at court. The dining hall will be full, I assure you."

"Cook, will we be able to feed them all?"

"Yes Your Highness, but it would've been nice to have had some advance warning," she grumbles. "I can't guarantee that we'll have enough venison, and we've run out of fresh pommeras." She sends a harassed look my way. I've been eating pommeras like they were M&Ms. "I don't know what I'll do for pies."

"I'm sure you will work your miracles as you always do," Mother cajoles. This pleases the chubby old curmudgeon so much she almost smiles.

"All right now, Jaden, go and bathe," Mother says. "I'll send Sylvia up with your dress.

"No! Not Sylvia. Send Maria," I say.

"Oh, all right. Maria. I don't have time to argue with you."

Once in my room I shower quickly, washing out my yards of hair. Maria arrives as I'm attempting to yank the tangles out with a comb. Two of my mother's young ladies-in-waiting are with her, one carrying a gorgeous lavender silk dress, the other carrying a stack of decorated boxes.

"Let me do that," Maria says taking the comb from me. "You need some of my special tonic."

She rubs tonic into the ends of my hair, and the tangles fall away smoothly as she combs. She styles it loosely down my back. I always have to be careful not to sit on it when she does that.

"The queen would like you to wear perfume and makeup tonight, Princess." She says, opening the first two boxes to reveal containers of both. "Sarah will apply it for you. She is very skilled."

"Perfume is okay. I mean all right," I say, sniffing at one of the tiny bottles. "But you know I'm not really that into makeup."

"Your mother would like you to look very special tonight for the prince," Maria coaxes.

"Why? What's the big deal?"

She looks surprised by my question and the two young girls behind her giggle. She shoos them out of the room, saying she will dress me by herself tonight.

"What's going on Maria? What am I missing?" She's a sweet girl, and we've become close in a way, even though technically she's my servant.

"Please do not tell your mother I said this," she whispers. "But I think she is hoping the prince will like you. You know—maybe for a wife."

"You're kidding, right?"

She shakes her head.

"But I'm supposed to be the Queen of Domerica after my mother. He lives in Dome Noir."

"Yes, but he would live here. His older brother will be king when his father dies. I think Prince Damien and his father do not get along very well. I believe Damien is a bit of a gambler."

"Oh, great."

"But he is very handsome, and he would be your consort. You know, so you can produce an heir."

An heir? Oh crap! I didn't sign up for that.

"So, my mother's playing matchmaker, huh? Well, I'm not ready to get married, and I'm definitely not ready to produce an heir! Maria, you've got to tell the queen that I'm deathly ill, and I can't come down for dinner." I have to find Ralston and make him hide me or help me fake a fever or something.

"Oh, but you must at least meet him." She looks alarmed. "It would be a great insult for you to snub him after he has come all this way to seek your hand. Nothing requires you to accept him."

TRANSCENDER: *First-Timer*

"Yeah, what about my mother? She can be pretty forceful sometimes."

"The queen wants a good marriage for you. Maybe it is with Prince Damien, maybe not. I think if you do not want him, she will not force you. Her mother did not force her. She had a choice."

I consider this for a moment. Maria's probably right. She knows more about Domerican traditions than I do. I guess I can be polite and pleasant to the prince and tell Mother later that there's not the slightest possibility I will consider marrying him or anyone else at this point.

"All right, all right," I groan. "We'll do a little make-up to make my mother happy. I'll wear perfume and the fancy dress, and we'll just get through this somehow."

I know I should probably be more careful about what I say to Maria, but I trust her, she's the closest thing I have to a girlfriend in this world—besides Ralston, that is. I've really missed having my BF, Liv, to talk to.

"The prince is said to be very good with the ladies," she says. "Maybe you will like him." She brushes some mascara on my lashes, swipes a little blush on my cheeks, and gloss on my lips. Finally, she dabs perfume on my wrists and neck, and then sends me to my closet to put on my under things.

"You will not need a bra tonight," she calls to me.

Huh?

Maria carefully holds up the lavender dress for me to step into. I wince when I see myself in the mirror. The fabric is exquisite, but it has a deep V neckline that shows a dangerous amount of cleavage.

"My mother wants me to wear this? Are you sure?"

"Yes, she selected it herself."

"But what if I, you know, fall out of it?"

"We'll make it a little more secure here," she says pulling the plunging neckline in a little. "I'll pin it for you." Her handiwork makes me slightly more confident that I won't have a wardrobe malfunction at dinner, but I still feel a little bare.

"The queen has sent you her amethyst necklace to wear," Maria says brightly. She opens the third box and removes the necklace. Oh momma! It's the most incredible piece of jewelry I've ever seen. It is made of platinum, with a trail of mega-diamonds running down each side and an enormous, pear-shaped lavender stone at the center.

"You will need to take this off." She points to Ryder's necklace.

I don't want to take it off, even for an evening, but I don't want to have to explain it to my mother either, so I pull it over my head and lock it securely in my jewelry chest.

The amethyst necklace fits perfectly into the deep V of my gown, and I look regal in spite of myself. I may be ready on the outside, but my insides have turned to mush. I feel like Cleopatra on her way to meet Caesar, or Daniel confronting the lions, I'm not sure which. I steady myself, straighten my posture, and go in search of my mother and the prince.

Mother is waiting for me in the music room when I arrive. I've never been to the music room, and I had to follow a tray-carrying servant to find it. The room is large with a mirrored ceiling, three enormous crystal chandeliers, and gilded carvings adorning the walls. It's called the music room, I gather, because a white, grand piano and several other antique-looking instruments are displayed prominently throughout.

A woman with long, curly brown hair and wearing a beaded dress sits at a harp by the window. She softly plunks and strums the scads of strings. Overstuffed seating is strategically positioned around the room, and a long table is laden with silver trays piled high with pastries, fruits and cheeses. Pitchers of colorful beverages and elaborate goblets have been placed along the sideboard. I wonder if others will be joining us, or if this embarrassment of riches is meant only to impress the prince.

"You look lovely, darling," Mother says when I kiss her cheek.

She's dressed in a gold satin gown that shows off her figure beautifully. Her hair is loose like mine, and she wears a delicate golden crown. As usual, she looks every bit a queen.

"The prince will be here shortly," she says. "Everything is coming together nicely." She's calmer and more assured than she was earlier this afternoon.

"Mother—" I say, wanting to let her know my feelings about this marriage thing before the prince shows up.

"Ah, here he is now!" I turn to see a tall, blonde man, dressed in black trousers and a shiny royal blue coat stride into the room. A horde of young men in dark suits follows closely on his heels.

He whispers something to the man on his right, who turns and herds the others to the back of the room. The prince walks directly to Mother and bows. He wears rings on every finger of both hands, and I'm shocked to see he's wearing more makeup than I am.

"Queen Eleanor." He lifts her hand and kisses it, staring deeply into her eyes. His lips linger a bit longer than is decent. "My Queen," his voice drips with counterfeit charm, "your beauty staggers me each time we meet."

Eww! I take an immediate dislike to this guy.

"Prince Damien, this is my daughter, the Crown Princess Jaden Beckett," Mother says ignoring the flowery compliment.

He turns to me and smiles, revealing a set of impossibly white teeth. He's probably a handsome guy, but whoever applies his makeup must have formerly worked for Lady Gaga because his natural good looks are obscured by layers of eyeliner, lipstick and bronzer that seem to have been applied with a trowel. I curtsey as I've been taught. He politely pecks my hand. Fumes from his thick, musky cologne fill my throat, and I cough involuntarily.

"May I offer you some refreshment?" Mother asks, nodding toward the sumptuous selections arrayed on the table. Samuel materializes out of nowhere to take our requests.

"A glass of sherry would be nice," Prince Damien replies, with only the slightest hint of a French accent. The light from the chandelier glints off the enormous diamond studs displayed in each of his ears.

"Water, please," I say.

"Nothing for me Samuel, thank you," Mother says, and he scurries away to fill our orders.

"Did you have a nice trip?" I ask the Prince.

"Very pleasant, thank you. I am looking forward to sampling the delights of your country, and I hope to become better acquainted with you, Princess." He nearly blinds me with his smile.

Samuel brings our drinks, and whispers something to Mother.

"Prince Damien, will you excuse me for a moment?" she says. "I have a small matter to attend to. I shan't be long."

"Of course Your Highness, and please take your time. I'm certain Princess Jaden will keep me entertained."

His eyes boldly follow Mother until she is out of the room, and his gaze returns to me. "Oh my!" he says, staring straight at my chest. "The famous Coventry Amethyst. May I?" He scoops up the center stone of my necklace, deliberately resting his hand for a moment against my exposed cleavage.

"Lovely. Just lovely," he smirks, obviously amused with himself.

My dislike for him shoots off the scale, and since Mother isn't around to hear me, I let him have it. "Okay dude, you just crossed a line here. I know you're a guest of the queen, but *I* don't give a crap who your daddy is. If you *ever* touch me again without my permission, I'll wipe that smarmy grin off your face permanently. Got it?"

"Oh ho!" He leers at me. "You're a feisty one. I like that. I was told you were rather dull."

"And I was told you were a gentleman. I guess we were both misinformed."

His arrogance seems to wane a little.

"Princess Jaden, I'm afraid we may have gotten off on the wrong foot. I apologize if I have offended you in any way," he says. "I have the utmost respect for you and the queen. Please, let us sit. I will try to make amends."

We sit on a brocade sofa. "Tell me everything about yourself," Damien says. "I understand you are a very accomplished young woman."

His pretended interest in me is completely unconvincing. His eyes dart around the room taking in every detail, but never resting on me.

"Actually, I don't really enjoy talking about myself," I say, still seething.

"Oh, you are too modest." He takes baby sips of his sherry and watches the door, no doubt hoping Mother will return soon. When he cranes his neck, I can see the faint outlines of a tattoo on the right side of his face. That explains the dense makeup.

"Very well, we will change the subject," he says, idly twisting one of his rings.

"Tell me about the queen. Is she seeing that vile lap dog of hers, General LeGare?"

"What do you mean?" I ask.

"They were inseparable in Dome Noir, always whispering to one another. They were very … I don't know, *intimate*. I wondered if he is to be her new husband."

"She's still married to my father."

"Ah, so it is the *affaire clandestine?*"

"If you're so interested in my mother's affairs, I suggest you ask her."

"Perhaps I will." He smiles and tilts his head, looking at me curiously. "I have heard of your abduction at the hands of that Unicoi thug, Blackthorn. It must have been a frightening ordeal for you."

"Not really," I say. "I was never in any real danger, and young Chief Blackthorn was a perfect gentleman the entire time."

His eyebrows shoot up and he focuses his gaze more intently on me. "Well, well, maybe you are one who enjoys a little danger, huh? Maybe that dark-haired savage has set your blood on fire?"

"You're so full of it." I fold my arms across my chest and turn away from him.

"I think not," he simpers. "I think maybe you have grown bored with your provincial life in Domerica. Maybe you crave a little adventure, eh?"

I glare at him in disgust, but he prattles on. "This cave-dweller, Blackthorn, though…please, he is just a stupid boy. I don't believe he is right for you." He slides closer to me on the sofa, and lowers his voice to a throaty whisper. "If you want danger and fire, if you want someone to make you feel like a woman, you need a man."

"Oh really? And I suppose you're that man?"

"There is but one way to find out." He moves even closer and his luminous leer makes my skin crawl.

"Not a chance!"

I'm beginning to feel like a trapped animal and my anger threatens to get the better of me. I want to lash out at him and tell him how much he disgusts me. I want to blast my mother for bringing this douche bag here and for making me wear these slutty clothes for him. And where in the hell is good old Ralston, the guy who is supposed to be guiding me through all this?

More than anything … at this moment, I just want to be home in Connecticut where life is so much simpler.

TWENTY-FOUR

I pop up from the sofa, searching for any avenue of escape. Prince Damien stands immediately—royal etiquette I suppose, since he obviously has no real manners.

"Where can Mother be?" I say, anxiously eyeing the door. "I must speak with her." I take two steps but, as if on cue, Mother glides into the room. Damn! I've got to get her alone. I need to tell her this little charade is officially over. I would never consider having a single date with Prince Damien, let alone marrying him. In fact, I can't bear to be in the same room with him.

But Mother is all smiles as she takes a chair, gesturing for us to resume our seats on the sofa.

"Mother, may I speak with you?" I ask, still standing.

"Yes, of course dear. But, please sit down. We'll speak before dinner."

I grudgingly plop down next to Damien.

"I'm glad you two had an opportunity to spend a few minutes alone. I trust you have gotten to know each other better," she says, looking from me to Damien.

"Princess Jaden is quite modest, and reluctant to speak about herself," Prince Damien says. "She is still an enigma to me."

Mother glances at me. I'm sitting, still huffy, with my arms crossed tightly over my half-naked chest.

"Darling are you all right?" she asks.

Without waiting for an answer, she turns to Damien. "Maybe I can help. What would you like to know about my daughter?"

"Thank you Your Highness. I have a great interest in Princess Jaden. I wish to know many things about her," he says glancing over his shoulder. "May I have my friend Luc join us?"

Mother narrows her eyes. "Isn't he your lawyer?"

"Yes. He is also my friend and trusted advisor. I value his opinion on things. As such, I wish for him to meet Princess Jaden and sit in on our conversation. He is also very charming. I assure you, you will like him."

"I had planned this private meeting so you and Princess Jaden could learn more about each other, but I suppose, if it would put you at ease …" Mother says.

"Thank you, Your Highness." Prince Damien nods to the group of men huddled in the corner. A dark-haired man breaks away to join us.

"Your Highness," Damien addresses Mother, "may I present Luc Canard, my close friend and associate."

"Monsieur Canard." Mother holds out her hand. He takes it, bowing low.

"This is Princess Jaden," Damien says. Canard also bows in my direction.

"Please sit down," Mother says. Damien and Canard sit on one sofa. Mother and I take its twin, facing them.

"Now, where were we?" Mother says to Damien. "Ah, yes, what can we tell you about Princess Jaden?"

"How old are you?" Prince Damien looks at me.

"Seventeen," I say. "How old are you?"

"Twenty-eight."

Geez, kind of old to be playing dress-up with mommy's makeup and jewelry.

"Does Princess Jaden reside with you at Warrington Palace, or does she have her own residence?" Damien asks Mother.

"She lives here at Warrington, but of course she has an estate of her own. Meadowood is southeast of here on two hundred and twenty-seven acres of some of the finest hunting and farming land in Domerica. It has a lovely manor house, as well as several guest houses. Currently only a small staff of groundskeepers inhabits the property, but you are welcome to visit if you wish."

I'm stunned. Ralston said I had a house. I didn't know it was a whole estate.

Mother continues, "When Princess Jaden marries she will live at Meadowood until she becomes queen, at which time, Warrington Palace will be hers as well." She smiles lovingly at me.

Luc Canard leans forward, extracting a notebook and pen from his jacket pocket. He jots down a few notes. "I assume Princess Jaden has received the finest education available in Domerica?"

Mother looks annoyed at the question. "She has received the finest education available *anywhere*, Monsieur Canard. She has been tutored by the most brilliant men and women in the world. No expense was spared on her education. She is fluent in several languages and has a vast knowledge of history, literature, and the fine arts."

"Very good." Canard says, smiling at Damien. "What is Princess Jaden's annual allowance at this time; and will it increase upon her marriage?"

Mother glances nervously at me. "These are matters which can be discussed at a later date with Prince Damien, should we mutually decide to move forward."

"But we are interested in knowing about the dowry and other assets the princess would bring into the marriage." Canard pushes. "Of course we would insist on the appropriate medical clearances before we can even make a determination whether or not to move forward." He looks to Damien who nods in agreement.

Mother's back stiffens and sparks glint from her eyes. "Monsieur Canard you are out of line. Prince Damien is here at my invitation, as a favor to his father. I shall decide the way in which these matters proceed."

"But, why not discuss it now?" Damien says lightly. "I have met the princess, and I find her acceptable. I am certain she finds me acceptable as well. Why not get these things out into the open straight away. Maybe I will not need to spend the entire week here."

Canard says, "I apologize Your Highness, but we are simply saying that certain things may strongly influence Prince Damien's decision one way or the other."

"Things such as the extent of Princess Jaden's wealth?" Mother says sharply.

"Well, Your Highness, he is being asked to give up a lot." Canard spreads his hands in an *it's-only-fair* gesture.

"Ha!" she says. "He is on the verge of being disinherited by his father. Marrying the princess would be considered his redemption."

"Madame, you wound me." Damien looks like he's been slapped. "My father would never disown me, he depends upon me. Besides which, I am currently in the process of pursuing a very lucrative business venture. Isn't that right, Luc?" His lipsticked smile is seriously disturbing.

In fact the whole *Prince Damien Show* gives me the willies, and this conversation is definitely pissing me off. I can't keep my mouth shut a second longer.

"Okay, people, enough!" I say, springing to my feet. The two men stand.

"Hello? Remember me? I'm sick of you people talking about me like I'm not sitting right here! Let me save everyone a lot of time and energy. The possibility I will ever marry Prince Damien is less than zero, zilch, nada, no-can-do, ain't gonna happen. First of all, I have no intention of marrying *anyone* for at least ten years. Second, if and when I *do* get married it'll be for love, not because someone is willing to help me pop out an heir.

"No offense Damien, but I don't even *like* you! You sit there with your smug expression, your fake tan, and all your royal bling— well, I've got a news flash for you, you ain't no Brad Pitt. I really don't know what my mother was thinking." I cast a withering glance her way. Then I turn my wrath on the lawyer.

"And you, Canard, you can take your little notebook and cram it up your … well, you get the picture. I'm out of here. Enjoy your stay in Domerica."

I hike up my hem and sprint from the room.

"Jaden, wait!" Mother calls, hurrying after me. "I want to speak with you."

I wheel around to face her. "Yeah, well, I want to speak with you too."

She takes my hand, pulling me down the hallway. "This way," she says, leading me into a small room off the corridor. She closes and locks the door behind us. "We won't be disturbed in here."

I've never seen this room either. It's cozy and smells like potpourri. Cheery glass logs gleam red and yellow in the hearth, and fake candles glow softly in every corner of the room. She pulls me down next to her on a nearby loveseat.

"Darling, I realize all this comes as a bit of a shock to you—"

I jump up, unable to sit still. "A bit of a shock? I'm astounded you would arrange all this without even discussing it with me."

"Jaden, please sit down."

I don't. I'm fuming.

"I had little choice in the matter, really," she continues. "King Philippe surprised me with this on the day before we left Dome Noir. Remember, I *did* send a messenger. He had a letter for you explaining everything. But apparently he met with some misfortune before he reached Warrington." She pats the seat next to her.

I sit down, resentfully.

"The king said he had given a lot of thought to this and felt you and Damien would make a good union. He believed Damien would enjoy a quiet respite in Domerica and might wish to adopt it as a way of life."

"With me thrown in as a little incentive?"

"Darling, Philippe requested that I bring Damien to meet you with the *possibility* of a marriage contract being reached by the end of the visit. Of course you have a say in the entire matter. I didn't commit to anything for you, but I couldn't turn him down. It would have been the ultimate insult."

"You could've told me all of this before I walked into that room, instead of leaving me in the dark. I felt like a total idiot!"

"I know, dear, and I'm truly sorry. But, I had no time. You saw the mess I walked into upon my return." She takes my hand in hers. "I apologize for the way this was presented to you, but perhaps you should not be so hasty."

"What!"

"I don't think you should turn down Prince Damien on the basis of one meeting."

"Oh, give me a break!" I'm on my feet again. "The prince is a pompous, conceited ass! You don't seriously want me to consider him as a potential husband, do you?"

"I know he has his shortcomings, but you would make a very handsome couple—one of the most powerful in the world. Don't forget he is a Prince of Dome Noir. One day you will be Queen of Domerica. Imagine the clout you would have as a pair."

"Mother, *please*, you need a reality check! He is much more interested in my money than he is in me. Not to mention that he obviously finds you the more sexually appealing of the two of us. Do you really want him for a son-in-law? Do you really think he could ever make me happy?"

She covers her face with her hands for a moment and shakes her head. "No. No, you're right, Jaden." Then she shocks me by laughing out loud. "He really is *dreadful*, isn't he?"

"The worst!" I crow.

"Can you ever forgive me?"

I sit down beside her and we hug each other, laughing. It feels so good to be in her arms, to smell her hair and feel her warmth. I hate it when we argue.

After we've composed ourselves again, Mother takes me by the shoulders and looks into my eyes. "Now Jaden, who is this other boy—this Brad Pitt? Is this someone you are seeing?"

I laugh at my *faux pas*. "No Mother, it was just... I've never even met him."

"Then what's this about your not wishing to marry for ten years time? You don't mean that do you?"

"Yes, Mother. I'm not ready to get married. There's still so much I want to do."

She looks confused. "What for instance?"

That catches me off guard. I can't very well say college, world travel, dating. Those things don't really apply in this world.

"I ... well, I ..."

Thankfully, the door knob rattles sharply at that moment. "Your Highness, is everything all right?" LeGare's voice carries through the door.

Oh great, another one of my favorite people.

Mother goes to the door and unlocks it. "We're fine, Charles. Just give us a few minutes more. Please make certain Prince Damien and his gentlemen are comfortable until I can accompany him to the dining hall."

"Yes, ma'am." He scans the room trying to figure out what we were doing in here. Glancing at me, he bows and leaves.

"I'm sorry, you were saying darling?"

"Mother, I just want to marry when I'm ready. And I want to marry because I'm in love, not because some out-dated law requires me to declare my betrothed on my eighteenth birthday."

She sighs wistfully, "I married for love, Jaden. I can tell you from experience it's not always the wisest thing to do."

"Well, at least you were allowed to make your own mistakes. I'm only asking for the same privilege."

Worry creases her forehead. "Yes, well, regardless, the law is the law. I believe we are entitled to a little latitude where you are concerned, but we cannot drag it out too long. Drew still has not declared a bride and he is nearly nineteen." She rubs at the crease nervously. "Both of the royal children balking at the marriage laws. It does not present a good example for our subjects. We must be sensitive to that."

"Maybe it's a law that needs to be reconsidered, Mother."

"That is something you may do when you are queen," she says. "Now, we really must see to our guests, dear. We have a number of dignitaries coming to pay their respects to Prince Damien, and I suppose I need to try to smooth things over with him before all the festivities begin."

"Do I really have to sit through all that?" I whine. "I don't want to be within ten feet of Prince Damien."

"Darling, I know the duties of your position can be taxing at times. It will be a public humiliation for Damien if you completely rebuff him. Please come to dinner. I will seat you next to Professor Ralston at the opposite end of the table from Damien. We will find a diverting dinner companion for the Prince—Lady Joanna, perhaps. I'll see what she is wearing this evening. Luckily, he is easily distracted by a pretty face and an ample bosom." She grins at me.

"I'll come to dinner. But I'm not going anywhere near that man or his lawyer again."

"Thank you, darling." She kisses my forehead and we hug once more. "I love you so much."

My heart squeezes at her words. *Oh, how I love her too.*

TWENTY-FIVE

I discover that *dinner* for Prince Damien is going to be an all night marathon, including ten courses of culinary delights followed, by dancing and local entertainment.

Damien causes a stir by showing up in the grand hall sporting a large gold-plated handgun in an elaborate leather holster, instead of the traditional ceremonial sword. The guy's such a gangsta.

Mother patiently reminds him that guns are strictly prohibited in Domerica. He politely removes the holster and turns it over to Samuel, who takes it in his gloved hand as though it were toxic waste. Samuel sets the gun on a silver tray, and carries it from the room. Mother assures Damien it will be returned to him upon his departure from Domerica.

As promised, Mother seats me at the opposite end of the table from Damien. Ralston's on my right and the attractive Sir Jason Fallon on my left. I've run into Jason only a few times since coming to the palace. It's good to see him again. He hovers around me all evening, looking after my every desire and making pleasant dinner conversation.

"May I get you one of those delicious looking cream desserts?" he asks after the main course is cleared away.

"Yes, I did kind of have my eye on one of those," I say. He hurries off to snag one before they're gone.

It's my first opportunity to confront Ralston about the whole Damien debacle.

"Thanks a lot for the heads up on the Prince of Darkness," I say.

He chuckles softly. "I am sorry about that, Jade. I didn't know about it ahead of time, I swear. As you know, we are operating in uncharted territory here. We didn't see this coming."

"Well, it was your basic train wreck! I could've used your help— the man is a total jerk."

"You appear to have handled it very nicely on your own," he says, nodding toward the head of the table where Prince Damien sits between Mother and the lovely Lady Joanna.

"Thanks to Mother," I say, watching her with admiration. She is at her diplomatic best trying to soothe Prince Damien's bruised ego. I'm sure that Lady Joanna's flattering attentions, as well as her plunging neckline also help the prince forget he traveled more than three thousand miles to be rejected by Queen Eleanor's strong-willed daughter.

Joanna is most guys' idea of a "Perfect 10"—long blonde hair, huge blue eyes, double-D cups, and a double-digit IQ. She giggles at Damien's every comment. She's the ultimate combination of *glitz* meets *ditz*.

The evening actually turns out to be nice for me. Jason and I dance nearly every dance together. I feel obliged to dance with a few of the old-geezer-types my mother has invited to the banquet, but by the end of the night it feels like Jason and I got to have our prom date after all.

When the evening draws to a close, Jason walks me to the staircase. He wishes me goodnight and leans in to kiss me. I turn, offering my cheek to him. Jason's cute, but he doesn't move me the way Ryder does. It scares me to think maybe no one else ever will.

"I had a real nice time, Jason. Thank you," I say, leaving him at the foot of the stairs.

As I near the top of the staircase, I hear voices coming from the guest wing hallway. The tones are low and secretive, like a private matter is being discussed. One of the voices sounds a lot like Prince Damien. I slow my pace as I reach the top step, and I see Damien's back. He is speaking with someone. The other person is hidden in the shadows, but it can't be Joanna, because they are speaking French.

I move quietly to the landing for a better look at the pair, in time to see Prince Damien take a package from the other person and slip it into his jacket. He says a curt *"bon soir,"* and then heads toward his room at the other end of the hall.

I'm curious to know who his companion is, so I duck into a darkened alcove and wait. Soon I hear the rustle of long skirts scurrying my way. I'm shocked when I catch sight of Sylvia hurrying toward the staircase, glancing cautiously over her shoulder.

That old witch! She is so busted! Looks like my mother's not the only one she's been spying for. I wonder what's in the package she gave Damien. What could he want that Sylvia would have access to? I can't come up with anything right away, but the whole scene is very hinkey. I need to talk to Mother or Drew about it.

~ ~ ~ ~

It's heaven to be back in my room and to just be myself. It gets so exhausting pretending to be a princess all the time, especially at these formal events. I'm always stressed that I'm going to slip-up by saying or doing something that'll give me away as a phony. I change into a soft white dressing gown and brush out my ridiculous hair. The simple act of washing my face helps to ease my tension and relax my frazzled nerves. I remove Mother's amethyst necklace, replacing it with Ryder's silver wolf. Much better.

Someone knocks softly at my door, prompting an internal groan. I just want to close my eyes and go to sleep.

"Jade, open up, it's me," Drew whispers from the other side of the door. Drew is probably the only person I would allow in my room at this moment.

"What's under your coat?" I ask, closing the door behind him.

"Chocolate!" he croons with an evil grin. "I purloined it from Mother's office. Prince Damien gave it to her."

I'm still full from dinner, but I haven't had chocolate since coming to Domerica, and I've missed it. We both flop down on my bed, and Drew opens the crimson box.

"Ooooh," I moan. It smells divine. I've never seen such elaborate chocolates. They look like little carved animals and flowers. It's almost a shame to eat them.

Drew plucks a dark chocolate dragon from the box, and I select a milk chocolate fargen. The taste is sheer bliss.

"Mmm, the Noirs really know how to make chocolate," Drew says, collapsing back on the bed, sinking deeply into the down coverlet. "So, I understand we won't be having a wedding at Warrington Palace anytime soon." he says, mouth full of dragon.

"Not unless *you're* finally getting married."

"You weren't swept away by Prince Damien's many charms, I take it"

"Ugh! Can you believe he actually brought a gun to dinner? The man is such a tool."

"A what?"

Oops. "A *fool*. The man is a total fool."

"He's a fool if he's willing to marry you," he says, selecting another candy.

"Hey!" I grab a pillow and swat him, producing a large brown streak on the satin cover.

"You'll never guess what I saw when I came upstairs," I say.

"Tell." He rolls over and props up on his elbows, ready to dish.

"Damien and that nasty old maid of Mother's, Sylvia, whispering in the hallway. She gave him a package of some sort."

"Sylvia and Damien? That's an odd couple. I wonder what they were doing."

"I don't know, but I think she's a spy. What could she have given him? Does she have access to anything important?"

He snorts. "No. She's a maid. And she doesn't really do much anymore, now that you've banned her from your chambers. Perhaps she was sending something back home to her family. Or maybe after you turned him down, Damien went to his second choice."

"Well they make the perfect pair," I laugh. "They both give me the creeps." Maybe I'm being overly suspicious, but there's something sinister about both of them.

Drew turns momentarily serious. "Joking aside, Jade, Damien is a swine. I'm glad you refused him. You should've seen him at court in Dome Noir. He was out of control—drinking and gambling and ... let's just say he didn't lack for female companionship."

"I'm not surprised. But I can't figure out why Mother even brought him here." I pop a chocolate orchid into my mouth.

"She felt obligated to. It was as if King Philippe were looking for a way to get rid of him by foisting him off on Mother. No doubt he was hoping Mother would order you to marry Damien."

"Like that would have worked!"

"The king is well aware his own son is an ass. He just didn't know that the queen's daughter can be stubborn as a mule," Drew says. We both laugh and greedily dig for more chocolate.

At least Drew is the same here as he is back home. It feels good to hang out with him. Mother is another story, though. I suppose the stress and strain of running a country can shape a person differently, but I want my old mom back. Ralston says everyone in this world is the same deep inside as their counterpart back home. So, I know my sweet, caring mother is in there somewhere. The problem is going to be finding her before I have to leave this land.

After Drew and I devour the entire box of candy, we're both yawning and ready for bed. I force Drew to take the empty box with him, so I won't be caught with the evidence.

"You're not going hunting with us in the morning?" he asks.

"No, I guess not. Mother thinks it would be kind of awkward."

"She's probably worried that Prince Damien might loose a stray arrow into your back when no one is looking!"

"I hadn't considered that," I frown. "I'd better stay clear of the prince when he's carrying lethal weapons."

"Sleep well Jade, and be sure to lock your door," he says, raising his eyebrows.

After Drew leaves, I climb between the cool sheets of my bed and turn off the light on my table. I'm so happy Mom's back from Dome Noir. Avoiding Damien for the next week isn't going to be easy, but I'll find a way to steal some time alone with her. Excavating all the complex layers of the queen is going to be trickier than I thought.

I yawn loudly, close my eyes, and instantly fall asleep.

TWENTY-SIX

When I wake the next morning, the castle is mostly deserted. I eat breakfast alone in the family dining room, where Samuel finds me and informs me that the hunting party left earlier this morning. They plan to be gone for the entire day, but Prince Damien and his entourage didn't accompany them. A messenger arrived at dawn, summoning the prince back to Dome Noir post-haste, due to some urgent business with his father.

I suspect Prince Damien actually arranged for the messenger, allowing him an opportunity to slip out of the country gracefully. After the way I treated him, he probably didn't feel like sticking around, and since he no longer had any hope of dipping into the Domerican royal coffers to support his gambling habit, he had no reason to stay. I'm elated to be rid of that viper in drag. My week's looking better already.

I beg Ralston to jettison our studies for the day and instead go straight to the old barn for another fencing lesson. I assure him I've learned more than enough about dome governance to bluff my way through any situation. I also remind him that he owes me big-time for not warning me about Damien. We compromise by agreeing to spend the morning reviewing the Unicoi form of parliamentary democracy and to meet right after lunch for another sparring session.

~ ~ ~ ~

The old barn is bright and smells of fresh hay this afternoon. One wall has been neatly stacked with new, green bales. We spend the first hour reviewing the moves Ralston already taught me. Then, he shows me a new attack called the *Imbrocatta*. He takes me through a few drills so I can get comfortable with the move. My favorite part is when he sets out some obstacles—a bale of hay, a sawhorse, and an empty barrel—and we practice some free-flowing fighting in between, and sometimes over, the obstacles.

"Good work today, Jade!" Ralston says, wiping the sweat from his brow with his sleeve. "I think you're getting the hang of it."

"I still don't feel totally comfortable swinging a big blade around," I admit, "but it's getting better."

"You study Tae Kwon Do at home, don't you?" he asks, taking a seat on top of the sawhorse.

"Yes, ever since I was six years old. My mom had to force me to go, but I'm glad she did. It's been a good sport for me."

He tilts his head and smiles at me. "You're a third degree black belt if I'm not mistaken. Quite an accomplishment, old girl. Why don't you demonstrate some moves for me?"

"Here? Are you serious?"

"Quite. I'd love to see you in action."

"Okay. Sounds like fun, but we need to clear a little floor space." Ralston and I move the obstacles out of the way.

"All right then." I pull off my boots, and position myself in the middle of the floor. "This would be more impressive if I were wearing my *dobok*—my uniform," I tell him.

"I understand."

I take a deep breath and stand at attention. I bow to Ralston and take my ready stance. After a cleansing breath, I begin. My routine includes a specialized series of stationary kicks, spinning kicks, blocks, punches, and knife-hand strikes. I designed and performed this routine for my last exhibition. The moves are second nature to me now, since I've practiced them at least a thousand times. The actions are powerful, yet graceful, and can be deadly in actual combat.

When I was a kid, I always wanted to take ballet. I've grown to love the flow of Tae Kwon Do, though. I tell my friends it's "tough chick's ballet." It feels good to let my mind relax and allow my body to take over, performing the familiar movements. I end the routine with a *Kihap*—a loud shout. Then I resume my ready stance, and bow to Ralston once again.

"Bravo!" He applauds vigorously. "I'm most impressed, Jade."

"Thank you," I say, out of breath.

He puts an arm around my shoulder and gives it a squeeze. "I've heard that Tae Kwon Do is more than a martial art—it is considered a way of life by many of its students," he says.

"That's true."

"What are its tenets?"
I recite the familiar words that begin every class. "Courtesy, integrity, perseverance, self-control, and indomitable spirit."

"And do *you* subscribe to these tenets, Jade?"

"I try to. Why?"

"I was just thinking that they must have contributed to your being the strong young woman that you are. The situation you've found yourself in requires enormous strength of character, which you have demonstrated admirably."

I don't feel totally worthy of the compliment.

"I'm not sure I've always shown you the courtesy you deserve," I tell him. "And I really haven't exercised a lot of self-control when it comes to my feelings about Ryder. It's just so hard not to care," I say, my voice cracking. "I know I need to do better in that department."

"Ah, don't trouble yourself too much about it, Jade. It's a good thing to be a caring soul. It will all be resolved soon enough anyway. Just keep up that indomitable spirit."

"Thanks for the pep talk, Rals." I peck him on the cheek and pick up my boots. "Let's head back. I need a shower."

"Yes, you do!" he heartily agrees.

TWENTY-SEVEN

*M*aria knocks on my door at exactly six o'clock. Mother has planned a quiet family dinner for us, but the royal family still dresses for dinner—even when it is just us three. Maria waits while I shower and wash my hair. She applies her special tonic to my wet tresses, and begins to patiently work out all of the tangles. She's easy to be with and I'm grateful for her company.

"You are having dinner with only your mother and Prince Andrew tonight?" she asks.

"Yes. Prince Damien was unexpectedly called back to Dome Noir, so the palace should be quiet tonight." I'm sure Maria knows more about the events of the past two days than I do, thanks to the palace grapevine. We play this little game anyway, where she asks me questions and I answer them, either confirming or debunking the latest palace gossip.

"The queen was not upset when you turned down the prince?"

"Nah. She probably thinks I could've been a little more tactful about it, but she agrees it was for the best."

"The entire palace is buzzing today—they say the prince left with a broken heart." She sticks out her lower lip making an exaggerated sad face.

"Empty money bags maybe. Definitely *not* a broken heart," I tell her.

"No? They say you told him you would marry only for love and that ... eh," she wrinkles her nose, "... you did not even *like* him."

"Well, that part's true," I say, amazed at the accuracy of the report. "What else do 'they' say?"

"Um, the rumor is that you turned him down because you are in love with someone else."

"Oh, that one's rich." I laugh. "Who am I supposed to be in love with?"

"Some say Sir Jason." She finishes combing the tangles from my hair and expertly weaves it into a single braid in the back.

"I like Jason. I'm not in love with him."

"That is what I thought." She twists the braid into a bun and fastens it with tiny pearl hair pins. She hands me a small silver mirror, so I can hold it up in back to see her handiwork.

"Some think you are in love with the young Chief Blackthorn," she says matter-of-factly.

"What!" The mirror slips from my hand, shattering to pieces on the marble floor.

"Oh Princess, I am sorry." She takes a towel and begins sweeping the shards of glass into a pile. "Be careful. Do not cut yourself."

I crouch on the floor next to her. "Maria, stop for a minute." I put my hand on her arm. "Why do they think I am in love with Ryder Blackthorn?"

Her eyes probe mine. "He is said to be very good-looking and very kind. They think that when he captured you, you escaped, but maybe your heart did not."

"And what do you think?" I ask.

She smiles. "I think they are wrong. I think you are in love with the one who gave you this." She touches the necklace at my throat. "A mystery man, eh?" She gathers the remains of the broken mirror and puts them in the wastebasket.

"Why do you think that?" I finger the delicate wolf-head pendant.

"Because you wear it always, but you hide it beneath your clothing. It means something to you that no one else must know—except him, of course."

I just stare at her, unsure what to say. I want to tell her the truth, I need a friend to talk to, but I worry that she probably already knows too much.

"In any case, I think it is no one's business but yours," she says. "Let's find a dress for you to wear." She heads for the closet, obviously willing to let the matter drop for now. Not another word is spoken on the subject of my love life while Maria finishes making me presentable for the queen.

Ralston arrives at my door just as Maria is leaving. "May I see you for a moment, Princess Jaden?" he asks, assuming a more formal tone in the presence of Maria.

"Yes, come in," I say, closing the door behind him. "What's up, Rals?"

"I brought you a book." He hands a small black volume to me. "I believe you will enjoy it."

"Thank you." There's no lettering on the cover or the binding, so I open it to the title page. "La Vita Nuova—The New Life." I read aloud.

"Yes, it was written in 1295, by Dante Alighieri for Beatrice, the woman he adored. A rather heartbreaking tale of unrequited love." He smiles wryly. "It's no Harlequin romance, but it has some fascinating elements."

"Are you trying to send me a message or something?" I ask.

"No, no. Actually, I just needed an excuse to see you for a moment. I was hoping you would speak with your mother tonight about your desire to visit your father at the Enclave. You know our

TRANSCENDER: *First-Timer*

time is limited, so we must schedule the trip as quickly as possible."

I grimace. "I know, I know. I'll talk to her. But can it wait until tomorrow? This is the first chance I've had to spend some real one-on-one time with her since she got back. I don't want to bring up anything that might upset her."

"All right. Tomorrow is fine, but no later."

"Thanks, Rals. And thanks for the book," I call as he leaves my room.

I'm a little late for dinner. Mother is pacing impatiently. Drew's already at the table snacking on some appetizers. They each look as if they're going to scold me for my tardiness, so I head them off with breathless apologies and hugs for both.

We sit at one end of the extraordinarily long dining table in the family dining room. Mother signals the waiters, and bowls of piping hot soup immediately appear in front of us. Drew tucks into his soup, but I'm more interested in visiting with Mother. She looks a little tired and a little more stressed than usual this evening, even though this was supposed to have been a day of recreation for her.

"How was the hunt, Mother?" I ask, eager to hear the sound of her voice.

"Oh, I'm afraid it was rather disappointing. I'm glad Prince Damien wasn't along. Our wildlife has been seriously depleted by poachers. I've asked LeGare to place extra patrols around palace lands."

"That's too bad," I say. "Who do you think is doing the poaching?"

"I don't know dear. Outlanders, maybe, or perhaps renegade Unicoi warriors trying to prove they can enter our lands whenever they wish. Another tunnel was found today in Hampshire."

Drew momentarily lifts his head from his bowl of soup. "Mother, it's probably just the forest people. How else are they going to get food besides poaching and stealing?"

"Yes, well, their numbers must be growing, based on the increased livestock and game thefts. I suppose it's time to clean out the forests again." She rubs her forehead. "It's just so troublesome to have to house them all in the prisons until they can be rehabilitated or reeducated." She shakes her head. "But really, darlings, I wanted to talk to you both about another matter tonight."

Something in the tone of her voice makes Drew put down his spoon and focus on her. "What is it Mother? Is something wrong?"

"No Andrew, nothing's wrong. It's just that King Philippe and King Rafael were making overtures again at the last Coalition meeting about constructing a new dome."

"They want to build a new dome? But why?" I say, secretly hoping they've decided to allow the Unicoi to have a dome of their own.

She takes a sip of water. "For insufficient reasons, in my opinion. Both countries are experiencing food shortages and serious overcrowding in the cities, along with the related rise in crime that those problems bring about. They want this new dome to be a sort of 'supplier' entity for the other domes—producing food and goods to be shared among the three dome nations—according to population, of course."

"Interesting idea," Drew says. "They've designed it to ensure they'll be the major beneficiaries. Sounds as though they've thought this through rather thoroughly."

"Yes. Unfortunately, I believe they've been meeting behind my back in an attempt to present this in a way that I could not refuse."

"But you did?" I ask.

"Certainly I did. The structure of the proposed system is all wrong. It rewards them for having ineffective population and crime control. But worse, they propose to send all of their prisoners and political dissidents to this new dome as workers. Unpaid labor. It would be a sort of *prison dome* with wardens and guards to oversee everything. They believe it is the magical solution to all their social ills."

"Seems like a pretty extreme solution," I say. "Are their problems really that bad?"

"Oh, they're convinced they are. I admit it would be desirable to have Wall's Edge prison emptied of the worst inmates, but I believe the domes should at least attempt to control their population and crime problems by enacting stricter laws and *enforcing* them. I told them as much at the meeting."

"How did they react?" Drew says.

"Not very well, I'm afraid. The conference grew quite contentious. Their position is that since the majority of the Coalition is in agreement on the matter, the Guardian should go along."

"And if you don't?" Drew says.

"I don't know."

She slaps the table with her open hand. Drew and I jump. "This is not supposed to happen! I am the Designated Guardian. Treaties governing this very situation have been in place since the inception of the domes. The dome plans and materials have always been under the protection of Domerica, and the Guardian is the only one who may decide if and when they shall be used."

I'm a little confused by the conversation. Ralston has droned on about a lot of stuff, and, yes, I've tuned him out on occasion, but I don't remember his mentioning my mother is something called a Designated Guardian.

"You don't think they will try to force your hand, do you?" Drew asks.

"I certainly hope not. We've lived in peace for so long, it would be a tragedy to come to a confrontation over this issue." She sighs, looking very pale. Drew and I exchange concerned glances.

"What does LeGare say about this?" Drew asks.

She looks at him with a pained expression. "What do you think he says, Andrew? He's a soldier. He thinks we should defend our decision, even if it means war. Unfortunately, that is the way men usually react, which is why we have women rulers in this country."

Drew looks wounded by her words.

"Oh dear, I'm sorry Andrew. I didn't mean to paint you with the same brush. I actually want *your* opinion, and Jaden's. That's why I arranged for us to dine together alone tonight."

"Sorry to disappoint you Mother, but I actually agree with General LeGare," he says. "If you let them take advantage of you in this way, who knows what they'll do next—try to take over the whole of Domerica, maybe. Where do they plan to construct this dome anyway?"

"Apparently a strip of land exists in the country formerly known as Algiers, on what's left of the African continent," Mother tells us. "The explorers say the land is large, fertile, and stable enough to hold a dome and the soil is apparently free of toxins."

"That's awfully close to Dome Noir," Drew says. "Maybe Philippe has other motivations."

Mother nods. "Believe me, I've thought about that. I believe King Rafael is being callously manipulated by Philippe."

I sit silently during this exchange trying to figure out what all this means for Mother and Domerica. The decision rests on her shoulders alone. No wonder she seems so stressed.

She turns to me. "Jaden, you've been unusually quiet, what are your thoughts?"

Gulp. My thoughts are mostly relief that I'm not the one who has to figure out how to deal with this sticky situation. I don't want Mother to know she'll probably get better advice from Fred and Ethel, so I take a sip of water and stall for time.

"Well," I say, "Ralston tells me you have a group of advisors ..."

Her brow creases. "Jaden, you know I do. You've known most of them since birth. What are you getting at?"

I figure I've already put my foot in my mouth big time, so I might as well forge ahead. "I guess I would talk to my advisors, and anyone else I trust, like Dad, er, Father, and even Ralston. I think the more intelligent views you get on this the better. Maybe someone will have an idea for a solution you haven't thought of yet. You shouldn't have to face these bullies alone. At least get your advisors behind you."

She turns and gazes at the fake fire for a moment. "I was hoping to keep this under wraps for a while. I felt no need to trouble anyone else about it at this point, but I suppose we must be prepared, should it turn into some kind of conflict among the domes. You are right, Jaden; I shall convene my advisors tomorrow."

She reaches a hand across the table to me and one to Drew. "Thank you both for your help," she says. "I feel much stronger knowing you are here supporting me." She squeezes our hands. "Now, let's finish our meal, shall we?"

She signals to the waiter in the corner to bring the next course. He's gotten an earful of our family conversation. I'm sure the palace grapevine will be humming tonight. So much for keeping things under wraps.

Mother swivels toward me. "Did you have a nice day while Andrew and I were hunting, dear?" All traces of her earlier irritability have vanished.

"It was fine," I say.

"What did you do all day?" she asks, as plates of salad are placed before us.

"Uh, I spent most of the day studying with Ralston."

"How do you find him as a teacher?"

"He's good— very knowledgeable." I take a few bites of lettuce.

"What did you study?" She stabs at her salad, but doesn't eat.

"The governments of the various dome nations ... and Unicoi."

"Unicoi?"

"Yes, they have an interesting form of parliamentary monarchy," I say, showing off some of my newly acquired knowledge.

"What they have is a mess. The whole country is failing, and we can do nothing but watch it die."

"Maybe there is something that can be done, Mother."

"What do you mean?"

"Well, if you ever do build a new dome, the Unicoi could move there."

"Don't be ridiculous, darling. They would contaminate the entire dome. The rest of the inhabitants would be dead or dying in no time."

"But, I understand the disease isn't contagious," I say. "It comes from the Uranium in the ground and walls of Unicoi. If the people move out of the caves, most of them will recover with little or no permanent injury."

"That is what the Unicoi would have us believe. It has not been proven," she says, pushing away her plate. "Until it is proven beyond doubt, the Coalition has ordered that no Unicoi will be allowed into any dome nation."

"But, how are they supposed to prove it if they can't get away from the source of the disease and if the Coalition won't even listen to their scientific evidence?"

Her expression hardens, and I fear I've pushed her too far. "Jaden, do not presume to speak about matters of which you have no knowledge. What they claim to be scientific evidence is nothing more than their wishful thinking."

Drew glances at me with a slight shake of his head, then focuses intently on his food.

"Mother, please, I'm sorry."

"Who is filling your head with such ideas? Is it Ralston?"

"No!" I say adamantly. "Don't blame him Mother. I've heard stories of Unicoi from many different places, and I arrived at my own conclusions."

"No doubt that criminal Blackthorn attempted to fill your head with lies and frivolous notions when you were his prisoner. I hope you have completely discounted everything he said to you. He was using you to get to me."

"I know. I'm sorry. Let's talk about something more pleasant, shall we?"

Mother sighs, "Forgive me children, I am a little weary this evening. I agree Jaden; let us not discuss politics any more tonight."

The salad plates are removed and the main course is served. I silently nibble at my food, while Drew wolfs down his chicken, and Mother sips at her water.

After a few moments, Mother turns to me. "I have a surprise for you dear. I hope you will enjoy it."

"A surprise? For me?" I say.

"Yes." She smiles sweetly. "I have a little excursion planned for you and Ralston for tomorrow."

"That's great! Where are we going?" I'm touched that Mother has taken time out from her momentous responsibilities to plan something fun for me.

"I can't tell you. It's a surprise." She cups my chin in her hand. "It's my attempt to make up for the whole Prince Damien fiasco."

"I'm just happy you're not angry with me over that."

"Nonsense. You were absolutely right Jaden; he was not a suitable husband for you." She dabs her lips with her napkin. "I've heard some disturbing reports about him from sources here at home, and I've concluded that King Philippe did not wish to encourage a political union as much as he wished to rid himself of a parasite."

She smiles at me. "Do not worry, dear, we'll find an appropriate husband for you."

"No, Mother!" I choke on a mouthful of chicken.

She holds up her hand. "All I meant was that *you* will find the appropriate husband when you are ready."

I whisper a relieved. "Thanks."

The rest of the dinner passes pleasantly enough, but Mother's obviously uptight and distracted. She divides her attention equally between Drew and me, and she seems interested in what we're saying, but the warmth that used to radiate from my Connecticut mom isn't there.

When dinner's over, Mother kisses my forehead and says goodnight. I hug her tightly, taking her by surprise.

"What's this about, Jaden?"

"I missed you when you were in Dome Noir. I wish we could do something together, just you and me. Soon. Maybe a picnic or a ride in the countryside?"

"Of course dear, soon. But tomorrow I need to gather my advisors together, and you have your excursion with Ralston, remember? Perhaps we can do it next week. I'm really awfully behind on everything this week." She bids Drew goodnight also, and disappears down the hall.

"Congratulations," Drew says, once she's gone. "You managed to find the one subject that could infuriate her more than King Philippe. Nice touch. What is it with you and the Unicoi anyway? Have you adopted a new cause, Sister?"

"I honestly didn't mean to upset her, Drew. She's definitely hassled over this whole new dome thing. Do you really think it could lead to war?"

He shrugs. "I don't think it will come to that. If it does, I know we can assemble a better army than either of the other two domes."

"What if they are allied against us?"

He rubs his chin nervously. "That might be a challenge, but I'll wager LeGare is working on it right now."

"I hope you're right."

"When have I ever been wrong?" He grins and scoops up a piece of leftover pommera pie. "Care to help me finish the dessert tray?"

"Not tonight, big brother. I'm still recovering from all that chocolate we ate last night."

"Your loss." He takes a huge bite.

"See you tomorrow, then."

"Not if I see you first," he says, mouth bulging with pie.

TWENTY-EIGHT

I can't sleep. I pick up the book Ralston gave me. I can't read either. My mind won't settle down enough to make either activity possible. Thoughts of my mother consume me tonight. I want to help her, but more than that, I want to be with her, to let her know how much I love her before I have to leave. Our time is slipping away. With only a few weeks left in Domerica, I'm worried I'll never have time to tell her all the things I wish I'd said to my Connecticut mom. I'm blowing my second chance and I'm not sure what to do about it.

Completely absorbed in these thoughts, I nearly jump out of my skin when I hear a soft tapping at the French doors of my balcony. My mouth goes dry, and a wave of fear shudders through me. All my senses flip directly to *code red*. Who the heck is at my second-story balcony doors at this time of night? I pray it's not another kidnapper or, worse, Prince Damien.

I grab my sword from the corner. Keeping my back flat against the wall, I inch my way to the edge of the glass doors. They are draped with filmy white curtains—which prevent me from seeing out, but provide no cover for me in the lighted room.

"Who is it?" I demand, attempting to sound brave.

"Jaden, it's me. Let me in," says a soft voice I'd recognize anywhere. I drop the sword and fling open the doors to admit a clearly agitated Ryder Blackthorn.

My heart catches in my throat when I see the anguish in his face.

"Ryder, what is it? What's wrong?"

He takes me in his arms and hugs me fiercely. "I'm so sorry Jade, I had to come."

"Ryder, look at me!" He lifts his head, and I take his face in my hands. "What's the matter? What's happened? Are you hurt?" I ask, panic rising inside me.

"Tell me quickly, Jade, is it true?"

"Is what true?"

"Are you *betrothed*?" The air seems to leave his lungs with that last word.

"What! Is that why you're here?" I try to push him away, but he doesn't budge. "Geez, Ryder, let go of me. You scared me half to death!" I squirm out of his grasp.

"I heard Prince Damien was in the palace, and that you two were engaged to be married," he says.

"You heard this all the way back in Unicoi?" I ask, totally pissed that he nearly caused me to have a heart attack.

He nods. "I know this may sound self-serving, but that man is the worst kind of scoundrel, Jade. He does not deserve to wipe your boots, let alone be your husband."

"Who told you I was engaged?"

"I have my sources."

"Well, they're not very good! The prince *was* here, but I refused his offer. He left this morning in a rather large hurry."

"He's gone? And you're not betrothed?"

"Correct on both counts."

He beams and scoops me up into his arms. "That's wonderful!" He says, twirling me around like a child.

"Put me down! And take off that stupid armor, it hurts!" He sets me down, and I rub my shoulder, which he has nearly crushed. He quickly removes his armor and tosses it into the corner.

"Do you know how dangerous it is for you to be here?" I say. "Mother has all kinds of extra patrols out tonight."

"Don't be angry with me Jade. I wanted to see you and ask you myself. I did have to subdue two of your guards, but they're fine. They'll be discovered in the morning."

"Ryder! They'll report you were here."

"No. They didn't see my face. I was careful."

He takes me up in his arms again and settles down into the overstuffed chair in front of my fireplace with me on his lap. It's such a joyful release to be in his strong arms once more, but my head is insisting that I send him away immediately. I promised myself I wouldn't let things get personal again between Ryder and me. Yet here he is in my room, with me on his lap. Nice work, Jaden!

"You are all I've thought about since our last meeting at the lake," he says. His eyes hold such sincerity, passion, and hope that the remainder of my resolve evaporates instantly and I rest my head against his chest. We sit silently a few moments, our beating hearts the only sound in the room.

"So tell me, is your mother terribly displeased with you for turning down Damien?" he asks, smoothing my hair with his hand.

"Actually, no. I'm sure a part of her thought the marriage would make good political sense. In the end, though, even she had to admit he isn't the best husband material."

"How did Damien take it? Your rejection, I mean?"

"It's hard to say. I told him I wasn't going to marry anyone for at least ten years, and when I do marry it will be for love. Oh, and I might have mentioned that I thought he was a pompous ass. I don't think he's a very deep person, so he's probably gotten over it already."

TRANSCENDER: *First-Timer*

Ryder's face darkens. "Did he try to pursue you—romantically, I mean?"

"Not at all," I laugh. "He wasn't the least bit interested in me romantically. In fact he was hitting on my mother, right in front of me."

"He struck the queen!"

"No! What I meant was he was flirting with her, you know, making advances. He was more interested in the size of my allowance than anything else about me."

"Ah yes, that's classic Damien. It's rumored that he has overwhelming gambling debts. His father has refused to continue to pay them. I imagine he viewed your fortune as a means to pay his creditors. I hear they are an unsavory bunch."

"That must be why he travels with so many bodyguards."

"Did you see his famous tattoo?"

"Not really. He had it covered up with makeup. What is that thing?"

"A serpent," he smirks. "It coils around his neck and whispers in his ear."

"Seriously? Well, I guess that's kind of fitting. He does sort of remind me of a snake. But how do *you* know Prince Damien?"

"In a purely business capacity. Unicoi is mostly self-sufficient, but when the Coalition cut off all trade with us, we were forced to rely on trade with your father and black marketers to get things we couldn't make or grow ourselves. You may be shocked to know that Damien and his henchmen provide protection for the black marketers in Dome Noir."

"Actually, that doesn't surprise me at all. He seems very shady. I still can't believe Mother agreed to introduce us."

"I'm sure she did it because Philippe pressured her into it. She is probably concerned that her power and influence with the Coalition have become diminished. A power struggle has been developing among the members of the Coalition. King Philippe has been playing your mother and King Rafael against each other. "

I'm impressed he knows so much about dome intrigue. "Yes, but trying to arrange a marriage for me with an obvious low-life slime is insulting. She should've known I'd never consider him." I push away from Ryder's arms. "I can't believe you thought I'd be taken in by him."

"You're right. Please forgive me. I should have known you would never accept such a lout. I don't know what came over me. I think I went a bit mad when I heard you were betrothed." He gazes at me with those unfathomable blue eyes. "I know I have no claim on you, but the thought of you marrying anyone but me was unbearable."

My heart squeezes in my chest, and a battalion of tiny pixies dance a jig in my stomach. His words make me outrageously happy. At the same time, I know this is a *disaster*. Ryder and I can never be together. Becoming closer now will only make things harder later— for us both.

I look into his heartbreakingly handsome face and steel myself to say what I know I must. "Ryder, this is an impossible situation—you and me. For more reasons than you'll ever know, we can never be together. Don't fall in love with me."

He half-smiles. "It's too late, I've loved you since the first day I met you, when you were twelve years old."

I break away from his embrace and spring from his lap. "No! Ryder, don't say that. You have to forget about me. You need to find a nice Unicoi girl. Stay as far away from me as possible. Loving me will only bring you pain, believe me. I know what I'm talking about."

He comes to me and wraps his arms around me again.

"Ah Jade, you have already brought me more joy and hope than I have had in years. Pain is nothing new to me. It's been a constant part of my life for a long while now. I'm not afraid of it. Really, I am not. I will walk through hell to be with you if that's what it takes." He puts his hand under my chin and raises my face to his. "You are the balm that eases my pain. You are the shining promise that makes it all worthwhile. Do you think it possible I could forget you? You are the reason I keep fighting."

"But you're not in love with *me*—not really. You're in love with a little girl with unusual eyes. You're in love with a princess who built an orphanage and lives in a castle. That's not me. I'm not that person." It hurts to look in his eyes, so I turn away.

"You're wrong, Jade," he says quietly. "I'm in love with *you*. I love your generous heart, your courage, and your fire. I love that you forgave me for what I did to you. I love that even when you're happy to see me, you are angry with me for taking the risk. I love that I am powerfully drawn to you, even from a hundred miles away. Forgive me Jade, but I love that you ache inside whenever we are apart. I love that you care enough to want to help my people, even at the risk of angering your mother. I love that when I kiss you, I feel powerful as a lion and weak as a lamb, all at the same time."

I put my hand to his lips to stop him. "No Ryder, don't say those things. Please believe me, this will never work. You and I can never be."

He takes my hand and kisses my palm. "We can find a way to be together if we both want it. I promise you that." Pulling me into a tight embrace, he rests his cheek on the top of my head, and I silently pray he's right.

A knock at the door makes me jump. Ryder pulls away, ready to bolt.

Frightened, I call out, "Who's there?"

"It's Ralston. I've brought Fred and Ethel to say goodnight." I heave a sigh of relief.

"Should I go?" Ryder whispers almost inaudibly.

"Stay. It's all right."

I open the door for Ralston. He steps into my room, a Skorpling in each arm. His face registers no surprise at seeing Ryder.

"Good evening Ryder," he says dryly. "News travels fast, I see."

Ryder smiles and rakes a hand nervously through his hair. Fred and Ethel squirm impatiently in Ralston's arms. Fred comes to me immediately, but when Ethel sees Ryder she turns shy and crawls onto Ralston's back, hiding her face behind his neck.

"Jay, Jay," Fred says in his Munchkin-like voice, fiddling with strands of my hair.

"Fred, I missed you," I kiss his furry nose.

Obviously astonished by the two exotic creatures, Ryder's mouth hangs open.

"Ryder, this is my friend, Fred," I introduce them. "Fred is a Skorpling. Have you ever seen one before?"

"No, I've heard about them though," he says, staring at Fred. "They're astounding! They speak!"

"Yes, they have a limited vocabulary, and they have trouble pronouncing some letters, but overall they're excellent company. Fred, shake hands with Ryder."

Fred holds out a tiny hand and Ryder shakes it. "Incredible!" he says.

"Ethel, come here," I coax. "Ryder is very nice. He has beautiful blue eyes and soft hair."

Ethel peers shyly around Ralston's neck and reaches out her hand for me. I take her in my other arm and carry her to Ryder.

She watches him for a second, then reaches for him. "Hair," she coos.

"Ryder, Ethel loves hair. Is it all right if she touches yours?" He looks uncertain at first, but holds out his arms to take her.

She goes to him, timidly fingering his silky tresses. "Pretty," she says.

"Yes." I agree with her.

She puts her furry hand on Ryder's face. "Oooh, eyes," she croons. "Ryer pretty."

"No. Ryder is handsome." I correct her.

She ignores me and puts her arms around Ryder's neck, planting a fuzzy kiss on his cheek. "Ethel like Ryer," she says, nestling deeper into his arms.

Ryder looks completely nonplussed.

"Yes, well, don't get too comfortable," Ralston says to Ethel. "You two need to go to bed." He takes her from Ryder's arms, and carries her to me. "Kiss Jade goodnight."

She obeys. "Goonight, Jay," she says. "Goonight Ryer."

Ralston takes Fred from me. "Goonight Jay," Fred says.

"Goodnight Fred, sleep tight," I scratch behind his ear.

With the two Skorplings in his arms, Ralston turns to Ryder. "I would be extra careful out tonight, if I were you. Additional patrols have been stationed around the palace grounds and on the village road. You might consider an alternate route."

"Thanks, Ralston, I will," he says.

"Oh, and Jade, apparently your mother has planned an early morning outing for us, so don't be up too late." Ralston looks meaningfully at both Ryder and me.

"I won't. Ryder's leaving soon."

"Good, I'll see you in the morning. Travel safely, Ryder."

"Goodnight Ralston," we say in unison.

When we're alone again, Ryder says, "Those Skorplings are

astonishing, where did you get them?"

"They were a gift from the King of Copula de Vita for my tenth birthday." I repeat what Ralston told me.

Ryder takes my face in his sturdy hands. My arms automatically wind around his waist. "Thank you for allowing me into your room tonight. My heart is much lighter than before. I shall leave you now and give you your rest."

"Stay for just a bit longer," I say, not willing to let him go yet. "How about a cup of Ralston's special chamomile tea? I have some right here." I step over to the kitchenette in the corner of my room and take two cups from the cupboard.

"I suppose it would be all right. I have missed Ralston's tea these past weeks. I do miss his company. It seems that you two get on very well, though. I am glad he is with you now."

This makes me feel a little guilty. "Well he may get tired of me very soon and be back on your doorstep. You never know."

We talk and drink tea in front of the fake fire for what feels like a few minutes, but in reality is two hours. At last Ryder gets to his feet and stretches.

"It's getting late, love," he says. "It will be light in a few hours, and I'd better be on my way. When will I see you again?"

"You mean when am I coming to Unicoi? Or when will it be convenient for you to sneak up to my room again?"

He laughs his delicious laugh. "Either one."

"I'll speak with Mother tomorrow about a trip to the Enclave. But, please don't come here again. I mean it! This place is getting to be as closely guarded as Fort Knox."

"Fort what?"

"Never mind. Just let me come to you." I twine my arms around his waist.

He brushes his lips along the side of my jaw stopping at my ear. "When?" he whispers.

It's hard for me to breathe, let alone think when he does that. "I'll try for next week," I manage to get out. "I'll send word through Lorelei."

"Thank you." He kisses me deeply, and my mind immediately begins devising ways to keep him here.

"Can't you stay just a bit longer?" I ask.

He shakes his head, "It will be a long journey home if I take the back roads. I'll need the cover of darkness until I get close to the tunnel."

"Go then, and please be careful."

"I'll see you next week." He scoops up his armor.

I walk him to the balcony doors. "Hey Ryder."

"Yes, love?"

"What would you have done if I *had* been engaged?"

He slips into his armor and fastens the sides. "I'm not really certain. Perhaps I would have pleaded with you to reconsider, or challenged Damien to a duel." A smile plays at his lips. "Or maybe I'd have kidnapped you again. I could do it better this time. I've learned a thing or two." He pulls me into another embrace.

"No way that could happen again. I've learned a few things myself!"

As he leaves, the familiar hollow, aching feeling immediately grips my insides. I put out the light and climb into bed. Ryder's smell is still strong on my skin, and I inhale deeply, recalling the feel of him. Lying in the darkness, I'm forced to admit to myself that for me it's too late also. I love him—and, worse, I need him.

Heaven help me.

TWENTY-NINE

*R*alston wakes me up at an ungodly early hour. He's fired-up for our little field trip, and much too cheery for this early in the morning.

He says Mother arranged for us to join her head stableman, Griffin Barksdale, for an excursion to a neighboring horse farm to choose some new horses for the palace stables. I've never been to a horse farm before. I guess it could be sort of fun. It has to be better than hanging around the palace and brushing up on my French.

The air is fresh and crisp as we walk to the stables. The pinkish-silver light of the Domerican sunrise slants through the morning shadows, painting everything a rosy shade. Since we have a few minutes alone, I tell Ralston about the Coalition meeting and Mother's concerns that Philippe and Rafael might try to force her into agreeing to build a new dome.

"We knew this would happen at some point," he says. "We did not foresee it occurring quite so soon. It could present a rather touchy situation for Domerica; I'll ask my people to do some checking into it."

"What did Mother mean when she said she was the Designated Guardian?"

"As Queen of Domerica, she is also the Designated Guardian of the only existing set of dome plans, specifications, and materials on this earth. The IUGA left them here at the time of the Great Disaster, should the construction of a new dome ever become necessary. The materials are kept hidden deep inside large caves, the location of which is known only to members of the Domerican Royal Family and the elite group of guards who dedicate their lives to protecting them."

"For real? So nobody can build a new dome without Mother's permission?"

"Exactly. Unless they use force. The dome walls are made from a clear material, harder than diamonds and non-existent on this planet. More importantly, the Xtron energy cell required to power the dome is stored with the other materials. It is extremely valuable and utterly irreplaceable—not to mention capable of global destruction in the wrong hands."

"Geez. No wonder Mother was so upset. This really could mean war for Domerica."

"Don't fret about it, my dear," he says. "These things have a way of working themselves out. You'll be home in Connecticut before any kind of compromise or confrontation takes place. Our director, Braxton Zarbain, is convinced that things will return to a predictable pattern once you are back where you belong."

His words don't comfort me. I'm not thinking about Connecticut at the moment, I'm worried about my mother, and afraid that somehow all of this is my fault. I want to help her, but maybe the best way to do that is to get the hell out of Dodge as quickly as possible.

We find Barksdale putting the finishing touches on saddling Roxanne. He's a crusty old codger who looks about a hundred and nine years old and smells faintly of manure. He bows courteously to me.

"Good morning Princess Jaden. Her Highness tells me you are in the market for a new horse," he croaks.

I get it now—that's Mother's surprise. The only problem is, I like Roxanne just fine and don't really want a new horse. "Maybe," I say.

"We shall be seeing some fine horseflesh today at the Selkirk farm. You may find a nice little filly for yourself."

"We'll see." I pat my sweet little mare on the neck. "It would be hard to find a better companion than Roxanne."

"Suit yourself," he sniffs, obviously disapproving of my current mount.

A slight chill lingers in the air as we start out for the Selkirk farms. I wonder if the temperature on the dome climate control gets turned down at night, or whether the outside temperature gets so cold that it cools the dome. I still have so much to learn about this land.

Mist settles in the lush green meadows. The distant chirping of an occasional bird is the only sound besides the clopping of our horses' hooves. Two palace guards trail behind us—near enough to lend aid if we're attacked, but far enough away so they don't intrude on our little group.

We ride for a little more than an hour when Barksdale says, "There's the edge of Selkirk's farm." He points ahead to where a post and rail fence begins. "The entrance is yonder about 200 yards."

Once we reach the farmhouse, Ralston and I wait while Barksdale goes in search of farmer Selkirk. We tie our horses to a hitching post and sit on a shaded bench under a spreading elm.

"Ralston, can I ask you something?" A question has been gnawing at me since last night, when I realized how totally gone I am on Ryder Blackthorn.

"You can always ask, Jade."

"Yeah, yeah. Meaning you might not answer me, right?"

"I'll answer if I can."

"Is there a Ryder back home? I mean, back on the earth where I come from?"

He's silent for a moment. I hold my breath. "Yes, Jade, there is a Ryder Blackthorn on your earth."

TRANSCENDER: *First-Timer*

"Will we ever, you know, meet each other?"

His eyes soften. "It's not really appropriate for me to reveal too much about the future—it could have some untoward consequences. All I can say is that if it is meant to be, you and Ryder *will* find each other."

That is something to hope for, at least. I swallow hard. "Ralston, I think I'm in love with him."

He presses his lips into a tight line and looks a little peeved. "What happened to exercising self-control?"

"I fought against it, Rals, I really did. But I lost."

He shakes his head, but his pique turns into something closer to amusement. "Oh well, you could certainly do worse."

"But this is a catastrophe! We can't be together. You told me so, yourself."

He raises his eyebrows. "Love doesn't come with a guarantee, Jade. Some people never find a great love. You are one of the lucky ones."

"Lucky? I don't feel lucky. When I'm not with him I'm thinking about him constantly, and when I'm with him, all I do is think about how I'm going to have to leave him in a little while."

"The poet Tennyson would tell you *it is better to have loved and lost, than never to have loved at all,*" Ralston says.

"Do you really believe that crap?" I say, frowning.

"Everyone must decide that for him- or herself. What matters is what you believe, Jade."

"I believe this is going to be an ocean of heartache—and not just for me, for Ryder too. But he doesn't really get to decide does he? It isn't very fair to him. I feel horrible about that."

"Ryder is a smart young man, Jade. He knows there are risks, great risks, in undertaking a relationship with you."

"Yeah, but he doesn't know *all* the risks, does he?"

Ralston chuckles, "No one ever knows all the risks of love, Jade. That's half the fun."

"But, he's already suffered so much loss, how will he ever cope with my death—I mean the death of the Jaden here—when I go home?"

"I didn't say your counterpart here was going to die," Ralston corrects me.

"You said she was supposed to have died from the fall off the cliff, the night I came. I thought that meant ..."

"As I've been telling you, we don't know what it means, that's the point," he interrupts. "This wasn't supposed to have happened at all. You weren't supposed to be here. The fact that you are has changed everything. You were never supposed to meet, and now that you have the entire course of this life has been rearranged. Frankly, we don't know yet where it will go upon your departure."

"Well, what are some of the likely options?"

He balks at the question. "Oh, I don't know really ... things could freeze in place, like your life back in Connecticut. I suppose a chance exists that your counterpart could be brought back. She is technically still alive, in body if not in spirit." He shakes his head. "The possibilities are too numerous to list. I really don't think I should speculate."

I feel a pang of jealousy that the old Jaden might come back and be with Ryder. Then I realize I'm feeling jealous of myself, which I can't quite get my head around.

I chew on my upper lip, afraid to ask the next question. "Rals, just tell me this one thing, could one of the possibilities be that I might stay here? Stay with Ryder?"

"No! That is not on the list of possible outcomes."

"But why not? It makes as much sense as any other option."

TRANSCENDER: *First-Timer*

His eyes are gentle, but his words are biting. "Because a number of very skilled agents are diligently working to get you back where you belong, working to get the universe back in order. Your being here is an *error*—one that needs to be corrected."

"I know that. I'm sorry. I just thought—" My thought is never finished, though, because the door of the farmhouse bursts open and a large, red-faced woman hurries toward us, her daffodil silk skirts billowing behind her. She curtseys deeply before me.

"Oh Your Majesty, Princess Jaden, we didn't know you were coming this morning. We only expected Mr. Barksdale." She blots her red face with a lace handkerchief. "I'm so sorry we weren't out here to greet you. Please, you must come inside and partake of some refreshment."

"Of course," I say getting quickly to my feet. She's so flustered I'm afraid she's about to stroke-out or something.

She leads us into her small but well-furnished foyer. Carved chests and rich oil paintings line the walls. We are ceremoniously seated in the front parlor. The large chairs are covered in fabric that looks imported from Dome Noir. Farmer Selkirk obviously does very well in the horse trade.

"The maid will be in shortly with a selection of juices and teas," Mrs. Selkirk says. "You must stay for luncheon after you have seen the horses. Of course we will have to make do with the provisions we have on hand. We weren't expecting you this morning," she repeats.

"Thank you Mrs. Selkirk," I say, "and please don't trouble yourself about us. Don't prepare anything special. Bread and fruit will be fine."

She looks like I just struck her. "Oh, Princess Jaden, surely we would never place such a mean meal before you." Two maids bustle into the room carrying large trays loaded with containers of juice, iced tea, a coffee urn, and a selection of honey cakes, blueberry tarts and oat cookies.

Ralston and I have barely enough time to sip at our drinks when

Barksdale hobbles into the room and says, "The horses are ready to be viewed."

We put down our glasses, thanking Mrs. Selkirk for her hospitality, and follow Barksdale out the door.

Farmer Selkirk has an amiable face, curly brown hair, and a well-fed-looking belly, straining at the buttons of his red velvet vest. He's flanked by two awesome looking horses. He holds one set of reins in each hand. A group of stable boys hovers behind him, all whispers and nervous energy.

"Welcome Princess Jaden." He bows deeply. "We are honored to have you."

"Thank you." I smile at the group. "What have we here?" I ask approaching the splendid jet black horse on his right. The animal's coat reminds me of Ryder's hair.

"Ah, you have a good eye for horseflesh, Your Grace," Selkirk says, handing the reins of the other horse, an Appaloosa, to a stable boy. "This is Gabriel, a three year old gelding."

"The Archangel, huh?"

"Just so, Your Majesty. This horse has near perfect conformation, and the disposition of a saint. Let me show you."

Farmer Selkirk proceeds to point out the finer areas of the horse's anatomy, from the muzzle to the withers to the hind quarters, most of which goes straight over my head. Next, we're treated to an examination of the horse's teeth. Selkirk points out how smooth and even they are.

"I just floated them last week," he declares proudly.

"What does that mean?" I whisper to Ralston.

"He filed them down," he whispers back.

Eww, too much information.

At last, Farmer Selkirk offers to let me ride Gabriel. He saddles

TRANSCENDER: *First-Timer*

the horse and hands me the reins.

"Would you like help up, Princess?"

"No thanks," I say, hopping on the horse's back. I pat him on the neck and speak softly to him, slowly allowing him to get used to my voice and my weight. I put him through his paces the way Ralston taught me: walking, trotting, cantering, and backing up. He's perfect at everything. Selkirk is obviously an expert trainer.

"He's wonderful," I say, trotting him back to the waiting men.

"Cut him loose, Princess," Farmer Selkirk says, "See how he can fly. He's faster than lightning!"

"Really?" I grin.

"Yes, run him out to the fence and back. Just give him his head and hold on tight."

I turn the horse around, snap the reins, and yell "Hah!"

Gabriel shoots like an arrow across the field, straight and smooth. The wind whooshes through my hair. My heart races almost as quickly as when Ryder kisses me. What a rush! Half fear, half wild excitement. It is the closest thing to flying I can imagine. I decide right then and there, I've got to have this magnificent animal!

"We'll take him," I pant, when I return to the men.

"Excellent choice, Your Grace," says Selkirk, "and might I add, you're a natural born horsewoman."

We stick around while Selkirk performs demonstrations of conformation and teeth examinations on five more horses before we get to eat lunch. Mrs. Selkirk has done a miraculous job of "making do" with what they had on hand. We're served venison roast and duck breast, accompanied by potatoes, squash, corn, and string beans. Dessert consists of peach cobbler, blueberry pie, and even some chocolate bon-bons imported from Dome Noir.

When it's time to leave, I'm so full my stomach aches. Farmer Selkirk says he'll deliver the horses and the appropriate papers to the palace in two days' time. He kindly offers to let me take Gabriel home now. I thank him and enthusiastically take him up on his offer.

To my great disappointment, though, Barksdale insists that I ride Roxanne and that *he* ride Gabriel home. He wants to observe him more closely. He seems suspicious of Selkirk's willingness to let us take him tonight.

Ralston and I ride abreast of each other, giving me an opportunity to speak with him privately.

"I told Ryder we would try to go to Unicoi next week," I say. "I hope that's okay with you."

"Of course."

"I *will* talk to my mother tonight about visiting the Enclave," I promise. "She was in a crappy mood last night. There's no way I could've asked her. I still can't predict what her reaction will be. She's so different in this world, but I'm going to do my best to get her to agree."

"Good luck." Ralston says.

When we reach the palace stables, I insist on watching while Barksdale inspects every square inch of Gabriel's sleek body, including his ears and mouth. At last, he pronounces him fit.

"He's a fine specimen, milady. He'll make an excellent mount for you."

I'm overjoyed with my new friend and companion—the second tall, dark stranger to steal my heart away in this weird and wonderful land. I thank Griffin Barksdale, kiss Gabriel on his velvety nose, and dash up to my room. There's something I need to do. Gabriel's name must be added to the princess' register of horses.

I compose his entry in my head on my way up the stairs: 'jet black mane,' 'swift as the wind,' 'likes to be kissed on the nose.' But when I reach my room and use my ring to unlock the desk, I find only the princess' daily calendar. The other book, the journal with her important information, is missing.

I check the top of the desk. Not there. It's not in the stack of books on my nightstand either. Where could I have put it? I've taken it out a few of times to check a name, or because I can never remember the damn combination to the jewelry chest, but I could have sworn I put it back each time.

It's possible that a maid moved it. Or Maria, maybe. I'll ask around. The princess will not be happy with me if I've lost her diary of essential information. I have a feeling she relies on it as much as I do.

THIRTY

*I*n the afternoon, I send word to Mother asking if she can spare a few minutes to speak with me. She responds, via Samuel, that she's having dinner with her council of advisors, but will see me in her office at ten o'clock.

When I arrive, she's sitting in one of the armchairs by the stone fireplace. I'm happy to find her relaxed and smiling.

"Jade, it's good to see you. Please sit down," she says. "Did you have a good day today?"

I take the chair opposite hers. "Yes, it was a wonderful day. The Selkirk horses are amazing."

"I hear you picked out a beauty for yourself."

"I did. An ebony Arabian gelding named Gabriel. He's gorgeous and very fast."

"Just be careful, dear. It takes time to get used to a new horse."

"I will Mother. Thank you so much for buying him for me."

"Let's just say I owed you a debt," her eyes sparkle with humor. "Now what did you wish to see me about, dear?"

"First, tell me how the meeting went with your advisors," I say, stalling for time.

TRANSCENDER: First-Timer

She tilts her head thoughtfully. "In the beginning, many conflicting opinions were expressed on what should be done. I was certain I had made a mistake attempting to involve so many strong-minded people. In the end, however, we arrived at a reasoned statement of the position of the Designated Guardian and of Domerica's unwavering pledge to uphold that decision. I believe every one of the advisors will sign it."

"That's wonderful Mother. May I read it when it is finished?"

"Of course, darling. I was hoping you would consider signing it also."

"You know I will."

"Now tell me what is on your mind," she says, her vivid green eyes searching my own.

My stomach feels instantly queasy and I forget everything I've planned to say. "I ... well, I was thinking..." I stammer.

"Is this about going to visit your father, Jaden?"

"Uh, yes."

"Ralston has already spoken with me about it. I think it's a good idea. You haven't seen him in weeks. It will do you good to get away. After your kidnapping ordeal and all the other excitement we've had around here, you could probably use a change of scenery. I do not like you being so near Wall's Edge prison, but your father's Enclave is perfectly safe."

Relief washes over me. Ralston's already cleared the way. "Oh thank you Mother," I say going to her chair and hugging her. "I do think it will be good for me to get away for awhile."

"Your father has already been informed of my little dispute with the other domes, and he has generously offered to lend his advice and support."

"That's great!"

"Yes. He still takes a keen interest in my welfare. He is also concerned about your well-being, child. I think it will ease his mind to see you. The only condition I have is that Drew and a contingent of guards go along with you. I understand you declined your escort more than once during my absence."

"But Mother—"

"I don't want to hear it, Jaden. The road to Wall's Edge has been plagued by highwaymen and Outlanders lately. I'll not have you traveling about unprotected. This is not subject to negotiation."

"Well, all right then." I'll just have to figure out how to deal with this twist in my plans later. "Thank you Mother. Should I send word to da—Father, or will you?"

"Your father and I will handle the arrangements. I assume Ralston is going with you?"

"Yes, if that's all right."

"Of course. What about Maria?"

I have no intention of dragging Maria to Unicoi. "No, I'll just borrow one of Father's servants if I need some help."

"Fine, but as you are aware, he doesn't have many. Everyone is considered 'equal' and all that nonsense at the Enclave. He still employs some household help, but they may not be of much assistance."

"I'll be fine, Mother."

"Is there anything else, dear?" She rises, obviously ready to dismiss me. That bothers me. I want to spend more time with her. This is the first time we've been completely alone for days, and I wish we could just talk. But, I'm grateful that she so easily agreed to let me go to the Enclave, so I just hug her again.

"No, that's all I needed."

An urgent knocking at the office door interrupts our goodbye. "Enter," Mother says.

TRANSCENDER: *First-Timer*

A pasty-faced messenger bows timidly, and hands her a gold and black envelope. She takes it and waves the man away. The puzzled expression on her face concerns me.

"What is it Mother?"

She sits in her chair. "I don't know. It's from King Philippe. This is his seal."

She rips open the envelope and begins to read. The muscles in her jaw tighten as she scans down the page. "Hmm, this is troubling news."

I kneel beside her chair. "What does it say?"

"Prince Damien has failed to return to Dome Noir. There has been no sign of him or his people. King Philippe is, of course, very concerned for his welfare. He inquires why his son left the palace so abruptly. Obviously he is unaware of the urgent message received by Damien—which means *he* did not send it."

"I sort of thought Damien might have arranged that himself, to save face," I say.

"Yes, that is certainly a possibility, but the messenger might also have been sent by someone planning to ambush the prince."

"Or someone planning some black market dealings with him."

She looks at me sharply, "What makes you think the prince is involved in black market dealings?"

"Just rumor," I say, shrugging.

"Well, whatever the reason, he has gone missing. The king has dispatched hydrofoils to search the ocean. Philippe wishes to send a delegation here to investigate the circumstances surrounding Damien's departure." She taps the envelope against her open palm. "I wonder if Philippe believes I may have had something to do with the disappearance. After all, what an effective bargaining chit—I return his son in exchange for his agreement to abandon the new dome proposal."

"That's a little extreme." I say, convinced she's being paranoid.

"Not for someone who thinks like King Philippe does. I need to speak with LeGare immediately." She gets quickly from her chair.

"Mother, I won't go to the Enclave. I'll stay here with you to speak with the delegation."

She puts a hand on my cheek. "No, darling. That is kind of you. It will actually be better if you are *not* here when they arrive. The delegation will reach Domerica on Wednesday, if Damien has not turned up by then. You and Drew should leave for the Enclave on Wednesday morning. I will not allow you to be interrogated about your decision regarding a marriage to Prince Damien."

She folds the letter and sets it on her desk. "We will offer our assistance in locating the source of the messenger and offer our resources to aid in a search, but we will not tolerate any implication that we may have had a hand in Damien's disappearance."

Opening the door, she signals to Samuel. "Fetch General LeGare for me, please." Turning to me she says, "Don't trouble yourself about this, dear. I am certain it will all be resolved by the time you return. Damien is probably just off on a gambling holiday in Cupola de Vita. Goodnight now."

"Goodnight, Mother."

When I reach the family quarters, I find Ralston reading in his room. I fill him in on the message Mother received about Prince Damien's disappearance. He groans, taking off his glasses, and rubbing his eyes. He stares at the ceiling for a moment. "Events are careening out of control, I'm afraid."

"What do you mean?"

He sighs and replaces his glasses. "A vanishing Damien, this proposal for a new dome ... none of this was anticipated. Circumstances are deviating from the path much further than we projected." He closes his book. "All we can do is take it one step at a time."

TRANSCENDER: *First-Timer*

"You're scaring me, Rals. What else is going to happen?"

"Who knows? Do not concern yourself about it Jade. You'll be fine."

"It's not me I'm worried about. What does this all mean for my mother and for Domerica?"

"It means things are unfolding exactly the way they are supposed to—it's just that we've not been successful at finding a reliable method of predicting where they will go next. It's confounding, really. Our usual methods of creating accurate prediction models have all failed. I've never seen anything quite like it."

"*Sheesh*, I thought you guys would have this all figured out by now."

"Sorry to disappoint you, old girl. IUGA is not omniscient. All we can do is work with the information we have, and try to keep things on track. In any event, the more pressing issue is getting you to Unicoi and back safely, so you can be returned home on schedule."

"Oh, yeah, and thanks for smoothing the way with Mother," I say. "She's happy I'll be gone when the Noirs arrive. The only problem is she's sending Drew and a bunch of guards with us. Not negotiable."

"Actually, that is probably a good development. We can use a little additional protection, with all this uncertainty."

I frown. "There is the small matter of what I'm going to tell Drew when it's time to leave for Unicoi. He'll have a fit. He'll try to stop me."

"Telling him the truth may be the wisest tactic. He might be curious enough to want to go to Unicoi with you. In the event he decides to tattle on you, you will already be in Unicoi by the time word reaches your mother. She won't be able to do much at that point, without creating an international incident."

"You don't think she would do that, do you?"

"No, I don't. Not with things so unsettled politically right now. She'd most likely attempt to keep it quiet until she can get you home and personally wring your neck."

I wince at the visual. Of course she's going to be furious with me. For a nano-second, I consider telling her what I'm really up to, but I just as quickly discard that idea. She'd probably chain me to my bed. I'll just have to find a way to make her forgive me later.

Ralston says he'll send word to Ryder, via Lorelei, that we'll be traveling to the Enclave on Wednesday and on to Unicoi by the end of the week.

With all the arrangements in the works, I'm starting to get excited about the trip. I've missed my dad more than I thought I would, and I'm looking forward to seeing the Enclave. But, most of all, it's the promise of seeing Ryder again that burns inside me. Only a few more days and the ever present longing will end—temporarily, at least.

The need to be with Ryder is with me constantly now. His presence is the only way to ease the hollow aching that afflicts me whenever we're apart. At first I cursed myself for not being strong enough to resist the desire. Lately, though, I've just accepted it and released myself to the sweet misery of my all-consuming need for him.

I touch the necklace that lies just above my heart. "Soon Ryder, soon," I whisper.

THIRTY-ONE

*O*ur little group is in high spirits as we set out for the Enclave early Wednesday morning. Drew and his men are all nervous excitement and chatter. Ralston seems exhilarated to be embarking on a new adventure. He whistles merrily as he tools along in the wagon. I'm thrilled to be out on the open road with Gabriel, and looking forward to the next few days. Even the crisp morning air and the vividly colored countryside foreshadow a pleasant journey.

As the day wears on, though, the road turns dry and dusty. Endless stretches of flowering meadow, cultivated farmland, and spectacular tree orchards become monotonous. The chatter dies down, and our party settles into a mild boredom. Occasionally, a deer or raccoon crosses our path, causing a bit of a stir, but then more of the same. By afternoon, I'm caked with dust, tired of being in the saddle, and ready to reach our destination.

Drew and I ride silently at the lead. Ralston and the guards follow closely behind.   I'm beginning to wonder whether it's actually possible to fall asleep in the saddle, when I'm startled out of my reverie by the sight of a figure stepping into the roadway a short distance ahead.

"Who's that?" I gasp.

Two guards automatically line up at our flanks. As we draw nearer, the man raises his hands to show he is unarmed. I recognize a familiarity in the movement.

"It's Ryder!" I cry.

"That filthy scum, Blackthorn!" Drew says. "We'll take care of him. You stay here, Jade." He draws his sword and the guards do likewise.

"No! Drew, stop! "He's here at my invitation."

"What!" He turns on me, his face contorted in fury. "Are you mad, Jade? That cave-dweller kidnapped you."

"I know, but things are different now."

"Different? How? Jade, you haven't done anything stupid, have you?"

"I'm asking you to give him a chance, that's all. He's come alone and unarmed. What harm is there in allowing him to accompany us to the Enclave?"

"Have you gone completely round the bend! Father will have his head if we take him to the Enclave. He comes as a prisoner, if he comes at all." Drew signals the guards, "Follow me."

"Stop," I shout, holding up my hand. "Sheathe your weapons." The guards hesitate a moment. "I command it," I say loudly. The men immediately put away their swords, and Drew glares at me. As the heir to the throne of Domerica, I outrank him.

"Young Chief Blackthorn will be joining us as our guest," I tell them. "Wait here." I climb off my horse and walk toward Ryder. Drew is at my side immediately.

"I may have to let him ride with us, but I do not have to trust him," he growls through clenched teeth. "You're still my little sister, and I won't let anything happen to you."

"Just lighten up, Drew."

When we reach Ryder, I can barely contain myself. The relief is exquisite. I hold out my hand, and he kisses my palm.

"Oh, Jade, no!" Drew groans, understanding a lot more than I give him credit for. "Please tell me you're not in love with him."

"Shut up Drew, you don't know anything about it."

"I know he's a kidnapper and a rogue," he says.

"I can only beg your pardon for my previous bad conduct, Prince Andrew," Ryder interrupts. "I assure you my motives were good. I understand now that my methods were wrong."

Drew ignores him. "Jade, why are you doing this? You know he can't be trusted."

"I know him, Drew. You don't. He's coming with us to the Enclave."

"But why Blackthorn of all people?"

"Because he's taking me to Unicoi after our visit with Father."

"What! No, Jade! You can't be serious." Drew takes hold of my arm. "This is some kind of trick. He's going to hold you hostage again. He's trying to use you in his scheme to save Unicoi. I'm taking you back to the palace right now."

I shake off his hand. "I'm going to Unicoi to see things for myself. I need to see if Mother's beliefs are true, or if half a million people are about to be obliterated from the earth for no reason other than they have nowhere else to go."

My eyes search Drew's. "Admit it, you've wondered too. You've heard the stories. You've heard Ralston's accounts of what is going on in Unicoi. Don't you want to see first-hand? Come with me. You can bring your men."

"*Your* men," he sneers.

"Look, you don't have to like it right now, just let Ryder accompany us to the Enclave peaceably. Talk to Father before you make up your mind."

"Father knows about this wild plan?"

"Yes. He's known Ryder for years. He's sympathetic to the Unicoi."

"I don't believe this!" Drew says.

"Prince Andrew," Ryder says, "Princess Jaden has found it in her heart to forgive me. She has decided to see with her own eyes whether my claims about Unicoi are true. I am here only to protect her and ensure her safe passage."

"*I'm* here to protect her," Drew jeers. "You're here only because Jade commands it. You'd better watch yourself Blackthorn. One misstep and you're dead. *Dead*, understand me? I don't care what Jade or my father thinks, the queen will thank me for it."

"Fair enough," Ryder says. He whistles for his horse.

Once Ryder is mounted, Drew says, "I'll take that sword and your knife. Father can decide whether or not you may have them back."

Ryder wordlessly unhooks the scabbard from his saddle and passes his sword and knife to Drew, who then assumes the lead of our party. Ryder and I drop back and ride abreast so we can talk. Waves of tension roll off Drew's back, but we ignore him. Nothing can throw ice on our happy reunion.

Ryder's mood is buoyant. He says Chief Blackthorn is pleased about my visit, although Catherine is beside herself making all the arrangements for a royal reception on such short notice. My spirits soar just having him near again.

Occasionally Drew casts an angry glance our way, but I just pretend not to notice. I'm pretty sure he'll thaw toward Ryder once we get to the Enclave. He'll see Ryder's not the villain Mother makes him out to be.

Ryder congratulates me on my choice of Gabriel, saying he has rarely seen a finer horse. We talk about everything and nothing. We're so completely engrossed in each other's company that we're utterly taken by surprise when the attack takes place.

TRANSCENDER: *First-Timer*

They come at us from above, dropping out of the trees. At first I think they're monkeys, but I quickly realize they're men—filthy, smelly, ragged men. One of them lands on my back, toppling me from my horse. We fall, wrestling to the ground. The stinky little man pushes my face into the hard-packed dirt, trying desperately to reach my sword with his bony fingers. After years of martial arts training, my reflexes automatically kick-in. The principles of *hosinsul*, or self-defense, help me control my fear.

I ram my elbow into the man's throat, and he momentarily loosens his grip on me. I scramble to my feet and face him. He agilely leaps to his feet, flashing a nearly toothless grin. I assume a fighting stance, shift my weight to my back foot, and ready myself for his attack. He pulls a shiny knife from his belt and makes a run at me. I hold my position until he's within a few feet, then I kick out quickly, thumping him squarely in the face. His nose cracks and blood spurts everywhere. He howls in pain, but he's still standing. Damn!

I intended to knock him unconscious, but my aim was off, so I take another shot at it. I swing my leg around, smashing my foot into the side of his head. He crumples to the ground, his face a bloody mess. One down.

I reach for my sword. It's still in my scabbard, but I remember Ryder is unarmed. I glance to my right. Drew and a tree man are fighting with swords. Drew clearly has the advantage. To my left, Ralston and a guard are defending the wagon against four tree men. Ralston is standing in the wagon bed, swinging his sword mightily. Anyone who gets in his way is likely to be decapitated.

I spin around and glimpse Ryder defending himself with a small tree branch against two knife-wielding opponents. I unfasten my sword and shout Ryder's name as I toss it to him. He looks up and catches it, unsheathing it with one smooth motion. My sword is smaller than the one he's used to, but he skillfully takes care of his two scraggly opponents in no time. Unfortunately, a dozen others are waiting for their turn.

A voice behind me cries, "Get the girl!" Three tree men immediately surround me. One man grabs me in a strangle hold from the rear.

"I've got 'er, I've got 'er," he squeals.

I hold onto the arms clamped around my neck, rear back and snap-kick the guy in front of me, making solid contact with his groin area. He yowls pitifully, grabbing his privates, before falling to his knees.

I smash my right elbow backward into the thorax of the guy trying to choke me. It knocks the air out of his lungs, and he releases his hold, giving me time to go on the offensive. I jump and spin my body clockwise, ramming a hard hook kick into his head. He sprawls face first onto the forest floor and slides about five feet before coming to rest against the trunk of a tree. Two more down.

Out of the corner of my eye, I see another tree man advancing from my right. This guy is bigger than the others, so I need to use a little more force. He lunges for me and I leap, swinging my leg and planting my right heel firmly into his temple. He falls to the ground with a heavy thud. I'm afraid I may have kicked him too hard. In tournaments we always spar barefoot or with foam footgear. After a second, though, I see his chest rise and fall and I know he's alive. Good.

To my left, I spot Ryder still battling three men. He's out maneuvering them, and seems to be enjoying the three-on-one fight. I consider joining the fray when out of nowhere another tree man charges me with a knife.

"Bloody witch!" he screams, murder in his eyes.

I spin in the air, using my own version of the 540 kick—a kick delivered while jumping and spinning the body 540 degrees, or thereabouts. My boot catches him cleanly under his right ear. The knife flies from his grip, and he's out cold before he hits the ground.

Two other tree men witness this scene and quickly scramble into the woods. One of them bellows out a signal that sounds like a shrieking bird call. The remainder of their accomplices retreat into the thicket, dragging their wounded companions with them.

"Is anyone injured?" Drew shouts, as we take stock of ourselves

TRANSCENDER: *First-Timer*

and our group. Other than some minor cuts and bruises, no one in our party is seriously hurt.

As I hurry toward the wagon, Ryder catches up with me. He's out of breath and smeared with dirt and blood, which thankfully is not his.

"What was that?" he asks in open astonishment.

"It must have been a band of thieves," I reply. "Mother says they're all over these woods."

He places his hands on my shoulders forcing me to stop. "Not the men, Jade. Where did you learn to fight like that?"

"Oh. It's a martial art. Uh, Ralston taught me."

"Ralston does *not* know how to do that!"

"Yes he does. Ask him. Hey Ralston," I call. "Tell Ryder about how you taught me Tae Kwon Do."

We walk to the wagon and Drew joins us, red-faced and juiced on adrenaline. "What in the name of Lucifer's hairy ass did you do to those men, Jade? I nearly wet my britches just watching. You were amazing! Is that what you and old Rals have been practicing in that abandoned barn?" He claps Ralston on the back, "You've *got* to teach me how to do that, man!"

Ralston's saved from having to respond by the arrival of one of the guards who announces, "They got away with two of our horses."

I quickly scan the area and catch sight of Gabriel. Whew!

"Damn, that means we'll have to double up, or—" Drew says.

"I'll go with Ryder." I quickly offer. "Someone can ride Gabriel."

"All right. One of the men can ride your horse, the other can go in the wagon," Drew says. "Did we lose anything else?"

"The wagon is still intact," Ralston tells him. "It appears the horses are the only loss."

"All right, we'd better get going," Drew says. "Father will be waiting, and it will be raining soon."

I'm glad to be in the saddle with Ryder as we continue our journey. I'm still shaken by the sudden attack, and it's reassuring to be near him. Even though I'm a little proud of myself for putting my Tae Kwon Do skills to good use, I feel weird—guilty actually—about inflicting so much injury. In all my exhibitions, even the sparring competitions, I've never really harmed anyone. It's not a good feeling.

Ryder slides a comforting arm around my waist, as if sensing my troubled thoughts.

Drew's still totally hyper from the fight. He replays his every move, and everyone else's, over and over, like the rest of us hadn't been right in the thick of it. His incessant chattering is beginning to get on my nerves. Ryder remains quiet while Drew prattles on, but I know sooner or later we'll have to discuss my little performance.

At three o'clock it begins to rain softly. Father will be worried about us. I'm sorry for that, but I don't mind the gentle shower. It has the effect of quieting Drew's diatribe, and I feel warm and safe next to Ryder.

He puts his mouth near my ear and says, "Jade, you astonished me. I didn't know you were such an accomplished fighter."

"Well, they weren't very tough opponents," I say. "They looked half-starved."

"Yet, I had the impression that you were holding back—that you could have killed them if you had wanted to?" He's not going to let me off the hook that easily.

"In Tae Kwon Do it's all about control," I say, trying to appease him. "What matters is where you strike your opponent and how much force is exerted."

"Then, you *could* have killed them." It's not a question.

"I didn't want to kill them Ryder. I only wanted to stop them from attacking us."

He's silent, and I have no idea what he's thinking. I wish I could see his face. I know some guys feel threatened or think it's unladylike that I train in Tae Kwon Do. I don't believe Ryder's one of those small-minded types, but I can't be sure.

After a few seconds, he says, "Jade, I wonder, do you think a man of my size could learn to fight like that?"

The question makes me smile. I squeeze the arm he holds around my waist. "I really don't think a man of your size *needs* to learn to fight like that. You have other advantages. I don't see why you couldn't learn, though. You're athletic enough."

"I believe it might be of some use if I ever find myself unarmed against multiple opponents again. You may not always be available to rescue me."

"Good point."

"I shall speak to Ralston about it when we arrive at the Enclave," he says.

Oh great! Ralston's going to be thrilled with me. He has two new Tae Kwon Do students. For all I know, he knows nothing about the martial art other than what he learned from me.

THIRTY-TWO

My heart beats faster when the white stucco walls surrounding the Enclave come into view. It's been weeks since I've seen my Connecticut dad, and the things I've heard about my Domerican father have made me eager to meet him. I'm nervous about seeing him for the first time, though. I hope he doesn't spot me as an impostor.

A large, double wooden gate marks the entrance to the Enclave. As we approach, Drew shouts, "Nathan, open up. It's Andrew and Princess Jaden. We've come to see Father."

A small door set in the larger gate opens, and a grizzled, white-whiskered face peers out. "Greetings Prince Andrew! Welcome," the old man says in a surprisingly robust voice. "The Governor has been expecting you." The small door closes and the gates open slowly inward.

A broad tree-lined avenue paved in cobblestones stretches out before us. Purple and yellow flowers bloom in well-tended beds arranged down the length of both sides of the street. The buildings lining the street are all of a similar Victorian style and appear to be freshly painted in pastel hues with white trim. Everything looks clean and new. It occurs to me that the entire village must be only ten to fifteen years old, since my parents couldn't have been separated for longer than that.

According to Ralston, the Enclave is its own little country within

TRANSCENDER: First-Timer

Domerica—not subject to its laws or my mother's rule. These were the terms of her separation with my father.

As we enter the town, the roads are empty. Only a few people with umbrellas scurry along the sidewalks, and I assume that, as in Warrington Village, most people use the hours from three to five on rain days for having tea or taking a siesta.

We make a right turn down a tree-lined lane that leads to a large Victorian mansion. I figure this must be Father's manor house. As we draw nearer, I see my father standing on the veranda. I can't help but smile at the sight of him. He's striking in his Domerican-style of dress: a puffy sleeved white shirt, black pants, and knee-high riding boots. His hair is a bit longer than it is back home, and he's sporting a closely-trimmed beard. He looks downright handsome.

We stop the horses near the foot of the stairs. Ryder helps me out of the saddle, and I run up the steps to give my father a soggy but heartfelt hug.

"Jade, it's good to see you," he says. "I expected you before rainfall. Why are you late?"

Drew, who had come up the stairs behind me, answers for me. "We got into a little scuffle with a band of highwaymen, about five miles from here. They got away with two of our horses."

"Was anyone hurt?" Father asks, alarmed. "Jade, is that blood on your trousers?"

"It's not mine, Father."

"None of us was hurt," Drew tells him. "But Jade inflicted quite a bit of damage on the ruffians. You should have seen her, Father. She nearly fought them off single-handedly."

Father's brow creases. "What's this?"

"Nothing, Andrew exaggerates," I say, frowning at Drew. "There were at least a dozen of them. We all had our hands full."

"Well, come inside all of you." Father puts an arm around my shoulder. "Let's get you dried off." A stack of towels sits just inside the door, and he hands one to each of us. "Andrew, have your men take your horses to the stables. And ask Peter to unload the wagon, please."

"Yes, Father," Drew says, skipping back down the steps to speak to his men.

Dad turns to Ryder and Ralston. "Young Blackthorn, it's good to see you again." He shakes Ryder's hand. "And you must be Professor Ralston. I've heard many good things about you. I am indebted to you for coming to Jaden's rescue. Welcome to the Enclave."

"Thank you, Dr. Beckett, and please call me Ralston." The two men shake hands.

"I shall, if you will call me John," Father replies.

We towel ourselves off at the foot of an elegant marble staircase. The entry hall is paneled in dark mahogany. The furnishings are heavy and masculine.

"Let's see to your comfort first," Father says. "Afterward, we shall have tea in the library, if you like."

"Erica!" he calls.

A smiling, dark-haired young woman emerges from a door to the right of the staircase. "Ah, your guests have arrived," she says in a husky voice.

Her face is striking and unusual, with slanted dark eyes and full, sensual lips. She wears a simple white blouse and a straight black skirt, neither of which conceals her stunning figure. I'm momentarily taken aback—is this my dad's girlfriend?

"Jaden, you remember Erica Hornsby, Captain and Missus Hornsby's daughter? She is helping me by running the household while her mother is visiting relatives in Cupola de Vita."

I pretend to remember Erica, the housekeeper's daughter, whom I've evidently met before. I smile and say, "Hi."

TRANSCENDER: *First-Timer*

She bows her head slightly.

"Erica, this is Professor Ralston." Erica makes a small curtsey. "I believe you already know young Blackthorn."

"Of course." She beams and steps toward Ryder. "Chief Blackthorn, I am happy to see you again. How is your arm?" She lays a long-fingered hand lightly on his right forearm.

"Much better, thank you," Ryder says smiling back at her, "and it's Ryder, please."

"Erica will take you to your rooms, so you can freshen up," Father says. "Jaden, I've changed some things around since you were last here. I've moved you into the room across from mine. It is larger and I think you'll find it more comfortable. Erica will show you."

Ralston, Ryder, and I follow Erica's tight skirt up the stairs.

"Tea in one hour." Father calls after us. "No rush."

The first stop is my room. Erica opens the door and ushers me in. "It is very lovely, yes? Your father has impeccable taste."

It's beautifully decorated in cream and aqua colors. While much smaller than my rooms at the palace, it's still spacious enough for a desk, sitting area, and large mahogany four-poster bed. "It's perfect" I say. "I love it."

She turns to go. "Where are their rooms?" I ask.

"Oh, just down the hall. Not far at all." I don't know whether it's her playful smile, her sensuous voice, or strictly my imagination, but everything she says sounds suggestive to me—like it has a double meaning. She closes my door and I experience a little pang of jealousy. I'm not sure I want her showing Ryder to his room. They've obviously met before, and shared some experience having to do with Ryder's arm.

I open the door a crack and peer out, watching the three of them walk down the hall. Erica glances over her shoulder, catching me spying, and I quickly retreat back into my room.

My boots and riding clothes are caked with mud and blood, so I need a change of clothes. My trunk is still in the wagon, but a few of the princess' things hang inside the closet, and I select a pretty, but simple lilac dress. I spend a little extra time on my hair, hoping that the contrast between the ravishing Erica and me won't be quite so noticeable.

I'm a few minutes late for tea, and when I reach the library Drew, Ralston, and Father are already sipping drinks, eating sweets, and deep in conversation. Actually, Drew is monopolizing the conversation by recounting, for the millionth time, our skirmish with the tree men.

I pour myself tea and pluck a blueberry tart from the tray. "Oh, Drew, give it a rest. I don't think Father wants to hear all of this, and I definitely don't want to hear it again."

"Actually, I'm finding it rather entertaining," Father says. "I understand you've gotten quite good at hand-to-hand combat. But where was your sword?"

"Oh, well, Ryder was unarmed, so I threw it to him. He was being attacked by two men."

"Why was he unarmed?"

"Your son wouldn't allow him to join us otherwise." I say.

"Where *is* Blackthorn, by the way?" Drew asks.

"He went to the lumber yard," Father says, "to arrange for a load of lumber to take to Unicoi tomorrow."

"Father, I can't believe you are allowing Jade to go. Mother would be furious if she knew."

"I'm quite certain you're right Drew, but Jaden makes up her own mind about things—in case you haven't noticed. Personally, I don't believe it's such a bad idea. She'll be safe with Chief Blackthorn, and it is my opinion that someone from Domerica's ruling family should have made such a trip long ago, rather than relying on secondhand and potentially unreliable information." Father eyes bore into Drew's.

"Are you implying that *I* ought to go also?"

"That is for you to decide, Andrew. I would go with Jaden, but I can't be absent from the Enclave at the moment. We have two very ill patients in the hospital, and I cannot risk leaving them. Perhaps you would be less worried about her if you went along. I know I would be."

Drew looks chagrined. "Do you actually trust this Blackthorn character?"

Father rubs the back of his hand along his whiskered jaw and nods. "I do, Drew. I've known him and his father for years. They are men of honor. Ryder made a foolish mistake attempting to kidnap Jaden, but he acknowledges that, and he seems truly remorseful. I believe Jaden agrees with me." He cuts his eyes to me. I smile and bob my head.

"Jade has been taken in by his charm," Drew says. "I don't trust her opinion on this."

"Drew!" I say.

Father holds up a hand for peace. "Your sister's always been a shrewd judge of people, Andrew. I wouldn't brush off her estimation of Blackthorn's character so lightly."

"I'm sorry," Drew says. "But I believe he has unduly influenced her."

"Ralston, what do you think?" Father asks. "Would this trip be an educational experience for young Andrew or just a boondoggle?"

Ralston sets his cup and saucer on the table. "I believe a trip to Unicoi would be most enlightening, a very good use of time for Prince Andrew.

"And what of Blackthorn?" Father asks.

"I trust him completely."

"There you have it, Andrew. You may go to Unicoi or stay here, as you wish. I ask only that you not alarm your mother by running off to tell her where Jaden has gone until she has returned safely to Domerica."

"I'm no snitch, Father. I'd like to think about it overnight, though."

"That's reasonable," Father says, standing. "Well, I've promised Ralston a tour of our little hamlet now that the rain has stopped. Would either of you care to join us?"

"Yes!" I say, excited to see the pretty little town, and glad for a distraction while Ryder is away.

"I have some things to attend to," Drew says. "What time's dinner?"

"Seven o'clock," Father tells him. "I'll just clear this up, and we'll be on our way." He begins stacking the empty tea cups on the tray.

"Let me help you with that, Father," I offer, picking up the tray. "Has Erica gone home?"

"Oh no, she has a room here. I sent her out with Ryder to do an errand for me near the lumber yard. They will return in time for dinner."

~ ~ ~ ~

The Enclave village is more modern-looking than Warrington Village, but it still has the quaint charm of a small New England community. The shopkeepers and tradesmen are cordial and welcoming to us. No one seems particularly impressed with having a princess in their midst, which is just fine with me. They're far more excited to see Governor Beckett—Father's official title here. It's nice being out of the spotlight for a change.

Father is animated, obviously getting a charge out of showing Ralston the many points of interest in the village. He seems proud of his community and its inhabitants. We stop in many of the little shops, so Father can pay his respects to the proprietors.

Under normal circumstances I'd be having a terrific time seeing *all this, but instead I find myself in a jealous snit because Ryder and Erica are off together somewhere. Someone once said: *He who is jealous is not in love.* I guess that means if I really loved Ryder I'd want him to hook up with Erica so he'll be happy when I'm gone. My heart doesn't work that way, though. It whimpers like a spoiled child at the thought of Ryder being with anyone but me. I have a sneaking suspicion whoever coined that phrase was never *really* in love.

We stop inside a hat shop so Ralston can check out the latest styles. I'm not much interested in bowlers, boaters, and berets, so I stare out the window and chew on my lower lip wondering where Ryder is right now.

As we're leaving, Father says, "Ralston, I would like to show you our library. I believe you will be pleasantly surprised by some of the rare volumes we possess. Our pre-Disaster section is larger even than that of Domerica's main library."

"I would be most delighted to visit your library," Ralston says. "I've heard of your impressive collection. I'd love to see it for myself."

"I need to make a quick stop at the apothecary to pick up a tonic for one of my patients," Father says. "I'll meet you two on the main floor of the library. Jade will show you the way."

Ralston and I exchange amused glances, since I obviously don't have the vaguest idea where the library is located.

"I believe it is at the end of the next block, is it not?" Ralston asks, pointing to a large granite building.

"Indeed it is," Father says. "I'll see you there in twenty minutes."

As Ralston and I turn up the street toward the library, a cluster of odd looking people appear in the walkway a short distance ahead. They're dressed in flowing white robes and each has very long, straight, white hair—men and women alike. I count a half-dozen of them in all.

I tug at Ralston's sleeve. "Who are they?" I ask.

"Ah, I see the Cleadians are in town. This could be a bit awkward, my dear. Perhaps we should make a small detour into one of the shops." His eyes dart up and down the block.

"They're coming this way," I say apprehensively.

"Yes, I'm afraid they've spotted us. It's all right Jade. They will know you are not the princess. They will not expose you, however, as they do not wish to be exposed themselves. They're not mind readers per se, but they can read a person's essence with just a touch of the hand."

"What? Who are they?"

"Actually they originate from the planet Cleadies," he whispers. "Their ancestors were stranded on this earth when the Great Disaster ruined their spacecraft."

"They're *aliens?*"

"Keep your voice down. That fact is not widely known. The story for public consumption is that the Cleadians are descendents of survivors from a town in Nova Scotia, who migrated to this area after the Great Disaster. They inhabit a colony about five miles outside of Domerica."

As the troupe draws nearer, Ralston puts a protective arm around my shoulder. "Steady, old girl," he whispers.

They stop directly in front of us, and an elderly man carrying a long staff steps forward from the rest. I'm struck by his milky blue eyes. On second look, they all have unusual, milky blue eyes.

"Professor Ralston, what a pleasant surprise," the old man says. "We did not expect to see you here."

"Nor I you, Melor," Ralston replies. "I trust you are well."

"Quite well. And you?"

"Just enjoying a small tour of the Enclave."

"Delightful. And who is your lovely companion?" he asks,

turning his milky orbs toward me.

"May I present the Crown Princess Jaden Beckett. Princess, this is Melor Thaddeus, elder of the Cleadian colony."

I offer my hand in greeting. He takes it in his own, and bows. Instantly, his head snaps up, his eyes wide in astonishment.

"Ah, but I believe you are trying to fool an old man," he says, an amused smile creasing the wrinkles of his face. "I see you are a long way from home, young one."

When he references *home* I understand he's not talking about Warrington. He glances over his shoulder at his companions. They immediately begin to whisper among themselves.

"The star of inter-dimensional travel shines brightly above you. You are a *Transcender*. How fortunate you are to see such wondrous things," he says, still holding tightly to my hand.

"Uh, thank you."

"I suppose this remarkable child would explain your presence in Domerica?" he asks Ralston.

"Quite so," Ralston says with a nod. "I go where I am needed."

"We wish you Godspeed on your journeys, young one. It is an honor to have met you," Melor says to me, bowing again and finally releasing my hand. He turns to Ralston. "Professor I trust you will be in touch if there is anything about which we should be informed."

"As always, Melor."

"Good day to you both," Melor says.

As the extraordinary little group prepares to depart, each member comes forward to take my hand briefly. Some of them bow silently, while others quietly "ooh" or "ahh" when their hands touch mine. Then they glide away from us down the sidewalk.

"Well that was kind of creepy," I say, a little rattled at having just pressed the flesh with six white-robed aliens. "What are they doing here?"

"They were stranded on this planet when the Great Disaster occurred. Their vessel was cruising in the vicinity when the dust cloud created by the meteor collision became so severe they were forced to make an emergency landing. Their craft was seriously damaged in the process, all of their communications equipment wiped out. So, you see, they had no way of letting their people know where they were."

"That's wild! They just got stuck here with no way to get home, kind of like ET?"

"Yes. For decades they tried in vain to repair their vehicle. Eventually they gave up and moved closer to Domerica to have a convenient source for food and supplies."

"They live outside the dome? Like the Outlanders?"

"No, not quite. Actually, they have a unique structure of their own which they built from materials salvaged from their disabled spacecraft. The architecture is quite inspiring. It looks something like the Guggenheim museum in your New York City. It is more for appearances than anything else, though. Cleadians have remarkable respiratory systems. The earth's atmosphere as it is currently composed is not toxic to them, and their skin is immune to ultraviolet rays. Consequently, they can survive just fine outside the structure's protection."

"Do they have any other special powers like the hand touching thing?" I ask, as we reach the doors to the library.

"Yes, a few. They do most of their communicating among themselves through mental telepathy. They are also known for being great healers. Rumor has it they can raise a man from the dead," he says lifting his eyebrows for emphasis. "I've not witnessed that myself, however. Otherwise, they appear to be quite human. They prefer to keep to themselves for the most part. In all of the years since the Disaster, I believe only a handful have ever married outside their colony."

TRANSCENDER: *First-Timer*

"Well, they seem nice, but they kind of gave me the heebie-geebies," I say.

"Yes, well, they probably had the same reaction to you, my dear—you being an inter-world traveler and all."

We step into the cool marble foyer. Soaring ceilings meet in a large dome with a skylight above the main lobby.

"What's that thing he called me?" I ask. "A Transcender?"

"A Transcender is an individual who is capable of traveling among the different dimensions at will," Ralston says.

"There are people who can do that?"

"A very small number, yes."

"But why did he think I was one of them?"

"I suppose he perceived you were not from this earth and assumed you were a Transcender. It seems a logical mistake," he says lightly. "Ah, I believe you father has arrived."

THIRTY-THREE

*F*ather spends the next hour showing off the library's most exceptional collections for Ralston. The architecture of the building is inspiring, and I'm sure the musty old books are fascinating to a scholar, but I'm tired from the long, eventful day. Fighting tree men takes a lot out of you. I'm ready for a rest by the time Father finishes our tour.

It is growing dark as we arrive back at the manor house. Ryder and Erica have not yet returned from their errands, and I'm disappointed and curious why they're out so late. I mean, how long can it take to order up a load of lumber?

"I think I'll go upstairs and lie down before dinner," I tell Father, knowing I'm not very good company.

"Are you feeling well, Jade? You look a little pale," Father says putting his palm to my forehead.

"I'm fine. Just tired from all the excitement today."

"It has been quite a day for you, sweetheart. Go and rest, I will call you for dinner."

"Thanks." I hug him and trudge up to my room.

I take a warm bath instead of a nap and actually feel much better afterward. In my quiet moments alone, I think over my meeting with the Cleadians. I'm still blown away that I actually spoke with

TRANSCENDER: *First-Timer*

extraterrestrials. My ideas about the universe are being stretched and challenged almost daily now, and I remind myself to enjoy every second of this exotic journey, because my time here is drawing to a close. I wonder what it must feel like to be a real Transcender, and have amazing experiences like this all the time.

~ ~ ~ ~

Dinner at the Enclave is a more casual affair than our dinners at Warrington Palace. My pulse quickens as I descend the stairs and glimpse Ryder in the dining room speaking with Father. His coal black hair is tied back with a beaded leather thong, and he wears a traditional Cherokee shirt of red and white fabric. The sight of him takes my breath away.

Erica is joining us for dinner tonight, and she enters the dining room at the same time I do, only from the opposite door. She has on a revealing red dress that displays her knock-out figure to its best advantage. She looks amazing, and I immediately regret that I put on the same plain dress I wore earlier in the day.

But when Ryder sees me, his entire face breaks into a smile, and he comes to take my hand. He seems not to notice Erica at all.

"You look beautiful," he says kissing the inside of my palm. The warm gentle current of his touch sends a shiver through me.

I glance at Father to see if he has noticed this exchange. I'm not sure he would approve of my feelings for Ryder. He smiles affectionately. "You look rested, sweetheart," he says.

"Will you sit with me?" Ryder asks. "I missed seeing you this afternoon."

He holds out the chair to the right of my father's at the head of the table. I sit down and he takes the seat next to me. "How was Ralston's tour of the Enclave? I hear you went along."

"I think Ralston had a great time," I say. "How was your afternoon?"

"Oh, it was mostly business, but it had to be done. One of the tribal buildings is in desperate need of repair. The Enclave is our primary source of lumber. I hope you do not mind that I had to leave you for a few hours."

"Of course not," I lie. "But I missed you too."

Drew and Ralston are the last to arrive, and Father announces that dinner is served.

The food is the most delicious I've tasted since coming to Domerica. Father's cook was once the head chef for the royal family of Dome Noir, but he was forced to leave the country to avoid imprisonment when it was discovered he'd been secretly diverting some of the palace food supply to the starving villagers. Drew claims Mother's been trying to steal him away for Warrington Palace ever since his arrival at the Enclave.

The dinner conversation is light and cordial. Ralston thanks Father for the tour earlier in the day and compliments him on his thriving little community. Father asks us about all the news from Warrington Palace, and Drew and I fill him in on Damien's disappearance and the imminent arrival of the delegation from Dome Noir.

Erica flirts with Ryder throughout the evening, but she also flirts with Drew and even Ralston on occasion. They all seem to thoroughly enjoy her attentions.

Father asks Ryder about his plans for our stay in Unicoi, and Ryder gives him a run-down of our schedule—the agricultural area, the fish farms, the warrior training camp, and finally the hospital, so I can see the toll the Uranium-related diseases have taken.

"I wish I didn't have obligations that prevent me from joining you," Father says. "It's been years since I was last in Unicoi, I'm certain much has changed."

I love seeing my dad so self-assured and relaxed. It's amazing to think that not only is he in charge of the whole hospital, but he's also the Governor of the Enclave—royalty in his own right. He's so different from my Connecticut dad, who always seems a little lost.

I'm proud of Father for all he's accomplished, even if it means that he and Mother had to separate. I can't help but wonder if my Connecticut dad might have been a little more dazzling if he hadn't always let Mom run the show.

To cap off the evening, the chef personally presents a luscious layered dessert shaped like a dome, with silver icing and white chocolate shavings on the outside. Father congratulates him on the fine meal, and the rest of us offer our hearty thanks, as well. By the time dessert is finished we're all pleasantly full and ready to retire.

Erica is the first to leave the table. She says a polite goodnight to everyone, and then asks Ryder if she can have a word with him. He escorts her to the door, where they speak briefly before she disappears.

Ryder offers to walk me upstairs, so I leave on his arm, kissing Father and wishing goodnight to Drew and Ralston before I go.

When we reach my room, Ryder opens the door for me. "Goodnight, love," he says brushing my cheek with his lips.

"Will you come in for a few minutes?" I ask.

"I shouldn't, Jade. I'm not sure what your father would think."

"Just for a minute." I take his hand and pull him into the room. "You can leave the door open, if you want. Or do you have somewhere else to be?"

"No. I'm going to bed. Where else would I go?"

"I thought you and Erica might have some more errands to run tonight."

He half-smiles. "Jade, it is late. We had both better get some sleep."

"What did she say to you downstairs?" I'm not about to let him leave until I know.

His brow creases and he shrugs. "Well, she asked me not to mention something to your father."

"What?"

"Jade, I don't know whether she would want me mentioning it to you, either."

"In that case you'd better tell me right now, or I'm going to think the worst."

He shifts uncomfortably on his feet. "She purchased a gift for John while we were out today. She didn't want him to know."

That surprises me. "Why would Erica buy a gift for my father?"

"She said his birthday is next week."

"Oh crap." I slap my forehead. "I forgot. I didn't bring him anything."

"Maybe you'll see something for him in Unicoi."

"Good idea. I've sort of lost track of the days lately."

He tilts his head to the side. "What did you think Erica was whispering to me?"

"To be honest, I thought she might be asking you to meet her later."

"I have done nothing to encourage the lady," he says.

"But you like her?"

"Yes, of course. She's a nice girl."

"Do you think she's pretty?"

"I don't believe it's a matter of opinion—she *is* pretty."

"So, that means you're attracted to her?"

He narrows his eyes as though sensing a trap. "What do you mean?"

"I mean … would you like to kiss her?"

TRANSCENDER: First-Timer

"I already have."

My stomach collapses in on itself. "You what? You've kissed her?" I ask, my voice rising an octave.

"Well, she kissed me, actually," he corrects.

"When was this? Today?"

"No, it was the last time I stayed here, while picking up supplies. We were loading lumber when a rope snapped, and a stack of wood fell on me. My arm was injured." He rubs his right forearm in the same spot Erica touched earlier. "Your father bandaged it for me and put it in a sling. He instructed me not to get it wet. So, that evening he sent Erica up to help me bathe."

"She bathed you?"

"No, she just helped with the preparations—running the water, undressing—"

"She undressed you!" I don't like the visual flashing through my head.

"I had the use of only one arm, Jade. Why are you upset?"

"Did you two ... I mean, was there more than just kissing involved?"

"No! I wouldn't disrespect your father that way."

"But, she saw you naked!"

"No. She didn't. I sent her away after we got my shirt off. That is when she kissed me. I assumed it would be less awkward trying to take off my pants one-handed, than trying to keep Erica at bay." He laughs.

I scowl.

He takes both my hands in his and sits on the arm of a Queen Anne chair, putting him on eye-level with me. "Jade, there is no need for you to be jealous of anyone. Ever. I love only you. You are the only woman I want to kiss." A smile plays at his lips. "You are the only woman I would allow to bathe me."

I roll my eyes, pulling my hands away. "Gee, thanks a lot."

He stands, still grinning. "Besides, what if she *had* seen me naked? What would you have me do? Disrobe right here so she would possess no greater knowledge of me than you have?"

I glare at him. "You know, that's not such a bad idea!" I snatch at the fabric of his shirt, pulling out the neatly tucked-in tails. I grab at his buttons, but he seizes my hands before I can reach them.

"I knew you were going to be trouble from that very first day," he says. We laugh, and I half-heartedly struggle to get free.

"Ahem." A small cough comes from the open doorway. My father is leaning against the door jamb, smiling. "I hope I'm not interrupting anything."

Ryder immediately drops my hands. We take an embarrassed step away from each other, and he tucks in his shirt tails.

"No, we were ... I just ...." I shake my head and shrug. "Oh, never mind. Hello Father, come in."

He steps into my room. "I came to say goodnight. It's getting late, and I retire earlier these days." He kisses me on the forehead and embraces me warmly. "It's good to have you here, Jade. I hope you're planning a nice long stay this summer. I feel cheated that you're here for only a short visit this time."

"I wish I had more time with you too," I say, sincerely desiring to know my remarkable Domerican father a little better.

"Goodnight, Ryder," Father says. He stops at the door and turns around, looking from Ryder to me and back to Ryder. "Don't keep her up late."

"I won't sir, I was just leaving."

"Oh good. I'll walk you to your room. I have a question about the new design of the healing wands we received from Keowe

Hospital."

Ryder kisses me chastely on the cheek. "Goodnight, Jade. Pleasant dreams."

"See you in the morning," I say wistfully, and my heart follows after him as he and Father disappear down the hallway.

THIRTY-FOUR

My sleep is deep and dreamless despite, or maybe because of, the day's many ups and downs. When I wake, my body feels like it's been trampled by a herd of runaway fargen. The scuffle with the tree men and the fall from my horse have left me battered and bruised. As I sit on the edge of my bed wishing for a couple of Advil, someone knocks softly at my door.

"Who is it?" I call, hoping it isn't Ryder, because I'm sure I look as bad as I feel.

The door opens a crack and Erica's stunning face peers around the side. "May I come in?"

"Sure," I say, hating her for looking so fresh and gorgeous this early in the morning.

"John thought perhaps you could use some help with your things. I'll repack your trunk if you like."

"That would be nice," I say. "I need to get out some fresh riding clothes first, though. My things from yesterday are ruined."

She picks up the muddy, blood-spattered pants I've thrown into the corner and *tsks* at me disapprovingly. "You really should let the men handle the fighting, you know."

Drew has obviously been regaling her with stories of yesterday's skirmish.

TRANSCENDER: *First-Timer*

"Yes, well I would've been dead or worse if I'd waited for the men to save me," I say, holding my head in my hands.

Her eyebrows pop up. "Oh my! Well, that is different, you had to defend yourself. And now you are feeling poorly?"

"I ache all over," I say, lifting my night dress slightly to reveal the bruises covering my shins and knees.

"Oh my," she says again. "Wait here, I'll be right back." She hurries out of the room.

I grasp the bedpost, pull myself up, and limp to the bathroom to splash some water on my face. A glance in the mirror tells me I was wrong—I actually look *worse* than I feel. My hair appears to have been styled with an egg-beater. Dark crescents are deeply imbedded beneath my eyes.

A smiling Erica returns a short time later and holds out a hand to me. In her palm are two greenish-brown pills. "Take these," she says, giving me the glass of dark red pommera juice in her other hand. "They will make you feel better."

I eye the pills suspiciously. "What are they?"

"They are pain relievers. Your father makes them from herbs. I take them during my time of the month. They are very helpful."

I swallow the pills and drink the syrupy juice, while Erica rummages around in my trunk.

"Here," she says holding out a light peach-colored sweater and a pair of doe-skin riding pants. "Put these on, then we will work on that hair."

I obediently take the clothes and hobble back to the bathroom, while Erica begins to neatly fold and repack my things.

By the time I've finished dressing, I'm starting to feel a little more human.

"Come and sit while I fix your hair," she says. "And finish your juice, you will need the strength for your journey."

I sip at the sweet nectar while she expertly uses a comb to tease the tangles from my knotted tresses. "You have lovely hair," she says. "So many different shades of gold."

"Yeah, well, I'm thinking of cutting it. It's too hard to manage on my own. I like the length of your hair."

"Oh no! You mustn't! You have princess hair. A princess must have long, silky hair." When she has detangled the unruly mess, she begins to weave my hair into a French braid. "This will be a pretty style for you."

"Thank you for your help, Erica." I say, and I mean it.

She makes a tut-tut sound with her tongue, brushing off my thanks.

"So," she says, changing the subject, "you are fond of our Ryder?"

"I am," I answer, not really liking the way she calls him "our" Ryder.

She makes a deep throaty *mmm* sound. "He is very handsome."

"Yes, he is."

"And a good kisser, no?"

"Yes."

"But not as good as Prince Andrew, I think."

"What?" I swivel around to look at her.

"Don't turn your head, I am still working," she scolds.

"You've kissed my brother?"

"I should say, he is more of a *willing* kisser than Ryder," she adds for accuracy's sake.

"Yeah, I'll bet. Do you kiss every man who comes to the house?"

"Only the good looking ones. And why not? I do not intend to marry, so I will have my fun while I am still young and beautiful."

This intrigues me. "Why don't you intend to marry?"

"Oh, I think men are mostly fools. A woman cannot be her true self if she is with a man. They love a woman to be strong and boundless when they are courting her, but when they marry her ... *pfft* ... she can no longer be that free spirit. They want to put her in a cage."

I consider this for a moment. "I guess that's true in some cases. I don't think all men are like that, though."

"Maybe not for a woman who is a princess. But for someone like me—a house servant—a man wants only to own me."

Her comments bother me. I thought the Enclave was supposed to be an enlightened community, everybody equal and all.

She turns me around to look in the mirror. "See, you are beautiful!"

I have to admit, I do look considerably better, and I feel better too. I guess Father's little pills really work. "Erica, have you spoken with my father about your feelings ... I mean about wanting to be more than a house servant?"

"Oh no! I am grateful for the job. John has been very good to my family."

"But what if you tell my father you want to help out in the hospital, that you want to study nursing, or become a doctor, or be some other kind of apprentice? Don't you think he would help you?"

She shrugs, "I don't know. He is a good man, but he might think I am trying to be above my station."

"No. He doesn't think that way," I say. I know he would help. I can speak to him for you, if you like."

"You are very kind, Princess. Let me consider it. Maybe when my mother returns to run the household again, it would be a good time to discuss it with John."

"All right, but let me know if I can help. Thank you so much for everything you've done for me this morning." I give her a quick hug. "And please call me Jaden."

We walk together downstairs to breakfast. Ryder is waiting for me. He awoke early to get things ready for our trip. Ralston is decked out in his travel attire and sporting a new brown fedora.

"Nice hat," I say.

"I got it yesterday while we were in town. Don't you remember?" he says. "You seemed a bit distracted."

"Oh, right."

We eat a quick breakfast with Father and are preparing to leave when Drew comes clunking down the stairs, dragging his gear behind him.

"I'm coming with you," he says. "If it's all right with Blackthorn," he adds, looking to Ryder.

"You will be most welcome in Unicoi, Prince Andrew."

"I wish to bring my men along."

"Of course," Ryder says.

Father walks with us outside and hugs me tightly. "Be safe, Jaden." He embraces Drew also, and shakes hands with Ralston. Turning to Ryder he says, "Please give my regards to Chief Blackthorn. If there is anything we can do to help him here at our hospital, please let me know."

"Thanks John," Ryder says. "I have implored him to leave Unicoi, if only for a month or two, to see whether his condition will improve, but he refuses to consider it until he can offer the same opportunity to the entire population."

"I understand," Father says, patting Ryder's shoulder. "In that case, let me know if there is anything *I* can do."

TRANSCENDER: *First-Timer*

"Thank you, sir."

The two men shake hands.

As I climb onto Gabriel's back, I hear Erica calling me from the veranda. "Jaden. Wait. I have something for you."

Loping gracefully down the front steps, she comes to Gabriel's side and holds up a small enamel box for me. I open it and find several of Father's herbal pills inside.

"You will need these for later today, and maybe tomorrow," she says.

I smile at her. "I'm sure you're right. Thanks."

I tuck the box into my pocket, wave goodbye to Father, and our small entourage sets out on our journey to Unicoi.

THIRTY-FIVE

It's a fairly short ride to Wall's Edge—so named because it is literally located alongside the dome wall. The lower part of the wall is overgrown with vegetation, but the upper wall is clearly visible. Up close, the swirling gases are a kaleidoscope of ever-changing shades of silver. It's mesmerizing to watch.

After a few miles, Ryder steers his horse onto a dirt pathway barely wide enough to accommodate our wagons. We ride along the wall for about a hundred yards, stopping near an outcropping of rock. Ryder climbs down from his horse and walks to the largest boulder in the outcropping. To my surprise, he steps behind it, and completely disappears from view.

When he reappears, he's accompanied by two men. They are nearly as large as Ryder, and wear similar leather body armor. As they walk toward us, I see Drew's hand go reflexively to the hilt of his sword.

"Princess Jaden, Prince Andrew," Ryder says. "These are my friends Alexander and Makoda." Both men bow their heads briefly.

Alexander looks like a platinum blonde version of Ryder. He's tall and graceful with light skin and nearly colorless blue eyes. I remember he was there the day I was kidnapped. Makoda, in contrast, looks very Cherokee. He's darkly handsome, with coffee brown hair and eyes to match. His skin, though pale, has a coppery hue to it. He appears wary of our group. Clearly, he was not expecting to see Drew and four members of the Royal Guard.

"Makoda will ride ahead and let my sister know of our impending arrival," Ryder says. "Alexander will travel with us to Unicoi."

"I prefer that they both accompany us," Drew says. "That way we will all arrive together. I wish to have no surprises awaiting us on the other end."

Ryder gazes at him, as if deciding whether to argue the point. He shrugs and says, "If that is your desire Prince Andrew, we shall do it your way. But I warn you my sister can be most unpleasant when her instructions are ignored." Alexander and Makoda both make snorting laughs at this comment. Ryder, however, seems genuinely concerned.

The three men walk again to the large boulder. Together they swing it open like a door. Alexander and Makoda disappear inside. Ryder remounts Tenasi waving us to follow him. When we are nearer to the entrance, I see that the boulder is attached to a large metal gate on hinges, allowing it to be opened and closed. When closed it's impossible to detect that it's the entrance to a tunnel.

Once inside the tunnel, I'm shocked to see Ryder's friends, Makoda and Alexander, seated in a small, engine-powered vehicle that looks like a go-cart. It glides smoothly along the dirt floor, making almost no sound. The tunnel is larger, brighter, and cleaner than I thought it would be. Rows of lights line both walls. There is more than enough room for our wagons to fit and for Ryder and me to ride side by side. The road descends in a steep incline, and it dawns on me that we'll need to travel beneath the dome wall to get out of Domerica.

"Nervous?" Ryder asks.

"A little," I admit.

He smiles. "The tunnels are perfectly safe, and the journey takes only three hours. Do not be troubled."

The trip passes more quickly than I expect. The road, which had leveled-off for most of the excursion now turns steeply upward, and I know we must be getting close to Unicoi. When we reach a small plateau, Alexander and Makoda park their vehicle to one side and walk to a large metal door. I realize anxiously that we've come to the end of the tunnel and are about to enter Unicoi.

Drew brings his horse up next to mine. "What are they doing?" he asks Ryder.

"They are announcing our arrival to the guards," Ryder says.

Alexander speaks into a gray metal box on the wall next to the door—some sort of intercom, I assume. Ryder climbs off his horse and helps me down from Gabriel's back. He tells us we must enter the town on foot. Our horses and the wagons will be brought in later.

The massive door opens automatically, and Alexander and Makoda lead the way inside. Guards line both sides of a long ramp ascending from the tunnel. Cheers and cries of welcome greet us. This is good. I find myself smiling, my jangled nerves easing a bit.

I can't see much until we emerge from the dimness of the entrance ramp into the city. In my imagination I pictured Unicoi to be dark and cavernous. Instead it's surreally lit and intensely bright. I squint against the harsh light, which casts bizarre shadows over everything, creating strange illusions.

When my eyes finally adjust, I'm immediately struck by the congested feel of the city. It's as though we've stepped into the middle of a teeming metropolis. The platform on which we're standing is crammed with a mish-mash of people in motion— brushing shoulders, turning sideways to get by—mothers with children, teenagers, business people, uniformed workers, shoppers, and many, many others. I hold onto Ryder's arm so I won't be carried away in the flow.

The contrast of the Unicoi people with the population of Domerica is remarkable. The styles of clothing here pop with color and panache. Some women dress in short skirts and sleeveless tops. A sprinkling of teenagers sport pink or purple hair. A number of people wear glasses with pastel-colored lenses—yellow, rose, and blue. Ryder tells me these glasses soften the garish light. He offers a pair to me, but I decline. I don't want to miss any sensations of this amazing city.

Buildings, several stories high, push up to the edge of the roadway, crammed so tightly together that no space exists between them. No trees or grassy patches surround them. In fact, I see no natural vegetation at all. Everything is wood, concrete, metal, brick or stone. The architecture is austere and utilitarian. Totems, sculptures, and painted murals add color and interest to the surroundings, but this environment is devoid of *all* green—not just green eyes.

The air around us is damp and smells earthy, but not in an unpleasant way. The temperature feels about ten degrees cooler here than in Domerica, and I shiver slightly. Ryder, who has stayed close by my side, asks if I would like a jacket, but I just shake my head, totally absorbed in the sights surrounding me.

"Where are we?" I ask.

"This is a conveyance station, for transportation of the public. The people come to this station and are able to ride to their destinations on village conveyances." He points to a line of large, blue vehicles. They are bus-like but open, without doors or roofs.

"Horses are not necessary for most travel in Unicoi," he says. "They are very expensive to own and stables are scarce—they take up too much room. In fact, horses are not allowed in town at all. Catherine will send carriages for us, once I get word to her that we have arrived."

"How are the conveyances powered?" I ask, pretty sure they don't use gas and spew pollution.

"By *elohi* energy. That is how everything is powered in Unicoi. *Elohi* utilizes the earth's natural energy to provide a clean, inexhaustible source of power."

Although our arrival hasn't been formally announced, the crowd begins to take notice of us almost immediately. Glances and whispers quickly turn into shouts of "Prince Andrew" and "Princess Jaden" and "Welcome to Unicoi." More people gather on the platform to get a look at us. I wonder, uneasily, if it will hold us all. Alexander,

Makoda, and the four Domerican guards form a protective circle around us. Many from the crowd reach their arms through to shake Drew's hand or to touch me.

"Look, at her eyes. They *are* green!" Someone says loudly.

"I was concerned this might happen," Ryder speaks into my ear. "Our escort would have been waiting had Makoda gone ahead. We will seek refuge inside the office until Catherine is able to dispatch the carriages for us."

He takes my arm and our group slowly shuffles its way through the crowd into a small building. Ryder waves to the excited assembly, and I do my best to look pleasant and regal, but I'm a little freaked out by the clamoring sea of humanity.

A uniformed man at the door speaks anxiously, "Chief Ryder, this way." He waves us inside the station, locking the door behind us. "Please take shelter inside my office. Is someone coming for you or shall I lend you a conveyance?" he asks, showing us into a tiny office. It's too small to hold all of us, so Drew and his men wait in the hall outside the door.

"Thank you, Stationmaster. I must contact my sister," Ryder says. "She is sending transportation for us. May I use your transceiver?"

"Of course. It's there on the desk," he says, gesturing to a small, silver oval object. "I will keep things locked up until you're safely on your way to Sequoyah Hall."

Ryder thanks him and picks up the silver object. He punches some buttons on its face and holds it to his ear. "Yes, it's Ryder, where is Catherine?" he says into the device. "We are at the station."

"You have telephones?" I ask in amazement. Out of the corner of my eye, I see Ralston wince at my *faux pas*.

Ryder smiles and holds up his free hand in a *just a second* gesture.

I hear Catherine come on the line. In fact, I'm sure everyone in Unicoi hears her.

TRANSCENDER: First-Timer

"Why are you there already? Makoda was supposed to come ahead to let us know when to send the carriages," she roars.

"Catherine, I do not have the time to explain," Ryder says. "The word is spreading that we've arrived. Crowds are beginning to form in the area." He glances out the windows of the diminutive office. People are swarming the station. "Please dispatch the carriages as quickly as possible. We have five extra guests, so you'd better send three. Goodbye." He presses another button at the base of the device.

"They will be here shortly. Sequoyah Hall is only two miles away. As I feared, Catherine is furious," he says, holding out the silver device for me. I take it and turn it over in my hands. It's curved and fits perfectly in my palm. It's completely wireless.

"This is so sick!" I say, examining the sleek little device.

"It is?" His forehead wrinkles. He takes the device from me and inspects it. "No, that is the way it normally looks," he says handing it back to me.

"I just meant it's amazing!"

"Yes, it is quite a convenient method of communication. Your father has actually ordered a similar system from us to be installed at the Enclave."

"Really? I bet everybody will want to own one of these." I set it on the desk.

"When the carriages arrive, we will need to use the front entrance. But do not be frightened, love. The crowd only wishes to catch a glimpse of you. You and Andrew are the first royalty to visit in twenty-five years."

In a few minutes, the stationmaster reappears and announces that the carriages are waiting for us. Ryder holds out his arm for me. Our group shuffles through the narrow hall to the front entrance. Several Unicoi guards are positioned on either side of three brightly decorated, open air carriages. For a second I wonder where the horses are, but then I remember the carriages are motorized.

When Ryder and I step out of the station entrance, a thunderous roar goes up from the crowd. My knees feel a little wobbly, and I'm glad to have Ryder's arm to steady myself. We board the carriages and begin our procession down the main street. Despite being loud, the crowds are orderly, lining the sidewalk, cheering and waving at our motorcade.

The street is decked-out with hanging baskets of paper flowers and hundreds of colorful Unicoi flags. Ralston taught me that each square flag is divided into four different colored triangles—blue, white, red, and black, representing North, South, East, and West.

"What's that?" I ask catching sight of a never-ending line of bright yellow cars, crawling like a caterpillar up one side of the street and down the other. The cars are filled with people sitting or standing and holding onto railings.

Ryder smiles, "They are called *Mosies*—short for Mobile Seating Units. The Mosies run constantly, up and down the street. People may step on or off as they wish in order to get to their destination on Main Street. The system was installed when the ban on horses went into effect. They run all the way to Sequoyah Hall and back down to the conveyance station."

As our carriages approach the end of the street, I see a perfectly round, three-story structure with a dome roof and gigantic tree trunks instead of pillars circling the building. This must be Sequoyah Hall.

"Why is it round?" I ask Ryder.

"The circle has great symbolic meaning for the Cherokee culture. It represents the circle of life, reminding us that we are all connected. You will see many Cherokee symbols throughout Unicoi."

The motorized carriages turn left in front of the hall, and proceed to a small cobble-stone courtyard in back of the structure.

"Sequoyah Hall is really a public building," Ryder says. "The family wing and the guest quarters are accessed through a private entrance in the rear. Catherine should have everything prepared for you."

TRANSCENDER: *First-Timer*

We climb out of the carriages, and Ryder escorts us to a large wooden door with giant animal totems on either side. Catherine steps out to greet us, looking spectacular in a flowing lapis-colored silk dress and strand upon strand of colorful beads around her neck. Her hair is loose and shimmers down her back like black gold. She's flanked by two older men dressed casually in slacks and white shirts.

She smiles graciously. "Peace be with you. Welcome to Unicoi, and welcome to our home," she says, bowing slightly.

Ryder says, "Catherine, may I present our guests, Princess Jaden, whom you have previously met; and this is her brother Prince Andrew." Drew steps forward, a goofy grin on his face and a gleam in his eye. I can tell he's already crushing on Catherine. As she places her hand in his, I think I detect a little spark on her side also.

"You are previously acquainted with Professor Ralston," Ryder continues.

Catherine manages a curt nod in Ralston's direction. "These are two senior members of our tribal council," she says. "Chander Longshadow," she nods toward a very tall man on her right, "and Daniel Wallace," the man on her left.

Daniel Wallace! I can't believe it. The man on Catherine's left is my Connecticut best friend Liv's father. He looks different with his brown hair grown long and pulled back into a ponytail, but it's definitely him. I shake hands with both men. I'm thrilled to see Liv's father. Maybe it means that Liv is here also. I've missed her so much over the past weeks. At home we were practically attached at the hip. I'd give anything to see her.

"Allow me to show you to your rooms so you may freshen up if you like," Catherine says. "You are invited to join us and other members of our tribe for an informal buffet luncheon in the dining hall." She leads us inside.

My room, on the second floor of Sequoya Hall, is charming and cozy. Dark wood dominates the decor; from the exposed ceiling beams to the log bed and chest of drawers. The furnishings are colorful with Native American patterns woven into the fabrics of the bed coverings and draperies. Thick wool rugs cover the stone floor. A small round fireplace holding a pile of glowing rocks is positioned in the center of the room, with two chairs and a table arranged to one side.

I quickly change from my traveling clothes into a cream-colored dress with lace sleeves. There's no time to tackle my hair before lunch, so I tuck the fly-away strands back into my braid and put on a woven gold headband. I pull out the gown I've brought for the formal dinner this evening, and hang it on the bathroom door so the wrinkles will have time to fall out.

Drew knocks while I'm unpacking, and I call for him to let himself in.

"Can you believe this place?" he gushes, flopping down on my bed. "It's phenomenal! Did you see those yellow wagon-like things moving up and down the street? How do they do that?"

"Ryder says they're called Mosies. Pretty impressive, huh?"

"Hey, why didn't you tell me Blackthorn has a gorgeous sister?" Drew asks. He's changed into clean slacks and a jacket and his hair looks freshly disheveled.

"She's not very nice once you get to know her," I say. "She can have a real attitude sometimes."

Another knock on the door cuts our conversation short, and Ralston enters with Chander Longshadow. They've come to take us down to lunch.

When we reach the dining hall, twenty or thirty people are already milling around chatting or sampling food from the buffet. Catherine says Ryder is occupied with some matters for his father and will not be joining us for lunch. I'm disappointed, but there isn't time to dwell on it, because Catherine immediately begins introducing us around to the Unicoi dignitaries—all of whose names I immediately forget.

My eyes flit around the room looking for Daniel Wallace. I want to find out whether Liv is here. I spot him at the other end of the room in conversation with two men and a woman. I recognize the woman as Liv's mother, Claire. The conversation appears friendly, so I gather that Daniel and Claire Wallace are still married on this earth—unlike back home where they've been divorced for several years.

I quietly slip away from Catherine when her back is turned, and wander over near the Wallaces. Daniel greets me cordially, and introduces me to his wife and their two companions. Claire Wallace curtseys stiffly, looking me over with a clearly disapproving eye. Her frosty behavior baffles me. I wonder if I have something hanging from my nose. I sniff and swipe it with my hand.

One of the men asks me if my journey to Unicoi was agreeable. I smile and say it was. We make this kind of small talk for a few minutes, and when I have an opportunity I ask Mr. Wallace if any other family members are at Sequoyah Hall. I'm elated to hear that their eldest daughter, Olivia, will be at the dinner tonight.

"I'm looking forward to meeting her," I say to Claire Wallace.

"Yes, I imagine you are," she replies icily.

Again, I'm not sure what she means by this, but her unfriendly tone bothers me. Before I can say anything more, however, Catherine latches onto me again, and drags me off for further introductions.

When the luncheon finally comes to an end, I'm exhausted. Catherine, with uncharacteristic thoughtfulness, suggests I go to my room and rest before the evening's festivities. I thank her and take her up on the offer. On my way out of the dining hall, I overhear her invite Drew to take a short tour of the grounds with her. It seems she just wanted me out of the way for a time. He falls all over himself accepting her invitation, and I wonder if the Blackthorn siblings have this same effect on everyone they meet. Poor Drew. He has no idea what he's in for.

THIRTY-SIX

*T*he butterflies that have taken up permanent residence in my stomach lately flutter lightly as I dress for the evening. The gown I've chosen from Princess Jaden's closet is beyond fabulous. Most of her spectacular ball gowns, and the queen's, are kept in a special wardrobe room in the palace, but she saved this one and kept it in her own closet. I bet it was her favorite. The first time I saw it, I promised myself I would wear it at least once before I went home. It's strapless and form fitting, made of white satin with a top layer of translucent fabric. Hundreds of shimmering crystals cascade in diagonal lines to the floor-length hem and along the small train in back. I'm not sure I'll be able to walk in it, but if I fall flat on my butt, at least I'll look fabulous doing it.

Thankfully, Catherine sends a woman to help me with my hair. I'm a little chagrined at how easily I've gotten used to having servants, but I'm grateful for the assistance. It's going to be weird when I get back home and have to do everything for myself again. The dark-haired maid is profoundly reserved and totally business. Without a word, she tames my unruly river of hair in no time, and arranges it into a sleek chignon at the base of my neck. I packed a delicate platinum and diamond tiara from the princess's jewelry chest, which my taciturn stylist expertly anchors in my hair.

"Do you think I should wear earrings tonight?" I ask.

She studies me for a moment. "Your eyes are like emeralds. You need no other jewelry," she says softly.

TRANSCENDER: *First-Timer*

I thank her for her meticulous work, and she curtseys and departs as quietly as she arrived. I smooth my gown, straighten my shoulders, and check myself out in the mirror. Not too bad. I may not be as stunning as the Unicoi women, but this is about as good as it gets for Jaden Beckett.

Drew and Ralston come to collect me at exactly seven o'clock. Drew is unusually complimentary about my appearance, making me suspicious that my zipper is broken or something. He informs me that Catherine has arranged for us to meet with Chief Blackthorn in a private room before the formal ceremonies begin. This news instantly transforms my fluttering butterflies into a flock of doves that tries desperately to escape through my throat. I'm not sure I'm ready to meet Ryder's father.

A formal escort of two men in military-like regalia arrives to usher us to the room set up for our meeting with Chief Blackthorn. Drew follows them and Ralston takes my arm, gently urging me forward. "You look splendid, my dear," he says.

I manage a small "Thank you."

"Courage old girl. You are the crown princess of Domerica. You can do this," he whispers.

Our escorts stop at the threshold of a large, white double door. They ceremoniously open the doors and bow, waiting for us to enter. I paste on my best Cinderella smile, and Drew and I step inside the cool, softly lit room. The furnishings are grand without being pretentious and a vague camphor smell hangs in the air.

Catherine and Chief Blackthorn are waiting to greet us. Ryder is not here. Catherine wastes no time launching into the formal introductions.

"Father, this is Princess Jaden Beckett of Domerica. Princess, this is Chief Seneca Blackthorn of Unicoi," she says.

Chief Blackthorn is a large man with raven hair that matches Ryder's, and deep chestnut eyes set in a drawn, but enormously handsome face. He wears a traditional Cherokee Ribbon Shirt of black, loose-fitting fabric with red ribbons running horizontally across the yoke and vertically down each side.

I step to his wheelchair and shake his hand. "I am very pleased to meet you, sir. Thank you for hosting us tonight."

"Welcome to you and peace be with you, Princess Jaden," he says in a raspy voice. "It is I who should thank you for making the journey to our country. May I also express my apologies and those of the Unicoi people for the way in which you were previously treated by my son. I am humbled by your capacity for forgiveness."

I blink, groping for a response to his apology, but I'm saved from having to reply by Ryder's sudden appearance in the room.

"I am terribly sorry for being late," he says breathlessly. "Last minute details …"

I have to steady myself at the sight of him. He is dazzling! I expected him to be in traditional Cherokee dress like his father. Instead he wears a crisp white shirt, a black formal jacket and a red tie. His hair is smoothed back and tied with a black ribbon. He hurries to my side, taking my hand in his.

"It seems she is constantly having to forgive you for one thing or another, my son," Chief Blackthorn says lightly. "Now, I was just about to meet Prince Andrew." He turns in his chair to Drew.

"It is an honor to meet you, sir," Drew says, shaking the chief's hand. "Thank you for having us."

"Welcome and peace be with you, Prince Andrew."

Chief Blackthorn asks about our journey and our initial impressions of Unicoi. His gracious manner puts me at ease, and I'm able to answer his questions without sounding like a total idiot.

"I trust that Governor Beckett is well. I am sorry he was not able to accompany you tonight," Chief Blackthorn says. "Please give him my regards."

"We will, sir. Thank you," I say.

TRANSCENDER: *First-Timer*

"I understand Queen Eleanor is unaware of your visit to Unicoi," he says.

I cut my eyes to Drew, clearing my throat, and taking time to choose my words. "She is preoccupied with important matters of state at this time, so we didn't want to trouble her about our plans."

"I suspect she would not approve of your being here," he says hoarsely. "And while I do not condone deception where parents and children are concerned," he glances at Ryder, "I am comforted by the fact that your father approves of your decision to visit our country. I am grateful that you both have come."

"Thank you, sir," Drew and I say in unison.

"We have quite an evening planned. I hope you will enjoy yourselves. Forgive me if my health requires me to retire early tonight. I thank you again for being our guests at Sequoyah." Chief Blackthorn nods, and Catherine takes the handles of his chair, capably wheeling him out a back door.

Our two uniformed escorts lead the rest of us to the dining hall entrance. Drumbeats announce our arrival, and the crowd inside quiets. An orchestra strikes up the Domerican national anthem as we are ushered to a long table where Chief Blackthorn and Catherine are already seated. The table is positioned on a slightly raised dais. I am given the place of honor on Chief Blackthorn's right. Drew and Catherine are seated together on the left. Ryder takes the chair next to mine, as the final notes of the anthem are played.

With obvious effort, Chief Blackthorn stands and speaks in a wheezy voice. "I am honored to have two esteemed guests with us this evening in Sequoyah Hall, the Crown Princess Jaden Beckett of Domerica and her brother Prince Andrew. I hope you will join me in welcoming them."

A cheer goes up from the crowd, and everyone rises to their feet. I flush with embarrassment at the boisterous ovation. Drew takes it all in stride, though, like this stuff happens all the time—and I guess it does, to him. He's a natural-born celebrity.

Again, I'm stuck by the eclectic appearance of the dinner guests. Some wear traditional formal clothing, while others sport feathered headdresses, beaded buckskin clothing, and other Cherokee party attire. Many of the younger crowd are even kind of punked-out, with short dresses, leather jackets, and funky jewelry.

A loud chime sounds, and the guests take their seats at elaborately-set, long dining tables. The hall is round, and the tables are arranged in a circle around a stage that dominates the center of the room. A spherical fire pit in the center of the stage blazes dramatically with a real fire.

Ryder squeezes my hand under the table and leans in close. "I have never seen you look lovelier," he whispers. My face flushes again.

"Where's Ralston?" I ask.

"Catherine still considers him a traitor of sorts, so she has relegated him to a lesser table on the other side of the room. Do not be concerned for him, though, he is among friends and I am certain he will be well taken care of.

The first course of our meal is briskly served by waiters dressed in black uniforms. The lights grow dim, and the evening's entertainment is about to begin.

A group of young dancers files onto the stage. They position themselves around the fire pit. The boys are dressed in Cherokee ribbon shirts, similar to Chief Blackthorn's, and the girls wear colorful blouses and skirts. Around the girls' ankles are bracelets that rattle when they move. Ryder whispers to me that these are called *shakers* and that the children will perform a variation of a Cherokee stomp dance. Drums beat out a rhythm, and a singer calls out the moves, as the children dance in a circle around the fire. They are totally synchronized—not one misstep. It's obvious that hours of practice went into their preparation.

When the dance ends, the children proudly take their bows. A girl of about ten or eleven walks shyly to our table and says she has a gift for me. I rise and gingerly make my way around the table, praying I won't trip over my train. I carefully step down from the dais and go to her. She holds up a set of shakers for me. I take them and give her a small hug. The other children immediately flock around us. They're so adorable and friendly, I hug each of them and thank them for my new shakers.

I'm barely back in my seat when the second course is served. Since I didn't get a bite of the first course, I hungrily dig into the delicious looking roasted meat.

"This is very good," I remark to Ryder between mouthfuls.

"Yes, rabbit is one of my favorites also," he says.

Before I can come to grips with the fact that I've just eaten a bunny, a loud war whoop fills the air, sending chills down my spine.

The second group of performers emerges onto the platform. They are all men—large, shirtless, strapping young men wearing black and white war paint, loin cloths, and not much else. Each man brandishes a large, fierce-looking battle axe.

The men crouch low to the ground. Drum beats reverberate throughout the darkened hall, and the dance begins. It's terrifyingly beautiful to watch.

"This is a traditional war dance, *tey yo hi*," Ryder tells me. "That's Alexander on the right."

Their movements are enthralling and frightening at the same time. I can't take my eyes off of the magnificent bodies swaying, whooping, and swinging their axes in a threatening cadence. The performance is gripping, and when it finally ends it takes me a moment to catch my breath.

Alexander approaches our table and bows to me. "We would like to make a presentation to Princess Jaden."

Again, I trundle around the table trying not fall over my feet. Alexander holds out a hand to help me from the dais. As I place my hand in his, Alexander's head whips around, and his astonished eyes lock onto mine. At that instant I know that he knows I'm not

Princess Jaden. But how can it be?

Then it strikes me like a bolt from the blue: the white-blonde hair, the pale blue eyes, of course. "You're part Cleadian," I say, as he leads me to the stage.

"Yes. You know about the Cleadians?"

"I know *everything* about the Cleadians."

He nods and helps me onto the stage. His face is expressionless, and I'm panicked—afraid he'll expose me to Ryder.

One of the beautifully built young warriors presents me with a satin-lined, dark wooden box holding a ceremonial battle axe. The dinner guests applaud, and I manage to maintain my cool long enough to shake hands with each dancer and thank them for my gift.

Alexander helps me from the platform, his face still unreadable.

"I want you to know that I love Ryder Blackthorn," I say, cold dread flooding through my veins.

"I know that, and I hope that destiny smiles on you both." He bows and rejoins his brother warriors.

What in the hell is that supposed to mean?

Ryder takes the wooden box from me when I return to the table and helps me into my chair. The next dinner course has already been served—fish with some kind of corn preparation. It looks good, but I've lost my appetite.

Lilting Irish violin music begins to play as a new group of dancers enters the stage. The piece is a traditional Irish step dance, which is executed beautifully by the talented ensemble. The costumes are striking and the performers first-rate, but I'm still shaken by Alexander's new knowledge of me.

Based on what Ralston said, I'm ninety percent certain he won't out me to Ryder. There must be some Cleadian code that prevents him from doing that. The question is whether his loyalty to Ryder is enough to force him to break that code. That niggling ten percent of uncertainty is making me a little nuts.

"Is everything all right, love?" Ryder asks, searching my eyes.

"Yes." I smile, and focus my gaze on the dancers.

As with the other performances, a gift is presented to me following the dance. It's an exquisite, creamy white shawl of handmade lace.

"It's lovely. I'll wear it often." I tell the dance troop.

"Would you care to join us for a reel?" one woman asks.

"Not in this dress!" I say. The crowd erupts in laughter and applause.

I return to my seat and place the lace shawl beside my other gifts.

"Coward!" Ryder whispers. "I would have loved to see you dance an Irish jig in that dress."

"Walking in this thing is challenging enough. A jig is out of the question." I answer with a lightness I do not feel.

"Coffee and dessert will be served soon, love. Afterward, I will introduce you to some of my friends. Perhaps you will consent to dance with me?"

"I'd love to," I say, squeezing his hand.

Catherine wheels Chief Blackthorn's chair to us so he can say goodnight. He reaches for my hand and pats it warmly.

"Thank you for being so gracious tonight," he says. "You have lightened the spirit of an old man."

I smile and bid him goodnight.

As the dessert course is served, several workers bustle into the hall and douse the burning fire pit. They fold up the stage into a more compact size and carry it from the room, leaving a large, open dance floor. The orchestra begins to play, and dinner guests leave their tables to dance or mingle with others.

"When you are finished with dessert, let us join the crowd," Ryder says.

"Actually, I'm not very hungry. I'm ready whenever you are."

He takes my hand and leads me onto the floor. We're greeted by two smiling couples who are obviously friends of Ryder.

"Brother, introduce us to the princess," a good-looking young man with long dark curls and sparkling blue eyes says. He's dressed like a hipster—tight black pants, black shirt, black jacket and a couple of impressive tattoos.

He and Ryder shake hands by clasping the right forearm of the other.

"I was hoping to avoid introducing you to her altogether, Thomas," Ryder says. "But I suppose since you come attached to the lovely Nunda, it cannot be escaped." He turns to me, "Princess Jaden Beckett, these are my friends, Thomas and Nunda." Nunda wears a short olive-colored lace dress with a full skirt, fishnet stockings and a headpiece with a sheer, black veil that covers her forehead and eyes. They make a stunning couple.

"This is Atian and Deidre," he says motioning to the other couple. They too are dressed very hip—he all in black, like Thomas, and she in a short, strapless maroon dress with a black velvet sash.

I shake hands with each of them, and we exchange the usual pleasantries about the delicious meal and the amazing entertainment.

"Ryder," a soft female voice behind us says. I'm thrilled when I turn to see my best friend Liv with her hand on Ryder's arm. She looks sizzling hot in a sleek black gown with colorful beaded Cherokee symbols. Her silver-blonde hair is loose and shimmers around her perfect face.

"Good evening Olivia," Ryder says. "I am pleased to introduce Princess Jaden Beckett."

I beam at her. "Liv," I say and hold out my hand—though I really want to throw my arms around her and hug her tightly.

She curtseys deeply, leaving my hand hanging in the air. "Olivia," she corrects me coldly. Ouch! Her dislike for me is clear from her expression as well as her voice. She and her mother obviously have something against me.

She leans in close to Ryder and touches his arm again, "May I speak with you? Alone," she asks, gazing up at him.

"Of course. Please excuse me," he says to the rest of us. Liv links her arm through his, and they walk to a secluded area of the room.

Nunda says, "I know everyone must tell you this, but you have the most astonishing eyes I've ever seen."

"I only hear that in Unicoi," I tell her. "My eyes are very ordinary in Domerica."

"And your gown is so stunning," Deidre speaks for the first time. "Is it from Dome Noir? I think the most exceptional gowns come from Dome Noir."

"I believe it is. I love your dresses, too. They're very chic."

I catch sight of Ryder and Liv across the room, deep in conversation. Liv reaches up and touches Ryder's cheek with such abject tenderness that it hurts to watch. It's obvious she's madly in love with him. My heart constricts inside my chest, and I can hardly catch my breath. Ryder and Liv together? Only my worst nightmare—the man I love and my best friend.

Ryder gently removes her hand from his cheek. He shakes his head, saying something to her. He cuts his eyes to me and I quickly look away, embarrassed to be caught staring at them.

"Would you care to dance, Princess Jaden?" It's Thomas with the glittering eyes.

"Yes. Is that all right with you?" I ask Nunda.

"I would welcome it," she says. "Just send him back when you tire of him."

The orchestra is playing a Viennese waltz, and Thomas is a wonderful dancer. I have to concentrate hard on my steps, which causes me to lose track of Ryder and Liv. When the song ends, I glance over to the place where they stood, but they're gone.

This night is full of troubling surprises—Liv in love with Ryder, Alexander a Cleadian—what next?

The orchestra members noisily stand and file off stage, as something resembling a pop band moves in to replace them. Three guitarists, a piano player, and a whole slew of drummers carrying several different types of drums, take up positions on the platform. After tuning-up for a minute or two, they proceed to rock the place.

The music, with its eclectic collection of percussion instruments, is exotic and infectious. The beat vibrates throughout my entire body. It's like nothing I've ever heard or *felt* before. My friends back in Connecticut would go wild for this.

Atian asks me to dance and I say *yes*—even though I have no idea how to dance to this music. I try to follow his movements so I won't look like a geek on the dance floor, but he's kind of free-form-all-over-the-place, and everyone else is too, so I just let the music move me, and go with the flow.

When I finally see Ryder again, he's dancing with Deidre and enjoying himself. Liv is nowhere to be seen. Good! My dreams of a best girlfriend reunion have been replaced by a baser instinct—protecting what's mine. I'm able to breathe normally again, and I actually begin to have a little fun.

As the music ends, someone behind me calls my name. I spin around to find Alexander, Makoda, and a willowy dark-haired beauty, who I'm guessing may be Makoda's sister. Alexander's war paint has been washed away and he's wearing formal clothing similar to Ryder's, his white-blonde hair tied back with a ribbon. He's ethereally beautiful.

"Alexander, Makoda. Hello!" I say

TRANSCENDER: *First-Timer*

"Princess Jaden, this is my wife, Meli," Alexander says.

His wife! I still can't adjust to people being married so young. "Nice to meet you," I say, extending my hand.

"It is very good to meet you, Princess Jaden." She shakes my hand. "Alexander has told me many good things about you."

"That's very nice of him," I say. "Your husband is an impressive performer. His war dance took my breath away."

She smiles shyly. "My husband has many hidden talents."

The band segues into a slow and airy tune, and Meli turns to Makoda. "You haven't danced all evening, Mak. Come dance with me." He looks abashed, but reluctantly agrees. They leave Alexander and me alone.

"Alexander, I'm not sure what you saw when you took my hand, but I would appreciate it if you would not say anything to Ryder that might—"

He interrupts me. "You have nothing to fear from me, Princess. I have seen your heart, and I have seen his. They are the same. That you are a Transcender is no one's affair but your own."

Relief floods through me. "I'm not really a Transcender, but thank you for your discretion."

He smiles. "I do not believe I could be mistaken about such a thing. In any event, it is sometimes best to keep some mystery in a relationship. Meli does not know certain things about me—Cleadian things."

"I understand," I say, wondering how Meli would feel if she knew about *all* of her husband's hidden talents. I also wonder, uncomfortably, what Ryder would think if he knew the truth about me. Would it change his feelings for me?

Sensing someone at my elbow, I turn to see Ryder's handsome face.

"*Do not* ask her to dance," he says to Alexander. "I have not danced with Jaden all evening, and it's my turn." He pulls me into his arms just as the last few notes of the otherworldly music end. The singer for the band announces that the evening's festivities have come to a close.

"I knew this would happen," Ryder says. "We never got our dance."

"It's all right. Let's go somewhere and talk for awhile," I say.

"Unfortunately, I must take my father's place in saying farewell to our guests. But I will come to your room later to wish you goodnight, if you are not too tired."

"I'm great—wide awake. Just come up when you can."

I scan the hall for Drew, but can't find him—or Catherine for that matter. I noticed they danced nearly every dance together tonight. Catherine is at least three inches taller than Drew, but they didn't seem to care. By outward appearances, they were totally into each other.

Ralston materializes by my side. "Did you have a nice evening?" he asks.

"Yes, did you? I heard you were seated somewhere in Siberia. I hope it wasn't too awful."

"No, it was fine. Not much of a view of the entertainment, but the food was good and the company delightful. May I escort you to your room?"

"Yes, thanks."

We walk together to the guest wing.

"Rals, did you know Alexander is part Cleadian?" I ask.

He stops and gazes at me with wide eyes. "Oh my, I had forgotten. You danced with him?"

"No, but he touched my hand, so he knows. He told me he wouldn't say anything to Ryder, though, and I trust him. But it's strange, he called me a Transcender like that other dude did."

I catch a trace of anxiety in his eyes. "Yes, well, I imagine that is the only way they have of classifying you ... sensing that you are not from this world and all. Ah, here we are." He deposits me in front of my door and quickly departs without even saying goodnight. Weird.

THIRTY-SEVEN

I hoped Ralston would have tea with me while I wait for Ryder, but I'm grateful for the time alone to rest and regroup. Although I loved wearing the princess' stunning gown, I can't wait to take it off. It's not the most comfortable item of apparel the princess owns. I long for some sweatpants and a hoodie to throw on.

I rummage in my trunk for something comfortable and pull out a soft, white wool jumper. I slip it on and wrap my new lace shawl around my shoulders. I pull out the hairpins holding my tight chignon in place and brush my hair out straight. Much better. I replace the princess's tiara in its velvet bag, and pack it away, along with her lovely gown. Then I curl up in an armchair by the glowing rocks and wait for Ryder.

A small publication has been left on the table, and I scan the headlines. The front page features an article about my visit, which the reporter calls a "Mission of Mercy." I silently pray that's what it will turn out to be, and not a total disaster. Who knows what Mother will do when I return. It's a good thing she doesn't subscribe to the Unicoi Times.

Someone knocks softly on my door. I toss the paper aside and hurry to answer it. Ryder has changed from his evening finery into casual clothes—something similar to a T-shirt and jeans, only the jeans are made of softest leather. He steps inside, pulling me tightly to him, and kissing me with more abandon than he normally allows himself. My blood is immediately on fire, and I respond with equal passion. He lifts me in his arms.

"They loved you, Jade!" he says, "especially Father. The entire country is singing your praises." He carries me to the chair, and cradles me in his lap. I rest my head on his shoulder. He lightly fingers the wolf-head necklace I put on over my dress.

"I love it when you wear this. It reminds me of my mother."

"Your mother?"

"Yes, my father gave it to her on the day I was born. Father's people are from the *Ani Wahya* –the wolf clan. The wolf is a Cherokee symbol of protection. Mother never took it off as long as she was alive. She said she wore it to protect me always. When she died it passed to me. I told you it is very special."

I study his face a moment. "You guys don't turn into wolves or anything like that do you?"

He laughs. "What would give you such an odd idea?"

"No, no … it's nothing," I say sheepishly. "But seriously, you shouldn't have given it to me if it was a remembrance of your mother."

"Who better to have it? You have saved my life more times and in more ways than one."

I smile. "I take that responsibility very seriously. I'll wear it always, to protect you."

"Well, I hope you will wear it at least until you will agree to wear my ring."

My smile vanishes. "Wait. What are you saying?"

"Ah, Jade, I love you. I want you to be my wife …when you are ready. I promise myself to you. There will never be anyone else for me."

"Ryder, no. That's … I can't …"

He touches a fingertip to my lips. "I'm not asking for the same commitment from you. I know you cannot give it now. But, I also know my own heart, and whether you *ever* accept my ring, the fact remains that I will marry only if and when you will have me."

I gaze into his honest blue eyes and in that instant everything becomes crystal clear. I know beyond any doubt that this man is it for me—the big *IT*, the love of my life.

In that flash of utter clarity my future is revealed to me, as though written on the book of life: I will return home to Connecticut. Eventually I'll find someone else. I will marry, and possibly have children, and I will be relatively happy, because that is who I am. But inextricably entwined within this sudden revelation is the absolute certainty that I will *never* love like this again. I will never love anyone as passionately and wholeheartedly as I love Ryder Blackthorn.

"I ... I love you too, Ryder," I whisper. "I know I will never love anyone else the way I love you."

He tries to read my face. "And this makes you sad?"

"No, of course not. I guess I just realized it."

"Well, I have known it for a while." He brushes the back of his hand gently across my cheek. "I knew the night you helped me escape from Warrington Palace. When I kissed your hand and you stroked my hair. I felt it in your touch, so pure and sweet, Jade. I knew we were meant to be together.

"Do you honestly believe that?"

"With all my heart."

"Ryder, will you stay with me tonight?" I ask softly.

He cocks a questioning eyebrow.

"I didn't mean *that* way. We can stay right here on the chair all night, if you like. I just don't want to be alone. I'm homesick, I guess."

He tilts his head, his eyes probing mine.

"All right, I'm lying! I just want to be with you tonight. Stay. *Please*."

"Jade, don't ask me …."

"Why not?"

"For many reasons, love, the primary one being that it would be unseemly. It would damage your image. Everyone in Sequoyah Hall knows I am in your room."

"I don't care about my image."

"Yes, you do. And so do I. I wish to act honorably and above reproach where you are concerned—although I haven't always done so in the past. I want to be worthy of you, Jade. I will wait forever for you if I must."

He takes my chin in his hand, turning my face to his. "There is also the minor detail of your mother. She is going to be difficult enough to deal with without ugly gossip reaching her ears. Trust me on this. If she believes your trip here was about anything other than a fact finding mission, she will have my scalp."

I know he's right, but I want him with me. I don't know how much time we have left, but it's not much.

"I still have arrangements to tend to for tomorrow, love. We have a long day planned, and I am anxious that all goes well." He kisses the spot just below my ear.

"I am sorry I can't stay longer, but we will be together all day tomorrow." He smiles. "We've never had the luxury of an entire day together."

"That's true, but we're going to have lots of company, aren't we?" I crawl off of his lap.

He follows, wrapping his arms around me. "It doesn't matter. We'll be together."

I sigh deeply. "I guess you're right. That's really all that matters."

"Sleep well, love. I shall see you in the morning." He plants a brotherly kiss on the top of my head, and slips out my door.

I mope around for a few minutes looking for a distraction, wondering how people survive without TV. I miss my favorite shows sometimes, but only when I'm not with Ryder. Being with him is completely absorbing. It's becoming difficult to remember my life before Ryder, before the essence of him seeped into my heart and mind and silently became the driving force behind my every waking thought and action.

I wonder what I'll do when I have to face life without him again. When I wake up each morning with no hope of seeing his face or feeling his touch ever again. Will I always feel the empty longing for him? It hurts so much to think about it now with my senses still so full of him.

Another knock at my door interrupts my thoughts. My heart thrills at the possibility that Ryder has changed his mind. I rush to the door and fling it open to find Claire Wallace standing there, still decked out in her ball gown.

"Claire, uh, Mrs. Wallace," I sputter.

"Were you expecting someone else?" she asks, stepping into my room uninvited.

"Um, no."

"I wish to speak to you about a most urgent matter." Her powdered face is taut and her expression unpleasant.

"All right," I pull my shawl tightly around me. "What is it?"

"I wish to know your intentions regarding young Chief Blackthorn."

"I'm sorry, my what?"

"Your intentions!" she snaps. "Do you intend to marry him?"

"He … I … Well, I don't see how that's any of your business."

TRANSCENDER: *First-Timer*

She glowers at me. "What are you doing with that necklace?"

My hand flies to the delicate pendant. "Ryder gave it to me."

"That was my cousin's necklace."

"Yes, and now it is mine." I say, annoyed with this whole conversation. "Please just tell me why you're here. I'm exhausted and I have a long day tomorrow."

She looks me up and down, evaluating me with her hawk-like eyes. The Unicoi version of Mrs. Wallace is much more menacing than the one who lives next door to me in Madison. She could be a little standoffish at times, but this woman is downright scary.

"You do not understand what you are dealing with here, do you? Poor little fawn. How long have you known Ryder Blackthorn? A month? You know nothing about him." She paces restlessly across the room, her full skirts swishing across the floor.

"He is ruthless when it comes to Unicoi. He will stop at nothing to save his people. *You* more than anyone should know this. Or have you forgotten how you two met? Since he was unable to sway your mother on his own, he has tried to snare you in his scheme."

She stops in front of me. "What would you say if I told you Ryder is in love with my daughter, Olivia? That they have long had plans to marry? He did not disclose that to you, did he?"

"I don't believe you. He would have told me," I say evenly.

"Not if he wanted to keep you in the dark. Not if it did not suit his purposes. He and Olivia have been seeing each other for the past two years. Their engagement is soon to be publicly announced. He is only using you to fulfill his plan, and after that you will be discarded like yesterday's refuse."

"If you have such a low opinion of Ryder Blackthorn, why do you even care? You couldn't possibly want your daughter to marry that kind of a man."

"My daughter will be fine," she shoots back. "*She* is the one he really loves. It is only that I am sorry for you, Princess. I feel it is my duty to warn you about him, before things go too far. That's all."

"Oh really? That's it? Well, thanks for the warning. You can leave now," I walk to the door and open it.

Her eyes become small slits. "Take my advice, *you* leave Unicoi as quickly as possible. You are not safe here," she simpers.

I gape at her. "Excuse me? Is that some kind of a threat?"

"Take it as you wish," she says, and turns to leave.

"Whoa! Hold on a minute, bitch!"

She wheels on me, her face a freakish mask of indignation.

"Do you even know who you are talking to? I am The Crown Princess Jaden Beckett, future Queen of Domerica. You may not have any respect for me, but you'd better respect the title, lady! And you'd damn well better show some respect for the Blackthorns. You *owe* them that. You think you can just waltz into my room and accuse Ryder Blackthorn, the most decent honest man on this planet, of using me and lying to me? You obviously don't know what I'm capable of."

I get right up in her face, so close I can see the makeup caked in her wrinkles. "If you ever threaten me again or talk trash about any of the Blackthorns, I promise you I'll do everything in my power to take you down. I'll see to it that you are brought up on charges of treason, sedition, and threatening a member of the royal family!" I'm not sure that last one is actually a crime, but I throw it in anyway.

Claire Wallace's face turns purple with rage. Her eyeballs bulge so huge I'm afraid they may pop out and roll across the floor. She turns abruptly and storms out of my room.

I follow her into the hallway. "And another thing, lady, tell your daughter to keep her slimy hands off my man!" I shout at her retreating back.

THIRTY-EIGHT

I eat a light breakfast in my room. I'm not in the mood for company, and I sure as hell don't want to run into any of the Wallaces this morning. I spent a restless night mulling over how to ask Ryder about his relationship with Liv. I have to know if there is, or was, something between them. It shouldn't matter, but it does. Over the years Liv and I have shared our deepest hopes and fears, we've borrowed each other's clothes and make-up, and we've been closer than many sisters are. But Ryder Blackthorn is the *one* thing I'm not willing to share ... with anyone.

The tour today is planned to be on horseback, taking some smaller roads not fit for conveyance travel. By the time I arrive in the courtyard, nearly everyone is mounted and ready to go. Our party is large and includes several tribal elders and their wives. Chief Blackthorn isn't among the group. I've been told he's no longer able to ride a horse. Catherine is staying behind also, to attend to some tribal matters.

Several warriors with halyards bearing the Unicoi colors lead the procession through a cobblestone street on our way to the first stop, the warrior training camp. The street is bright and theatrically lit. Many townspeople line the road to wave or gawk at our little pageant. Ryder and I ride side by side near the front of the group. He looks refreshed and in high spirits.

"Did you sleep well, Jade?" he asks, as we make our way slowly through the densely crowded street.

"I was a little restless," I admit. "I had a troubling visitor after you left last night."

"Oh? Who?"

"Claire Wallace. She warned me away from you."

He grins. "She did? What did she say?'

"She said you and Olivia are in love and have plans to marry." I watch him closely, but his expression doesn't change.

"Claire is my mother's cousin. It is her fond desire that her daughter and I marry one day. My feelings for the girl have never been more than mere kinship, though."

"I believe her feelings for you may be a bit stronger. I've seen the way she looks at you."

"How does she look at me?" he says, still smiling.

"Well, not lustfully like Erica does, but more longingly, like she loves you."

"If that is so, it is her misfortune, because only one woman will ever have me. I told you that, Jade. I've asked you to be my wife."

"Claire also said you were just using me to get what you want from my mother, and that you will stop at nothing."

He pulls up on his horse's reins, bringing the entire procession to a halt. The smile has vanished from his face. "And you believe that?"

"No, Ryder honestly, I don't. The problem is, I think she really does."

He slides off his giant gray and lifts me from Gabriel's back. He takes my hand, leading me to a small clearing near the side of the road. Sensing an unfolding drama, the crowd immediately parts and gives us a wide berth.

Ryder takes my face in his hands. "Do you trust me, love?" he asks quietly.

TRANSCENDER: First-Timer

"Of course, but what—?"

"Listen to me. Certain people here, in Domerica, and elsewhere will believe it in their best interest to try to keep us apart. We cannot allow those people to touch our feelings for each other. Do you understand that?"

"Yes, but—"

"Good."

He leans down and presses his mouth to mine, kissing me sweetly at first then pulling me tightly to him and kissing me in a way that clearly communicates to any observer that he means business. He releases me after a moment and turns to our captivated audience. "I love this woman!" he says loudly.

The crowd erupts in appreciative applause.

Hot blood floods my cheeks from equal parts embarrassment, anger and, well, passion.

"What was that?" I hiss, as we walk to our horses, the crowd tittering around us.

"In Unicoi, we call that a public display of affection," he says. His smile has fully returned.

"Oh, yeah, well what about my *image* you were so concerned about protecting last night?"

"It is more important that the people of my country know the nature of my feelings for you. I do apologize if it made you uncomfortable."

"Did you really have to be so … *demonstrative?*"

"Yes," he says, glancing back over his shoulder. A lone horse and rider break away from our group and speed toward the palace. I recognize Claire Wallace's back as she makes her swift retreat.

We reach our destination within the hour. The Unicoi warrior training grounds are made up of an old fortress-like building, a large barracks, and a vast training ground. It's the only open field I've seen since arriving in Unicoi. We're told we'll be given a guided tour of the training facilities, after which we will be treated to a small demonstration by the trainees.

The camp commander, Simon Greystone, a trim man with salt and pepper hair, conducts our tour. Drew hangs on his every word as he guides us through the facility, describing the rigorous training process. Greystone tells us the camp houses all current warriors in training, around two thousand young men and women. He explains that upon reaching the age of fifteen, every Unicoi boy or girl has the opportunity to be instructed as a warrior. It's not mandatory, but any boy or girl who successfully completes the program becomes eligible for a variety of tribal jobs, so most young people choose to participate.

"Why do you train warriors when there are no wars?" Drew asks. "I mean, the world has been at peace for three hundred years."

"It is a deeply ingrained part of our culture," Commander Greystone says. "It is always better to be prepared than to be sorry later. Our trainees receive instruction in hand to hand combat, swordsmanship, archery, marksmanship, and more."

"You use firearms?" Drew asks.

"Yes. We have a firing range in the corner of the grounds." He points to a steel framed structure.

"May I give it a try?"

The commander looks to Ryder, who nods his approval.

"I'll get you set up," Greystone says. He and Drew break away from our group and head to the firing range.

Ryder takes over as guide for the last leg of our tour. He trained at this camp a few years earlier and is familiar with the camp's lay-out and procedures. He shares some stories of his two years as a warrior-in-training. Although he's modest about his accomplishments, when we view the display of trophies, awards, and record holders for the camp, I notice that Ryder's name appears on a number of them.

TRANSCENDER: First-Timer

Drew catches up with us again as we are being seated in the reviewing stands to watch the demonstration. He's flushed and smiling, clearly exhilarated by his experience on the shooting range.

"Jade, you should have come with me," he says. "It was the most thrilling experience ever. They have a target of a man and I shot a hole right through his heart. You would have loved it!"

"Guns aren't really my thing, Drew," I say dryly. "And shooting someone through the heart isn't a skill I'm anxious to acquire."

He shrugs. "Oh right, I forgot. You'd rather just kick their heads off."

Ouch! I flinch at the bitingly accurate zinger.

The demonstration by the young warriors is impressively choreographed. Their uniforms are colorful and kind of funky. Instead of being designed to blend in with rocks and trees, like standard cammo, they're printed with slashes of colored war-paint. Ryder tells us the different colors represent the specialty of each warrior: black for hand-to-hand combat, red for swordsmanship, green for archery, and so on. The trainees are surprisingly skilled for being so young. It's amazing to think that nearly every Unicoi citizen has received this type of instruction.

We eat a small lunch of meat and vegetables at the camp before moving on to our next destination. I skip the meat portion, afraid it may be bunny rabbit again. Some members of our party depart right after lunch, but more than a dozen of us travel on to the agricultural district.

As we ride, I'm constantly amazed by the fact that every square inch of Unicoi is utilized for something. Every structure, scrap of land, and patch of flat surface is employed for one or more purposes. The crushing scarcity of space explains Ryder's awe at the lushness of the Domerican countryside and Catherine's hostility at seeing so much unused land.

A short distance outside the agricultural district, we stop and leave our horses at a public stable. We travel the last quarter mile on foot. The agricultural district consists of metal warehouse-like structures, several stories high, and packed closely together. We're told these structures are utilized for growing vegetables and fruit, and housing fish farms and livestock.

We enter one of the growing houses, and Ryder directs our attention upward. From our vantage point on the ground floor we can see five levels of growing space. Thousands of tomato plants are suspended seemingly in midair. Their exposed roots are being sprayed by automated watering machines. Workers in overalls tend to the plants, picking the ripened fruit and removing the dead leaves.

The growing house manager greets us cordially and offers us a short tour. We use an elevator to reach the upper floors. Our guide tells us that the crops are grown hydroponically—meaning no soil is needed—only the nutrient-enriched water continuously distributed by machine. Special lights are used to accelerate the growth cycle and shorten the time to crop maturity. The result is that five times the amount of tomatoes or zucchini or whatever can be grown in a one acre building as on one acre of land. It strikes me as pretty advanced technology for this planet.

The fish farms are every bit as amazing as the growing houses. Enormous clear tanks holding millions of fish line the walls of the multi-leveled structures. The temperature inside is very warm and the smell is far from pleasant, but it's like visiting a huge aquarium. The fish are fascinating to watch. Schools of rainbow trout, salmon, and steelhead make endless circuits round and round the tanks. Ryder tells us the fish waste is captured and used to enrich the water in the hydroponic growing houses, and that much of the fish food comes from the vegetable waste. It's an ingeniously efficient way to feed a lot of people using only a small amount of land.

By the time we finish touring the growing houses and fish farms it's late afternoon. I'm rapidly reaching information overload, and Drew's looking a little glazed. Ryder suggests we skip the livestock houses and go directly to Keowe Hospital, the last stop on our schedule. I readily agree since I know the only livestock in Unicoi consists of rabbits and domesticated deer. I'm not thrilled with the idea of eating either Thumper or Bambi.

The hospital won't allow our entire group to tour the facilities at once, so Ryder, Drew, Ralston, and I make the short journey alone. We're met at the entrance to the enormous white building by Dr. McAfee, a jovial man whose looks match his Irish name. He's shorter than most Unicoi at an even six feet. He has a ruddy complexion, a thick shock of strawberry blonde hair, and dark blue eyes surrounded by multiple layers of laugh lines.

"I'm so happy to meet you, Princess Jaden," he says shaking my hand heartily. "I've heard so much about you, mostly from your father. I am a great admirer of Dr. Beckett."

He gives Drew an equally warm welcome, and greets Ralston as an old friend. "Constantine, I've missed seeing you these past weeks. I miss our late night discussions over that delicious chamomile tea of yours."

Hospitals all look alike to me, and Keowe Hospital is no exception. It is clean and bright and, even though colorful paintings hang on the walls, it is still unmistakably a hospital, complete with white walls, linoleum floors and the strong odor of disinfectant.

Dr. McAfee rubs his hands together eagerly. "Well now, Ryder, where shall we begin?"

"Our major purpose in being here is to see the Uranium sickness patients. Later I would like Princess Jaden and Prince Andrew to see our research findings on the disease," Ryder tells him.

"Well, that should be easy," Dr. McAfee says, "since the majority of our patients are suffering directly or indirectly from Uranium poisoning. Shall we start with adult wing?" He leads us down a long corridor. As we walk, Dr. McAfee explains a little about the disease.

"Uranium is a metallic chemical element that occurs naturally in rock and soil. About fifty years ago, a Unicoi expansion project uncovered a major deposit of Uranium. At the time we were completely ignorant of the dangers and built housing, agricultural, and manufacturing facilities on the site. It wasn't until years later, when residents and workers in these areas began to fall ill at an alarming rate, that we realized we had a major problem. By that time,

I'm afraid it had spread throughout the country."

"Exactly what is the problem with Uranium?" I ask.

"It is a highly toxic metal. If it gets into the soil and water, it can be ingested by humans and build up in the body. Over time it can affect normal functioning of the kidneys, liver, brain, and heart. Although it may not become symptomatic for years."

"My mother was a patient here after being diagnosed with renal failure," Ryder says. "We took her home when it was clear all hope was gone."

"Yes, Caitlin Blackthorn was a great lady and her loss was felt by us all," Dr. McAfee says. "Unfortunately Chief Blackthorn is now suffering from the effects of radon gas—the gas released as Uranium decays. We have found cancer in his lungs."

Ryder's mood has turned somber. The stark reality is that his mother has already died from the disease, and little hope remains for his father. It's likely that in time he and Catherine will be affected also.

Dr. McAfee stops in front of a set of double doors. "We have many wards of people who are sick and dying from the Uranium poisoning. I've chosen this one because the patients here have a variety of different heath issues, all relating in one form or another to Uranium. I warn you that some are very ill and it may be difficult for you to see, but they will all be delighted to make your acquaintance." Dr. McAfee opens the door and we follow him inside.

I'm completely unprepared for the dire sight that meets my eyes. The ward is roughly the size of a large ballroom, and is filled to overflowing with row upon row of cots, each one holding a seriously ill patient. Doctors, nurses, and other hospital personnel scurry among the rows attempting to care for thousands of patients. Uranium poisoning has obviously hit epidemic proportions in Unicoi.

I hear Drew's sharp intake of breath behind me. He puts a hand on my shoulder. "This is unbelievable," he mutters. "I had no idea things were this bad. Is there nothing that can be done?"

TRANSCENDER: *First-Timer*

"As you will see later, even with all of our research and the clinical trials we have run, we have found no medicine to even slow down the progress of the disease, let alone cure it," Dr. McAfee says. "The air purification and water filtration systems we have put into place have improved matters, but have failed to return the air and water to safe levels. There is simply too much of the stuff."

"But why don't you just tear down all the buildings in the expansion and cover the whole thing back up again?" Drew asks. "Won't that stop the spread?"

Dr. McAfee shakes his head with a frown. "We've done that to the extent we can, but it's not that easy. You see, the contaminated earth, rock, and ore extracted from the mountain were transported to various parts of the country and used as building materials. That is why the problem has become so wide-spread.

"In addition, Prince Andrew, the sad truth is that we are simply out of room. Too many people would be left homeless. We've no place to put them. Unicoi cannot expand in any other direction. It's quite a predicament. If we don't get out of this mountain we will all die."

Drew gazes out over the sea of sick and dying humanity, while Dr. McAfee's ominous prediction sinks in. His face is ashen, and I'm afraid he's going to faint.

"Drew, are you all right?" I ask, taking his arm. "Do you need to sit down?"

He shakes his head slowly. "I'm sorry, but I don't think I can look these people in the eyes. Our mother and the other dome rulers have known about this for years and have done nothing. They've done nothing ..." he trails off, a tear slipping down his cheek.

Ralston steps to Drew's side. "Why don't I take Prince Andrew over to the research building? The walk will do us both good, and we can get a head start on reviewing all of the information."

"That's an excellent idea," Dr. McAfee says. "Just ask for Dr. Reed. She is our most knowledgeable epidemiologist and will assist

He turns to Ryder and me. "Come along. I'll introduce you to some of our patients."

We move slowly down the rows of cots greeting patients, shaking hands with those who are able. Some of them appear excited to see us, others are too ill to care. Family members are allowed to pay short bedside visits, and some are present in the ward. Children hold the hands of their dying mothers. Husband and wives soothe and comfort their ailing spouses. I have to choke back tears at many of the more heartbreaking bedsides.

I'm glad to have the opportunity to look into the faces of these brave souls—the casualties of a world looking the other way. I know now what I have to do. I silently vow that I will make Mother listen.

When we finally leave the ward, Dr. McAfee asks quietly, "Would you care to see the children's ward, Princess?"

I bite my lower lip. I'm mentally and emotionally drained, and I'm pretty sure I won't be able to control my tears if faced with a room full of dying children. "Would you think I was a total coward if I said no?"

"Of course not, child. You are already a hero for doing what no other royal has had the courage to do. You've come here to see things with your own eyes, and I commend you for it."

I thank Dr. McAfee with relief. I've already seen enough to leave an impression on me that will last a lifetime.

Ryder and I say our goodbyes to the doctor and set out for the Research Building to find Drew and Ralston.

Outside, the lighting has dimmed to a soft yellow-gray—twilight in Unicoi. Neither of us speaks as we hold hands and walk to the research center. Drew and Ralston are coming out of the building at the same time we arrive. Drew's carrying a large file stuffed with papers, and I'm relieved to see some color back in his face. He appears to have recovered himself.

TRANSCENDER: *First-Timer*

"Jade, I went through everything with their scientists," he says, patting the file. "I have all the information right here. No one can seriously claim this disease is communicable in light of these findings. I know we can convince Mother to take some immediate action, even if King Philippe and King Rafael refuse to do so."

I smile at his enthusiasm. "I hope you're right big brother. And I'm glad that both of us will be doing the convincing, instead of just me." I turn to Ryder, "This has been an incredible day. Very eye-opening. Thanks for arranging it for us."

"It has been my great honor to show you my country, Ryder says. "But we have one more stop before returning to Sequoyah Hall."

"Where?" I ask, trying not to groan out loud.

"Let's find a place to eat. I'm starving!" he says.

"Sounds good to me!"

Drew and Ralston wholeheartedly agree.

THIRTY-NINE

We stop at a local eating establishment along the road home. The restaurant is jam-packed, just like the rest of Unicoi. We receive more than a few shocked glances from the patrons as we shuffle through the door. A woman in a long black dress with a thick rope of pearls and flaming red hair rushes to greet us.

"Peace, Chief Blackthorn, welcome," she says bowing slightly. "We weren't expecting you tonight. May I seat you and your guests?"

Ryder smiles at the woman. "Peace, Judith. I am sorry to arrive unannounced, but we are hungry and thirsty. I wonder if you have a private room available where we may dine quietly." He glances around the main room and nods to the patrons, acknowledging the curious stares we're receiving.

"Yes. Yes, we do," she says. "Please follow me." She leads us down a short hallway and opens a wooden door revealing a small room with a table for six. It's chilly inside and smells musty and unused, but it is private and I'm thankful for that.

"Let me turn on the fire." She hurries to a small fireplace on one side of the room and activates the glowing stones inside. The room instantly becomes cozier. "Please make yourselves comfortable. We'll have everything readied for you straight away."

The efficient restaurant staff bustles around the room, setting our table, filling our water glasses, turning on additional lamps.

TRANSCENDER: *First-Timer*

While these preparations are taking place, I hover near the fireplace warming my hands over the stones. Ryder orders food from Judith, and she hustles her staff from the room closing the door behind them. Ralston and Drew sit at the table and continue a conversation they've been having about the Uranium research.

Ryder holds out an empty chair for me. "Are you ready to sit, love?"

Before I can join him, though, the door opens again, and a young man appears in the shadow of the door frame. He's tall and handsome with dark hair and translucent, sea-grass-colored eyes. He stares at me curiously for a moment and nods.

"I'm sorry, wrong room," he says, quietly reclosing the door.

Something about him is familiar, but I can't place him. "Do you know that man?" I ask Ryder.

"I'm sorry, love, I did not see him? Why?"

"I don't know. I think I've met him before. Maybe in Domerica. Did either of you see him?" I ask Drew and Ralston. They both shake their heads. I open the door again, but the man is gone.

"You and your people are the only visitors presently inside Unicoi," Ryder says. "I would've been informed otherwise."

"But he has green eyes. He can't be Unicoi," I say.

"Are you certain, Jade?" Ryder asks. "It may have been a trick of the light."

"Could be. I am tired," I say, but I know what I saw, and I'm sure I've seen him before.

"Would you like me to go find him?"

"No. No, it's not important. I'm hungry, let's eat."

The food is hot and delicious. We pass the time chatting about all the wondrous and terrible things we've seen throughout the day. Drew's newfound zeal over the plight of the Unicoi people is heartening, but he insists on going over the research findings ad nauseam, and he presses me for an opinion on the best way to approach Mother.

I tell him I need to think about it, but I wish he would just give it a rest. It's our last night in Unicoi, and all I really want is some quiet time alone with Ryder.

~ ~ ~ ~

On our arrival back at Sequoyah Hall, we're met by Makoda and another Unicoi warrior. They've been waiting for us to return.

"Ryder, peace." Makoda says. Ryder slides off of his horse, and they clasp each other's forearm.

"There was a skirmish at the east entrance this evening," Makoda tells him. "A band of intruders attempted to break in. Two men were killed."

"Two of our men?" Ryder asks in alarm.

"No, two of theirs. We think they may have been Outlanders, but it was impossible to tell. We have no idea what they were after."

"Thank you, Makoda. Have reinforcements been sent to the east entrance?"

"Yes. Alexander went down to inspect it himself. He says to tell you not to worry. He has everything under control."

Ryder nods. "I am certain he does. I'll need to speak with him upon his return." He turns to Drew and me. "Let us take your horses. Makoda and I will see that they are cared for tonight."

"Ryder, is everything all right?" I ask. "Could this have something to do with our visit?" It occurs to me that Mother may have discovered where we are and sent a rescue team for us.

"This happens on occasion. I do not believe it relates to your visit. If your mother knew you were here, I'm certain she would have sent the entire Domerican army to Unicoi," he says reading my thoughts.

TRANSCENDER: *First-Timer*

Drew turns over Glacier's reins to Ryder and Makoda takes Gabriel.

"May I come up and say goodnight, later?" Ryder asks me.

"Yes. I'll be disappointed if you don't."

He kisses my cheek, and Drew and I trudge off to our rooms.

I peel off my dirty, sticky riding clothes and run a hot bath. I soak for a few minutes, relaxing both body and mind. It's been another extraordinary day for a high-school girl from Connecticut.

I slip into one of my silky under-dresses and pull a soft white sweater over the top. The outfit is a little unconventional, but comfort is the main goal tonight, and nobody but Ryder is going to see me anyway.

When he arrives at my door, Ryder has changed into a light blue shirt and doeskin jeans. In one hand he holds a small black box with buttons on the face.

"What's that?" I ask.

"A surprise!" He sets the black box on a table and pushes one of the buttons.

To my amazement music begins to play. "Wow! What is that thing?"

"It's a music machine. Only a few are currently in existence, but we are building more. Isn't it remarkable?"

"It is. I like this music! It's a lot like rock 'n roll." The music is full of energy with a driving beat, due mostly to the Cherokee tom-toms which can be heard above all the other instruments. I laugh and perform a little dance for him, my body moving rhythmically to the music.

"Is that a traditional Domerican dance?" he asks when the music ends.

"It's more like the funky chicken meets Jade Beckett," I tell him.

"Very nice. Rock and roll you call it?"

"Yes, very popular where I come from. But do you have anything slow in there that you and I can dance to? We never did get our dance."

He pushes another button, and a soft sexy song wafts from the tiny box. He holds out his arms for me, and I melt into him, dancing slowly, coaxing his body to respond to mine. I close my eyes, clearing my mind and allowing all my senses to be focused only on Ryder—his scent, his strength, the gentle current that connects us whenever we touch.

I reach up and pull the leather tie out of his hair, letting it fall loosely across his shoulders. I run my fingers through his silken mane.

"What are you doing?" He smiles down at me.

"I love the feel of your hair. I like the way it tumbles around our faces when you kiss me."

He leans down and places a whisper-soft kiss on my lips. I feel its effects all the way down to my toes. Hot blood floods through me. I tug off my sweater and toss it on a chair—one less layer of fabric between us. Our bodies sway sensuously together, in time to the music. I move my hand to the front of his shirt, and begin to unfasten his buttons one by one.

"Now what are you doing?"

"I want to feel your skin against mine." He doesn't stop me. When I finish with the buttons, I pull his shirt open and wrap my bare arms around him, caressing the smooth skin of his back. Pressing my cheek against his chest, I find his heart pounding as wildly as my own.

I reach up and circle his neck with my arms. "Lift me up." I say softly. He lifts me into a kiss, and my legs twine around him. My breath is ragged now, and I'm feeling lightheaded.

"Jade," he whispers hoarsely. "I have never desired anyone the way I desire you. You are my obsession."

"And you are mine," I say. I run my tongue lightly along his lower lip.

He moans softly.

"Ryder, I want you now," I say, placing my mouth near his ear. "Don't tell me no. You promised yourself to me. I need you now."

His heavy-lidded eyes stare steadfastly into mine. "I am powerless to refuse you."

He carries me to the bed, gently laying me on top of the coverlet. He slides languidly out of his shirt, and I tremble at the sight of him. The air between us quivers with magnetic tension. We reach for one another, crashing together in unrestrained passion.

I drown in the intensity of him. His taste, his strength, and the urgency of his touch. Yes. This is what I've waited for. "Yes," I whisper softly.

A loud, insistent pounding erupts at my door.

"Ryder, open up! It's Catherine."

Ryder pulls his lips from mine. "Not now, Catherine. Go away!" he shouts.

"Open this door *now*! Father wants to see you," she calls.

Ryder looks up at the ceiling and shakes his head. "I don't believe it," he says.

The pounding resumes.

He climbs slowly from the bed, cursing under his breath. He rakes a hand through his hair. "I am so sorry," he says. "I'll be right back."

I slide off the bed and follow him.

He flings open the door. "What do you want, Catherine?"

She stares at him in his shirtless, disheveled state. Glancing into the room, she sees me standing barefoot in my slip.

"Well," she says folding her arms over her chest. "It looks as if you two have been busy cultivating diplomatic relations. Sorry to interrupt your little tryst, but Father wants to see you, now."

"Why? What's this about?" Ryder asks.

"Claire Wallace is in Father's quarters. She is positively apoplectic, ranting about you and Olivia. You'd better hurry; things were turning rather ugly when I left."

"Oh, all right," he sighs.

"And for God's sake put on a shirt," she calls over her shoulder.

He turns to me, anxiety marring his handsome features.

"Go," I tell him. "You don't want to upset your father."

"I'm so sorry Jade." He takes my hands in his. "I promise I will come back as soon as I can."

"I'll be waiting."

I help him into his shirt. He buttons it and tucks it into his jeans.

"Here, you might need this," I say, holding out the tie for his hair.

"Thanks." He smoothes his hair back and skillfully ties it in place. "I'll return soon."

"Good luck!" I call after him.

FORTY

After more than an hour, there's still no sign of Ryder. I've seen Clair Wallace in action, so I know she can create quite a scene. When he finally walks through my door at midnight, though, he's smiling.

"I'm sorry I had to leave you, love. The timing couldn't have been worse. Are you all right?" he says.

"Yes, I've been anxious about you though. What happened?"

We sit in the chairs next to the fireplace. "Claire went to see my father. She demanded that I declare my intentions regarding Olivia immediately. She claims I have led Olivia to believe we have a future together, and I have *trifled with her affections*, to use her words."

"Have you?"

"No, Jade! I've never discussed a future with her. I've never even kissed the girl. I treat her with the same polite courtesy with which I treat all the other girls in Unicoi."

"So, what did you tell your father?"

"I told him I would be happy to declare my intentions toward Olivia. I have no intention of marrying her—ever." He reaches for my hand. "I told him I love you, and I have promised myself to you. I said that I've asked you to be my wife, and that if you will not have me, I shall never wed."

"You told him that?" I ask, crawling over to join him in his chair. "What did he say?"

"He asked whether you feel the same about me and whether we have plans to marry. I said that I believe you feel the same, but that you do not intend to marry for another decade or two." A smile plays at his lips.

"You did not! Did you really say that?"

"Yes. That is what you told me, isn't it?"

"Oh, hell. I might have said something like that. So how did he react?"

Ryder smiles and smoothes my hair with his hand. "Father said he respects my decision, and will happily welcome you to our family when you feel the time is right. He also said he will pray to the gods and the spirits of our ancestors that your mother will not have me executed before we can be together … or something to that effect."

I bury my face in his shirt. "Your father must think I'm an idiot. Is he really all right with this—you and me together?"

He holds me tightly. "Yes. I told you, they all fell in love with you last night."

"Not *all*," I correct him. "Catherine still hates me."

"She doesn't hate you, Jade. She just doesn't know you, that's all. She's afraid you are going to hurt me."

"Hurt you? How?" I look up at him, concerned.

His eyes are gentle. "She thinks you will make me fall helplessly in love with you, and then you will leave me."

My heart drops into my stomach at his words. Catherine is right. That's exactly what I'm doing. I cover my face with my hands and silent tears leak through my fingers.

"Jade, what is it?"

I keep my face hidden from him and continue to cry.

He strokes my hair. "Shhh, Catherine will come around. Don't worry about what she thinks." He rocks me gently in his arms.

After a moment I'm able to look at him again. "Ryder, you know I love you?"

"Yes. I know."

"You know I would never deliberately hurt you?"

"Yes. Of course." He softly brushes the tears from my cheeks. "What is this all about?"

"Tomorrow is our last day together," I sniffle, knowing that it may be the last time I'll ever see him.

"Is that what is making you so unhappy?" he asks, relief in his voice. "It's only for a short time, love. I have to be back here for the Council meeting tomorrow night, but we will be together again soon, at the lake, or the Enclave, or I will come to the palace. I'll find a way to be with you, I promise."

"I just hate to be away from you, even for a short time." I touch his face, my fingertips tracing the outline of his lips. He bends to kiss me, and my heart is instantly flooded with longing and desire. "Ryder, stay with me tonight. In my bed. Stay with me all night."

He holds me to him. "Oh God, Jade, it's what I want more than anything on earth. But, I cannot."

"Why not?" I ask, searching his eyes. "You were prepared to stay before Catherine came for you."

"It's my father. As I was leaving him this evening, he cautioned me not to make you pregnant in order to persuade you to marry me sooner, or as a means to get your mother to consent to our union."

"But—"

"He's right, Jade. That would not be the right way for us to begin our life together."

I stare up at the ceiling and sigh. "All right, I agree. I don't want to get pregnant. But don't the Unicoi have any form of birth control?"

"Of course," he smiles. "I don't happen to have any with me, however. I did not expect to have a need for it."

"Oh hell," I say, defeated. "In that case, will you just stay with me for awhile, here in the chair? I promise I will not try to seduce you. Please?"

"Yes, I'll stay as long as you like." He kicks off his moccasins and pulls my shawl from the back of the chair, wrapping it around me. "Try to rest, love. We have another early morning tomorrow."

I snuggle into his chest, allowing his comforting warmth and familiar scent to seep deeply into every pore of my body, to be stored and remembered in the months and years ahead. I wonder if there will ever be a time when I stop thinking of him, longing for him. I push the overwhelming sorrow into a small corner of my heart, knowing I will have to confront it sometime very soon.

~ ~ ~ ~

I don't know how long Ryder holds me before I fall asleep. I awake in my bed in the light of early dawn, covers pulled closely around me. A note from Ryder is propped against my pillow. *Sleep peacefully, love. Though I had to leave, my heart is here with you. Always, Ryder.*

With a heavy sadness I pack my clothes and other belongings back into my trunk. Thankful I've witnessed first-hand the plight of the Unicoi, I'm determined to convince my mother to help them. It's a matter of life and death for the Unicoi people, a matter of honor for me.

I bathe quickly and change into my traveling clothes, tucking Ryder's note into my pocket. The dining hall is already alive with activity. Drew and his men are noisily eating breakfast. Ryder is not in the hall with the others, so I grab a pommera and quietly duck outside to find him.

I spot him in the courtyard helping with preparations for our departure. Watching him from the top of the steps, I memorize his every move. His hair is laced back and the fabric of his shirt strains over his powerful shoulders as he works to saddle Tenasi, his efficient hands fastening cinches, straightening stirrups, and patting the great beast on the head. All vibrancy and laughter, he banters with the men as they pack saddlebags and ready the other horses. For the thousandth time I marvel at how amazing it is that he loves *me*.

He smiles up at me and waves, striding to the stairs. "We're nearly ready to go. Did you sleep well?"

"Yes. Thank you for tucking me into bed."

"At your service, lady." He bows. "Shall I send someone up for your trunk?"

"Yes, I'm packed."

 Drew and his men clatter onto the veranda. "There you are Jade," Drew says. "We need to be on our way soon. Father will be waiting for us."

"I'll get your things," Ryder says to me and disappears through the doorway.

Drew takes my arm, pulling me to one side of the veranda. He leans against the railing, arms folded over his chest. "Jade, I want to thank you for bringing me here. I am ashamed that I did not possess the intestinal fortitude to have come before now. My eyes have been opened to a number of things. Mother must be told the *truth,* and she must accept the fact that we cannot escape the truth by simply ignoring it. Forgive me for being such a pig-headed ass."

"Hey, I'm used to it big brother," I say. Drew rolls his eyes.

"No really, thanks for coming with me, Drew. It'll help to have you as my witness when I have to speak with Mother about all of this. I don't know what she'll do to us. We may be spending some quality time together in the Warrington dungeons when we get home."

He lays a gloved hand on my shoulder. "I'm not only your

witness, but your ally, Jade. She'll have to listen to us."

Ryder appears on the veranda with my trunk. He carries it down to the courtyard and stows it in the back of the wagon where Ralston is busy organizing our things. I turn to join them, but Drew catches my arm.

"One more thing, Sister, about Blackthorn," he cuts his eyes to Ryder loading my trunk in the wagon. "I guess he's not the scoundrel I once thought he was. I still don't excuse him for kidnapping you, but I believe he is essentially a decent man." He smiles at me, eyes twinkling. "And fairly sane, except for the fact that he appears to like you a great deal."

I shrug his hand off my shoulder. "You never change, do you?"

"Then I wouldn't be me!" he chortles.

We join the others in the courtyard and get ready to mount up, when a relaxed and smiling Catherine appears. This morning she wears a buckskin blouse with turquoise trim and a matching skirt. Her raven hair is held in place by an elaborately beaded headband. She looks remarkably like a young Pocahontas, instead of her usual Xena the Warrior Princess persona.

She makes a small curtsey and speaks to me. "Chief Blackthorn wanted to be here to see you off, but he is not well this morning. He has some gifts for you, which he has given to Professor Ralston to place in your wagon. He sends you his highest regards and his thanks, and he bids you have a safe journey home."

I bow my head in acknowledgement. "Thank you Catherine. Tell Chief Blackthorn we appreciate his kind hospitality and his gifts. We hope he feels better." I hold out my hand and she shakes it.

She turns to Drew, smiling sweetly. "Prince Andrew, I brought this for you." She holds up an eagle feather tied with a beaded string. "It will bring you luck."

His eyes light up, and he removes his glove, taking the feather in his hand. "It's beautiful. Will you put it on for me?"

She gently loosens a curl from his mop and ties the feather in place. He smiles a little forlornly. "Thank you, I will treasure it always."

She holds out her hand to him, and his lips graze her skin.

"Be safe," she says softly.

FORTY-ONE

*R*yder and I ride side by side as our group makes its way down a back road to the conveyance station. A few townspeople watch and wave as we pass, but most of the town is still sleeping, and we're not the same novelty we were two days ago.

Ryder has arranged for some large conveyances to take us, our horses, and wagon through the underground tunnel back to Domerica. He says it's faster and more relaxed than going on horseback. I sit next to him in the roomy, comfortable vehicle. The others sit at the opposite end, giving us our own space. I'm happy it's now public knowledge, among these people at least, that we're in love.

Ryder and I talk about trivial things and snack on hydroponically grown peanuts during the ride. I've made up my mind that once we reach Domerica, I'm going to ask Ryder not to accompany us back to the Enclave. It'll be easier and more private to say goodbye to him at the tunnel instead. I don't need my father and the rest of the household to witness me falling apart as Ryder leaves me, maybe forever.

But, when we reach the end of the tunnel and I ask Ryder not to come with me, he refuses to stay behind.

"Jade, no! I'm going to see you safely back to your father."

"It's only a short distance," I tell him. "We'll be fine. I'm well guarded by Drew and his men. Besides, it doesn't make sense for you to ride all the way there, just to turn around and come right back."

"No. I'm coming with you."

"But, Ryder—"

"Jade," his voice is strained. "I need more time with you. You're not the only one who suffers."

I put my arms around him and hold him close. "I'm sorry. Please come with me."

"I thought we might ride together on Tenasi," he says.

"Yes. I'd like that."

He ties Gabriel's reins to the back of the wagon and helps me onto Tenasi's back. Climbing up behind me, he takes the reins in his right hand and wraps his left arm around my waist. He nods when we are ready, and our little group sets out for the Enclave.

We ride in silence most of the way, enjoying each other's warmth and sharing the same melancholy at having to part again. When the walls of the Enclave come into view, my stomach twists itself into a knot. According to Ralston, I have a week left, at most. I don't know how I can leave Ryder. My whole body trembles at the thought.

Ryder's arm tightens around my waist. "Are you all right, love?"

"Ryder, promise me we'll see each other again, within the week," I say. "Just promise me, please."

He leans in close, his lips in my hair. "Of course. Yes, I swear it."

My trembling stops on the promise that I'll have one more chance to see him again.

As we approach the wooden gates of the Enclave, they open for us without our having to announce ourselves. We ride inside and turn onto the tree-lined lane to the manor house. It soon becomes apparent that my father has visitors. At least a dozen horses are tied to the hitching posts at the side of the courtyard.

Drew pulls his horse to an abrupt stop. "Mother's here!" he says to me.

I quickly slide down from Tenasi's back. "Leave now," I hiss to Ryder.

He hastily turns his horse around, but the gates have already closed behind us, and twelve mounted soldiers of the Queen's Royal Guard are positioned across them.

Ryder swings Tenasi back toward me and, to my shock, he dismounts.

I run to him. "Ryder, what are you doing? Get out of here. Go!"

He shakes his head, his features taut. "Any attempt to escape now would be suicide, Jade, which may be exactly what she wants. The queen and I have unfinished business to attend to. Now is as good a time as any." He strides determinedly toward the house, and I trail after him, pleading for him to reconsider.

Father's front door opens, and Mother flies out onto the veranda with LeGare close on her heels. A dozen more Royal Guards file out behind them.

"Seize him," Mother cries, and the guards hustle down the steps, converging on Ryder. Two men take hold of his arms and remove his sword and knife from his belt.

"Drew, Jaden, in the house now," Mother says.

"No Mother! Stop!" I turn to the guards. "Let him go," I shout. They pay no attention to me, and I tug at their arms trying to free Ryder.

"Jaden, come in the house this instant," Mother says. "That man is a murderer and a thief. He tricked you into trusting him by lying to you and manipulating you."

"That's not true, Mother. You don't know what you are talking about. Let him go," I shout again more loudly. I reach for the hilt of my sword.

TRANSCENDER: *First-Timer*

"Jade, let it be," Ryder says, in a tense voice.

I hesitate for a moment, not sure what I'm going to do with the sword anyway. All I know is that I have to do something.

"Eleanor!" Father appears around the eastern corner of the manor house, accompanied by a small regiment of heavily armed, mounted men. "Perhaps you've forgotten you have no legal authority here."

"John, what are you doing?" Mother is incredulous. "We know this man is a murderer and has stolen the Xtron cell. He must be arrested and interrogated immediately."

"Call off your men, Eleanor. I would like to hear what young Blackthorn has to say before I decide whether he needs to be arrested."

"This is outrageous!" Mother cries. "He could escape again."

"I hardly think that's a possibility. He's greatly outnumbered, and this *is* a walled city. Call them off Ellie. Now!" Father climbs from his horse and goes to Ryder who is still being held by Mother's guards.

"Release him," Mother says, glaring at Father. The guards let go of Ryder's arms and step back.

Father places a hand on Ryder's shoulder. "I beg your pardon for this rather excessive display of brute force, Ryder." He scowls at Mother's guards still hovering nearby. "But you have been formally accused of stealing the dome energy source from the Sacred Caverns and with murdering two guards in the process."

"That's absurd," Ryder says. "I have never been to the Sacred Caverns. And I am no *murderer*."

"The two guards who survived the attack have given sworn statements identifying you as the leader of the intruders. Will you agree to come inside and speak with us about it?"

"Yes, of course."

"Fine." Father sweeps an arm toward the house. "Let's all go inside, shall we?"

"Father, this is so wrong. Don't let her do this," I say, agitated and frightened.

"Come inside Jaden, and we'll discuss it," he says calmly. "Andrew, come along. Eleanor, your men may wait out here. Captain Hornsby will require them to surrender their weapons until this matter has been resolved." Father signals to the captain of his little brigade. Hornsby and his men immediately dismount and prepare to collect the weapons of the Queen's Royal Guard.

"John!" Mother protests. "This is intolerable."

"Eleanor, you are in *my* community, we'll do this my way."

She nods stiffly to LeGare, and he orders his men to turn over their arms.

"General LeGare is welcome inside, of course," Father says, "as long as he leaves his weapons out here. I think we'll all be comfortable in my office."

He speaks to Drew and me, "You two should remove your swords also. You'll have no need of them in here." He pats my shoulder reassuringly.

We unfasten our swords and give them to Erica, who is positioned at the doorway. She's smiling and openly delighted with the high drama being played out in this normally quiet little hamlet.

We file into Father's office, and he asks everyone to be seated. He takes his own chair behind an enormous, ornately carved desk. LeGare refuses to sit, choosing instead to lurk behind Mother's chair near the floor to ceiling bookcases. Father pays him no heed and speaks directly to Ryder.

"Again, I apologize for this Ryder, but Queen Eleanor arrived this morning with the sworn statements of two surviving guards who were stationed at the Sacred Caverns. They report that a band of armed men broke into the caves and killed the two men posted at the front entrance. The statements allege that they then surrendered their own weapons and were restrained while the thieves made off with the Xtron power source. The guards have identified you as the leader of the band of thieves."

Ryder bolts to his feet. "It's not true! I swear it."

"Please stay calm," Father says. "You'll have ample opportunity to speak your piece."

"What would I gain by stealing the dome power source?" Ryder says. "Unicoi's own energy source is much stronger and more efficient than the power used by the domes."

"You could hold it for ransom as you intended to do with my daughter," Mother says.

"I never intended to hold your daughter for ransom. She knows that. Your son and daughter have been in my country these past two days of their own accord. It was my hope to convince them in a peaceful way to help us find a solution to the problems of my people."

"But it would benefit you, would it not, to have some insurance, just in case your efforts failed?" Mother says.

Ryder shakes his head in apparent frustration and turns to my father. "John, when did this theft supposedly occur? I've been here and in Unicoi for the past three days."

"It was prior to that," Mother answers. She opens a file on her lap. "It was the night of May 17th, around midnight. The theft was discovered the following morning. Due to a breakdown in communication, I was not notified of the theft until the 23rd."

"Five days after the fact, Ellie?" Father says. "That's quite a communication breakdown. What happened?"

"Captain Carver, former head of security for the Sacred Caverns, made the decision that it was best not to deliver the news to me while the delegation from Dome Noir was present at the palace," she says tightly. "In a further exercise of poor judgment, he decided that he

VICKY SAVAGE

and his men would attempt to recover the Xtron themselves. Based upon the information given him by the two surviving guards, they made an ill-fated attempt to break into Unicoi. A small battle ensued, in which we lost two additional men."

"We heard about the skirmish when we were there," Drew says. "The Unicoi assumed the intruders were Outlanders. They had no idea they were Domerican."

"Yes, well, Captain Carver has since been relieved of his post and will soon take up residence at Wall's Edge Prison," Mother says.

While this exchange is taking place, I do some quick calculating in my head. "Mother, wasn't that the day Prince Damien left the palace? May 17th, I mean?"

She thinks about it and glances at LeGare who nods. "I believe it was. Why?" she says.

I jump to my feet. "Then it can't have been Ryder! He was with me that night."

FORTY-TWO

Mother is clearly taken aback. "What! He was where?" she sputters.

"Ryder was at Warrington Palace, with me, in my room," I say. "Ralston saw him there ... and so did Fred and Ethel."

"At the palace? In your room!" Mother rises to her feet. "What was he doing in your room? How did he get in? Were you alone?"

I ignore her questions. "Father, get Ralston in here. He'll back up what I'm saying."

Father goes to the door and speaks a few words to someone in the hall. "Everyone, please sit down," he says. "Let's hear what Ralston has to say, and perhaps we can resolve this matter."

Ryder and I sit, but Mother remains standing, fists clenched tightly at her sides. "Jaden, this is disgraceful! How could you?" She whirls around on LeGare.

"How did he get past your guards? You assured me the palace was impenetrable."

"We had a small security lapse that night," LeGare says. "Two guards were overpowered and locked in a garden shed. They could not identify their attacker."

"And, I was not informed?" Mother roars.

He opens his mouth, but Father cuts him off. "Ellie sit down!

You too, General LeGare."

Mother grudgingly complies. LeGare perches on the edge of an empty seat. Father turns to me. "Sweetheart, are you certain Ryder was with you that particular night? May 17th?"

"Yes, absolutely! It was the day Prince Damien left the palace. I'm positive. He stayed until well after midnight."

A sharp knock on the door makes all heads turn toward Ralston as he walks cautiously into the room.

"Please sit down Professor Ralston." Father gestures to an empty chair. "I am sorry to involve you in this matter, but there have been some rather serious charges leveled against young Chief Blackthorn, and we are attempting to establish the facts. Will you help us?"

"Certainly," he replies.

"Thank you. We were discussing a visit Ryder paid to Princess Jaden at Warrington Palace. Do you recall an evening when you saw Ryder with Jaden in her room?"

"Yes, I do."

"Do you remember what night it was? The date, that is?"

"It was a week or so ago. I don't remember the exact date," Ralston says. "But it can easily be checked. It was the same day Prince Damien departed Domerica."

"Yes!" I cry. Both Father and Mother look at me sternly, and I hold my tongue.

"Professor," Father says. "May I ask why you did not report this meeting to the queen or to one of General LeGare's men? You were aware that Blackthorn was wanted in Domerica."

"I didn't report it because I knew Ryder's motives for being there were … shall we say friendly and not hostile. I knew he would never harm Princess Jaden, and I was unwilling to hurt two decent young people by turning him in."

TRANSCENDER: *First-Timer*

"Humph," Mother grunts. "It seems everyone has been keeping secrets from the queen."

Disregarding this, Father continues, "To your knowledge, did anyone else see him?"

"Only Fred and Ethel." Ralston smiles. "As I recall, Ethel took quite a liking to him."

Mother groans. "Oh, saints preserve us! Skorplings cannot serve as alibi witnesses."

"No, but our daughter and Professor Ralston can," Father says. "I believe they make very strong witnesses. Do you question their truthfulness?"

"I don't know what to believe anymore," Mother says. "Why would the only survivors of a bloody massacre lie?"

"For any number of reasons, Ellie. It may be a case of mistaken identity, they may have thought young Blackthorn would make a convenient scapegoat, or they may have been paid off themselves. The whole situation is troubling." He rubs his knuckles across his bearded jaw. "The most important question may be why they were spared by the thieves. It's not likely, after killing two men, they would leave witnesses."

"The guards are being brought to Warrington Palace as we speak," LeGare pipes up.

"That would be prudent, since there appear to be a number of holes in their story," Father says. "In any event, I believe we have adequately established that Ryder Blackthorn could not have been involved. The Crown Princess and Professor Ralston will swear to that, effectively refuting your sworn witness statements, Ellie."

He addresses Ryder. "You are free to go, with our apologies."

"Wait," Mother cries, rising from her chair again. "I am not finished here. Jaden, what were you and Andrew doing in Unicoi?" She wheels on Drew. "Did you convince her to make this foolhardy trip?"

Drew's eyebrows fly up. "It wasn't me."

She cuts her eyes to Ryder. "It must have been you. What have you done to my children to cause them to deceive me in this way? What are you doing to my family? You have put them and all of Domerica in harm's way by your recklessness."

This new accusation against Ryder is more than I can bear. "Oh Mother, shut up!"

She stares at me as though she doesn't know me. "You would tell the queen to shut up?"

"I'm sorry, but you've got to calm down and listen, instead of hurling wild accusations at innocent people."

"If he is innocent, what are you? What were you doing with this man, Jaden? He abducted you once, for pity sake, why would you allow him into your room? And why were you in Unicoi?"

"I'm not afraid of him, Mother. We've become … friends."

"Friends! You mean that night was not the first time you had seen him since your abduction?"

I shake my head. "No."

She gazes at me with eyes that hold both anger and fear. "Oh Daughter, what have you done?"

"I haven't done anything Mother, except what you should have done long ago. Drew and I went to Unicoi to see with our own eyes the truth of the situation. We need to talk about that. You can't avoid it any longer."

"Oh, we shall discuss that," she says. "Your deceitful behavior will be thoroughly addressed. But first I must know what is between you and young Blackthorn."

I glance at Ryder. He comes to my side and takes my hand in his. The comforting electrical current flows through us, uniting us. We stand facing the furious queen.

"If you'll allow me, Your Highness," Ryder says. "I went to Jaden's room that night because I had heard she was engaged to be married."

"Of what significance is that to you?"

"I love your daughter," he says. "I came to her because I had to know if it was true."

"Surely you are not serious," Mother says. "She is heir to the throne of Domerica."

Ryder turns to Father. "I am sorry, John. I know I should have spoken with you before, but an opportune time did not present itself. I have asked Jaden to marry me."

Mother's sharp intake of breath is the only sound in the room.

Father studies Ryder soberly. "Well, that is momentous. Such a union would have significant implications for both Unicoi and Domerica. I assume you have thought this through?"

"To be honest with you sir, while I have certainly considered the implications, I cannot pretend to know what it will all mean. What I know with certainty is that I love Jaden. I will do whatever must be done to persuade her to marry me."

"I take it that means Jaden has not yet accepted your proposal?" Father asks.

Ryder glances sideways at me. "I do not wish to speak for Jade, but she told me she is not yet ready to wed."

"Oh, thank goodness," Mother says clutching her throat. "And you two have not … Well, there is nothing that … Jaden," she says to me. "Would you still be considered marriageable to someone else?"

"I'm still a virgin, if that's what you mean, Mother," I reply, prickling at the question. Her relieved smile is infuriating. Ryder squeezes my hand, and I lower my eyes, gazing at his long golden fingers intertwined with mine. In that moment I realize that regardless of what tomorrow brings, I must speak my heart.

"Hold on a minute. I have something to say to you both." The back of my throat aches with emotion as I speak. "It's true that I told Ryder I'm not ready to get married right now. But don't be misled by that. You need to understand that when I am ready to marry, I *will* marry Ryder. There will be no one else."

Ryder raises my hand to his mouth and presses his lips into my palm.

"Oh, Jaden." Mother groans softly, crumpling into her chair.

Father comes to me. "You're certain of this Jaden? It is an enormous decision."

"I am absolutely certain. I'll announce publicly that he is my betrothed. I'll sign whatever papers you like to make it all legal. And we will marry before my twentieth birthday, as the law requires."

"Jaden, wait," Mother says. "Please do not be so hasty. Think about what you are saying."

"I know what I am saying, Mother. I love Ryder. I'll always love Ryder." I gaze at his amazing face, an exquisite pain piercing my heart. I know I'll never be his wife, but at least I can make this gesture of love for him, so he will forever know how much I cared.

"I can't imagine life without him," I say quietly, knowing that the truth of those words will cost me dearly.

Mother slumps as though defeated, hiding her face in her hands. She seems more human and less queen than I've seen her since my arrival in Domerica. It doesn't make me happy to hurt her this way, but for my own peace of mind there are certain things I must say to my mother before I leave this realm. And not only how much I love her.

Father puts an arm around my shoulders. "Jade, it's hard to believe you have found your husband. I think you've made an outstanding choice. I'm happy for both of you." He hugs me and kisses my forehead.

"Congratulations," he says, shaking Ryder's hand. "Have you

spoken with your father about this, Ryder?"

"Yes sir, he has given us his blessing."

"Excellent!" He looks to my mother for her response. "Ellie?"

Her face is still buried in her hands. LeGare crouches beside her chair, whispering softly to her. I know she's angry, but I pray she won't cause an ugly scene by disowning me or something.

When she finally removes her hands her expression is sphinx-like. Collecting her skirts, she rises regally, the queen once more. "Please come here Jaden," she says, and I walk to her on wobbly legs. She presents an imposing figure.

"What if I forbid you to marry this man?"

"I'll do it anyway," I say defiantly.

She scrutinizes my face as if trying to gage my resolve. I raise my chin and return her stare.

"This is not the way you were raised to conduct yourself," she says. "You are royalty—a future queen, no less, not some scullery maid. This sneaking around behind my back is enormously disappointing." Her voice is sharp and cold.

"How long have you been seeing this boy? Was that whole kidnapping escapade just a stunt so the two of you could be together?"

"No Mother! I swear. That was the first time we'd met, other than when we were children."

She places her hand under my chin, her eyes probing mine. "And I suppose you had nothing to do with his escape from the palace?"

My face burns scarlet, and I lower my eyes. "I was responsible for the escape," I say quietly.

"Jaden! How could you?"

"How could I? How could *you*?" I throw back at her. "I'd do it again if I had to. It's beyond barbaric to wipe out a person's mind—their past and all their memories. It's cruel and unusual punishment," I say borrowing a few words from the United States Constitution. "It should be outlawed!"

She twists her mouth into a taut smile. "Well, fortunately for us all, you do not get to make those decisions until you are sitting in my chair. And in light of your recent lapses in judgment we can only hope that is a *very* long time from now."

Her words hurt me, but I continue. "Mother, I'm not trying to take over your throne. I never asked for any of this. All I can do is follow my conscience and try to do the *right thing*, not the easy thing. *That* is the way I was raised! Lately I've wondered about your motivations, though. Do you really care about doing what's right? Or do you care only about doing what's in your best political interest? Thousands of people in Unicoi are dying because you have refused to help them. You should look into their faces Mother, because I know that if you do, you could not continue to be so cruel."

She collapses into her chair, sobbing, and my heart falls into my shoes. I've made my mother cry. My dearest mother, whom I have missed every minute of every hour of every day for the past year. I drop to my knees and hug her.

"Oh Mother, I'm sorry. Please don't cry. I love you. I didn't mean it. I'm sorry I hurt you. Don't cry. Please."

She wraps her arms around me, and we hold each other tightly. "I love you too, darling," she sniffs. "You will find when you are queen that it is not always easy to know what constitutes the *right thing*. Many others besides oneself must be taken into consideration."

"I know, Mother. I know it's hard. I know you're doing the best you can. I'm sorry I've caused so much trouble. Please forgive me."

She looks at me with a melancholy smile. "I think we must try to forgive each other, Daughter. I am not without fault, I know. You must think me cold sometimes, but I do love you dearly. I want only what is best for you."

"This is what's best for me, Mother! Truly. Ryder is what's best for me. He makes me happy."

She smoothes back my hair with delicate fingers. "Beautiful Jaden, you have always been the headstrong one. Let us hope your Ryder knows what he is getting into."

She rises and puts an arm around my shoulder. Together we walk to Ryder. He looks uncomfortable at having witnessed such an intimate family scene, or maybe for being the cause of it.

Mother peers up into his face. Her brow wrinkles, and she laughs unexpectedly. "Oh, for heaven's sake man, kneel down so I can see your eyes." He kneels before her, raising his eyes to hers.

"Do you love my daughter?"

"Yes, Your Highness."

"Do you promise to care for her and protect her?"

"Yes. With my life!"

"Then you have my permission to marry, when Jaden is ready, of course. Things will not be easy for the two of you. You are from different cultures and many will object to your marriage, but you are part of our family now and we will do our best to smooth the way for you." She holds her hand out to Ryder and he kisses it.

"Thank you, Queen Eleanor." He gets back to his feet, and gathers me up in a bone-crushing embrace.

"Ryder," I wheeze. "Can't breathe."

"Sorry," he sets me down gently. "I'm just so happy!"

His enthusiasm is infectious, and I have to laugh. But my head is reeling with the awareness that I've just become engaged to be married. I don't dare to even glance Ralston's way. I doubt he considers my behavior appropriate considering my imminent departure, but I don't give a crap anymore.

"I believe this calls for a celebration," Father says. "Ryder, can you stay on?"

"Yes. I'll need to send word to my father that I cannot attend the Council meeting tonight. He will understand, under the circumstances."

"What about you, Ellie?" Father asks. "Celebration dinner for the newly engaged couple? Will you stay the night?"

"Oh no," she shakes her head vigorously. "I couldn't possibly. The theft of the Xtron has global implications. I must get to the bottom of it without further delay. We are woefully behind in our investigation due to Captain Carver's irresponsible actions, and we no longer have a prime suspect." She smiles nervously at Ryder.

"We were in the middle of preparing our response to the demands for a new dome when the theft occurred. Now I am certain Philippe and Rafael will call for my resignation as Designated Guardian."

"Ellie, these are pressing issues, all of which will keep until tomorrow," Father says. "I have some thoughts on the theft I would like to share with you, but in the morning. Send LeGare back to Warrington to get started on the investigation. Our daughter has just become engaged! Surely you can take an evening off."

She frowns like she's going to argue, but soon her face relaxes. "Oh, I suppose you are right. It will keep until morning. Our daughter becomes engaged only once. Do you have room for me here?"

"Of course, we have plenty of room for everyone. We'll get you comfortably settled, and then I have a party to plan."

FORTY-THREE

My Domerican father continues to impress me with his talents, this time as a party planner. When Ryder and I join the others downstairs for our celebration dinner, we find the dining room completely transformed for the occasion. The table is covered with an Irish lace cloth and set with fine bone china, gleaming silverware, and sparkling cut-crystal stemware. Electric candles glitter like starlight from every available space. Vases overflow with white roses, hydrangeas, and fragrant gardenias. Pine boughs laced with white ribbons hang above each door. Tinkling music wafts from the living room, where Father has hired a string quartet for our evening's entertainment.

In addition to Erica and Captain Hornsby, Father has invited a few additional residents of the Enclave who have known Princess Jaden since childhood. I actually recognize one guest from my life back in Connecticut, my mother's cousin Henry Balfour. In Domerica he is "Lord Balfour," and he's much more formal and distinguished in this role. I'm happy to see him, and I hug him warmly. As far as the others go, I just pretend to remember them all.

Father gets the festivities underway with a champagne toast and well wishes for the betrothed couple. Mother seems relaxed and lighthearted in spite of all the heavy problems weighing on her shoulders. I'm surprised at how graciously she has accepted my engagement to Ryder. But I should have known that she only wants me to be happy. That's my mom—unconditionally loving.

The evening is filled with happy laughter, pleasant conversation, and a superlative meal. As dinner is winding down, Father mentions to the others that Drew, Ralston and I have just returned from a visit to Unicoi. Mother's back stiffens slightly at this shift in the conversation.

"Oooh, you must tell us all about it. It must have been fascinating," a sweet-faced, plump older woman, named Miss Charlotte, says. Miss Charlotte served as Jaden's nanny during her childhood visits to the Enclave.

"It was all so amazing, I don't know where to begin," I say.

"Well, I do," Drew chimes in." They have a huge, highly trained army of warriors. Most men and many women belong to the armed forces, at least part-time. Ryder says it is the Cherokee tradition that all young men, and even most of the girls, become warriors when they reach their mid-teens. They receive training in many forms of combat, and they conduct realistic war games."

"Goodness, are they expecting a war?" Miss Charlotte asks.

"No. They just wish to be prepared." Drew says.

Ralston speaks up. "Yes, well, the army is rather impressive, but the strides in agricultural production are what impress me the most. Crops enough to feed the entire country are grown within the confines of a few hundred warehouses. The hydroponic methods of farming, along with the shortened growing cycle, are astounding, to say the least."

He turns to Father. "John, I understand you are utilizing some of the Unicoi methods here at the Enclave."

"That's true," Father says, "and so far the results have been remarkable. We hope to learn more of them."

"I guess I was most impressed by the technology," I say. "They have these things called transceivers you can use to speak to people miles away." A collective gasp goes up from the table.

"You mean you can actually hear one another's voices?" Miss Charlotte asks.

"Yes, mind-boggling, huh? And, they have motorized trolley cars that take people up and down the main street, so you don't need a horse, and there are conveyances for public transportation in the city. In fact, horses aren't even allowed on the main roads. Isn't that so, Ryder?"

He chuckles. "Yes it is. It seems they have no manners when it comes to being in town. We couldn't keep up with the mess and the smell, no matter how many street cleaners we employed. It's much better this way."

"How do the vehicles run?" Lord Balfour asks.

"On *elohi* power, like the rest of Unicoi," Ryder says.

"Oh yes, I've heard of that," Lord Balfour says. "Remarkable stuff. Uses the earth's own energy. It seems Domerica has a way to go to catch up with the Unicoi in several respects."

"It does appear so from what we saw," Drew agrees.

"But what did you find out about this insidious disease?" Captain Hornsby asks. "Weren't you at all concerned for your own safety?"

Mother, who has remained stoic throughout this entire exchange, winces at Hornsby's question.

"No never," Drew says. "The disease has been confirmed to be completely attributable to the presence of the element Uranium in the soil, walls, and even the water of the underground cities. Some victims suffer from radiation poisoning, and others become ill from the radon gas emitted as the Uranium decays. I have the research if you would like to see it. It's indisputable. A person cannot catch Uranium poisoning from another. Don't you agree Ralston?"

"Yes, quite so," Ralston says. "The research is solid. The difficulty is that the only known cure for the disease is to physically remove the victims from the contaminated environment. In other words, to relocate the entire Unicoi nation. Otherwise, I am afraid they are all doomed."

Miss Charlotte utters a small cry, while others at the table shake their heads in concern.

"That essentially confirms what our independent research has shown," Father says. "Ellie, I sent a copy of that report to each member of the Coalition two months ago. I hope you had the opportunity to discuss it at your last meeting. It's quite persuasive."

Lord Balfour swipes his napkin across his lips and speaks to Mother. "Yes Ellie, what are we going to do about this? I understand these people are desperate. If this thing really is not communicable, don't we have a moral obligation to take some action on their behalf?" All eyes turn to Mother.

"Henry, I'm afraid the Coalition has been preoccupied with other important matters recently," Mother says quietly, "and I have not personally reviewed John's report. So I have just received this information tonight, as have the rest of you. Of course, I must consult with my advisors before I can make any decisions regarding the fate of the Unicoi."

Pastor Langford of the Church of the Chosen, speaks for the first time. "But these people are running out of time. They should be brought to Domerica immediately."

"Don't be absurd, Pastor," Mother dismisses this suggestion. "We do not have enough room for them all."

Another guest, a thin man with a thick swath of dark hair, whose name escapes me, speaks up. "Besides, Pastor, these people are not among the Chosen. Should we really be sheltering them?"

"That is a gross mischaracterization of Church doctrine, which has grown into popular belief." Pastor Langford says with conviction. "*All* survivors of the Great Disaster are considered to be 'Chosen.' Nowhere is it written that only dome residents hold this distinction." This elicits some surprised "ohs" from the guests.

"Mother," I say. "I'd be willing to let them have Meadowood. They could settle there."

"Jaden, don't be foolish," she says. "Meadowood is just over two hundred acres. The Unicoi would need at least two hundred *thousand* acres."

"Ellie, nearly three hundred thousand acres lie between here and Warrington Palace that are being used for little more than fargen grazing," Father says. "As you and I have discussed on a number of occasions, the Unicoi could establish themselves there without taking up valuable farmland or displacing anyone except a few forest people."

Mother stares uncomfortably at her plate.

"Of course, substantial time and planning would have to go into constructing such a settlement," Father says, "but we managed to do it here at the Enclave, and I would be willing to assist in any way that I can."

"These people are Princess Jaden's kinsmen now," Miss Charlotte adds. "You can't just let them die." She looks at Mother with watery eyes.

Drew adds his voice to those of the others. "Mother, you wouldn't believe the things Jaden and I saw: thousands of men, women, and children affected by the disease. They are dying horrible deaths, and they have no hope whosoever of surviving unless we step in. The situation is desperate beyond belief."

Mother glances at Drew and then at me.

"Please Mother, we must do something." I say softly.

"Please," Drew echoes.

Mother straightens herself and surveys the faces around the table. "I have heard what all of you have said. You have made some compelling arguments. I admit that I was very angry when my own daughter was abducted in order to further the Unicoi cause. That may have rendered me less sympathetic than I otherwise might have been." She pauses and looks at Ryder and me. "That situation has resolved itself, however, and I am willing to take a fresh look at the matter. I also admit that in the past I may have been overly influenced by the position of others in the Coalition, rather than arriving at my own conclusions."

I hold my breath, waiting for the "but."

"But, Jaden has reminded me today that it is the obligation of the queen to do what is right, not what is politically expedient."

She meets the eyes of each guest in turn, and continues. "I promise you that I will revisit this issue as soon as I am able to turn my attention from other more compelling matters. If my scientists and city engineers tell me it can be done without endangering or displacing our own people, I will propose that we offer two hundred thousand acres to the people of Unicoi for the purpose of relocating them to Domerica, should they wish to do so."

A cheer goes up from the table. Ryder hugs me. He stands and raises his glass to Mother. "This is exceptionally good news. I thank you on behalf of my father and all the people of Unicoi. A toast to Queen Eleanor, a wise and merciful ruler."

"Hear, hear," Lord Balfour says.

"Hear, hear," the guests join in.

Mother accepts this tribute with a nod and a modest smile.

The rest of the evening passes like a dream. Ryder holds my hand under the table, his excitement and joy flowing into me like a rejuvenating tonic.

Miss Charlotte asks if I'm planning a traditional Cherokee ceremony in addition to the grand state wedding Mother will throw at the palace. I have a wonderful time pretending it's all really going to happen, imagining what my wedding will look like and how I will feel. I even imagine the dress I am going to wear. I'm so totally absorbed in the festive atmosphere of the evening that all thoughts of leaving vanish from my mind.

I know that no matter what happens after today, nothing will ever change this magical night. Future generations of this world will know that Princess Jaden of Domerica was once engaged to be married to young Chief Blackthorn of the Unicoi nation. My heart clings to the knowledge that we will be forever linked, at least in that small way.

TRANSCENDER: *First-Timer*

The guests stay late and are reluctant to leave until, at midnight, Father announces that the queen has urgent business tomorrow in Domerica and must get an early start in the morning.

As they depart, Ryder and I thank each guest for helping us celebrate our joyful news. When the last goodbyes are spoken, I'm beyond exhaustion. I secretly wish Ryder would offer to carry me up that long flight of stairs to my room, like Rhett sweeping Scarlet away in *Gone With the Wind*. But I'm sure he's as tired as I am. Instead, he walks me to my door and kisses me chastely on the forehead.

"Goodnight love. This has been the happiest day of my life," he says with a tired smile.

"Mine too," I say.

FORTY-FOUR

I fall into bed nearly comatose and do not move an eyelid until the smell of frying bacon wakes me in the morning. When I reach the dining room, which has been restored to its former self, a small group is already seated at the table. Breakfast is laid out on the sideboard, but I notice nobody is eating.

"Good morning, Jade," Father says. "We were going to let you sleep awhile longer."

"What's going on?" I ask groggily. Ryder greets me with a kiss on the cheek and guides me to the chair next to him. Mother and Drew are sitting across from us. Ralston and Captain Hornsby are quietly sipping tea at the opposite end.

Father stands at the head of the table and addresses the group. "I hoped to share some thoughts with you on the theft of the Xtron. But first Ellie, now that Jaden is here, perhaps you should fill everyone in on the message you received this morning from General LeGare."

Mother remains seated, her expression tense. "Yes I will. General LeGare informs me that the surviving guards from the Sacred Caverns have, under further interrogation, recanted their story that Blackthorn was involved in the theft of the Xtron energy cell. In fact, the guards were not even present when the theft took place. They had abandoned their posts to visit a local pub.

"They returned in time to see a band of men dressed in black retreating to the east on horseback. They discovered their two dead comrades and the missing Xtron cell and concocted a scheme to dispose of their own weapons and bind each other's hands, making it appear they had simply been spared by the thieves. While waiting to be rescued, they hatched the plan to accuse Ryder of the crime, knowing that he was already wanted in Domerica."

"Thank you Ellie," Father says. "At least that part of the mystery is cleared up. I have another possibly related question for you. Have you received any news regarding the whereabouts of Prince Damien?"

"No," Mother says. "He has simply disappeared. Our investigation, and that of the delegation from Dome Noir, determined that he and his entourage left the palace at around 8:00 a.m. on the 17th. They boarded their ship and departed from the harbor around 10:00 a.m., according to the Harbormaster's log. Damien has not been seen or heard from since that time."

"Why did he leave the palace so abruptly?" Captain Hornsby asks.

"He received a message, which he reported was from his father, summoning him back to Dome Noir immediately," Mother says. "King Philippe denies sending such a message, however, and we have been unable to locate the messenger. The hydrofoils, which were sent out from Dome Noir to search for Damien, have turned up no signs of his ship."

Father rubs his chin in thought. "And the theft at the Sacred Caverns took place around midnight on the date of Damien's disappearance?"

"Yes. Do you think the two incidents are connected?" Mother asks.

"It's too coincidental not to be connected," Father says.

"You believe the same person is responsible for both?"

He half-smiles. "Yes. Actually, I was thinking Damien himself might be responsible for both."

Ryder speaks up. "I've been thinking the same thing. The men dressed in black, the gun, the fact that they rode east, *away* from the tunnels—all these facts tend to implicate Damien and his men."

"Wait," Mother says. "Do I understand you to say that you believe Damien engineered his own disappearance, stole the Xtron from the Sacred Caverns, and killed two guards in the process?"

"Let's say that is the theory I am putting forth," Father replies.

"But you cannot accuse a prince of Dome Noir of theft and *murder* based on such flimsy evidence."

Drew snorts. "That didn't seem to concern you when it came to accusing the son of the Unicoi Chief of the identical crimes."

Mother glares at him. "It is not the same, Andrew, and I have apologized for that."

"Sorry," he says quietly.

"Ellie, hear me out," Father says. "A number of factors make him the most likely culprit. He was already here; he had armed men and horses with him. It would have been easy for his ship to circle around and anchor in some secluded spot off shore, while he and his men reentered Domerica through a tunnel. He may even have left men waiting inside Domerica to help them get back in."

"But why?" she asks.

"Damien has any number of reasons to want that Xtron cell. We've heard he is in desperate need of funds. After Jaden turned him down, he had few other options for getting them. Another possibility is that he was looking for a way to regain his father's esteem. Handing him the key to his new dome in the form of the Xtron would accomplish that. Also, we must face the fact that the Xtron holds an enormous amount of concentrated energy. It is capable of being turned into a weapon or weapons. If the person in possession of the stolen energy cell is inclined to use it for nefarious purposes, he just may be the most powerful person in the world at the moment."

TRANSCENDER: *First-Timer*

"What about Outlanders?" Mother says. "They could have discovered the caves and taken it."

"A possibility, but not very likely," Captain Hornsby answers. "We would have received their demands by now. Also, they are not that organized or well-equipped, and how would they have known the location of the caves? I understand they are extremely well-hidden."

"But the same question would apply to Damien," Mother says. The site of the Sacred Caverns has always been a closely guarded secret, even from the other members of the Coalition. How could Damien, or anyone for that matter, have known their location?"

Father shakes his head. "That is one piece of the puzzle I cannot sort out. Perhaps they bribed a guard. It may be the reason the two surviving guards abandoned their post in the first place."

"Wait a minute!" I pop out of my chair, nearly knocking over a glass of juice. "I think I know what happened."

Everyone stares at me. "On the night Prince Damien arrived, I saw Sylvia secretly give a package to him. They were whispering in the hallway. They didn't know I was there, but she passed something to him and he put it in his jacket."

"Sylvia?" Mother says.

"But how would Sylvia get directions to the Sacred Caverns?" Father asks.

"Oh no," I groan and slump back into my seat. "My book, my diary—it has a map to the Sacred Caverns inside. It was missing from my desk when I went to write down Gabriel's name. I thought I'd just misplaced it, but she must have stolen it."

Mother clutches the table for support. "I can't believe it!"

"Oh Mother, I'm so sorry," I say.

"Sylvia of all people," she says. "I trusted her completely and she betrayed me. She had access to everything and … oh, Jaden, please forgive me for trying to foist her on you. You might have been placed in danger. I'll have her arrested immediately."

"Ellie, you have ample time to deal with Sylvia," Father says. "Right now we must focus on the issue at hand. All indications are that Prince Damien has stolen the Xtron and has killed two men in the course of doing so. His whereabouts are currently unknown to us. He could be anywhere, but he is probably still in Domerica. We need to find him quickly and establish what his motives are. It's crucial to know whether King Philippe is involved."

"Oh, you don't think he could be?" Mother says.

"At this point, we must consider all possibilities," Father tells her.

"Excuse me, John." Erica steps into the dining room. She has been unusually subdued since Ryder and I announced our engagement, but she looks lovely this morning in a yellow spring dress.

"Yes, what is it?" Father says.

"Nathan is outside for you. He says it is important."

"Nathan? The gatekeeper?" Mother asks.

"Yes, I'd better see what he wants." Father excuses himself and follows Erica out.

He returns a few moments later, his features tense. "Ellie you have a visitor. Crown Prince Gilbert of Dome Noir."

"Prince Gilbert is here?" she asks.

"Yes, he joined the Dome Noir delegation at Warrington Palace last night. He says he urgently needs to speak with you. I told Nathan to send him up to the house."

Mother looks a little green. "You don't think Philippe has learned of the theft of the Xtron do you?"

"Let's hear what he has to say, Ellie. We'll know his objective soon enough."

We wait only a matter of minutes before Erica announces the arrival of Prince Gilbert.

He strides into the room with purpose. Spotting Mother in her chair, he bows deeply. "Your Highness. Blessed be the Chosen."

Gilbert is an impressive figure, tall and elegant, with features more ruggedly handsome than those of his younger brother, Damien. Rather than the usual black or brown leather armor, his is gold-plated metal with the Dome Noir coat of arms embossed in black on the chest plate.

"Prince Gilbert, welcome," Mother says. "You remember my family?"

"Yes." He holds out his hand to Father. "Governor Beckett, thank you for allowing me to interrupt your family gathering."

"Good to see you, Prince Gilbert," Father says.

The prince swivels slightly to face me. "Princess Jaden, you are looking well," he says with a bow. His dark eyes burn with intelligence and, unlike Damien, he wears no makeup or jewelry.

"Nice to see you again, Prince Andrew." He shakes Drew's hand, and glances up at Ryder.

"This is young Chief Ryder Blackthorn of Unicoi," Father says.

The slightest ripple of Prince Gilbert's brow is the only indication that Ryder's presence comes as a surprise to him. "Chief Blackthorn, I am pleased to make your acquaintance," he says.

"My daughter and Chief Blackthorn have recently become engaged," Father tells him.

Prince Gilbert smiles warmly. "Well, that is good news. I congratulate you both." He looks at Mother. "But I thought …"

"I shall explain later," Mother says.

Father introduces Ralston and Captain Hornsby. After shaking hands with the two men, Gilbert turns again to Mother. "Your

Highness, I must speak with you regarding a very important matter. May we have some privacy?"

"I would like my family to be present for our discussion, Prince Gilbert," Mother says.

"As you wish, Madame."

Ralston makes a small cough. "Why don't Captain Hornsby and I wait in the library?" He and Hornsby push in their chairs and walk to the door. Ryder follows after them.

"Ryder, please stay," Mother says. "You are part of the family now."

He nods. "Yes, ma'am. Thank you."

Father offers Gilbert a chair, which he accepts, perching on the edge of the seat. He looks seriously stressed. "Queen Eleanor, I've come on behalf of my father. He wishes you to know that we are aware of the theft of the Xtron energy cell from its place of security."

Mother makes no reply and registers no emotion on her face.

"He also wishes me to tell you that we know who is responsible for this theft. Unfortunately, it is my own brother, Damien."

"And how do you know this?" Mother asks.

"Damien has been in contact with my father. It appears that on his recent visit to Warrington Palace, he bribed a member of your staff with ties to Dome Noir to steal directions to the Sacred Caverns. He feigned a reason to leave the palace early, while actually remaining inside Domerica. He and his men found their way to the Caverns and took the Xtron. We have heard that two men were killed in the commission of the theft. For this we are terribly sorry."

"Yes, they were murdered by the thieves," Mother says. "We had already suspected some of what you have told us. What we do not understand, however, is why Damien would resort to this."

For the first time, Gilbert breaks eye contact with Mother. He stares at the rug and speaks softly. "Damien has always been

358

troubled, from the time he was very young. As an adult he has developed many destructive habits: drinking, gambling, and associating with the criminal element in Dome Noir. Now he has gotten himself into serious trouble with organized criminals and black marketers in Dome Noir. Until recently, we were unaware of how serious it actually is."

Gilbert returns his gaze to Mother. "We do not know exactly when Damien devised his plan to steal the Xtron. We assume it was sometime prior to visiting Domerica. When Princess Jaden proved unreceptive to a marriage contract, he made the decision to follow through."

"What does Damien want with the Xtron?" Mother asks.

"He has demanded that my father abdicate his throne and name Damien his rightful and legal heir. In other words, he wishes to be king of Dome Noir."

"Is he mad?" Mother says.

"It would appear so," Gilbert replies grimly. "As you can imagine, Father is beside himself with grief, anger, and worry. That is why he did not come to you himself. He sends his deepest apologies for all of the sorrow and disquiet Damien has caused, and he offers the full resources of Dome Noir to assist in the capture of Damien and his men and in the recovery of the Xtron."

"What does Damien plan to do if his demands are not met?" Father asks.

"He has threatened to destroy the domes one at a time, beginning with Domerica. We do not know precisely how he plans to do this, or whether he is even capable of turning the Xtron into a weapon, but in light of his recent unstable behavior, we feel his threats must be taken seriously. My brother Jean Louis is meeting with King Rafael as I meet with you, to make him aware of the situation and of Damien's threats."

Mother grips the arms of her chair. "This is disastrous," she says quietly.

"We have reason to believe Damien is still hiding out in Domerica," Gilbert says.

"What makes you believe so?" Father asks.

"His messenger disclosed as much under rather strenuous interrogation, and it stands to reason that if Damien plans to destroy Domerica first, he is likely still nearby."

"Clearly we must find Damien as swiftly as possible, before he has time to convert the energy cell into weapons," Father says.

"We are in agreement then," Gilbert says. "Tell me what we can do. What resources can we provide to assist in the search?"

"I'd like Captain Hornsby and Professor Ralston to be a part of these discussions," Father tells him. "We will need their input in devising a strategy."

"Of course," Gilbert replies.

Father looks to Mother, and she nods her agreement.

"John," Ryder speaks up. "I would like to send for trackers from Unicoi. My men are the best trained in the world. I believe they would be a great asset in the search for Damien."

"By all means, Ryder. Thank you," Father says. "The sooner they can get here the better."

~ ~ ~ ~

We sit at the conference table in Father's office while he fills in Ralston and Hornsby on the information Prince Gilbert has given us. Mother appears to be in shock. She sits silently, staring ahead while Father stresses the urgent need for a wide-ranging plan to quickly locate Damien.

"John, if I may?" Captain Hornsby says. "While finding Damien is undoubtedly of the utmost importance, it may be wise also to shore up security at some of our most vulnerable sites in the meantime. We don't know what he may be planning, and Queen Eleanor has reported that he left Warrington Palace with a decent-

TRANSCENDER: *First-Timer*

sized contingent of armed men."

"That's a good point," Father says. "Ellie, we should identify all areas in Domerica that are most susceptible to attack and immediately assign additional security to those sites."

"Oh, I wish LeGare were here," Mother says, clutching at her throat.

"If you wish to send for General LeGare, Ellie, feel free to do so," Father says impatiently, "but this cannot wait. We must put together a strategy now. The Enclave is at stake here also, and I will not have it destroyed because we failed to act decisively."

Mother stares fiercely at Father and rises to face him. "I have never failed to act decisively where my people are concerned. Any implication otherwise borders on treason."

"I did not mean to be insulting, Ellie. But, I do not feel we have your full attention."

"Well you have it now!" she barks. "Ralston!"

He jumps about five feet out of his chair. "Yes, ma'am?"

"Find some paper. We are going to need a record of our plan. You shall act as scribe."

"Yes, ma'am." He scurries off to get something to write on.

A strategy begins to take shape among the seven of us at the table. Everyone offers contributions to the overall plan. Prince Gilbert promises two regiments of soldiers to assist in the search for Damien and more aid if needed. Father agrees to assign some of Hornsby's men to guard the Sacred Caverns and work with LeGare's men to reinforce the security at the main entrance of the dome. Ryder volunteers a contingent of Unicoi Warriors to guard the Dome Operations Center in Wall's Edge, in addition to the trackers who are to be assigned to each search party.

"We need to block all tunnels leading in and out of Domerica," Father says. "Ryder, do you have up-to-date maps for these?"

"Yes, I can get them for you."

"Good. We may ask to borrow your explosive experts to ensure that the job is done correctly."

"Of course. We'll send you our best," Ryder says. "We've developed a new type of explosive, KXT. It is very precise, and a small amount goes a long way. I shall send a box of that also. Would you like us to provide firearms?"

"No!" Mother says firmly before Father can answer. "We'll have no need of firearms. I do not want them in the country."

"Ellie—" Father begins.

"It's not open for discussion, John."

Father shrugs at Ryder. "No firearms, but perhaps some crossbows and archers if you can spare them. We'll need them if Damien has guns."

"Consider it done." Ryder says.

"Can I say something about the tunnels?" I ask. "We need to leave at least a couple of them open to bring the Unicoi people to Domerica."

"The Unicoi are being brought to Domerica?" Prince Gilbert asks, seemingly stunned by this news.

"It has been taken under advisement," Mother says, casting a stern glance my way. "We have determined that the disease is not communicable, as once thought, and we feel a moral obligation to aid these suffering people, if at all possible. They are Jaden's kinsmen now."

I smile at how she has been converted to the Unicoi cause. This is more like the Eleanor Beckett I've always known!

"In any event, we should leave two tunnels open between here and Unicoi," Father says. "We need an open conduit between our two countries, for the help and supplies Ryder is sending us. We must make certain they are more than adequately secured, however."

TRANSCENDER: *First-Timer*

"Let me handle that," Ryder offers.

"Excellent!" Father says.

"Ellie, you and Andrew may wish to return to Warrington Palace today to ensure that security there is tightened up. That is probably the first location Damien will strike. If I were you, I would do the same for your food storage facilities. We will add additional security to our vulnerable sites here at the Enclave as well."

"Yes, I think I shall return to Warrington later today," Mother says. "I wish to brief General LeGare on our discussions. Our search efforts must begin immediately."

~ ~ ~ ~

It is well after lunchtime before everyone is satisfied that all potential issues have been discussed and effectively dealt with.

Mother stands and addresses the group. "I am confident that we have covered everything, based upon what we know today. Thank you all for your insights and offers of assistance. Prince Gilbert, I know this must be terribly difficult for you and your family. Thank you for being here and for helping us to coordinate our efforts. Will you be staying on at Warrington Palace?"

"If that meets with your approval," he says. "I would like to stay until Damien is found and the Xtron recovered."

"Very well. You and your men may accompany us back to the palace. I think it is time that Andrew and I depart."

"Mother," I say nervously, "I realize we're in crisis mode here, but I don't want to let any more time pass before the Unicoi can be brought to Domerica. They're in crisis too, and we need to get things rolling right away."

She sighs heavily. "Daughter, I know you will vex me about this until a relocation is underway, and I have other pressing concerns to which I must give my undivided attention at the moment. Accordingly, I am assigning the entire project to you and Professor Ralston. You may have access to my city engineers, surveyors, builders, social workers, whatever you need. When you have adequately established that such a relocation of the Unicoi population is feasible, and when a workable plan is in place, we will begin the transfer process. Does that satisfy you?"

"Yes, it does," I say, smiling.

"Fine. Now kiss me goodbye, dear. And promise me you will not go outside of the Enclave walls without several armed guards." She looks to Father for his agreement.

"I'll make certain she is safe," he says.

Ryder comes to my side and takes my hand. "Jade, I'm afraid I too must leave at once. Much has transpired since yesterday. My father must be informed of Queen Eleanor's willingness to consider our relocation to Domerica. Also, Father must be made aware of Damien's threats against the domes. I'm certain he will join me in offering whatever assistance your mother requires. We both have a great deal to do." He smiles and tucks a strand of hair behind my ear. "You must discover a means and method for shifting an entire population from one location to another through two small tunnels. I think you have the more difficult task."

He's right! What was I thinking? Suddenly I'm feeling in way over my head. How could I sign up for something I'm so pathetically unqualified to do? I'm just grateful I have good old Rals to help me. What would I ever do without him?

FORTY-FIVE

*R*yder has been gone for three days now, and the longing to see him is like a raw wound throbbing in my heart. Occasionally I'm clutched with fear that I won't set eyes on him again before IUGA whisks me back to Connecticut. I wonder if he remembers his promise to see me within the week. My insides churn each time the thought of leaving him crosses my mind, so I push those thoughts away spending my days in a kind of blissful denial. Maybe if I don't think about it, it won't happen.

Drew returns to the Enclave and updates us on developments at Warrington. He tells us the Unicoi trackers arrived, and search parties have been hastily organized throughout Domerica. The two regiments of soldiers from Dome Noir are scheduled to reach Warrington Palace within a day, and will be dispatched in search of Damien also.

A grid of the entire land mass under the dome has been drawn up by government engineers. The master plan calls for a search of every square inch of land, including the hundreds of caves located in the hills. Wanted posters with Damien's face and his distinctive snake tattoo have been distributed throughout the countryside. All shopkeepers, farmers, and ranchers are being interviewed for any information that might shed some light on the whereabouts of the Noirs.

"It will be impossible for a group of men that size to hide from us in Domerica." Drew says. "Eventually they will have to acquire food and water. When they do, we'll have them."

"Let us hope they're not encamped somewhere in the Outlands," Ralston says.

"If they are, we'll trap them when they attempt to reenter." Father replies. "Ryder is due back this afternoon with his explosives experts. He's also bringing some new KXT explosive to assist us in closing up the tunnels."

"That's fantastic!" I say, dashing for the stairs. "I need to clean up."

I can't remember the last time I ran a brush through my hair or paid any attention to my personal grooming. I spent the last three days and two nights working on the plan for the exodus of the Unicoi nation into Domerica.

Two days ago, a quietly beautiful and brilliant woman named Chimalis from the Unicoi Council of Elders arrived to act as liaison and assist us in coordinating the plan. I think Ralston has developed a little crush on her. Not only does she have luminous ebony eyes, golden skin, and an elegant manner, but she also appreciates Ralston's wry sense of humor. It makes me wonder if IUGA agents ever date.

In the short time she has been here, the two of them have sorted out many of the sticky issues relating to the transportation of humans, young and old, healthy and infirm, to a stretch of land that is currently used mostly as a buffet for fargen. They developed a strategy for clearing the land and preserving the lumber. Construction plans for a new Unicoi Village are being drawn up by government architects, and provisions for temporary housing are in the works. True to her word, Mother has made her experts available to us, and things are coming together nicely.

I wash my face, change into fresh clothes, and start to work on my hair when sounds of a great commotion downstairs make me stop my primping and open my door to see what's going on. Frantic voices rise from the landing below. Someone calls urgently for my father. I run to the top of the stairs and meet Ralston on his way up

TRANSCENDER: First-Timer

to get me. His face is white as a ghost.

"What is it, Rals? What's wrong?" I ask.

"Jade, it's Ryder. He's been hurt. Come quickly!"

I take the stairs two at a time and catch sight of Alexander and two Unicoi warriors standing in the front hall speaking with Drew. Both warriors are wounded and bleeding.

"What's happened? Where's Ryder?" I ask.

"He's been captured by Damien," Alexander says. "We were ambushed as we emerged from the tunnel. Damien's men overwhelmed us and took our weapons. The KXT was on my horse, and they took that too. Ryder was shot attempting to rescue me."

"Shot!" Father says, striding into the hall. "They had firearms?"

"Only one handgun that we could see," Alexander replies. "They may have more. Once they captured Ryder and the KXT, they rode off. Makoda is tracking them, but Ryder is badly injured. We must find him quickly."

Father examines the two wounded men. "These men need medical attention," he says. "Erica can take them to the hospital. Where did this happen?"

"At the west tunnel entrance. They retreated toward the hills at Wall's Edge."

"How many of them?" Father asks.

"Many," Alexander said. "Twenty, maybe more."

"Drew, you and your men go with Alexander. Make sure to take weapons for the others. I'll find Captain Hornsby, and we'll meet you there with reinforcements. We'll bring some firearms with us, just in case we need them."

"You have guns?" Drew asks.

"Captain Hornsby has a small store of them. You needn't tell your mother, though. This is the Enclave, Drew. We are equipped to protect ourselves. Swords are no equal for guns, so wait for us before engaging them."

"Father, I'm going with Drew," I say.

"No. Jade, it's better if you stay here. They have explosives and at least one gun."

I stare at him. "Father, its Ryder—I'm going."

He nods. "Get your sword. I'll have Peter saddle your horse. What about you, Ralston?"

"Yes, I'd like to go along," he says.

"Very well, we'd better get moving."

~ ~ ~ ~

Alexander leads us to the foot of the hills where Ryder was last seen being carried off by Damien and his men. Makoda is there with Ryder's friend Atian and three other warriors—the explosives experts, I assume.

"Have you found their trail yet?" Alexander asks, jumping from his borrowed horse.

Makoda shakes his head, frowning. We can follow their trail as far as the base of that hill. Then it disappears."

"Could they have climbed the hill?" Drew asks.

"Not on horseback," Atian says. "It is too steep and there is too much vegetation.

"More men are on the way," Alexander tells them. "But we cannot afford to wait for them. We must split up and search the area." He passes out the swords we brought.

"They are probably hiding in a cave," Atian says, as he straps on a weapon. "We will never find them. They could stay hidden for days."

TRANSCENDER: *First-Timer*

Alexander glowers at him. "Ryder does not have days. He will die if we do not find him soon. We must act now."

Alexander's blunt words send a wave of hot panic through me. I clasp Ralston's arm and pull him to the side so the others can't hear. "Ralston, you've got to find him. Get in touch with IUGA, ask them where he is. They must know. They know everything, right?"

"Jade, they won't know where he is. I told you it doesn't work that way. Since your arrival, everything we once knew is useless. We're operating in the dark."

"No! I don't accept that. We've got to find him. He could die!"

"You can do it, Jade," Ralston says quietly. "You can find him."

"Me? Are you out of your mind? How am I supposed to find him?"

He takes my arm and leads me to a large flat boulder. "Sit down for a moment and listen to me." I sit, reluctant to be wasting time.

"Remember when Ryder described the pull he feels toward you?" Ralston says.

"Yes. He said it was like a magnetic thing. So what?"

"Well, it's real Jade, and you have it for him also."

"No, I don't. It's different for me."

He shakes his head. "Listen to me, it is the same. You just believe it's different. A connection exists between you and Ryder. A bond, if you will. You are each powerfully drawn to the other. It is complicated to explain, but it's something that can be worked out when two souls have a long history together and wish to be reunited in other lifetimes. It's a contract between them—a Perpetual Contract. It doesn't mean they are intended to be together in *every* lifetime. But when two such souls do happen to meet, the connection becomes activated. It ensures that the purpose of the contract will be fulfilled."

I gape at him in anger and amazement. "Oh really? You knew this all along and you just forgot to tell me? You spent a whole lot of time trying to convince me that Ryder and I aren't supposed to be together. Was that just a bunch of crap?"

"No, no! It is true you are not meant to be together in *this* existence, and if you had not accidentally come into contact with Ryder, the connection never would have been established between the two of you. But since you did meet, the connection is present. The point is—you can use it to find him."

I shake my head. "I don't believe this. That's it? That's all we have to work with?"

He nods.

"Okay, what am I supposed to do?"

"I know it sounds impossible, but try to calm your mind. Focus on the feeling you have when you and Ryder are apart."

I close my eyes and suck in a deep breath, letting the air out slowly.

"Do you feel it, Jade?"

"Yes. It's kind of hard to find under all the panic, but it's definitely there."

"I think our best chance of tracking him is to attempt to work backward from that feeling. If the feeling begins to ease, you are getting closer to Ryder. If it worsens, you are getting farther away. Do you understand?"

I peer at him skeptically. "I understand what you are saying— kind of like the *hot-and-cold* game. I just don't know if it'll work."

"It has to," he says with finality.

I get to my feet, and we quickly rejoin the others.

"What's going on?" Drew asks.

"Jaden thinks she may be able to locate Ryder," Ralston says.

TRANSCENDER: *First-Timer*

Drew looks doubtful. "How?"

"By tracking him, in a way."

"That's absurd! Jade is no tracker."

"With respect, Prince Andrew, you don't know as much about Jaden as you think you do," Ralston says. "I'll wager that a week ago you would have said she was no fighter either. She has the ability; give her a chance."

Drew shrugs. "We can't do much until Father gets here anyway. Go ahead, Jade. Find him."

Alexander speaks up. "Princess Jaden, I hope you will understand that our first loyalty is to Ryder. We are experienced trackers. We must split up and cover as much ground as possible to find him."

Ralston begins to object, but I hold up my hand and speak to the Unicoi warriors. "I know you're all very skilled, but we don't have much time. Makoda, Alexander, do you remember the night I escaped with Ralston?" They both nod. "Ryder knew where I was. It was dark, and he wasn't tracking me in the traditional way, but he knew which cave I was in. Remember?"

"Yes, but he did not want us to recapture you. He wanted to allow you to go home," Makoda says. "We did not understand, but we stayed with him."

I smile. "Yes you are good friends. Ryder let me go home for the same reason he knew where I was. A unique connection exists between us. It's very strong, and I'm trying to use that same connection to find him. Please just give me a little time. We've got to stay together because we'll need your help if we find him."

Alexander and Makoda glance at each other and at Atian. They each nod in turn. "We'll stay," Alexander says speaking for the group.

"Thank you. Take me to the spot where the trail disappears."

I pause on the spot and close my eyes, concentrating on the hollow feeling in my chest. I turn to my right, no change. I turn left, same thing. Great! Now what am I supposed to do?

I take several paces to the right, pivot and walk several paces in the opposite direction. I sense a slight difference. "It feels better going left," I tell Ralston.

"Then let's go left," he says.

I move to the left along the base of the large hill, keeping my mind only on the feeling. After ten yards or so, the feeling begins to worsen again. I stop.

"Wait. We need to go back a little." I turn around and retrace my steps for a few yards. I sense he is close, but I don't know where to go next. I examine the side of the hill for a hidden cave or trail, but something inside of me says this is not the place.

I rub my temples, trying to concentrate harder. Ralston comes up behind me. "Jade, what is it?"

"There's something about this place—if I go east, the feeling gets worse, but it's the same if I go west. I'm stuck."

"This is madness!" Drew says. "We're wasting time. If you really want to save Blackthorn, we must find Father and have Hornsby's men fan out all over these hills."

"Look at this," one of the guards says. He points to a thick growth of trees and bushes near a shallow stream which flows from the hillside. A brown and white feather lies atop the branches of a bush about three feet from us.

"That's Ryder's," I say, snagging it from the bush. I hand it to Alexander, who nods in agreement.

Ralston pokes around in the bushes looking for other clues. A tiny droplet of dried blood clings to a leaf of a small sapling. He parts the tangled thicket with his hands. "What about in here, Jade?"

A narrow cleft has been carved in the hillside by the flowing stream. The cleft is virtually invisible from where we stand because of the overgrowth of trees and bushes.

TRANSCENDER: First-Timer

"Damien and the Noirs may have entered here and traveled down the middle of the stream," Ralston says. "That's why we can find no tracks."

I step into the shallow water. Ralston and Drew follow me. We wade a few yards up stream, and the raw feeling inside my chest begins to ease. A tiny spark of hope flares inside me.

I stop and look up toward the inside of the cleft. "He's here, Rals. There must be a cave off that ridge up there. See? They could ride their horses along that path to the north."

"You may be right," Ralston says, examining the ridge through a small telescope.

"No. I *am* right. I know he's there."

Drew blows out a long breath. "All right, Sister, what do we do now?"

"I'm not sure," I say. "We can't just go storming up the hill. They'll have a lookout. If they see us coming, I'm afraid they'll kill Ryder."

"Let's get the others and formulate a rescue plan," Ralston says. "The Unicoi will want to move quickly."

We tell Alexander what we've found and he follows us up the middle of the little stream. I show him the spot where Ryder is being held. He squints at the ridge and the path leading to it.

"I believe you are right," he says. "We should travel up the opposite side of the hill, and come from above them. It will be difficult terrain, but our chances of surprising them are better if we go that way."

"I agree," Drew says, and we wade back to join the others.

Squatting on the ground to scratch a diagram in the dirt, Drew uses a twig to draw a bell shape like the hill. "We will travel up the backside of the hill, and split up to approach the cave entrance from both sides, blocking any escape route. Our best strategy is to trap them inside."

Alexander nods and everyone looks to me.

"Let's do this," I say.

FORTY-SIX

*T*he horses slip and strain up the rocky slope of the hill. There's no path to speak of, and the terrain is steep and craggy. Father and the others will arrive to find us gone, but we can't spare anyone to stay behind to give them directions. We stop just short of the crest of the hill to rest our horses. Alexander dismounts, waving for Makoda to join him. The two of them disappear into the thick foliage on the side of the hill.

The short break is long enough for me to wonder just what in the hell we're doing. We have no plan, really. There are only twelve of us and more than twenty of them. They have at least one gun, maybe more. They'll probably pick us off like ducks in a shooting gallery when we come busting through the small entrance of the cave. The smart thing would be to wait for Father and the others, but my gut tells me we've got to find Ryder fast. We don't have a choice. I know Alexander feels the same.

Alexander and Makoda return a few minutes later. "We will leave our horses in that clearing ahead and approach them on foot," Alexander says, pointing to a bare spot among the trees. "We will make less noise that way. Only one man guards the cave entrance. I will go over the crest of the hill and drop down on him from above."

He looks to Drew. "Prince Andrew, I suggest that you and two of your men accompany two of my men and approach from the east. The remaining men and Princess Jaden will approach from the west."

375

Drew agrees, and we ride our horses to the clearing, where we quietly dismount, taking our weapons with us.

"I will wait until I can see you nearing the entrance before I take out the guard," Alexander says. "We must enter the cave swiftly. The ridge is barely wide enough to accommodate a man on a horse. Fighting there should be avoided if possible." We all nod and Alexander waves us forward.

My heart is bonging like Big Ben, but I'm strangely calm inside. I don't know what will happen in the next few minutes, only that it will be momentous. I know I may be killed or someone I love may be killed, but I also know in my heart this is something I must do. Ralston says it's all about the choices we make, and I am at peace with my choice.

We creep silently along the ridge, single-file. Makoda heads up our group. I follow behind him, then Ralston, two Royal Guards, and a Unicoi warrior at the rear. Drew, Atian, and the other men approach similarly from the other side. The Noir guarding the cave is stationed on our side of the entrance and as we draw closer, Makoda signals for us to hang back. We hug the side of the hill, out of sight.

I hear rather than see Alexander drop down from above. He lands on the guard with a loud thud, and they fall to the ground, struggling. Alexander clamps onto the guard's arms, rolls to the side, and pushes him off the cliff.

The commotion doesn't arouse any unwanted attention from inside the cave, so Alexander waves us toward the entrance. We pick up our pace, running quietly to him.

As we near the opening, Alexander takes the lead, bursting through the cave entrance, bellowing a thunderous war whoop. Swords drawn, the rest of us quickly follow.

The startled Noirs are taken completely unaware. Most of them are eating, sleeping, or just lying around. Drew and Atian easily disarm and subdue two men near the entrance, but the remaining men hastily find their weapons and the battle is engaged.

TRANSCENDER: *First-Timer*

The scene quickly becomes one of chaos—flailing swords, shouting men, flying fists. It's immediately clear to me that my newly-acquired fencing skills are pathetically inadequate against these trained fighters. I wouldn't stand a chance and would probably lose an arm or some other appendage within the first few minutes. So, instead of jumping into the melee, I make it my mission to find Ryder.

Cautiously clinging to the cave wall, I creep past the struggling combatants, holding my sword with both hands, and praying that no one notices the trembling girl in the shadows. All my senses are elevated to *DEFCON 1,* as sounds of clashing steel and raging men erupt all around me. A flood of adrenaline courses through my veins, propelling me forward.

I'm nearly knocked to the ground when Atian skewers a Noir in the leg and the guy tumbles backward into me. I shove him away with one hand and continue skulking along the wall toward the back of the cavern. In a darkened alcove to my right, I see a stone bench sticking out from the wall. Something or someone is heaped on top. It has to be Ryder. I can feel it inside.

As I reach him, my heart sinks at the sight of his waxen face. His right pant leg is black with drying blood. I fall to my knees, stroking his forehead with shaky fingers. His skin is hot to the touch. I feel under his chin for a pulse. It's there, but it's thready and weak.

"Ryder," I whisper, my mind grasping for a way to get him out of here. Before I come up with anything, though, I'm grabbed roughly from behind and yanked to my feet by a burly, bald Noir with rancid breath. My attacker pins my arms behind my back and swings me to his right, bringing me face-to-face with Satan himself.

Damien's hair is greasy and matted. His unmade-up face looks pasty and pock-marked. Cave living has taken an obvious toll on the prince's narcissistic ways. He raises his right arm stiffly, pointing a menacing handgun directly at my face. My heart stops beating for an instant, and the thought flits through my mind—*if I die in Domerica do I die in Connecticut too?*

"Hello, Princess, it's so good to see you again," Damien smirks.

"You have come to rescue your lover, I see. And now I have two high-value hostages instead of one. How thoughtful of you."

"Yeah, good to see you too, Damien," I say. "Nice snake." His serpent tattoo is clearly visible now, slithering up the side of his cheek and whispering in his ear. He leers at me, but his mega-watt grin is not quite as dazzling as it once was.

My mind shifts to overdrive, calculating my chances against Damien's gun. But before I can act, a Unicoi battle cry cuts through the air and I glance up to see Makoda hurtling toward Damien, his sword held high. Damien swivels slightly, steadies his aim, and coolly pulls the trigger. A loud blast echoes through the cave, and Makoda crumples like a broken doll.

"No-o-o!" I cry.

Unfazed, Damien turns the gun on me again. "These brave Unicoi warriors ... no match for a gun, eh?" His laugh is chilling.

"So, what do you think of your boyfriend now?" he asks, jerking his head toward Ryder. "I told you he was just a stupid boy. I think that soon he will be a dead stupid boy, just like his friend there."

I glare at him but don't reply. My blood sizzles with hatred and determination. I will not allow this monster to win! I will find a way to kick his ass and get Ryder out of here, or I will die trying.

He lowers his weapon, stepping closer to me. I flinch away from him, and the bald guy pulls my arms tighter from behind. The wolf-head necklace slips out of the neckline of my top.

"What is this?" Damien asks, grasping the dangling pendant with his left hand. "A trinket from your lover?" He lets it slide from his grip, and then he slowly traces the curvature of my breasts with his filthy fingertips. "I told you what you need is a real man," he says, licking his lips suggestively.

"And I told *you* what would happen if you ever touched me again without my permission."

I rear back, throwing all my weight against the burly guy behind me. Summoning every ounce of strength I possess, I spin my body to the left, kick up with my right leg, and clock Damien under the chin with the heel of my boot. I feel his jaw crunch as it fractures. His eyes roll back in his head, and he collapses in a heap. The gun clatters to the stone floor, skittering away from him.

The beefy guy still has my arms pinned, as Damien hits the ground, and I'm about to try a reverse kick to his groin, when an object comes flying through the air, and lands squarely on top of his naked head.

He yowls loudly, releasing my arms and grasping at the thing on his head. It looks like a mess of straw to me, but it's hissing and spitting, and clawing the hell out of the guy's chrome dome. In a flash of recognition, I realize it's the hungry Hillcat from my first night in Domerica. It pays to have friends.

I dive for Damien's gun, scrabbling on my hands and knees across the hard floor, while the cat makes mincemeat out of the guy's scalp. I grab for the gun just as a hand scoops it up and out of my reach. Shit!

I sit back on my haunches, half expecting to find the barrel pointed at my face again. But the guy who snagged it is holding it out for me to take. He isn't a Noir, but he isn't one of us either; then I place him—the hottie with the pale green eyes from the restaurant in Unicoi. I seize the gun.

"Who are you?" I ask.

"I'm Asher, a fellow Transcender," he says. "We need to talk." Then *poof.* He vaporizes into the air at the same instant an enormous sword slices across the spot where he was just standing. He reappears at once, three feet to the right and deftly kicks the sword from the hand of a startled Noir. Catching it midair, he uses it to impale the man through the arm.

"What the …?" I say, not believing my eyes. "What are you doing here?"

"I need to speak with you," Asher says.

"I'm a little slammed at the moment."

"I know. I'll find you afterwards." And he disappears again.

I don't have time to look for him. The battle is still raging all around me, and I know I have to find a way to end it—now—before anyone else winds up dead. I need to get Ryder out of here and to a hospital fast.

I've never fired a weapon in my life, but I use both hands to point Damien's golden gun at the ceiling, and I squeeze off a round. The report creates a deafening explosion inside the cave. Dust and debris from the ceiling fly everywhere. The Hillcat high-tails it out of there, leaving baldy moaning and clutching his head.

"Listen up," I shout. "The next person who moves gets capped." I steady the gun. "Everyone drop your weapons." Swords and knives clatter to the ground. With relief I see more of our guys standing than Noirs.

"Drew, get over here!"

He springs to my side. "Take this thing." I hand him the gun and he scans the crowd for anybody going for a weapon.

"I'm getting Ryder out of here."

"I'll help you," Alexander says, lifting Ryder from the bench.

"What about Makoda?" I ask.

"Dead," he replies.

"Oh, God, I'm so sorry."

Another explosion rocks the cave, this one louder and messier than the gun report. I duck the flying debris, but a thick cloud of dust makes it difficult to see what's happened. Someone must have set off a KXT charge.

A noisy clatter of hooves erupts to my left, and the Noirs' horses stampede from their pen. Damien's remaining men take advantage of the pandemonium to flee the cave also, concealing themselves among the frightened animals.

Drew pops off a random shot at the escaping herd, but doesn't hit anything. He curses loudly.

"Send your men after them," I say. "And make sure Damien's tied up," I jerk my chin toward his unconscious figure on the floor. "We've got to get Ryder to the hospital—now. Alexander, can you carry him to our horses?"

"Yes." Ryder is draped over his shoulder.

"Drew, I'm sorry to leave you with this mess. I'll find Father and send him to help. The Xtron may still be in the cave. You'll need to search for the rest of the explosives too. Let's hope the Noirs didn't run off with it."

Sheer bedlam reins outside the cave. Terrified horses crash over the cliff, while others run madly along the trail. A number of scuffles have broken out along the treacherously narrow spit of road. As we weave our way along, dodging the tumult in our path, another explosion sends rocks and chunks of bushes and trees shooting from the side of the hill.

Alexander and I move quickly to the horses. He carefully lays Ryder over his saddle and climbs up behind him. The ride is rough, and I'm thankful Ryder is unconscious and can't feel the pain of being jostled down the rocky terrain.

We meet Father and the others on their way up the hill. They followed the sounds of the explosions to find us. I quickly explain to Father what happened, and describe the location of the cave to him and Captain Hornsby.

"But, be careful," I tell them. "Several of Damien's men got away. They may still be nearby, and they have explosives."

"Jade, I'm coming with you," Father says. "Hornsby and his men can handle this. Ryder needs immediate attention."

"Thanks, Father."

"One of my brothers is dead up there," Alexander says to Captain Hornsby. "We must see that his body is returned to his family for a proper burial."

"I'll take care of it, son. I give you my word," Hornsby replies.

Once we reach the bottom of the hill, we ride swiftly to the Enclave hospital. On our arrival, several nurses and aides rush out to help us, but Alexander insists on carrying Ryder inside. Father directs us to an operating room, where Alexander gently settles Ryder's unconscious form on the table.

For the first time, I notice that Alexander's arm is bleeding. "You're hurt!" I say.

"It's nothing." He shrugs it off.

"You need to get that taken care of." Father calls to a nurse.

"See that his injury is tended to," Father tells her, and she leads a reluctant Alexander from the room.

Father immediately begins to work on Ryder's leg. He uses scissors to cut through the fabric of his pants. The congealed blood causes the material to stick to the skin, but Father expertly peels it away revealing a deep gaping wound.

A middle-aged woman with steel-gray hair and kind brown eyes steps to Father's side. "What can I do, doctor?" she asks.

Father instructs her to start an IV. "He's lost a lot of blood," he tells her.

"This is not going to be very pretty, Jade," he says. "You may wish to wait outside. It shouldn't take long."

"I'm staying."

"Then you might as well make yourself useful." He pulls a tray of instruments next to me. "Everything we need is there. Put on some gloves." He fills a syringe with what I assume is a local anesthetic.

"When I ask for something, it will be on the tray. Locate it and

TRANSCENDER: First-Timer

hand it to me. Sally will help you." He looks to the nurse with the kind eyes. She smiles and nods at me.

"Got it," I say. "Just make him better."

"I'll do my best, sweetheart."

Although the wound is deep, Father is able to locate the bullet quickly and remove it from Ryder's thigh. He tells me there is no irreparable damage, but there's so much blood I don't know if I believe him.

I lose count of the number of stitches it takes to join the tissue together again. Sally places a fresh gauze bandage over the incision and wraps the leg with additional bandages to keep it stable. The whole procedure takes about two hours.

"I think he'll be more comfortable at the house than he will be here," Father says. "And I can more easily monitor him throughout the night if he is there. Please arrange for the orderlies to transport him on a stretcher," he says to Sally. "Jaden, you go on ahead and see that his room is ready."

"Yes, Father, but are you sure he's going to be all right?"

"If he remains unconscious for long, we will consider giving him more blood. It was lucky you found him when you did, Jade. If he had bled much more, the result may have been different. As it is, I believe he'll have a complete recovery."

"Thank you Father. I don't know what I would have done if ..." I trail off.

"Best not to even think about that," he says, kissing my forehead. "Now go and get his bed ready for him. And sweetheart..."

"Yes?"

"You make a damn fine nurse."

~ ~ ~ ~

When the hospital orderlies place Ryder in his bed, he begins to come around a bit. "Jade," he mumbles.

"Right here, love," I say taking his hand as I sit in a chair I've placed next to his beside.

"Where am I?" he asks, groggily.

"At Father's house, in your room."

"Where is Alexander?"

"He's at the hospital, but he's fine, Ryder. He just needed some stitches."

"And Makoda?"

I bow my head and bite my lower lip. "He ... he didn't make it," I say with a sob.

Ryder stares at the ceiling, and a tear slides down the side of his face. "Anyone else?" he asks quietly.

"No, everyone else is fine."

"This is a very sad day, Jade."

"Yes, I know. But Ryder, we did get Damien."

"Was he responsible for killing Makoda?"

"Yes. Damien shot him too."

He turns his eyes to mine. "Did I lose my leg?"

"No! Father treated it. You're going to be fine."

"I guess that is a small consolation," he says. "I do love dancing with you."

I raise his hand to my lips and kiss it. "Get some sleep, love."

"Don't leave me," he whispers.

"I won't, I promise." I stroke his forehead, and he closes his eyes.

FORTY-SEVEN

*R*yder drifts in and out of wakefulness through the night. The medication seems to control his pain, but occasionally he moans softly or tries to move. I spend my time holding his hand, watching the rhythmic rise and fall of his chest beneath the sheet. I gaze at our intertwined fingers, thinking back to a few days earlier when we stood in front of Mother, and I announced my intention to marry him. It feels like eons have passed since then. I lift his hand and hold it to my cheek, breathing in his familiar scent.

"Jaden," Father says quietly from the doorway. "You should be in bed. You are probably suffering from shock yourself."

I smile and shake my head. Father has assured me over and over again that Ryder will be fine, but I can't bring myself to leave his bedside for fear he may need me. Father crouches beside my chair. "I won't force you," he says. "But at least climb up on the bed next to him and lie down. I'll put a blanket over you."

"Do you think that would be all right? I don't want to hurt him."

"He's heavily sedated. He won't feel a thing."

"And, it's fine with you? I mean, if I sleep next to him on the bed?"

"I'm not particularly concerned about propriety at the moment." He pulls a coverlet from the bottom dresser drawer. "Up you go."

"Thank you Father." I carefully crawl onto the bed and rest my head on the pillow next to Ryder's.

"Try to sleep for awhile. I'll check on you both later." Father spreads the soft blanket over me and I close my eyes.

~ ~ ~ ~

I pass the next two days in a kind of haze, camped out at Ryder's bedside. I've completely abandoned my responsibilities on the Unicoi migration project, dumping the whole thing on Ralston and Chimalis. Ralston tells me they're making excellent progress, though, and I figure they're probably better off working without me, anyway.

By the afternoon of the second day, Ryder is improved enough to eat solid food. We share some lunch and talk a little.

"Has the Xtron been recovered yet?" he asks.

"No. But everyone in the country and scores of soldiers from Dome Noir are looking for it. We'll find it, Ryder. Don't worry."

"Any progress in the search for Damien's men and the KXT?"

"Not that I've heard, but I'm sure they'll be captured soon. They can't stay hidden for long."

The news seems to disappoint him, and he loses interest in his food. I remove his tray and tuck the sheets around him as he drifts off to sleep again.

The house is unusually quiet today. Father's at the hospital, and Erica has the afternoon off. Ralston stopped by earlier to say that he and Chimalis were going into town for a few hours. I'd like to go outside and take a walk or ride Gabriel, but I don't dare leave Ryder, so I retrieve my book from the nightstand and settle myself in the bedside chair to read.

I sense rather than hear someone behind me in the doorway. As I turn, I'm shocked to find Asher leaning against the doorframe watching me.

"What are you doing here?" I say in an alarmed whisper.

TRANSCENDER: *First-Timer*

He smiles a lazy smile. "I told you I would find you. I could never get close to you at Warrington Palace. This place is much easier."

"What's that supposed to mean? What do you want?"

"Can we talk for a minute?" He nods toward the hallway. I put down my book and follow him, pulling Ryder's door closed behind me.

"Are you some kind of stalker or something?" I say, although he doesn't seem menacing at all. "Because I warn you, one scream from me and an army of servants will come running."

He's dressed in unusually modern clothing, blue jeans and a leather jacket. He laughs a sexy little laugh, green eyes twinkling. "I should think you would more likely just clobber me yourself. I understand your Tae Kwon Do skills are rather impressive."

"How do you know about that?"

"I know a lot about you—possibly more than you know about yourself. I've been trying to get you away from Agent Ralston so we could talk. The IUGA won't let us near you. I thought you would want to know that they're manipulating you Jaden, and they're lying to you."

"What do you mean?" I ask skeptically. "Lying about what?"

"The fact that you are a Transcender, for one thing."

Now it's my turn to laugh. "That's ridiculous. I can't travel between worlds at will. I'm here by accident."

"You have the ability. You only lack the training," he says. "Your showing up here couldn't be called intentional, but it isn't the kind of cosmic accident they're telling you it is either. It was an uncontrolled shift. Not bad for a first-timer, actually." He tilts his head and one side of his mouth quirks up.

"You're not supposed to end up in the body of your mirror, though. That's a big Transcender no-no. We can teach you how to use your gift—how to control your travels so you know where you're going and how to take your own body along."

He grins broadly. "Just think of it, Jade. Think of the things you can see and do if you have the ability to shift in and out of different dimensions and different worlds as you please, and then go home whenever you please."

"Is that how you did your little disappearing act in the cave the other day?" I ask. "You just shift in and out whenever you feel like it?"

"Yeah. Kind of cool, huh? You can learn to do that too. We can teach you."

"Who is *we* exactly?"

"The other Transcenders, Jaden. We want you to join us. At least come and speak with us. We'll tell you more about your gift and how to use it. Then you can make an informed decision."

"Now? You want me to come now?"

He gives a little shrug. "Why not?"

"Seriously? Well, for one thing, my fiancé is all banged up in the next room. I'm not leaving him alone. And for another thing, I'm not going anywhere with *you*. I don't even know you. I shouldn't be out here talking to you right now. If Ralston's trying to keep you guys away from me, there must be a good reason."

I hear the front door open and my father's voice downstairs. "You'd better go now. My father's home, and I need to get back to Ryder."

His translucent eyes turn cloudy. "I accept that as your answer for today Jade, but you can't run away from who and what you really are. Eventually you'll want to know more. We'll be back in touch when you're ready."

He walks to the top of the stairs and turns. "And don't let IUGA control you. Their motives are not as noble as they want you to *believe. Don't let them prevent you from living the life you were meant to live."* He skips down the first few steps and vanishes.

I quietly open Ryder's door. He's still sleeping soundly. Thank God he didn't hear any of that conversation! I'm shaken up by the whole thing myself.

What if Asher is telling the truth? What if I have a special gift and that's how I got here in the first place? It's a little thrilling and more than a little scary to think about. But why would Ralston lie about that? And do I really want to know if I'm some kind of freak of the universe?

It's too much to think about right now. The important thing is to get Ryder back on his feet. After that, I'll deal with Asher, and Ralston, and everything else.

Father appears in Ryder's doorway. "How's the patient?" he asks.

"He's good. He ate a little lunch, but he's still so weak … Hey, did you see that guy, uh man, just now?" I ask.

Father wrinkles his forehead. "What man?"

"Oh it was nobody. Someone looking for Erica," I lie.

"She is not working this afternoon."

"I know. That's what I told him."

Father checks Ryder's vital signs. Everything is normal. "He should be well enough to have visitors tomorrow," Father says. "Alexander has been by and is anxious to see him."

FORTY-EIGHT

*R*yder passes a peaceful night and seems to be feeling better in the morning. Some of the golden glow has returned to his cheeks. We share a small breakfast, after which I excuse myself to take a much needed shower and to dress for the day.

On my way back to Ryder's room, I run into Alexander coming to pay him a visit.

"I'll take you," I tell him. "He's looking forward to seeing you."

"I've missed him," Alexander says. "Thank you for caring so well for him."

Ryder seems cheered when Alexander walks in.

"Peace, Ryder. How are you feeling?" Alexander asks, beaming. He seems to bring the fresh air with him, a wave of cleansing energy.

"Better now that you are here," Ryder says. "Please sit and keep me company. How is Meli?"

"She is well." Alexander says. "She ... we ... I am going to be a father."

Ryder grins. "That's wonderful news! Congratulations. Please give my best to her."

"I will. She sends her love and wishes for your rapid recovery. Your father does, as well."

TRANSCENDER: First-Timer

"How is he?" Ryder asks.

"Concerned for you, but otherwise his condition is unchanged."

"Tell him I love him and will see him soon."

"I will, brother."

"What is the news on the search efforts for the Xtron?" Ryder asks Alexander.

"The cave where Damien was holed-up has been thoroughly searched, but the Xtron was not found. Damien's men must have taken it, along with the KXT."

"The Xtron is the most important thing," Ryder says. "But the KXT is capable of inflicting great damage."

"Be at peace. We will locate them," Alexander says.

"And what has become of Damien?"

"He is still at Wall's Edge Prison until his fate can be decided. King Philippe desires that he be returned to face judgment in Dome Noir. Queen Eleanor believes that since his crimes were committed in Domerica, he should face his punishment here. I think the queen may have the upper hand in that argument. Prince Gilbert supports her position."

"Gilbert is a decent man," Ryder says, "unlike his youngest brother. Has Damien been questioned about the Xtron? Has he made any kind of a statement?"

"No. He has not uttered a word since his capture. Of course, that may have something to do with the fact that his jaw was badly broken and is wired shut," he says, shooting a smile my way.

"How did that happen?" Ryder asks.

"Let us just say that your fiancé is clever on her feet, and *with* her feet."

"Jaden?" Ryder looks quizzically at me.

"Never mind," I say. "We'll talk about it later."

Ryder asks about Makoda, and Alexander tells him the body was taken back to Unicoi for a warrior's funeral. Ryder expresses his regret at not being able to attend and pay his respects to the family.

"Do not trouble yourself about it," Alexander says. "You were there for him in life. Everyone knows how much you loved him."

"I still can't believe he is gone," Ryder says.

"His death will not be in vain," Alexander says. "Damien will die for this."

"Let us hope the queen does not see fit to sentence him to reeducation instead. He is still a prince of Dome Noir."

"If she does, it will not prevent justice from occurring. The Unicoi are not bound by Domerican laws. It will mean only that Damien's death will be delayed."

Ryder places a hand on Alexander's arm. "We both loved Makoda. But I caution you, brother, not to be consumed by thoughts of revenge. We must act with care right now. Do not give the queen an excuse to change her mind about providing a refuge for our people."

Alexander stiffens in his chair and looks ready to argue the point.

"You're going to be a father soon," Ryder adds. "You must think of your new family."

At the mention of this, Alexander's face relaxes into a smile. "Do not worry about me. I have a feeling justice will find Damien, whether it is by my hand or not.

"And now, you must rest." He gets up from his chair. "Catherine sends her love, and eagerly awaits your homecoming. She is compiling a list of urgent matters for you to attend to immediately upon your return, so you may wish to take a few extra days to recover."

They grasp each other's forearms and Alexander leaves,

promising to come again tomorrow. Ryder seems exhausted by the short visit, so I arrange the covers around him, and he quickly falls asleep.

I gaze out the window for a moment, looking forward to the day when Ryder will be up and about again. Taking my book from the nightstand, I open it to the page I've marked and nestle back in my chair. Catching up on the classics has been one perk of not having TV, music or the internet to distract me. Soon I'm so engrossed in *Robinson Crusoe* that I don't even hear Ralston's footsteps on the stairs.

"Good evening, Jade," he says, standing in the hall, silhouetted by the midday light.

"Hey Rals," I say softly. "Come in."

"How is he today?" he whispers, peering at Ryder's slumbering form.

"Actually, he's better. Father says he can get up tomorrow and start using that leg."

"That's wonderful. I'm happy to hear it. May I speak with you for a moment?"

"Oh sure." I close my book and lay it on my chair. Ralston and I step into the hallway and he shuts Ryder's door. When he turns to face me, his eyes are gentle but his expression is serious.

"What is it Rals? Is something wrong?"

He hesitates for a moment. "Jade, I'm very pleased that Ryder is so much better, and that he will undoubtedly enjoy a full recovery."

"Okay ... that's nice," I say, waiting for him to get to the point.

"That should reassure you and make it easier for you to leave him now."

"What do you mean?" A knot of dread begins to form in my stomach.

"I mean that you and I depart for Warrington in the morning. I've told your father that we are going to personally deliver the Unicoi transition proposal to Queen Eleanor. In reality, I've received word that it is time."

"Time? No. It can't be time yet."

He clasps both my hands in his and smiles. "You are going home, Jade, at last!"

I jerk my hands away. "No! I'm not going back. I can't go home right now. I can't leave Ryder like this. You need to tell them." My legs quiver beneath me, and tears well up in my eyes.

He puts an arm around me. "I know it hurts, my dear, but you knew this day would come. You understand this is how it must be. It isn't your decision, or *mine*. IUGA has gone to great lengths to arrange your transportation home, back to your own world and your own body."

I pull away from him. "No, no, no!" I shake my head violently, hugging myself to stave off a growing wave of nausea. "It has to be my decision; it's my life! You can't interfere with my free will. You told me that. I don't want to go home. My life here means something. I can make a difference. I *have* made a difference."

"Free will cannot be allowed to supersede destiny, Jade. Your destiny is not in this world. Your continued presence here amounts to an unwarranted interference. The events of this universe must be allowed to unfold as they were preordained. Without you."

Torrents of tears cascade down my face. "But there's nothing for me back in Connecticut. *I* am nothing in Connecticut."

"That's not true. What about your family? They need you."

"My family is here. I can't leave them, not in the middle of this crisis. They need me more." I glance at Ryder's door. "*He* needs me."

He shakes his head sadly. "Jade, you have your whole life ahead of you. You have important things to do with that life. Things which are unimaginable to you right now."

TRANSCENDER: First-Timer

"I can't leave him, Ralston," I choke through my tears. "I love him. We're connected. Tell the director about our Perpetual Contract. He'll have to figure out another plan—a plan where I stay here."

"He knows about the contract, Jade. It's not valid under these circumstances. There is no other way. You must leave now."

I narrow my eyes at him. "I don't believe you. Asher says you're lying to me. He says I'm a Transcender, like him. He says I can travel among the different worlds at will like he does, and return home whenever I want to. So why do I have to leave now?"

Ralston's face turns an ugly shade of red. "Asher was here? He has no approval to be here! What did he tell you?"

"He says my being here isn't a cosmic accident. He called it an uncontrolled shift. He says he can teach me how to control my travels, so that I can come and go whenever I please. Is it true, Rals? Am I a Transcender like he is?"

He stares at me for a moment, his jaw muscles clenching in and out. "Yes. It's true. You are a Transcender. We kept it from you because you still have a chance at a normal life, Jade. The life of a Transcender is no life for you. They are galactic nomads, showing up where they are not wanted, making a mess out of everything.

"Listen to me, Jade, if you cooperate with us, you can still resume your life back in Connecticut exactly the way it was. The odds of an uncontrolled shift ever happening to you again are less than zero."

His eyes lock onto mine. "But, if you refuse to cooperate, IUGA cannot guarantee the outcome, either here or back in your real home. The results may be dire."

I glare at him. "You lied to me after you promised you wouldn't. I can't trust you, and I'm sure as hell not going with you. You can't make me. IUGA can't make me go home, either. You listen to me. You are leaving alone tomorrow, and I don't ever want to see you around here again. Do you understand? You're fired!"

He blinks once and bows his head slightly. "As you wish," he says. "I will leave you. That does not alter the fact that you must return home without delay."

"If you send me home against my will, I'll just come right back."

"Do not even think of trying it, Jaden. You are playing with fire. You do not know how to use your gift. You may find yourself in a hostile universe where your very life is placed in jeopardy. Or worse, you could interfere with the course of events in yet another world and cause irreparable harm to that realm. You must not misuse your gift! The forces for order in the universes will not tolerate a Transcender run amok." He turns on his heel and hurries down the stairs.

I slump against the wall and slide to the floor. What have I done? I'm sick inside, utterly miserable. Not only have I renounced my former life completely, but I've banished my guide, mentor, and friend forever. His final warning echoes in my ears. Hell, I barely know what a Transcender is, now I'm about to become some sort of inter-galactic outlaw.

"Jade." Ryder's voice carries weakly through the door. I leap to my feet and wipe away my tears.

"Coming," I call, realizing none of that really matters. My destiny is with Ryder now. We can make it through anything as long as we're together.

FORTY-NINE

*B*oth Father and Ryder insist that I sleep in my own room instead of in the chair next to Ryder's bed, and I have my first good night's sleep in days. I wake up feeling refreshed and optimistic about the future, if a bit guilty about the way I treated Ralston.

I don't know how to explain to Father and Chimalis and everyone else why Ralston has bailed on us before the relocation proposal has been presented to my mother. Creative differences, maybe? It's probably best just to tell them that Ralston got word of some urgent business elsewhere and had to leave. But I haven't figured out how to word it without it sounding totally bogus.

As I brush out my hair, pondering this dilemma, someone knocks softly at my door.

"Jade, are you up?"

It's Ryder! I rush to the door and find him leaning on a crutch and grinning lopsidedly.

"Good morning, love. Before he left for the hospital, your father said I could get out of bed this morning if I use this crutch. I believe I need some help on the stairs, though, so I fear you are stuck playing nursemaid again."

I'm overjoyed to see him on his feet. "This is great! I'm happy to help you downstairs if you promise not to overdo."

"I solemnly swear," he says, holding up his free hand.

He places his arm around my shoulder, and we carefully hobble down the stairs one step at a time. I guide him to Father's great room.

"Where would you like to sit?" I ask. "In Father's chair with the ottoman?"

"No. Help me to the window seat. I would enjoy a view of the grounds. I feel rejuvenated just looking at them."

The generous window seat runs the entire length of an enormous bay window. I situate Ryder in one corner and gently prop his injured leg on the bench.

"Come and sit with me," he says, opening his arms.

I balance on the edge of the bench, careful not to push against his leg. His arms wind around me and I rest my head on his chest, happy to be in his protective embrace again.

He strokes my hair tenderly. "I've missed holding you so much," he says.

"Me too."

"They tell me it was you who found me in that cave. How did you do it?"

"I guess that magnetic pull thing works both ways," I say. "So I just followed my heart."

"Can you even imagine how much I love you?" he whispers.

I raise my head and study his face. "I'm not sure I can. In my wildest imagination I never dreamed I could love like this."

He holds my head against his chest and sighs. Our hearts beat in perfect rhythm. I'm at one with him again, my love, my soul mate.

After a moment he speaks softly. "When I was wounded and feared I would die, my thoughts were all of you—the touch of your

TRANSCENDER: First-Timer

hand, the warmth of your mouth, the depth of your heart. And believe it or not, I was happy." He kisses my hair. "I knew I could die a happy man for the outrageous good fortune of having been loved by you."

I marvel at his courage. I've shown myself to be a sniveling coward when it comes to thoughts of leaving him. "Thanks for coming back to me," I say, holding him tightly.

We sit in silence for a moment and he asks, "Have you any news of Damien's men?"

"No, I'm afraid not. There've been a couple of reported sightings, thefts of food, things like that, but the leads go nowhere. Damien did speak for the first time, though, to Father, when he was rechecking Damien's jaw."

"Anything useful?"

"Not really. He says if he's not released soon, his men will come for him. In the meantime, they'll *wreak havoc on Domerica*. That's a direct quote."

"So he believes his men are still here and still operating on his instructions?"

"Yes, and that scares me. We know what Damien is capable of, but do you think his men would really try to destroy Domerica?"

"I don't know, love," he says, placing his finger under my chin and lifting my face to his. "But you should not worry. We will find them, I promise you."

"I know. I'm fine."

"What does your mother intend to do with Damien?"

"She hasn't made that decision yet, but I believe if Damien agrees to tell her where the Xtron is, she may just send him home as his father is demanding."

"She is in a difficult position," Ryder says. "She is dedicated to administering swift and sufficient justice. King Philippe would probably do no more than place Damien under house arrest at the Chateau. To allow him such slight punishment would make your mother appear weak. But the return of the Xtron is essential to ensure the safety of Domerica. It is not an easy choice."

"I'm glad it's not my call to make," I say.

"Someday, when you are queen, you may be faced with an equally difficult dilemma," he says.

I draw in a deep breath, processing for the first time that my decision to stay with Ryder means I'll someday succeed my mother as queen. I can't truthfully say it's a job I desire or one I'm capable of. I only hope I'll have many years to grow into it.

Ryder gazes out the window distractedly. "What time is it?" he asks.

"Around 10:30, I think. Why?"

"It almost looks as though it's going to rain." Concern creases his brow.

"Way too early for that."

He nods, but still appears troubled.

"How are your plans for the Unicoi migration coming along?" he asks, changing the subject. "Father has sent word that our people are making their preparations and are anxious for the day when we will be free of the Uranium scourge forever. Although, I fear it is too late to save him."

"You never know, Ryder. There may still be hope." My heart hurts for him. "The proposal is on its way to my mother and your father. I think it's a workable plan, thanks to Ralston and Chimalis. I'm sure the transition will go smoothly."

"Where *is* Ralston, by the way?" he asks.

I'm about to launch into my half-baked story about Ralston's sudden vanishing act, when Ryder and I are nearly jolted from the window seat by a loud, rumbling noise.

"What was that?" Ryder asks. "An explosion?"

"It sounded like thunder," I say.

"What do you mean? Thunder? Inside the dome? That's impossible!" But as he says it, the dome grows darker and raindrops begin to pelt the window glass. I stand, helping Ryder to his feet. We both stare out the window in astonishment.

"Ryder, what's happening?"

A bolt of lightning splits the air.

"It must be the Noirs! They've breached security at Dome Operations and are manipulating the weather. My men are stationed there. I must go at once."

"That's crazy. You can't go anywhere with your leg like that."

"I have to." He grabs his crutch and hobbles toward the door. "Go find your father. Tell him to send reinforcements."

"No, Ryder!" I clutch his arm. "You're still too weak. I'll go."

"Jade, you are *not* going! Find your father quickly. That is the most useful thing you can do." He tosses the crutch aside, limps out onto the porch, and whistles for Tenasi.

I run to the kitchen calling for Erica. She and the kitchen staff are huddled around a window watching the freak storm.

"Erica! You've got to go to the hospital and find my father, now."

"What is it? What is happening to us?" she asks, her features drawn together in fear.

I take hold of her arms. "I don't know, but listen to me. Ryder thinks someone has sabotaged the Dome Operations Center. Find Father and tell him Ryder has already gone there and needs reinforcements as soon as possible. Do you understand?"

"Yes," she says, trembling. "Send reinforcements," she repeats.

"To where?" I quiz her.

"To the Dome Operations Center." she adds more forcefully.

"Good girl. And hurry!" I rush out the back door, and dash for the stables. Another lightning bolt pierces the air, followed closely by the deafening roar of thunder. I'm drenched by the time I reach Gabriel's stall. I quickly saddle and bridle him, and he's already in motion when I jump onto his back.

"Throw me your sword!" I shout to Peter as I bolt from the stables.

"Princess, what's wrong?" he calls.

"Throw me your sword!" I shout again. He unbuckles his scabbard and tosses it to me. I catch it and wedge it between me and the saddle. I urge Gabriel into a dead run, praying Ryder hasn't gotten too far ahead of me. I'll never find my way to Dome Operations by myself. I know the general location, but I've not actually been there.

The rain falls in sheets, obscuring the road in front of me. I can barely make out Ryder's form in the distance. He'll be angry that I've followed, but I can't let him face the Noirs alone.

I'm pissed at myself for telling Ralston to get lost last night. How will I get through this without him? He'd know what to do, or at least he'd make sure I came to no harm. God only knows what's going to happen now.

Ryder turns his horse into the hills and I follow. This new road is rough and narrow with a dense thicket of trees running the length of both sides. Wiping the water from my eyes, I strain to keep him in sight.

Lightning rips the sky above me, and Gabriel rears up, nearly throwing me to the ground. I manage to hang on, but he's spooked by the storm and slow to calm down. Ryder is quickly disappearing in the distance—I'm losing him.

I pat Gabriel's neck and speak soothingly to him. Once he has quieted, I gently urge him forward again, but by now Ryder has completely disappeared from view.

I don't know what to do. The rain is so intense I can hardly make out my surroundings, and the road is rapidly becoming a river of mud. I pick my way along slowly, looking for a road sign or a structure or anything that might help me to know where I am, but soon I'm hopelessly lost. I don't even know if I'm still going in the right direction. Maybe I missed a turn somewhere. I'm about to give up and turn around, when the rain stops abruptly, as though someone has turned off the faucet.

Able to see again, I look over my shoulder trying to get my bearings and, as I do, all thoughts of being lost are immediately replaced by sheer panic at the sight behind me.

Fire! A colossal fire blazes in the forest to my rear. Ferocious red flames shoot high into the air. Thick plumes of black smoke billow into the dome. It must have been sparked by the lightning, and it appears to be raging despite the previous soaking rain. It's a disaster of epic proportions! Nothing can destroy the ecosystem or suck the oxygen out of the dome faster than fire.

Fear tears at my insides. Father and his men will never be able to make it around the fire to the Dome Operations Center, if they even try. But, they, and every other available man, woman and child in Domerica will be needed to help put out the fire and save the dome.

I momentarily consider returning to help douse the fire myself, but I can't turn back now. I must find Ryder and the Operations Center. He's all alone, and I'm all he's got.

I frantically knee Gabriel forward and swing my gaze back to the road in front of me, but all I see is the blur of a low-lying tree branch before it slams into my forehead, sending rockets of pain through my skull. My body is violently thrown backward.

The last thing I remember is the sensation of tumbling— tumbling from Gabriel's back and tumbling from the face of the earth.

FIFTY

I awaken in the quiet darkness of my room. A troubling dream flits across the edge of my mind before I can grasp the retreating wisps. My thoughts immediately go to Ryder, as they always do when I first wake. Then I remember. The fire, the storm!

I sit bolt upright in bed, wincing at the pain in my forehead. I recall being knocked from my horse. But what happened after that? I reach for the lamp on my table. It's not there.

Wait a minute—this isn't my room at Father's house, or at Warrington Palace. This room has boxes stacked everywhere. I'm momentarily disoriented, and then dreadful recognition seeps into my brain and a cold wave of horror shudders through my body. I know this room. I'm back in Madison, and this is moving day.

I clutch at my chest for Ryder's necklace, knowing it's not there.

"No-o-o!" I howl, springing from my bed. I fly downstairs and out the back door. It's raining heavily, but the lightning storm has vanished. I search the sky. No sign of horsemen in the clouds.

Winding my way through the boxes, I find the section of porch railing where I dove to the other side. Maybe if I jump in exactly the same spot, I can find the wormhole or Transcender door or whatever it was, and be transported back to Domerica. I have to try.

I climb to the top of the railing and leap into the air, only to splat hard in the mud and thorny bushes. A cry of pure anguish breaks from my throat as the full impact of the truth is driven home. He's gone. My love, my life. I've lost Ryder, forever.

Grief, raw and wild, envelopes me. Not the dull, sickly grief I felt when Mom died, but an untamed, uncontrollable madness. I turn my face to the sky and keen like a wounded animal, the pounding rain drowning out my mournful cries. I feel my insides have been ripped out, leaving only an empty, dying shell.

I lie in the mud wishing only to sink deeper and deeper into the soil, into my final resting place. The weight of my dire situation presses me further and further into the earth. I wonder if it's humanly possible to survive without a heart and soul, but in truth, I don't care. Surviving would be the cruelest fate of all.

I lie there, crying, for what feels like hours. Eventually, the rain subsides, and the sky lightens with the first rays of dawn. I know I need to go inside, I can't lay in the mud in my pajamas forever. So I pull my sorry carcass off the ground and drag myself to my room, trailing dirty water as I go. I strip off my wet clothes, tug on a nightgown, and make a half-hearted stab at rinsing the soil from my hair before climbing back into bed.

In the darkness I picture Ryder's face the last time I saw him, riding off in the rain, his expression grave and determined. It's unbearably painful to think of him, but I force myself to relive every moment of that last morning. I vow never to forget any detail of our time together.

I think of Mother and all that she is going through. I pray she'll be all right. I never got to say goodbye to her this time either.

I cry until it seems I can't possibly have more tears inside me. I cry until morning has fully broken, and I hear a muffled knock at my door. And still I cry when the door opens a crack to reveal my dad's worried face.

"Jade, can I come in?" He asks quietly.

I sit up and wipe my nose with my sleeve. "Sure Dad. I'm sorry if I woke you."

He sits on the side of my bed. "Sweetheart, I know this is hard for you. It's hard for all of us." He's trying to be so kind, but he doesn't have a clue what the real source of my anguish is, and I can never tell him.

"I've tried so hard to hold things together since Mom died." He shakes his head sadly. "I guess I haven't done a very good job. I wish we could stay in this house. I know how much you love it. There are so many memories of Mom here." He lowers his head. "We just can't do it, though, and send you kids to college. I had to decide what was best for the family. You may not be able to see that now, but I hope someday you'll understand."

He raises his head, eyes brimming with tears. "I miss her so much. It's killing me to leave behind everything Mom and I shared and worked so hard for. It's like a part of me is missing, and I don't even know how to get it back." His voice breaks. "You and Drew are the only things that keep me going."

I gaze at my dad, and for the first time I get it. I understand the acutely unbearable pain he's going through. He lost his wife, his love, his life. I throw my arms around his neck, and we cry together.

"I'm so sorry, Dad. I should've been more understanding."

"You had your own grief to deal with, sweetheart. Don't apologize."

"But I couldn't see past my own pain. I couldn't see the hell you were going through."

He squeezes me tight, and then pulls away to look at me. "Don't worry about it. We're all doing the best we can." He wipes the tears from his cheeks.

"What happened to your forehead?" he asks, pushing my hair away from my face.

"It's nothing. I just bumped my head last night."

"Did you clean that cut?" he asks, always the nurse.

TRANSCENDER: *First-Timer*

"Yes, Dad. It's nothing, really."

"I do have one bit of good news for you," he says, surprising me with a smile.

"What?"

"I spoke with Mr. Padget at the school district yesterday. They've agreed to let you stay at school through the end of the year, even though we're moving out of the district. I convinced him that since you only have a couple of months left, it wouldn't mean much to them, but it would mean a great deal to you. He was pretty nice about it."

"Dad, that's great," I say. I couldn't care less about school at the moment, but I want Dad to know I appreciate his efforts.

He gets up and pulls a tissue from the box on my dresser. "Okay, sweetheart, we have a big day ahead of us. I'm going to fix us some breakfast. I'll see you downstairs."

"Okay Dad, and thanks."

~ ~ ~ ~

It is a big day—a very long and busy day. I'm thankful for the distraction of moving. It doesn't keep my mind off of Ryder and Domerica, but it does keep me from crawling back into that black hole of grief and wallowing there.

Thoughts of using my Transcender gifts to return to Domerica float through my mind, but I discard them for now. The fact is I have no idea how to deliberately shift from one world to another, and the fear of what might happen if I do it wrong scares the hell out of me. I could get lost in the universe forever. I wonder if Asher will ever show up again. I could kick myself for not going with him when he asked.

I'm furious every time I think about Ralston lying to me, and the IUGA forcing me to go home against my will. I know Ralston thought he was doing what was best for me and the galactic order, but it was cruel not to give me a choice.

I try to make myself feel better by recalling what Ralston said one day: "If it's meant to be, you and Ryder will find each other." I cling to that hope for strength every time I'm about to break down again. I believe with all my heart and soul (or what's left of them, at least) that Ryder and I are meant to be together. So we will be. End of discussion.

The new townhouse isn't terrible. It's small, but cute and clean, with fresh paint and new carpeting. It even has a tiny back yard and a matchbook-sized patio. Drew's bedroom and bath are in the basement. I'll inherit that space when he goes off to Duke in the fall. Dad's room, my room, and a small shared bathroom are on the second floor. A living room, dining room, and kitchen make up the main floor. Lots of stairs to climb—but not as many as at Warrington Palace, I remind myself.

The hole in my heart throbs constantly while I unpack boxes of our family stuff. By outward appearances only my address has changed. No one could ever guess the real truth—that *I* have changed completely. My experiences in Domerica are an indelible part of me now. They will influence my view of the world for the rest of my life. The love I shared with Ryder will be my eternal beacon. The hope that I'll someday see him again will keep me hanging on. No matter how many years come between us, he'll forever be the love of my life.

It makes me a little crazy not knowing what happened after my disappearance. I hope and pray that Ryder is safe and will somehow find happiness again. I'm glad and a little proud to think that he and the rest of the Unicoi nation will soon be living in Domerica— assuming the dome survived. I refuse to consider the alternative.

I work without a break throughout the afternoon, and get most of the boxes unpacked. I organize the kitchen and set up the shared family living space, saving my room for last.

My new room is about half the size of my old one. I gaze at the stacks of boxes, and wonder how I'll ever get all my things to fit. Sure they're just things, but each one of them represents a treasured piece of my old life. I won't easily give them up.

I lose all track of time while I work. Old memories are revived by each new item I unwrap. These are the things that make up my little world in Madison: my music, my books, my photo albums, my jewelry box (miniscule compared to Princess Jaden's). I unconsciously reach for the silver wolf necklace now missing from my neck, and a sharp pain pierces my heart.

Around midnight, Dad pokes his head in my room. "It's getting late, Jade. Why don't you call it a night?" he says.

I sit on the floor placing my books in the half-size bookcase I've managed to wedge inside the already over-stuffed closet. "I will Dad. Just a few more things to do."

"All right. Don't make it too late, though." He smiles, and the corners of his eyes crinkle the way they always did before Mom died. He seems different. Maybe it's getting out of that house full of memories, or maybe it's the moment of understanding we shared this morning. Whatever it is, I'm glad to see him smile again.

"I won't be much longer," I say. "Hey Dad?"

"Yeah."

"Have you ever thought of growing a beard?"

He rubs his chin. "I don't know. Do you think I need one?"

"It might look nice."

"I'll give it some thought," he says. He glances at my disorganized desk. "Has Drew hooked up the network yet?" he asks. "You guys are going to need it for school."

"I don't think so, but I'll remind him tomorrow."

"Okay, g'night, sweetheart."

"G'night, Dad."

I look over at the top of my desk, my eyes resting on my laptop, and suddenly it hits me—if there's a Ryder Blackthorn on this earth, I can find him! I can't believe I didn't think of it before. I don't have to sit around waiting for fate to take its course. This isn't backward Domerica. I have the internet!

I know his name, birth date, and his parents' names. That's enough to get started. If I have to contact every Blackthorn in the United States, or the world for that matter, I'll do it. It might take years, but I don't care. A surge of shiny new hope swells inside of me.

I have a plan! If I can find Ryder and arrange to meet him somehow, the bond between us will be activated. According to Ralston we have a contract to be together. I know if I set my mind to it, I can make it happen! I *will* make it happen.

EPILOGUE

ONE YEAR LATER

*T*he doorbell rings. Ten-thirty on Saturday morning. Kind of an odd time for visitors. Dad's working the early shift at the hospital because he has another date with Lisa tonight. They've been seeing a lot of each other lately. Drew's still in Durham taking finals at the end of his freshman year at Duke.

I check the peephole and reluctantly open the front door to a uniformed police officer.

"Good morning, Miss Beckett. Nice to see you again," he says, smiling broadly.

"Hello, Officer Wilson. Can't say I'm thrilled to see you."

"May I come in?"

I step back from the doorway and gesture him inside. "Have a seat."

"Thank you, but this should only take a minute," he says, pulling his little black notebook from his belt. He flips to a page in the middle of the book. "I'm sorry to say the department has received another call about you." He looks up from his notes, his eyes a warm chocolate brown. "You know, Miss Beckett, I kind of thought you'd finally given up the ghost; things have been so quiet these past few months." He continues with a disappointed shake of his head. "But now we get this call from a lady named ..." He checks his notes, "*Catherine* Blackthorn. Ring a bell?"

I fold my arms across my chest and stare at him without responding.

"She says you've been harassing her for the past two weeks. First on the phone and then at her home in Glastonbury." He taps a finger on the notebook page. "Even says here you accosted her in Saks Fifth Avenue while she was shopping in Manhattan. I assume that wasn't just a chance meeting?"

"No, I followed her," I say. "But that's out of your jurisdiction."

"Be that as it may, it's still part of a pattern of harassment. Sounds like stalking, if you ask me."

"I'm not harassing her. She just said that because she's never liked me."

"She claims she's never even *met* you, Miss Beckett!" He spreads his arms in a *gimme-a-break* gesture. "She doesn't know who you are, and the lady's scared. You can't blame her."

"Has she filed a complaint?"

"Not at this time." He closes his notebook and puts his hands on his hips. "I managed to convince her you're harmless. I assured her your offensive behavior would cease immediately. Do I make myself clear on that?"

"Well, what exactly would be considered offensive behavior?"

"Miss Beckett! I don't want you having any contact with this woman *whatsoever*. That means no phone calls, no visits to her neighborhood, no showin' up in her favorite department store, either."

"Oh come on, what if it's just a coincidence? Maybe we have the same taste in clothes."

"Look Miss Beckett, I would hate to have to arrest you. I know you're starting at Yale in the fall, and I don't believe they would consider stalking an acceptable extracurricular activity."

Okay, now he has my attention. "I'm not stalking her, I just want to know where her brother is."

"I don't get it," he says, scratching his head. "What made you latch onto this woman?"

"She's his sister. After a year I finally found his family, and it turns out they're right here in Connecticut. But he's not living with them, and she won't tell me where he is."

"Well, of course not. She's petrified. She thinks you're some kind of loony-tune. She's not going to tell you how to find her brother."

"I just want to know where he is," I say through gritted teeth.

A year's worth of frustration and disappointment threaten to overwhelm me. All that time, and not one iota of evidence had surfaced that Ryder Blackthorn was anything other than a dream. At moments during the last twelve months I even doubted my own sanity. But then I saw her! I saw Catherine with my own eyes. That's all the proof I need. I'm so close—closer than I've ever been. I can't stop now even if it means not going to Yale. Hot tears sting my eyes.

Officer Wilson stands with his hands on his hips, watching me for a moment. "Look Miss Beckett," he says gently, "are you sure this is even the right guy? You've had a few missteps already."

"Yes! It's him. I know Catherine. I know she's his sister."

"Why does she say she's never met you before?"

I wave my hand dismissively. "She just doesn't remember. It's been a long time, and she never liked me anyway," I repeat, swiping tears from my cheeks.

He looks skeptical. "Yeah, well, she also says anyone who is *really* a friend of her brother would know where he is."

"What?" I spring from the couch. "She told you where he is?"

"Whoa." He holds up both hands. "You know I can't give you any of that kind of information. That would be viewed as facilitating the harassment. I'm here to put an *end* to it. Besides, I can guarantee you won't find him by following Miss Blackthorn around."

"Why do you say that? Is he okay? He's still alive isn't he?" Fear grips my insides, and I begin crying in earnest. "Please just tell me that much."

"Miss Beckett, calm down, please. He's fine." Officer Wilson takes my elbow and eases me back down onto the couch.

I hold my face in my hands, sobbing. "Thank you," I choke. "Thank you. If you only knew what I've been through this past year, not knowing where he is, or whether he is even alive. It's been torture."

He pats my shoulder. "Can I get you a glass of water or something?"

"No, thanks. I'll be okay." I sniff and wipe my nose with my hand.

He pulls a snowy white handkerchief from his pocket and gives it to me. "You've had a rough stretch these last couple of years, haven't you? What with losing your mamma and now this boy ..." he trails off.

"You know about my mom?"

"Course. Everybody knew Judge Beckett. She was one classy lady. Tough-minded, but always fair." His voice softens. "I bet you miss her, don't you?"

I nod, blotting my tears with his handkerchief.

"Oh, what the hell," he says, pulling out his notebook again. "If anybody asks, you didn't hear this from me."

My heart stops beating for a second. I can't believe it. He's going to tell me where to find Ryder.

He flips through a few pages and pauses. "Okay, according to his

TRANSCENDER: *First-Timer*

sis he joined the Peace Corps about a year and a half ago. He's been in Africa—Zambia to be exact. Got six months left to go. Should be back by Christmas."

He points a finger at me, accompanied by a stern look. "But I'm warning you young lady, I don't want to be getting any calls from *Mister* Blackthorn come December. If the man doesn't want to see you, you got to accept that, child."

His tone turns fatherly. "Don't go making a fool of yourself, all right? You got too much going on to be throwing it away on some man."

Joy and relief flood through my heart. I bounce up and down like a kindergartener and hug Officer Wilson's neck, causing him to drop his notebook. I close my eyes and silently thank all the angels in heaven. I resolve to donate all my earthly belongings to charity, become a vegan, and go to church every Sunday. Yippee! I've found him!

"I promise you won't be getting any more calls about me," I say. "I swear I'll never harass another Blackthorn for as long as I live. I'll be the best law-abiding citizen you've ever seen. Just thank you!" I try to hug him again, but he holds up his hands and takes a step back.

"That's not necessary," he says. "Keep your promise to me, and we'll both be happy." Officer Wilson retrieves his notebook from the floor and heads for the door.

I'm still dancing with delight, as I show him out. He smiles and shakes his head.

"This guy must really be somethin' special."

"He is. Take care, Officer Wilson, and thanks again."

"Don't mention it," he says, and walks back to his cruiser.

Yes! Ryder's alive! He's in Africa, and he'll be back in Connecticut by Christmas. Now the question is: Can I wait until Christmas to contact him? The answer is a resounding *NO!* The acute pain I've suffered over losing him has settled into a dull, throbbing ache over the past year, but it's always with me, and Ryder Blackthorn is the only cure.

I consider contacting the Peace Corps to find a way to get a letter to him. But what will I say in the letter? "You don't know me, but I love you with all my heart ..." No, that'll never work. I need to do this in person. I need to see his beautiful face again, and the sooner the better.

The outline of a plan begins to form in my mind. Graduation is only a few weeks away, and I've got a couple of months off before classes start at Yale. I'll go to Zambia and find Ryder. It's the only reasonable thing to do. Of course it will require a lot more money than I currently have stuffed in the envelope in my dresser drawer, and Dad will have a fit about the whole thing, but I'll find a way to do it. Nothing can stop me now.

My laptop is on the kitchen table, and I *Google* Zambia. Several sites pop up on the screen. Before I can check them out, though, the doorbell rings again. Probably Officer Wilson back for his handkerchief. Where did I put that thing? I pat my pockets.

I swing open the front door and gasp. He's wearing a charcoal gray business suit and his sandy hair is a little thinner, but there's no mistaking my old friend, Agent Ralston.

"Ralston!" I squeal, throwing my arms around his neck.

He chuckles, nearly thrown off balance. "Hello Jaden. Still as exuberant as ever, I see."

"What are you doing here?"

He straightens his crushed lapels. "May I come in?"

"Of course. Come in." I hold the door for him, and he steps into the small living room. I catch a glimpse of a long black limousine idling in the driveway.

"Hmm, nice ride. Is that how IUGA agents are getting around these days?"

"Not really, but I needed reliable transportation today."

I motion for him to sit on the couch, and I take the chair across from him. "Rals, it's good to see you," I say. "I'm still pissed at you for sending me home against my will, but I've missed you over the past year. I want you to know I appreciate the way you took good care of me while I was in Domerica."

"Don't mention it, old girl. I'm sorry about the little deception, but my director at the time felt things would be easier for you and your family if you were able to resume your life exactly where you left off. He envisioned unrestrained chaos if the Transcenders had been allowed to intercede, or if you had been allowed to remain in Domerica."

"Well, I didn't want to come back at all. But you're probably right—it was probably best for all of us."

He sits on the edge of the couch, resting his elbows on his knees. "You seem happy, Jade?"

"I'm happy *today*. Ralston, I've found him!"

"I suppose I don't have to ask who?"

"Ryder! I found Ryder."

"Yes? And I presume you've already worked out a way to get to Zambia?"

"Actually, I was just looking at that. Wait a minute. You knew he was there?"

"Of course."

For the first time I notice that Ralston seems a little keyed-up. "Can I get you some tea or something?" I ask, hoping he plans to stay for a few minutes. I have tons of questions for him.

"No, thank you." He looks at his watch. "There is really no time for that."

"Okay. So I assume you didn't come here just to check on me, and I know you didn't come to tell me where to find Ryder, so why are you here?"

"Has anyone else been to see you?"

I narrow my eyes at him. "What do you mean? Like who?"

"Like Asher or another Transcender."

"No. Why?"

He brushes off the question with his hand. "Never mind." His mouth forms a taut line and his eyes lock onto mine. "The thing is, Jade, I've come to take you back."

I blink at him. "Back? Back to Domerica?"

"Yes."

"But no ..." I say, confused. "I've just found Ryder, and I'm home now. I'm going to Yale in the fall. Hey, weren't you the one who told me the whole entire universe would be totally screwed up if I didn't come home where I belong? Didn't you say there are laws against Transcenders interfering with the natural order of the universes? That scared me, you know."

"I might have implied that once or twice." He sits, nervously bobbing his legs. "But things have changed. IUGA has sent me here to take you back."

"Changed? How? What's changed?"

He lifts his glasses and pinches the bridge of his nose. "It has been determined that procedures were not properly followed during your stay in Domerica. You should have been informed of certain things earlier, and given the opportunity to choose whether or not to return to your life here."

I gawk at him. "No shit? Who decided this?"

"Let's just say *the powers that be*. Braxton Zarbain has been relieved of his directorship as a result of the incident, and I have been demoted to *Junior* Guidance Agent. I've been offered a chance to redeem myself, if you will consent to return with me."

"But what about my life here? What about Dad and Drew? I can't just disappear."

"You'll be given thirty days, with no consequences to your life on this earth. After that time, you must decide whether to stay in Domerica, return home, or ..." he trails off.

"Or what?"

"I'll let the Transcenders explain the third option to you."

"My life here will just freeze in place again?"

"Yes."

"I'll get to see Ryder?" My heart surges at the thought.

"Yes."

"And my mom?"

"Yes. And, in fairness, Jade, I must tell you, she is not well."

"What's wrong?" I ask alarmed.

He rises from the couch. "There's really no time to go into that now. I'll explain everything on the way."

He holds out a hand for me. "How about it, old girl? Are you game?"

I take his hand. "Let's go!"

To be continued ...

ACKNOWLEDGEMENTS

There are so many people I *could* thank for contributing to my drive and desire to complete this project—beginning with my fourth grade teacher, Mrs. Binns—but I decided to stick to the essentials in the hope that someone will actually read this. First, thanks to my family, for all their love and support: To Mike for always believing in me no matter what harebrained thing I wanted to try next. To Jessica for never allowing me to quit. To Colter for being my "teen" consultant and sounding board. To Shelly for being my guardian angel and trusted advisor. To Mark for being the transmitter of positive vibrations. To my daemon, Bella, for keeping me grounded, and to Katie for making me smile. Additional thanks go to Jaydn Diane Sanders for lending me her lovely first name.

The comments and expertise of several people helped me along the way to publishing this work. Thanks to Jim Swain who empowered me to initially epublish this book myself. Thanks to Carrie Parker for her editing assistance. Thanks to Kaye Coopersmith for suggesting I make the *Prologue* into Chapter 1. Thanks to Joyce Bowden for her copyediting services. Thanks to Saxon Andrew for his valuable advice and counsel. Thanks to Marsha Quinn for introducing me to this genre and for being my friend. Thanks (again) to Jessica McDonald and Shelly Savage for their invaluable final comments. And a special thanks to Carrie Drazek, actor, writer, producer, and creative genius, for her support and encouragement and for designing a fabulous new book cover.

ABOUT THE AUTHOR

Born and raised at the foot of the Wasatch Mountains, Vicky Savage became irresistibly enchanted by the spell of the ocean when she attended law school in Florida. She practiced law for several years before taking time off to raise her two children. She is now an author and publisher of young adult books. She lives on the water on the west coast of Florida with her husband, son, and two dogs.

Made in the USA
San Bernardino, CA
13 July 2014